The Briefcase

The Briefcase

Jackson Kerr

Copyright Information

The Briefcase
By: Jackson Kerr
©2020

Published by:
Good News Fellowship Ministries
220 Sleepy Creek Rd.
Macon, Georgia
ISBN-13: 978-1-7344999-5-7

Printed in the United States of America

Format by : Lisa Walters Buck

Contents

Chapter 1

"All right," he said, "now what have we got so far?" Timothy was standing behind one of the graphic designers who worked to carry out his visions. Timothy worked in marketing for a company that made house appliances. Their patent product was the blender that they made. Timothy's job was to explain to the customer what the product was, it's capabilities, it's uses, and why they should buy it - all in 100 words or less. To be more specific he oversaw marketing, which meant writing advertisements and package text, as well as overseeing package design for new products.

Timothy took another look at the package design in front of him.

"This is my favorite." Said Kendall. Kendall used his knuckle to push his glasses back up on his nose. Timothy never understood why Kendall didn't just get prescription lenses. Timothy noticed a roll of tape on the desk which matched tape on the man's glasses, as well as a tiny phillip's screwdriver. He didn't know whether the man had his glasses broken recently or was simply interested in maintaining them well.

"As you can see, this box's design by moi utilizes the box's rect-angular shape to draw attention to the blender's extra-large capacity."

"That's nice Kendall. What about this text box here?"

"The orange-on-white draws the customer's eye to the genius of our company's engineering which-"

"It's too bright. When I look at it it's like a warning sign. Do you have something a little more subtle?"

The neon orange text box was set against a dark grey backdrop.

"The design won't do any good of the reader's eyes have to adjust to look at the picture."

Kendall silently clicked about at his computer in front of which he sat. Tim stood over his shoulder. With a few clicks the orange text box disappeared and a light grey one replaced it. His computer screen showed the potential product box as though someone had unfolded it and laid it out on the floor, splayed.

Timothy nodded. "That one is better, easier on the eyes. Keep up the good work, man."

Stepping away, Timothy looked at his mug and realized that he could use a refill. The company was large enough to have their own café with specialty drinks, smoothies and espresso. Instead the company pinched those pennies and made sure that each floor had access to a coffee machine that was made in the last century. H.R. needed to pick up the slack.

Someone was already brewing some extra-dark roast as Tim approached. The smell grabbed him by his olfactory sensors and pulled him to the coffee machine. Slowing, he glanced about. There were several people who drank the extra-dark roasted coffee. But only one or two brought the special blend from home. He glanced over his shoulder to see a figure looming over his shoulder.

"Why hello there Timothy."

"Hey Will, how's it going?"

"I would say that today's proceedings have been a jolly good time."

William's problem wasn't that he watched a lot of television. William's problem was that he brought his shows with him to work every day. Today, for instance, William's put-on British accent was passionately over-the-top.

"Timothy my dear fellow, how awww you today?" The overly-modified r's in the sentence slurred into one long vocalization that was closer to a speech impediment than an actual accent. Downton Abbey did not look good on some people.

"How aww you today?"

"I'm doin' fine Will." Timothy replied. "How's that marathon going?"

"Just splendid. I finished season two last night and just had to go on with it."

Timothy poured himself some coffee. "That's nice." He said as he watched the cup fill with the steaming brown liquid. Will's eyes wandered over Tim's shoulder and his eyes widened.

"Tim." He said, all 4% of his British heritage gone with the accent. "Don't look now, but it's Marsha." Tim groaned. It had to be today.

The woman's high heels clicked rapidly across the tile flooring that lined the office space. Tim didn't like some of his fellow office workers, but they were ones with little quirks and habits which annoyed him.

Marsha was another case entirely.

"Good afternoon gentlemen." She said, displaying her blinding smile. "How are we today?"

"Hey Marsh." Tim said. "How's stuff in H.R.?"

Titles, assignments, roles, these were something that Marsha took too seriously and everyone in the office knew it.

"Well," she said, clearing her throat, "I don't know about 'stuff' or how it's going in "H.R.' I do know that as Head of Employee Relations to the Human Resource Department I spend my time-"

"-acting as a liason between us and management." Will said. "Got it."

Tim nodded. "You can let H.R. know that we are A-OK down here. If anything happens we'll send a messenger raven."

Marsha, despite being in charge of H.R. communicating with the office, never answered her e-mails in faster than three days. That's why all questions to her were forwarded through the intern. That way their question was answered quickly or referred quickly to Marsha. At least that way it would be less than three days before she saw the message.

Her brow furrowed at Tim's raven joke.

"I've never found difficulty with using modern methods in communication. Is there anything that you're having trouble with? Perhaps there is some way that H.R. could be of assistance?"

Tim nodded, despite the fear in William's eyes.

"Yes, there is." He said. "If you could check about how quickly it takes for our e-mail browser to download messages, that would be helpful." Tim saw the look of terror give way to despair on Will's face. Marsha looked carefully at Tim.

" You have trouble receiving e-mail?"

Will was shaking his head 'no'.

"Not exactly." Tim said. "I've been sending out e-mails for work. But I'm having trouble getting in touch with others."

Marsha looked truly fascinated now. "What others?"

"I'm not sure." Tim said, picking up steam. "It could be anyone. Or half of them. Or all of them."

Marsha made what she must have thought was a sly gesture out onto the work floor. Tim nodded. She looked between the two for them, an intensity in her gaze. "You believe this may be a widespread problem?" She was in full Covert Operations mode. Tim shook his head with a grim expression.

"I can't be sure."

She nodded. "And what is the nature of the problem?" She asked with intensity.

Tim kept himself from rolling his eyes and told her again. "Just this," he said, matching her intensity. "That sometimes, when I send an e-mail – I don't get a response the same day."

A heavy silence fell over their corner of the room. Will's grimace was plain but Tim ignored it, eyes locked with Marsha She stood still, not moving at hair's breadth. Then she thanked both of them, turned, and made her way to the elevator. Will turned to Tim.

"What was that all about? Are you looking for ways to cause trouble?"

Tim shook his head. "Relax," he said, "Nothing will keep her out of here besides a good challenge. Besides, what's more challenging than looking for yourself?"

Will shook his head. "If she finds out that you know about that, she's going to be mad."

Tim waved it off. "She'll never notice. Besides, she's the go-to person for all complaints. By the time she can think about what I said she'll have forgotten it."

Will shook his head again. "I'm not sure about that."

Tim laughed "You worry too much. I'm telling you by the time she gets around to remembering what we were talking about ten other people will have needed something from her." Will took his coffee and headed back to his desk, with another word of warning about Marsha.

As he headed back to his desk, Tim thought through what he had to do today. He knew that his workload wasn't heavy. His work was done by project; each week he had a quota of work to get done, rather than a regular time to work. But the work was demanding enough that he was working regular hours. There was one project that he had to look over, and another that he was drafting. Something about a new set of knives the company was looking to manufacture. They were moving from appliances to other kitchenware for their home and kitchen department. Trying to figure out whether this would work or be a flop was a coin-flip without some good planning. And good planning involved good marketing.

Though Nikola Tesla was an incredible inventor he was a quiet man. It was Thomas Edison with his public displays that got people's attention. Because of it, Edison was the man remembered by the population and Tesla was all but forgotten. Grandstanding as the nation's patent "Mad Scientist" did wonders in the field of marketing.

When Tim paged through the papers on his desk, there was one request which had been improperly routed. He made a note to send it to the right people. After a few more minutes of taking notes for himself and the secretary in charge of the marketing department, Tim grabbed his coat and headed for the door. Locking his office behind him, he stepped through the office to the floor's front desk.

"Hello Katelyn."

"Good afternoon Mr. Runn. How are you doing today?" The twenty-something year old was good at her job and maintained a bright cheerfulness that many people found hard to keep up with.

"I'm doing fine. I've made a few notes about some work to get done. Can you pass these notes on to Will for him to look over? I've sketched out a few things for the video advertisement on the Spin-ister Six." The comic reference hailed from the nerdy heritage of many of the designers. Those who were working to design a new blender spent much of their childhood reading adventures of the super-powered protectors of cities like theirs.

Katelyn smiled and nodded as she took the papers. "I'll be sure to pass this onto him."

"Thanks Kate." Tim gave a little wave and stepped to the elevator.

He was out a little earlier than usual, but his workload and time spent at the office varied. Today he was glad to get out of the office earlier than usual. The run-in with Marsha hadn't boosted his mood much. His interactions with her always seemed like some kind of challenge, like staring down a wild moose. The marketing department was well-structured enough that a check-in was sufficient with the work that went on in the designing process. He wasn't desperately needed for the rest of the day. Besides that his wife had asked him to pick up some ribs on the way home.

Tim stepped out of the office building and took a breath of air. It was good to be out of the office. The parking lot was just the same as it had always been, and his car right where he had left it.

Pulling down the street, he reminded himself of what was going on in his house. His oldest daughter, Lynn, had dance practice tonight. She decided that she wanted to learn ballet and Mom agreed, so it was settled. He wondered about the annual salary in the field of dance. Of course he didn't know if she wanted to be a dancer when she grew up, but it was best to keep all doors open now and decide later.

Little Michael was in preschool now, spending his time coloring and building towers out of his blocks to knock the over with his dinosaurs. He was the rambunctious one, always running, 'Here daddy, take this,' he'd say, shoving a stuffed bear into his hands and running off to grab something else. His little eyes gleamed as he saw worlds beyond what Tim could experience in a day. He sailed along, carried by the power of his son's imagination.

Tim parked in the market's parking lot and checked his pockets for his wallet. Finding it in his pocket he locked the door behind him and made his way inside. As he stepped through the door his ears caught the sounds of many voices. Some siblings shouted at each other as they ran around their parents. One baby's crowing could be heard halfway across the store.

The store's management had poor taste in music and apparently wanted everyone to know. The speaker system was pulling its weight as sound careened around the room and into Tim's eardrums. He grimaced but kept moving. He noticed a few women pushing their carts as they tried to imitate fashion models with loud lipstick and erratic wardrobe choices. Tim shook his head. Let the designers have their moments on the page with the models. They all went through with the outrageous costume choices so that regular people wouldn't make the same mistake. Some fashion choices were not universally attractive.

Tim made his purchase and made a quick exit, hoping to get home early. As he stepped out of the building he felt the sun hit his face. He took a breath and slowly broke into a smile. The sun shone down on him and warmed him over. He stepped towards his car, bag in hand, when he heard a noise down the sidewalk. There was some kind of commotion. People were shouting and he could see through a small crowd that usually lined the sidewalk they were being pushed aside by someone unseen. As he watched a man broke through.

The man was very tall, certainly pushing past six feet. He had an angular face that was very long, eyes that were bright and used to taking in detail. He wore a suit which clearly fell into an upper category for quality and price. The man's feet were huge. Tim wondered where the man found a place that made shoes in his size.

And the man was bleeding. He held a hand at his lower ribs on the left side and Tim could see blood seeping between the man's fingers.

The buildings in this area were close together, and alleyways ran in between. The man rushed past Tim, bumping into him and nearly knocking him over as he did so. At that moment Tim looked into the man's eyes and saw the wild animal desperation that panic brings on. The man had rushed past him already and Tim stepped forward, looking for what the man was running from. Two men were pushing their way through the crowd.

The first man had been very tall, but very thin as well. These two weren't the same. They also pushed past six feet in height, but they were huge and muscular. If they worked out daily for years, Tim wasn't sure how they could get to be this large. Tim had decided to help the man, but he wasn't sure a face-to-face confrontation would be his best way of helping. Turning around, he began to run in the direction of the first man. He didn't hear or see if the two followed him or even noticed him. The observation and decision to run, took only a moment.

Running along, he spotted a vending machine on his right. As he approached, he ducked behind it. He tried to catch his breath. Adrenaline rushed through his system to boost his senses and strength and sending tremors through his body. Sweat speckled his forehead. Hearing footsteps approaching he took a breath and counted to three. Then he swung out, using the bag of meat in his hand as a kind of blunt mace. It caught one of the men squarely in the jaw. Turning, he sped down the sidewalk before either of him could catch him.

As he began to run, bag of meat in his hand, he weaved his way through the busy sidewalk. Moving along, he spotted an alleyway on his left hand side. He looked around. Besides stepping into a store, there was no way that the man could find another placed to hide. With a bit of hesitation, Tim ducked into the alleyway, hoping that the men hadn't seen him yet.

He found the lone man leaning against the wall with a hand pressed to his side. With a glance, Tim could see the man was dying. The man looked at him and motioned him closer. Tim was silent as he hurried to the man.

"Are you all right? What happened? Who are those men? And who are you?"

The man took a breath and spoke. "My name is Williams, Agent Williams. I'm a special operations agent with the FBI." Tim's head reeled, but the man pressed on. "I've been doing some intelligence work for the last several years. On my own. The agency doesn't know about it." A wave of pain crossed the man's face and he slid to a sitting position, breathing heavily. He pointed to a case on the ground.

"That case," he said, "contains all of my research. Someone is about to make a strike at America."

"What kind of a strike?"

The man shook his head. "I couldn't learn. But the strike could happen in a matter of days. I'm not going to make it." He nodded to the case. "Take it. Get it to the Federal Beaureau of Investigation, they'll know what to do about it." Tim glanced up to the alley's entrance.

"What about those men in black? Who are they? What do I do about them?"

"I don't know who they are. I got a tip that someone was after the intel I had gathered and was coming after me. I got my things together. Sure enough, they broke in and I've been running since."

"For how long?"

9

"About three days." He waved at Tim. "Go. I'm not going to make it. This information has to get to the agency as soon as possible. Our society will collapse without it."

Tim looked at the man in the eyes. The wild animal instinct was gone and his gaze was soft. But he was clearly aware of his surroundings. Tim stepped around the man and picked up the case.

"Did you drive here?"

Tim nodded.

"Where's your car?"

"In the market parking lot."

The agent gestured around the building. "Head out the other end of the alley and circle around to your car." The man began to lift himself off the ground with a groan. Tim helped him to his feet. There was a commotion at their entryway to the alley. The two men stood at the alley's entrance and he saw them tense.

"Go!" shouted Williams. Tim turned and ran down the alleyway. He heard as Williams ran forward to meet his opponents, all pain forgotten, all fear lost. As he reached the end of the alleyway he glanced back. The agents had doubled down on Williams. Tim turned away and began to run.

Chapter 2

Circling around the corner of the building, he glanced both ways down the back street. This one ran behind the building, allowing employees to reach the back warehouse for load-ins and deliveries.

Tim's mind reeled and he felt sick. There was not a chance of William's helping him here. The man was probably already dead. He looked at the case in his hand. What was he supposed to do with it? But Tim shook his head. Now wasn't the time for questions. He sprinted back behind the market building as he heard footsteps approaching from the alleyway behind him. Breaking out into a run, he rounded the back corner of the building heading to the front again. He heard a shout from one of the men but didn't look back.

Spotting the parking lot, Tim glanced at incoming traffic. It was clear. Clear enough. A white SUV laid on the horn as he jumped in front of it, hands out in the traditional "I'm walkin' here' stance. He dashed across the other half of the street and looked about for his car.

Of course now was the perfect time to forget where he had parked.

He looked and looked. What did he drive again? It was a sedan, a blue sedan. Where was it? He pulled out his key fob and clicked the unlock button. A familiar clicking sounded on his left. Turning, he sprinted in the direction of his car. As he did so he saw the two men emerge from the alleyway, guns in hand. Tim ducked down, hoping they didn't see him. Looking forward again, he spotted his car.

With a grunt he sprinted to his car. Opening his door, he almost dropped to the ground when the first shot rang out. Opening his car, he threw himself into the driver's seat. At this moment he wanted one of those new cars with just the key fob. That way you didn't have to put an actual key in, you just had to have the key fob with you. But she insisted that if he didn't have an actual key with him he would forget the key fob and leave it somewhere. Scrabbling through his pockets he found his key as another shot rang out over his car, followed by another. Tim got the engine started and shifted into reverse.

He laid on the gas and tore out of his parking spot, scraping the parked car on his left as he did so. More shots rang out, and he heard one make contact with his car. Tim shifted into drive and floored the gas. Tim's car screamed away from his parking space and onto the road where he worked to make as much distance from the two men as he could.

He glanced out the back window and saw the two men watching him. A car horn brought his attention back to his front. A thousand questions rumbled through his head at five hundred miles per hour. Who were those men? The men in black? The mafia? Could they be rogue accountants?

Tim needed some coffee. He took a left at the next intersection and headed for his favorite coffee shop. There were several coffee shops that he went to on a regular basis. Which one he chose depended on who was coming and the occasion. There was a very nice one on Fifth street which was known for its foreign touch and exotic flavors. But that's not what Tim needed now. He needed a regular cup just to steady himself.

The coffee shop was on the left. Tim pulled into the parking lot, grabbed the case, stepped out of the car, closed the door and locked the vehicle without a thought. Tim crossed the street and entered the building. The familiar scent soothed his nerves. He took another breath just for the smell of the coffee and felt the stress of the day already beginning to melt a little. But it didn't go any farther than that. He made this order at the front and took a seat in the back, away from the front window. He needed to think. What was he dealing with? He realized now that he didn't know anything. Grabbing the case off of the floor, Tim set it on the table before him. There weren't many people around, so he felt relatively confident about his safety at the moment, unless the two agents found him. He didn't know whether they would risk shooting with a crowd around. Nothing much seemed to deter them. He turned his attention to the case.

It was a standard-looking briefcase. He looked it over for any special markings. None were present. He looked at the lock to open it. There was no keyhole. He tried to open it. It might as well have been welded shut along the seam. He took another look. It was a plain black briefcase made of leather. The handle was what he expected, a leather-covered handle with metal parts for the connection to the case itself. Everything about the case was sturdy. Tim sighed. The information in this case must have been very important for this fight to be going on about it.

Williams said it was some kind of intel. All Tim knew of cop films and secret agent shows came back to his mind. "Intel" was short for 'intelligence', information that an agent had gathered for some purpose. What in the world that purpose could be was beyond Tim. His head was still reeling. He felt as though he had awakened from a dream suddenly and found that he was falling, but he didn't know when or where he started, or how high up he was when he slipped off the ledge. Or when it would stop.

Sitting at a table with his drink he rubbed his temples before taking his first sip of coffee. After several more sips and half a cup of coffee gone he felt ready to face the situation again. The first obvious step was to take a second look at the briefcase in his possession. He glanced out the large front window. No sign of any darkly-dressed men. Or any big, black SUV with tinted windows. He looked back to the table in front of him, took a breath and lifted the case onto the table.

Again, it was a standard-sized briefcase with no special markings. The outside was leather, but he could tell from the weight that the interior was reinforced with metal of some kind. Looking at the clasps that held it shut he saw no special lock. But there was no apparent mechanism for getting the thing open. He sighed and took a sip of coffee. So he was stuck with a briefcase holding vital information for the Government of the United States. Information which could save the nation. And he couldn't get the stupid thing open.

He gave one of the sides a knock. It was definitely reinforced somehow. He checked the bottom. The hinges on which it opened were as sturdy as the rest of the case. Tim was just about to finish his coffee and move on when a man approached, settling himself across from Tim.

"Hey there, the name's Dean, how's it going? You come here much?"

Tim looked the man over. Dean looked as though he had just emerged from his single-bedroom apartment after a month-long marathon of some sci-fi show so that he could stock up on coffee and have another look at the sun before his next marathon. At least that's what Tim thought. He was about to speak when Dean beat him to it.

"Yeah I come here pretty often. I've been working on a project. Something big." His voice lowered as he leaned in. "This is something that might revolutionize our world as we know it. A technology that could change the world overnight." Tim sat mesmerized and thoroughly confused at the man's prattling. He was about to speak when the man started laughing.

"I'm kidding, I'm kidding." He said. "That's all I do, I kid, I joke, I'm a comedian, a standup I make the people laugh. My name's Dean Meare, Rhymes with pear, and don't forget to bring a pair of earbuds, 'cause people tell me you can go deaf from listening to me too long." The man stopped, for a moment, to breathe. "What's your name, kid?"

Tim looked Dean over. The man couldn't be older than twenty-five. He smiled and quietly offered a hand to the man.

"My name's Tim."

"Well, Tim, it's good to meet you." Tim grabbed the case and began to set it on the ground. Dean caught sight of it and began to prattle again.

"Say, what's that there? Is that what I think it is?"

Tim's hair stood on end as he began to make an excuse, but Dean laughed.

"I'm joking, I'm kidding. I know you, you know me. Not very well, but we know each other. I'm sure you don't have anything sensitive or secret in that case-" the man stopped and turned again to Tim. "-or do ya?"

Again, Tim's hair stood on end. How much did this guy know? Finding it hard to breathe he swallowed and opened his mouth to speak.

"I… I mean…" Dean sat there for a moment and there was silence. Then he started laughing again.

"Man, you must be tightly-wound or something man. The jokes keep coming, and that's another strike on you, the balls fly right past." Dean leaned back in his chair, looking to other customers. "Am right? Look at this guy, all wound up."

"Would you keep your voice down, please?"

"Hey man, I'm sorry, I didn't realize that this is a private conversation."

'What is your problem?"

"I'm a comedian, I got jokes, I got to tell 'em."

Tim sighed and decided that giving up on this conversation was his best option. He stood up. "Well Dean it was nice to meet you, but I've got to go." He picked up the case and his cup of coffee, tossing the cup as he passed the trash can.

"Hey Tim." Tim stopped and turned where he stood, looking at Dean. The man's face was now somber as he observed Tim. Dean looked him over and made eye contact. He spoke, but his voice was soft now.

"Take it easy. OK?"

Tim smiled a little and nodded as he exited the building.

He tried to slow his mind down as he drove home. At this point he was just trying to wrap his mind about what had happened. Everything was fine until he decide to help a man he didn't know from two thugs who looked ready to kill him. He thought back to his run to the alley.

The man, Williams, had turned to face the assassins – Tim couldn't think of another name for them – as they had come to kill him. Tim didn't doubt that the men would have no hesitations about killing Williams - or a civilian.

He pulled into his drive as the sun was beginning to set. He stepped from his car and around the front of it. Looking at the bumper, he saw one indentation. The bullet. One of the shooters had left a bullet hole in the front of his car. Should he call the police? Tim almost laughed. He hardly believed what had happened today. How would he convince a policeman of the same?

Chapter 3

There was nothing special about the next morning. The regular routine; get up, get coffee, get ready for work. Tim had spent some more time examining the case last night, but he couldn't find anything unusual about it. However, there was no apparent way of opening it. He tried prying it, looking for switches, and seeing if there were hidden buttons. Nothing worked. It was just a very solid, apparently standard briefcase containing secrets that could keep the nation from a national disaster. He signed. All plans for a stress-free workday were flying out the window.

Tim gathered his things and headed for the car. Grabbing up his things he headed for the door. As he reached it, he hesitated and took the case. He wasn't sure what he was going to do with it yet. Going straight to the FBI sounded like a fairly good option if this wasn't a hoax. The only thing he knew to do was study the case more to see if he couldn't find something wrong with it, or find a way to open it up.

The drive to work was uneventful, save Tim's looking out for apparent secret agents everywhere. He nearly jumped at the sight of a man in a suit with sunglasses. After a second glance, however, he saw that the man had a different build and was clearly not interested in his vehicle.

As he stepped into the office, he was greeted by Katelyn.

"Good morning Mr. Runn. Here are some things for you to look over."

"Thanks Kate." He took the stack of papers, not the least bit interested in them. They would either be copies of something he didn't need or requests he couldn't meet for something he didn't have.

He sidled up behind Kendall.

"Hey Kendall, I need you to take a look at something."

The man looked over his shoulder and made eye contact with Tim. "I'm not critiquing your design if you're looking into packaging." Kendall said.

"No, this is something different. Meet me at my office." He stepped away, entering his office at the near side of the room. One of the things Tim most appreciated was the fact that his office had a closing door. He knew of some managers who simply had a desk in the open set a few feet apart from the others.

He stepped inside and shut the door from the noise without. Clearing off a portion of his desk, he set the briefcase on the one clear side and looked at it again. Was there anything that was missing? He didn't want to embarrass himself, but this is why he was working with an engineer.

Kendall showed up a moment later, and stepped inside.

"What do you need, boss?"

Tim gestured to the case. "I need your help with this. He said. "Does it look unusual to you?"

Kendall stepped to the desk and inspected with briefcase. He turned it this way and that, inspected the handle, the latches, hinges and outer shell, and finished with a once-over. "I can't say there's anything starkly obvious about something gone wrong. I can tell you that it's heavier than a regular suitcase."

"Well, wouldn't the weight change with something inside of it?"

"Yes, unless the case itself had been changed or build differently than other cases. On the other hand, someone could have stuck a bunch of metal bars in here and made it twenty pounds to carry round.

Assuming it was a practical joke.' Kendall looked at him with expressionless eyes.

Tim shook his head. "I have no reason to believe that this is a practical joke of any kind."

Kendall nodded. "Unless this is a practical joke on me." He said. Kendall watched as Tim shook his head.

"No joke." Kendall went back to inspecting the briefcase.

"Look here." He said, pointing at the top underneath the handle.

Tim leaned in. "What do you see?"

"Nothing."

Tim looked at Kendall. "Is that supposed to help with anything?"

"It could. We know that the case is locked, correct? Which means that there must be a method of securing it shut."

Tim nodded. "I'm tracking so far."

Kendall gestured to the case. "Since there is no obvious outside lock and it's sealed shut somehow, there must be a mechanism inside which keeps the case shut. That means it can't be tampered with. At least not easily."

They both looked it over. Kendall followed this information with other assessments. The case was certainly not cheap. From the materials on the outside it could well have been a custom order. Which meant that whoever manufactured it, as well as the customer, had a good amount of money. Kendall turned to Tim.

"What do you know about this case?" A sigh escaped from his lips as Tim sat in his chair. He collected his thoughts before speaking.

"I was given this case yesterday."

"By whom?"

Tim hesitated. He didn't know what he was getting into, and whether to involve anyone else. His gut told him to keep it a secret. But he needed to learn more about this case, and the best way to do that was to understand what the case was. Tim sighed and responded.

"A man who said he was part of the FBI. He was running from two other men. They could have been agents of a foreign government, or of some private enterprise. He was wounded when I found him. He gave me the case and talked about getting it to the FBI. Apparently it has something to do with intel he was gathering privately and needed to turn in. But someone must have got wind of it. He talked about this stuff and how the country might collapse without this information in the hands of the FBI. A collapse of society, he called it."

"And you believe him?"

Tim felt the first pang of doubt hitting him. "I had good reason to. He was clearly running from those men. For all I saw he died to cover my escape."

Kendall looked him in the eyes. "And you're sure he's dead?"

Tim's expression was answer enough.

"What do I do now?"

Kendall turned to him again. "Turn it in."

Tim looked at him and spoke. "You think I should head to the FBI office and tell them I have some vital information for the security of our country?"

Kendall shrugged. "What else are you going to do? You can't do any good on your own. All you can do is get this to the right people so they can get what they need out of it."

Tim nodded and thanked the man as he left the room. It was good to have another voice to process what he was going through. He sat and considered his options. At this point he didn't know much about what was going on. He needed to know what was going on. What was this project and what was is about? The words 'national catastrophe' were pretty vague.

Eventually Tim tired of the unanswerable questions and decided to go for lunch. Between intermittent periods of real work he came to the case again and again. What was the purpose? And who was this man running from? He took the bunch of sticky notes with to-do tasks stuck to his desk and worked on each as he could. He set the case behind his desk, next to his right foot.

Through the afternoon he would glance at it every once in a while, trying to crack the code, to reason through what it could be. But every time he wound up in the same position - he didn't have enough information. He didn't know what it was for, who created it, and for what purpose it was created. He was dealing with something bigger than himself. He remembered the time he tried working on his first big project in college. At the end of his first year he was supposed to work with a team to put together a presentation so they could exercise their knowledge about marketing new products.

He had been scared brainless. He didn't know what to do with himself. He worked on writing up some ideas, but he felt enveloped by the scope of trying to do, what he thought at the time, an enormous task.

After some work at the office, Tim decided that the thing to do would be to head back to the scene of Agent Williams' death. He decided on this course of actions for a couple of reasons. The first was that he needed to know more about what was going on, and about the Williams himself. The second was that he needed to assure himself that the agent was actually dead. If Williams was still alive, he felt an obligation to do something. This third was that he needed to assure himself that he wasn't dreaming.

After grabbing his coat, Tim checked his office once more. Seeing nothing else important, he grabbed the case and stepped out of his office, locking it behind him. His rise to the job of marketing manager had been quick. He started out as a designer. But as he worked people took notice of his output. And his keen eye. He had an understanding of design matched by none. This talent was put to use outlining and designing packaging. Soon enough someone approached him and recommended him to be promoted to management. The move had been unanimous on part of the committee.

As he stepped to his car he took a look around. People kept walking to wherever their feet were taking them. Cars passed by, their tires on the asphalt grumbling as they rolled along. He climbed in and pulled out of his parking space. Pulling onto the street put him in downtown traffic. It was early afternoon, maybe three o'clock, which mean he had an hour before the rush.

The sun shone fiercely down on him. He pulled out his sunglasses. Tim hardly liked to use them, but when necessity begged he answered the call. The drive was short, and uneventful. When he looked up he found himself in the parking lot across from the market store. It was busy with mothers running errands and others making quick stops before coming home. He stepped out of the car and took a look around.

Everything seemed normal enough. He took a closer look, scanning all about for any mysterious looking vehicles. Seeing none, he deemed it safe enough to investigate. Closing the car door behind him, he stepped across the street.

Chapter 4

She watched as the car pulled in. Same description, Red sedan, four doors, no older than three or four years. The subject stepped from his vehicle, taking what he thought was a good look around. But he didn't know what to look for. He bent over, reaching back into his vehicle. When he emerged, she gasped, surprising herself. She had known that Agent had given the case away to someone. To see it with someone else put her on edge.

The Subject locked his vehicle and stepped across the road. She waited a moment before emerging from her vehicle.

As he walked, he tried to keep his eyes open. The sidewalk was pretty busy with a good amount of foot traffic. What had the agent been doing here? Why pick the store, or the place outside the store, to be carrying around such an important item?

Making it to the alley he stepped in and stopped. He tried to recreate the scene in his mind, seeing the agent slumped against the wall, the attackers rounding the corner. Tim stepped over to the wall to take a look. There was nothing special about the wall.

The alley ran the length of the store and was wide enough for a car to pass through. Tim looked around. There had to be something that was missing. The Agent had been there for a purpose. The question was whether there was any way Tim was going to discover that purpose? He had passed the case off to Tim. Was there someone else involved?

Tim sensed the person before he turned to look. A woman who appeared to be in her mid-thirties stood at the entrance to the alleyway. From the first glance he could tell the woman knew what she was doing.

Her dark blonde hair was pulled back tight into a bun. He clothing was professional but clearly practical. Slacks and flats were the choice of the day. No heels to kick off if someone want to run. She was staring at him. Tim swallowed.

"I'm sorry miss, I was just-" he bent over. "-looking for something." With a sudden movement, he sent a bag of garbage flying in her face. That's what he attempted to do. Instead the bag gave a little hop and landed about four inches from where it had been. Tim stuttered.

"I- I- I'm sorry, I meant to say-"

She stepped forward. He was scrabbling around on the ground for some thing.

"That is-" His hand gripped a piece of wood. He swung it up towards her head. She brought her right arm up and blocked it as it almost came in contact with her head. But her left was already in motion and caught him in the ribs. She swung again and whaled away at him. He gave the wood another wild swing at her head, but she ducked out of the way and whaled on him again. Tim lost his breath and collapsed to his knees.

"Who…" He expected the woman to attack again but she stood still, looking down on him. When he could breathe again he spoke. "Who are you?"

"I could ask you the same question."

He nodded. "Fair enough." He glanced up at her. "So are you going to kill me now? Do I make a last plea?" No reaction. With a groan, Tim stood up, holding his ribs. He stepped over a garbage bag lying in the alley.

"Stay down."

He nodded, but stayed upright. "Okay." Tim spread his hands. "What do you want to know?

"Who are you?"

"Is this the part where I confess to the crime? Because nothing has happened yet."

"Answer the question."

"My name is Timothy Runn. I'm a marketing manager."

"What are you doing here?"

"I'm here looking for a friend."

"That's pretty vague."

"All right." He said, but he paused. "But might I ask what you're doing here?"

She reached into her coat and pulled a gun out for him to see.

"OK," he said, "I was at the store yesterday, I was just leaving. I saw a man running by the front door-"

"Give a description."

"Well, it's made of metal and glass, it slides back and forth. There's usually a good number of people-"

"The man."

From the tone of her voice it was clear the woman's patience was wearing thin.

"He was really tall, very thin. Knew how to handle himself. As he ran by, two men were following him. I took a swing at one of them and knocked him in the face. I followed the first man in here. And he gave me this."

Tim stepped over to where he had dropped the case and he held it up. She stepped closer. He was nervous but held his ground. She looked like she was about to speak, but remained silent as she looked at the case. He could tell all of her attention was on the object in his hand.

She stepped forward again and reached towards it. He retreated a step and she paused.

"What would you say if I told you that this case was important?"

He nodded. "I've heard a few things about it."

She grunted. "Look are we just going to stand here all day doing nothing, or are we going to get something done? Are you giving me the case or not?"

"He entrusted me with the case." She sighed and raised her hands in protest.

"He was dying. He had to give it to someone."

"How did you know that? Who were those men who were after him? And how do I know that you aren't one of them? I told him that I was going to protect this thing."

She studied him for a moment. Then she turned, waving him on.

"Come on."

He glanced around. "Where are we going?"

"If we're going to do this, I'm going to need some coffee."

Chapter 5

Fifteen minutes later they sat in the same coffee shop. She chose a table in the corner, with a good view of the door, but out of the way of most prying eyes. There was an intensity about her that Tim found almost funny. Almost. Even when she sipped her coffee, she was completely alert. When she sipped her coffee, her eyes remained up, looking intently about her. To say that she was alert would be an understatement. High-strung would be a closer description. Caution read in her glances. She didn't have the nervous energy that would make him think of a squirrel or a rabbit with their eyes wide open with their little nose working. Tim shook his head and decided that was not a particularly flattering idea and dropped it.

"So," he said, "What do you want to know?"

"How you got your hands on this case. Why my partner gave this case to you if, in fact, that is what happened. Who were those two men you mentioned? And what are your intentions?"

"There isn't much else to tell you." He said with a shrug and took a sip of coffee. The woman waited. Tim shifted in his seat. "I've told you what I know. The man gave me the case before he died, I suspect, because I was the only person within reach who wasn't trying to kill him. And as far as what I'm going to do next-" Tim glanced over his shoulder before turning to the woman in front of him. "-lady, if you could fill me in about what is going on, I'd really appreciate it. I have no idea what to do next."

The woman leaned in from her seat, looking into Tim's eyes. He began to turn away, but her gaze held him. He felt exposed, as if involuntarily revealing himself and his depths to her. Tim shifted in his seat again, thinking to glance around the café, but keeping his eyes locked with hers. If anyone was staring at them, she was unaware of it. They sat in silence for what must have been a full minute, eyes locked on one another.

It was over. Blinking, Tim sat back in his seat. The woman took a sip of her coffee now, and gestured a silent toast to him. He nodded in acknowledgment. With her momentary fix, she sat up and spoke again.

"My father always told me that if you want to know someone – really know them – you have to know one thing about them first." She paused as an invitation for him to comment, but he refrained. "Every one of them you meet is only human. We have our fears, our doubts. If I'm going to trust you, it has to be on that basis. I don't know you any other way. So I must trust in as much of your humanity as I can access in the next fifteen minutes."

"There is my testimony- my words, what I've told you."

"Yes, but words are easy – easy to speak, easy to bend, easy to throw away. Character is something different entirely." She went for another sip of coffee. "I believe you."

This caught Tim's ear, but he held back his knee-jerk happiness at being acknowledged. "Why would you believe me?"

She shrugged. "A gut feeling. And I've seen the look in your eyes before. In others."

"'Others' is a bit vague."

"In other people I trust. I've seen it in their eyes as they confide in me. In the eyes of victims looking for help. In people who are looking for someone to listen to them." She paused and looked at the table. "My name is Gemma Erskine."

"It's nice to meet you Gemma. Now could you please tell me what's going on?"

She sat up, took a breath and thought for a moment. "You know already that at least two enemy agents are after this briefcase." Gemma took a breath. "What you don't know is that Agent Williams is supposed to be dead."

"Dead?"

She nodded.

"How do you know?"

"News spread about a car crash he was involved in, about seven years ago. The story ran through the entire agency."

Tim didn't know what to say, so she continued.

"There was a project several years ago which involved research into wireless tapping. Williams disappeared soon after and was presumed dead. The device you talk about sounds like an overpowered wireless access point. But the man you talk about sounds like Williams."

She paused and gathered her thoughts before continuing.

"This briefcase we're after contains a piece of technology that could revolutionize the process of gathering information. Now, when you do something online where you have to store information on the internet, you usually set up an account for the website you're using. You make an account, and the website acts like another filing folder on your computer, storing information for you. But it's not on your computer, it's on the web, which is why you could access it from any computer with an internet connection.

"Now there are plenty of examples I could give of connections between different devices, allowing them to share information wirelessly. So now I can use my phone to get into my computer and look at that document that I was writing on my computer. Some technology allows me to search for devices other than my own, to see if they can share information with the devices I already have. Then I can connect to speakers, phones, any other kind of wireless device." She glanced casually over her shoulder. Tim took a subtle look around as well, but saw nothing unusual.

"Now," she said, getting back to her explanation, "think of this device as an overpowered wireless modem. Its primary purpose is to connect whatever device you choose to others devices. What's different here is that this machine can access anything with a wireless connection, secure or not. If you've got your special website for your Star Trek figurine collection and you've got internet security and five passwords, those will be useless in trying to protect your information. This device will bypass all of it."

Tim sat back in his chair and gave it some thought. She continued to speak.

"This machine could end the world as we know it. Anyone who has this device would have any kind of information that he wanted – access to the FBI's data on all criminals and potential threats to the U.S. All information about terrorists and their locations, the weapons they're using, people we think may be involved in acts of terror.

"This machine goes beyond taking information that stored only on the internet. I'm sure we will be making progress with this."

"So you're saying that my information isn't private online. Didn't we know this before?"

"Yes, but when hackers get into a website, they're only into that one account on that one site. So they might be able to steal from your online bank account if they get your online password. But with a device like this, they could take everything – everything you've ever written online, all of your dental and health records, all of your information about financial wellbeing would be an open book. Banks would be vulnerable. Anything they have stored online – check images, account information, currency through the web, the owner of this device would have access to it all."

"So why hasn't anyone used it yet? It seems to me that if I knew how to use a thing like that and I had the intention of stealing some secrets, I'd go right ahead and hook up my computer."

"That's the other problem." She smiled. "The computer which uses this device has to have a great capacity for dealing with information. I'm talking about processing power."

"The ability of a machine to handle large amounts of data in a reasonable time and without crashing."

"Precisely."

"All right."

Gemma was about to continue when she felt someone behind her. She tensed, ready to spring.

"Well hey there sweetie, how's it going? If I didn't know any better, I'd guess you guys were talking state secrets or something." Gemma's eyes widened and Tim could see the energy building. He shook his head but it was too late.

In an instant she gripped the man by the shirt and with a pull she had him flying over her head only to the table, where he landed on his back, spilling coffee everywhere. Tim jumped from his seat. Dean, the smalltime comedian, lay on the table, staring at the ceiling with a stunned expression. Their subdued conversation had been quiet enough to keep attention away from all except the most nosy people in the building. Now everyone's eyes were on them. No one pretended to be busy with something else. She had him by the collar and was raising a fist when Tim spoke up.

"Gemma, this is Dean, an acquaintance of mine from yesterday." Her hard look at Dean provoked a laugh from the man.

"Hey look at that, a Grumpy Cat impression. Hey Tim, who's this, is this your friend, is she a friend of yours? Say, you two aren't spies are you, like a team of spies who are working together to save the word and are totally in sync, huh? You've got her back and she's got yours?"

She looked up to meet Tim's gaze as she held her arm around his neck. "You want me to take him out?" Tim smiled for a moment before he realized what she was asking.

"No! No, no, don't hurt him." Everyone was staring. He spoke up. "Dean, I've told you a thousand times, don't scare her like that. She's jumpy." Most people settled for this and turned back to their food or coffee. He turned to Gemma, who had her arm around Dean's neck.

31

"What do we do with this one?" she said with a smile.

"Let him go." Tim said, gesturing to Dean. "He won't give us any trouble. You won't give us any trouble, will you?"

Dean shook his head vigorously. Gemma released him, but not without hesitation. Dean took an eager breath and stood upright.

"Gemma, this is Dean. He's an acquaintance of mine for about twenty four hours. He's a comedian."

Dean nodded a greeting and Gemma responded in kind. She spoke again.

"I take it that sneaking up on people is a regular part of what you do?"

Dean pointed to her and spoke to Tim. "Does she always talk like this?"

Tim nodded. "Her job is to identify threats. That's what she does."

Dean turned to Gemma and, placing his hand over his heart, spoke again. "Ma'm, I can assure you that you are in do danger from me. I am a comedian and though I am a comedian I am an honest comedian."

"You managed to identify yourself as a comedian three times in that statement." she said.

He turned to Tim again. "And she's quick on the pickup."

"So," Gemma said, "just what kind of secrets are you expecting to hear from us by hanging around here?"

"I dunno." Dean returned, matching her eye contact. "People tell all kind of secrets in little cafes all around the world. Secrets about love, about family, about secretive operations with secret code words and names – it's mostly the nephews and nieces that talk about that kind of stuff-" Tim wondered at the man's choice of words. Nephews and Nieces sounded a bit specific. As he watched the man he suspected the comedian had quite a range of young relatives. Of course family gatherings were good for all kinds of interesting stuff. He realized his mind was rambling at this point and that he didn't have any idea what Dean was currently talking about. He also realized that Gemma was just as much n the dark as he was. He cleared his throat.

"Dean."

The man stopped in the middle of his best Guinea Pig impression.

"This business is kind of private, so if you wouldn't mind…" he made a shooing motion and Dean took the hint.

"Right. Sorry. I'll be out of your way in a jif."

Somehow Dean made the situation more awkward by taking another moment or two to get himself together before completing his task of walking away. Just before he left, however, he turned back.

"I must ask, though," he said, "would it do you any good to have a man with you who knows about locks and safes and things? Y'know, devices that people use to lock things up and keep them safe?"

Tim looked at him and said "Yes, actually, that would be very useful. Can you give us a recommendation? Where is the guy?"

Dean stood before him, hands clasped in front of him and gave a bashful blinking of his eyes to make his eyelashes flutter.

"Oh no…"

"No, no, it's all right, I know what you're thinking. Can this man be more funny than he already is? And the only way-"

"I don't need to know if you're any funnier than you were twen-ty-four hours ago. What I need is a competent human being who knows something about picking locks and mechanisms."

Tim stood and approached Gemma with a little huff. "If we're going to get anything done, we need to go."

The front window shattered and Tim heard the crack of gunfire. Someone screamed and panic ensued. There was another shot, but

Gemma had already pulled him to the ground. Looking up, she spotted the door to the kitchen.

"On my mark, you run for the kitchen, all right? Not before." Timothy realized that they were crouched behind a table. While he tried to reconcile the moment of lost time from lying on the floor to crouching behind the table, Gemma pulled out a gun. Seeing it, Tim blanched and shook his head.

"No, you can't…"

Prepared, she took a breath, popped up from behind the table and took two quick shots. Tim leaned in.

"Did you hit 'em?"

She shook her head, checked her gun, and rose to fire again. "Go now!"

"What about you?"

"I'll be fine."

"Are you sure? Isn't there anything I could-"

"Go!" she shouted as she rose to take another shot at the unknown assailant. Tim needed no more encouragement. Crouching low, he half-crawled, half-shuffled across the floor to the kitchen door. He listened to the crack of guns as fire was returned with fire.

As he stood behind the door, he glanced through the small, square window in it. Gemma was exchanging the clip in her gun for another one. He considered his options. He could run now, and make it to his car before the fighting was over. He considered calling the police. But if he called the police they would start asking questions, as their job entailed. Questions about the gun fight would lead to the conversation they had before, and-

Tim almost screamed. The case. The case was resting in the dining room still, beside the overturned table. People were cowering everywhere, the few children present were crying. He didn't know about the staff of the building. Tim didn't see the staff anywhere. He looked

through the window again. He could see Gemma, who was just standing up to take another shot through the front glass which was shattered. The case was still out there. He was about to make a charge out to the dining room, when he heard another door slam. Glancing in the direction of the sound, he looked and groaned. Dean stood against a second kitchen door, case clasped in his hands.

"I want in." he said after he had caught his breath.

Tim raised his arms. "I think this qualifies as being involved for you." There was a moment of silence in the kitchen as the two men listened to a series of shots ringing out through the building.

"Well," Dean said, "this could be worse."

Tim sighed and shook his head, wondering how this man's thought process led him to speak those words. Dean continued.

"I mean, y'know, it could always be worse. But I have a distinct feeling that this situation is really not as bad as it appears."

"So what you mean to say is that you are a blind optimist." Tim answered.

"I can see perfectly, thank you."

The gunfire stopped.

There was some scuffling sound from the front room. Tim moved to the window and was about to peek in when the door swung open violently and smacked him in the face. Tim blinked as stars hovered before him in his vision. Gemma, who had just stepped through the door, was glancing about as if looking for something. She spotted Tim.

"He's out of rounds." She said. "I think they're your buddies from yesterday, which means we haven't seen the second one yet. Apparently they have a winner-take-all mentality." She looked from Dean to Tim. "Is everything all right here? You both seem a little quiet."

"Quiet?" Tim's voice was muffled by his hand held over his nose. "Nothing wrong with being quiet when you've got someone shooting at you from the next room."

"Well, that's my worry. I think he might be in there already which means we have to move now. Where's your car?"

Tim waved his head in the direction of the store front. Gemma groaned. Then she sighed and walked over to the wall on her left, near Tim, and leaned against it.

"So what are we supposed to do now?" Tim asked. "Their second agent is probably covering the back door. So we're likely to get shot whichever door we pick. It's like that show, what was it called, the Monty Hall show, where's he's got three doors and you have to-"

"I know what the Monty Hall show is, thank you very much." Her fingers massaged her temples. She looked at Tim, then looked at Dean. After a moment of looking between them she looked at the floor as she thought. The two men stood in silence as she did so.

After a moment or two, Gemma spoke up again.

"I don't know why I'm hesitating. Our odds really aren't that bad."

"You don't think so?" said Tim. "Should I remind you about what's going on? Among the three of us we have only one gun. There are at least two agents out there, both of whom surely have guns, and we don't know where at least one of them is. We are also trapped in here."

"The second one is probably driving the car." She replied. "He may be just trying to scare us out into the open."

"Or he could be trying to kill us."

"And he's already had that chance." She said. With a glance at the two of them, Gemma stepped to the door. Tim reached to grab her arm, but she was already through the door. Tim waited in agonized silence for the sound of a gunshot, a scream, anything. Dean's eyes were on Tim, as he listened at the door. Then Tim heard a whistle from the front of the café.

"Come on out boys." Tim breathed a sigh of relief and stepped through the door. The frightened customers had fled, abandoning the cafe. Glass littered the front of the store. He scanned the room and, as expected, didn't see any employees.

"So you were correct this time. What's the plan, chief?"

Dean was peering nervously from behind the door.

"Everybody but us must have seen them drive away and they ran for it."

Overturned tables littered the floor and expensive cups of coffee were spilled. Chairs rested on their sides or against walls. Some tipped precariously against tables. An exceptional few stood upright as they had been placed that morning. The scene was in complete disarray.

"Will it be safe to go out there? Won't they find us?"

"Well, they'll certainly find us if we stay here. Come on." Gemma began picking her way to the door. Tim followed. "You too!" she called back to Dean, who stood rooted to the ground, nervously clutching the case. Tim spoke.

"Dean! Let's go, unless you want to be target practice again. You said you wanted in, right?"

Dean pulled his eyes away from the overturned tables and scrambled after them leaving the café in silence.

"We'll be taking your car." Gemma said.

Tim hesitated. "My car? Are you sure that's a good idea? They've seen me in it, they might be tracking it."

"Maybe, but it's the only car we have right now."

"You're searching after something that could - how did you put it?"

"Revolutionize the process of gathering information."

"Yeah, that. You've been tracking this device and you don't even have a car? How do you get around?"

"Public transportation has some benefits."

"I'm going to stop you right there." He said. "I don't want to know."

"Your loss. If we're going to make it, it will be by using our heads. These unknown agents have all the manpower. What are you doing?"

Dean was attempting to hide himself behind a light-post.

"Blending into my surroundings. Don't you know that catching your enemy by surprise is nine-tenths the battle?"

"Yes, but as soon as we left that building we became sitting ducks. If they were still around we'd be caught already." Gemma turned to Tim. "Where's your car?"

Tim gestured to the parking lot.

"In the front parking lot."

"All right. That will work for now, but we'll have to dump it as soon as we can find another one."

"Wait, wait, wait – 'dump it'? You mean drop it off, right? Like at a friend's house – hey look after my car for me – that kind of 'dump it' right?"

"As long as by 'drop it off' you mean off a high cliff – without us in it- but we don't have any of those handy. We will have to ditch the car. If those agents know you were here it probably means that they've been tracking your car and they can continue to track it. We'll have to find another vehicle if we're going to get out of town."

"'Get out of town?' What do you mean?"

Gemma turned to Dean and gestured at Tim. "Does he have to have everything spelled out for him?" She turned back to Tim and spoke again, as she would to a child. "I mean we can't stay here. Those agents or others will be back." She gestured him onward. "We'll talk in the car."

Chapter 6

"Are you sure you know where we're going?"

"Trust me, just keep moving."

"That's funny," said Tim, his hands on the steering wheel, "because the last time I trusted you we ended up in a one-sided shootout with these agents. Who are they?"

"Turn here." Tim followed Gemma's instructions.

"Y'know," Dean piped up from the backseat, "it might be easier to get out of town if we headed towards the city limits."

"Pipe down back there." Gemma said.

"'Pipe down', that's your word choice?"

"Make a left at the next light."

"I mean if I was going to quiet a man, I can think of more appropriate word choices than that, can't you?" If Dean knew that the last question was for him, he didn't acknowledge it. Gemma ignored his running talk. Tim turned to Gemma.

"So what are we doing? And when are we dropping of Mr. Funnybones?"

"We're not. He's one of our key witnesses. As the highest-ranking agent working this case-"

"Translate to 'the only agent on the case.'" Tim chimed in.

"-it is my responsibility to protect you two and your cooperation would be most appreciated. Turn here." Tim felt around in his pocket and handed something to Dean.

"What's this?"

"It's my card. I feel like it might be a good idea if you had someone to call. Y'know, if you got stuck in an elevator or something."

Dean huffed. "I'll have you know that I only get stuck about every other month." he said, but pocketed the card anyways. Sidewalks were laid out on either side of them, like two unrolled reels of film. Tim's mind was filled with protests, but questions were all that would come out in speech. His mind raced in a hundred directions at once, and no single thought would settle on top and present itself to be answered.

They wound their way through the city streets. As Tim became less sure of what he was doing, an uneasy feeling rose in his gut.

"You said before that this technology we have would make internet security a non-issue, right?"

"For anyone who is in control of it, yes."

"So any private access to my social media profile page would be an open book."

"Along with all of your banking information, your social security account, investments, home security information – any information stored on any kind of device with access to the internet."

"Well, what if I shut it down? Or stopped using my computer?"

"It doesn't matter. All that information is stored-"

"On the internet. If we're going to be on the run like this, I think it would be good to know a little more about what's going on. Who were those spies?"

"They could be anyone. Someone may have learned what's going on and wanted it for their own business. Or someone who is looking to sell to the highest bidder."

The glass behind Dean's head exploded with the sound of gunfire from behind.

"Get down!" Gemma shouted to him.

"What do I do?" Tim said. The woman's was loading her pistol.

"Drive." She said. "And don't get us killed."

"How did they find us?" Dean's muffled voice sounded from the backseat. Gemma was taking aim at an SUV behind them.

"They never lost us. Our walking out the front door wasn't the smartest idea."

"'Wasn't the smartest'?" Tim cried as he swerved to avoid an oncoming car.

"Keep it steady!" Gemma replied.

"I thought you were supposed to be the best at this sort of thing." Gemma fired two shots and Tim heard tires screech behind them. "For an agent in training…" He turned to speak and nearly swerved off the road. At this moment the pursuing vehicle gunned its engine and swerved to approach by the driver's side of the vehicle. Tim glanced in that direction and almost clipped an oncoming pickup truck.

"Who taught you how to drive?"

Tim tried again.

"For an agent in training you sure seem to be the one in charge, bossing us around."

Whether she heard him or not, she didn't acknowledge it. Tim tried to cut over, blocking off the vehicle behind them, but was persuaded by an oncoming vehicle to get back into his own lane.

"Get out of here." Gemma said. "We've got to lose them. They don't need us alive to get the case."

"Hang on." Tim said, and gunned the engine before swerving around another corner.

Dean piped up again from the backseat. "Have we lost them?"

Gemma's eyes scanned the space behind the vehicle. The wind whipped through the car.

"Gemma?" Tim asked, slowing the car down to merge with the current traffic. She watched with a raised hand, for a moment, before turning back to face forward.

"Go." She said. Tim needed no more encouragement. He gunned the engine again and roared around two cars in his own lane before moving into it again at the insistence of the oncoming car.

"I thought she told you to keep us from getting killed." Dean said.

"Well, that one didn't kill us, did it?"

The revving of an engine behind them had everyone turning their heads. The pursuing vehicle approached from behind, pushing up against other passenger vehicles as it did so. The first vehicle let out protesting honks as the SUV pressed further up against the sedan. The driver of the sedan made the mistake of hitting his brakes. The SUV's driver gunned the engine, pushing the sedan around out of the way. Carrying his forward momentum, the SUV's driver careened forward into the tail of the next vehicle, sending it spinning off onto the side of the road.

"These guys don't take a hint, do they?" Tim's voice was tight as he maneuvered the vehicle down the streets. Gemma tapped his shoulder.

"Go that way." Tim craned his neck.

"There? Why?"

"I've got an idea."

"Oh, an idea," Tim said as he cranked the wheel around to take a sharp left, "that's all we need right now."

"We've got to get away from all these two-way streets. It's too tight here."

Tim whipped around a corner and headed away from the city's heart. Whizzing through stoplights and angry horns, Tim made record time through downtown traffic. As they reached the city's outskirts, Gemma pointed ahead.

"There." She said. Seeing it, Tim nodded and took the entrance ramp to merge onto the highway. "Now we take this onto our territory."

"Our territory. You make it sound like you grew up on the road itself."

"My territory's out east." Dean piped up from the backseat. "I've hardly been in the city for a month."

"Can it." Gemma said.

"You pick this moment to give us your life's story?" Tim asked, glancing back at the man.

"I need your eyes on the road, not a running commentary or biography from you two."

"Hey guys," Dean piped up again, "they're back." As if on cue, Tim heard an engine roar behind him. A few cars either hurried to pass Tim or dawdled in the fast lane. Gemma's eyes were on their pursuers.

"Come to mamma." She said.

"Don't encourage them." Tim replied. "Also, where'd you hear that?"

"Why do guys get all the macho sayings?"

The back SUV roared and approached from behind. Gemma leveled her gun.

"I'm not saying they do, I'm just saying I've never heard that one before."

"Stay down." Gemma told Dean. He needed no encouragement.

Taking a moment to line up the shot, she let one loose through the back of their vehicle at the driver of the SUV. A simple tok sounded below the sound of the pistol's report, and a scuff mark appeared on the windshield. Changing her tack, she took aim at the engine of the vehicle. At that moment one of the men rolled down his window and leaned out to take a shot. Gemma whipped back around to face forward just as a bullet whipped into the car's interior roof, followed by another in the taillight.

In one motion, Gemma turned in her seat, straddling the center console between the front seats and took a shot at the pursuing vehicle's front engine grill. Fumes began pouring forth from the car and the engine sputtered but the vehicle pressed onwards. Tim swerved and Gemma was thrown against her own passenger window.

"Watch it." She said. Tim was too busy keeping the vehicle on the road to respond. Gemma righted herself. Tim was speeding along, his head swinging this way and that, his breathing labored. Gemma's eyebrows scrunched.

"Do you drive much?"

"Not more than I need to."

She grabbed the rearview mirror and adjusted it Tim began to protest.

"What are you doing? I need that, what are you trying to-"

"Keep your eyes on the road."

At that moment, the report of a gun sounded, two shots off the rear of the vehicle. Gemma's eyes were on the mirror.

"Y'know," said Dean, "I think you might want to contact your insurance company about this. I don't know what your warranty covers-"

"Whatever it covers, it's not this." Tim replied as he screamed by a car in the fast lane.

"Now you…" Gemma paused and turned to Tim. "Who's your friend in the backseat?" she said.

"Dean."

"Dean, I need you to-"

"Head down, mouth shut, got it."

Gemma locked her eyes once more on the rearview mirror. Tim finished whipping around another sedan. The wind roared through the back window. Tim flinched. She had already whipped around, delivering another three shots to the back SUV. His ears were ringing. Gemma took a breath and sat back in her seat, checking her weapon Tim grabbed the rearview mirror and adjusted it to his position. Looking into the reflection, there was a black SUV receding, smoke billowing forth from its front.

"Watch your speed." She said to Tim. "They're not going to catch us on foot. By the time they report in, clean up the mess, and get back on their feet, we'll be out of here. Tim eased off the gas. They took a collective breath.

"Now," said Tim, "would you please explain just who you are? I caught that 'agent-in-training' line that slipped out earlier."

"You did catch that, didn't you?"

"Yes we did." Dean mustered from the back in what he must have thought was a serious voice. Gemma sighed and reached for the band holding her hair up. Pulling the band out, she shook her hair loose and sat back in her seat.

"What do you want to know?"

"Who were those men? Why do they want the case? Couldn't they be FBI agents? And who are you?"

"I am Gemma Erskine. I am an FBI agent-"

"You said something about training. What was that about?"

"I'm still in training."

"In training? So they let you off the leash or what?"

"Something was wrong with Agent Williams He was one of the instructors at the academy. I grew to like him." She caught Tim's eye. "As a teacher. Then he was called away which is unusual – they hardly call instructors from the academy unless they're desperate, or the instructor has specific knowledge which they can use. I didn't see anything of him for a month afterward. I began to worry about it."

"Why would you worry? I'm sure the man knew what he was doing." She shook her head. "Sometimes you have to go with your gut."

Tim sighed and turned his attention to the road.

"I suppose this is a bad time to mention it," Dean said, "but I've had to go to the bathroom for the last twenty minutes."

"What now?" Tim asked, ignoring Dean.

"We have to find cover – and get rid of this car."

"Get rid of it?"

"Yes. As long as we're in this vehicle, we're advertising our presence on every passing street camera, to every bystander."

"Do they have access to street cameras? That seems a little far-fetched."

"We can't be sure. Until we know more we have to assume that they have every available resource at their disposal." She paused for a moment. "We need to get off the grid." Cars flew by on their left, the highway a means of escape from the city. Sleek sedans, rumbling trucks and pickups and the occasional compact all in competition to get out. The sun shone own, reflecting its piercing light off of each car and into the eyes of the next driver.

Dean cleared his throat.

"Well," he said "if you guys are looking to get away, I might be able to find a place."

"Not your home." Gemma said. "If they find out who you are, your home won't be safe. Besides that, we're in this together. You are part of this as well. I'm sorry for you both," she said, "but now I need you two safe so you can testify."

"Testify?" Dean asked.

"You are my only witnesses of an attack on our lives and the death of one of our agents." She pointed ahead. "Get off at this exit. Until we know more, you two are going to have to be off the grid. No contacting your families, at least until we know what's going on."

Chapter 7

None of them spoke much after that except for Gemma, to give directions to Tim. The general plan, as he understood it, was to slip out of the city quietly and find someone within the agency who could help them. Whatever resources she had could only be guessed.

Tim relaxed as the buildings thinned out and trees speckled the landscape. He knew that as they got further away from the city there would be more open fields, but the sight nearly took his breath away. It was only at the sight of so much natural beauty that he understood how crowed he felt in the city. But they weren't completely removed from civilization.

At the sign of the next suburb, Gemma directed Tim to pull off the highway. As they pulled through town, she directed them to a used car lot. At first glance, the place reeked of pushy salesmen and markups.

They stepped out of the vehicle and were met with a loud voice.

"Hello folks, welcome to Lenny Frasier's cars, 'If you've got a need, you're at the right place indeed.'" The swarthy man's voice sounded at least a register too high for his build. The well-built man stood at five-foot five and made up for his height difference in volume and appearance. His clothing was typical for a 1980's film shoot. His physical frame sagged beneath the violently colored drapery. Tim stifled a laugh.

"Hi Mr. Frasier," Gemma said, "we're here looking for a quick deal and we were kind of hoping for a trade-in." Tim almost did a double-take. Gone was the terse, tightly-wound ball of wire he had met only a few hours ago. Now the woman had his arm in hers, leaning on him, giggling, flapping her arm around like a marionette. But he smiled and played the straight man.

Though the woman spoke about settling the deal quickly, nothing was pressed or forced. He kept in rhythm with her and followed her lead.

"-and the kids were just all over it." She was saying.

"I see," said Mr. Frasier "So you two are looking for…" Mr. Fraiser let the sentence and participles dangle as he waited for a reply.

"Oh, we haven't even talked about that," she said, "I mean we have, but we can't decide on anything."

"It'll have to have good gas mileage." Tim put in. Gemma gave him a look. "What? It's one of the first thing you told me."

The salesman laughed.

"Well, I'm sure I can help you find something. Now what have you got here?"

"Oh, this is my car. It's in good shape, except the back window, drives well." As the man stepped closer , the door opened and Dean stepped out. Seeing the salesman, he gave a nervous smile and glanced at Tim and Gemma before sidling over to them. Gemma stayed loose, but Tim caught the quick, catlike look at Dean. Tim swallowed, hoped Dean caught the look, and turned his attention to the salesman who was inspecting the car.

"Your back windshield is clean out." The man said as though he were the first to discover it. "Y'know if you guys are looking to buy you'll want a warranty with your vehicle."

"We're not interested in the warranty, thank you." Tim said, and Gemma trailed in just after him.

"Just the car. What do you have?" she asked.

"If you're budget cruncher, I've got some 2005 models for you to look at."

"Oh no!" Gemma cried with a little squeal. Tim nearly did a double-take, but she elbowed him in the ribs. He kept a straight face. "No, we can't be driving in something that old." Her voice dropped to a lower register with the utterance of the word.

"Don't worry miss-"

"Watcher." She said, looping her arm through Tim's, "Mrs. Watcher."

"Mrs. Watcher." Mr. Frasier said, "Let me show you a few more models I think we might have something that's just right for your needs." He led them over to a vehicle which must have been at least a decade old, not much better than their current vehicle.

But it was better.

After a discussion with the dealer, they spoke about the vehicle they had picked. Tim pulled Gemma aside.

"Look, this seems nice, but we're not going to get a car without paying the man." She laughed loudly and stepped further away from the salesman.

"Keep your head on," she said with a growl. "Keep smiling and let me handle this."

She turned, pulling him around to face the salesman.

"So," she said in an uncharacteristically bright voice, "we're thinking about this one and we're ready to sign. But we wondered if you could tell us a little more about the trade-in value of our car."

"Well, for your car Honda Civic in its condition, I'd say I can give you a $1,000 credit."

"Oh come on now!" Tim turned at Dean's outburst. "$1,000 for a car like that? We could go to any dealer in the area and get at least twice as much for it."

"Well, whatever you might claim, if someone told you that you'd get more than $1,000 for it, they'd be lying to you." The salesman said.

"Well then we may just have to go to another dealer. Come on guys, this guy's a ripoff."

Gemma dropped Tim's arm and strode over to Dean.

"Dean?" she said. "Can I talk to you for a moment? Tim watched as she stepped away with the man. He cleared his throat and tried to make conversation with the salesman, but he didn't take interest. The conversation lasted about thirty seconds. When they returned, Gemma was smiling, and Dean was as well, but all the color had drained from his face. Tim guessed the conversation had something to do with the space between Dean's ears and working to grasp a concept.

Gemma now directed her attention to the salesman, as though Dean didn't exist. Now Dean might smile and nod, but not a peep escaped from his lips for the rest of their conversation.

Tim nodded at the vehicle in front of them

"So what can you tell us about this one?"

"Gently used. The mileage isn't too high, it has some nice features for a car in its model period. The back seats flip down for storage."

"That's nice." Tim said, with a glance at Gemma.

"So," she said brightly, "where do we sign?" The salesman's eyebrows popped up and he masterfully hid a grin.

"Right this way."

As they stepped inside, Tim caught some sly glances from the salesman. They stepped into the small building and through the waiting room into a smaller office. The wall was lined with photos of 1970s and 1960s vehicles. Rusty orange carpeted furniture and shaggy carpet screamed 'remodel'. Lenny Frasier slid some papers around his desk which Tim guessed had been there for a while.

Some high shelves lined the upper wall. These had glass cases with model cars and magazines in plastic covers, as though the wall art was not enough. He expected a musty smell, but despite the age and clutter, Tim was surprised that the office didn't smell like stale fast food and cheap air freshener.

"Have a seat," Mr. Frasier said, gesturing to the chairs in front of the desk. Seeing the two chairs, Tim gestured for Gemma to take a seat. As she stepped by him to sit down, she grasped his arm and pulled him into the seat next to her.

Dean shuffled his feet and remained standing by the door.

After some browsing on the computer, Mr. Frasier found the car they were looking for, and detailed the vehicle's model and make, fetching the keys from the back.

"All right. Now as far as payments go, I think what we can-"

"We can pay cash." Tim's head whipped in her direction, but a firm hand on his knee stopped any protest he may have put forward.

"Remember I told you sweetie that I would get the cash for this." Tim's tried to think of something clever to say.

"Thanks sweetie." he said and watched as she proceeded to pay cash for the vehicle, signing all of the legal documents.

"I'll need to see your license and registration please." Gemma rummaged about in her purse and pulled two cards from it, handing them to the salesman. As she did so, Tim saw the name printed on one of them and caught his breath. A Ca printed at the beginning of her given name was all he glimpsed. He looked at her and she smiled back at him, giving his hand a very firm squeeze. The message was clear and he held his tongue.

After the salesman finished with the papers, he slid them across the desk to Tim. "I'll have you sign there, Mr. Whitmeyer." Tim was about to protest when Gemma nudged him. He looked at her and she nodded to the paper.

"Come on Tim."

He looked to the paper and saw a name printed underneath the line: Timothy Whitmeyer. Looking above that line he saw another printed name with a signature above it - Candice Whitmeyer. Tim swallowed, picked up the pen, and forged the signature.

"All right, thank you all, I will get you the title and keys to your new used vehicle."

After the salesman got them the required papers and keys, Tim emptied his own vehicle and turned over the keys of his own car. He transferred the license plate to the new vehicle.

Without much more from the salesman, they were off in their new vehicle. Looking over the document, Tim saw that the car was in his name, but that Gemma had co-signed.

"All right, now let me ask you." Tim said. "What is your real name?"

"Which one?" Gemma replied.

"Your given name, the one your parents gave you when you were born."

"I don't know what to tell you."

"Let's start with the truth." Gemma sighed and pulled at her hair. Dean leaned toward the front seat, but didn't say anything. They were rolling down the highway now at 55 mph, blending in with the rest of the traffic. Tim had made sure to get everything from the trunk of the vehicle as well.

"You both know that I am an FBI agent."

"Right, you told us that." Tim pointed to the papers in her hand. "When you signed those papers, you put down Candice Whitmeyer. Why did you do that?"

"I didn't want to leave a paper trail. It may be easy enough for those agents to find the vehicle, but if we leave our signatures and copies of our driver's licenses behind they'll find us much more quickly."

"But they have your driver's license."

"They have a driver's license."

Tim nodded. "I see." Silence settled in the car for a moment. The car drove well, the wheels hummed smoothly over the pavement.

"So what is your real name?"

"My name?" She looked at him and grinned for a moment. "If I tell you, can I trust you to keep it a secret?"

"Why would I need to do that?"

"Are you undercover?" asked Dean.

"Yes Dean." She said. "I'm not flashing my badge around as an FBI agent, and I'm not going around by my given name - it's safe enough to assume that I'm undercover."

"All right, I hear you." he said. "Did you hear the one about-"

"Not now."

"Got it."

They sat in silence for a minute. Tim felt like pressing her for more information, but held himself back. She wasn't going anywhere. She sighed and started.

"My name is Gemma."

"Gemma." Said Tim.

"Yes."

"So, what go you into the world of espionage, Gemma?" Tim asked.

"Now's not the time for life stories, unless you want to explain why you stepped out to assist a man being chased down by those agents."

"What is there to tell? He was outnumbered and clearly needed help."

"And that's your reason for interfering with what was clearly professional business with trained law enforcement agents?"

"Well, if he carried some kind of identification that might help your case."

He flipped his turn signal on and merged into the left lane. "I guess my point is that if he was dressed as an officer of that law that would be one thing, but a man walking down the street in business dress is just another face in the crowd." Passing a few cars, he merged back into the right lane and three cars whipped by him.

"So what's the game plan? Where are we headed?"

Gemma shook her head. "Well, that depends on several things. How quickly can we get you of the state? How far are you two prepared to go?" She looked at the two men. Dean shrugged.

"I'm in. I mean, I don't think I'd volunteer for this again, but you guys look like you need some expert leadership, so here I am."

"How soon do you think those agents will be back?" Tim asked.

"That depends. We're trained to move quickly, we can be halfway across the country in a few hours. I don't know what training these agents have. Do you know if they said anything? Was there anything that they did or said that could help identify them?"

Tim shook his head.

"No," he said, "nothing about the rich furs, heavy accents, fur hats and speaking in foreign language indicated anything unusual." Her look weighed him down. "I didn't hear anything from them." He said, and turned his attention to the road. She gestured to an exit ramp off the highway.

"Head east. We've got to get out of here and the further along we are if or when they catch up to us, the better off we'll be."

They began their trip heading from a definite treat only toward a vague hope. Tim's mind raced as he tried to fit together the events leading him to this point in time. He drove a traded car with two strangers from an unknown danger into an uncertain hope that they might find a way to save their society from certain collapse.

After some hours on the road, Tim pulled over into a gas station parking lot to stretch and fill up the tank. The car ran well, and he was happy with how it handled. He stepped out of the vehicle and took a breath, conscious of the cooling air around him, breezing by his jacket. Gemma headed straight inside. Tim watched and Dean worked his way out of the vehicle, blinking at the fading sunlight.

"Sunshine's fading fast." Tim said. Dean nodded but didn't say anything. Tim wondered what had happened to the ball of energy he had first run into less than forty-eight hours ago. Dean looked as though he had aged ten year in that time. Tim wondered how the man handled stress. He knew that as a comedian the man's job was to laugh at life, and to encourage others to do the same.

"Are you doing all right? I could swear that yesterday you were a ball of energy.

"No, I'm always like this when I get involved in a deadly plot involving unknown agents seeking a mysterious case that may or may not cause the destruction of our civilization. Yeah, I'm usually pretty cool about that sort of thing."

Tim shrugged. "You said you wanted in."

Dean looked at the ground and mumbled. "You didn't take me seriously did you?"

He stepped up to Dean and put a hand on his shoulder.

"I'm glad you're involved. We need all the help we can get."

"I'm well aware of that. In fact, let's recap." Dean stepped away from Tim and began to pace. "Out of the three of us, we know each other best and we only met for the first time less than forty-eight hours ago. You've discovered the case of a dying man who may or may not be an FBI agent. A woman comes by who may be an agent, a spy, or a lunatic saying she wants our help and off we go on a rollicking adventure to return the missing case to the FBI so we can be met with thunderous applause and awards by governors and maybe the president of the U.S.

"On top of it all, the case that we have found may well have the technology to throw society as we know it into complete chaos. We have the most slim chance of getting this case back where it belongs, as only one of us, perhaps, is trained in espionage.

"Now, if Gemma is a liar, the case is not real, and the agents that have been chasing us are just some lunatics, then I'm on the run for no reason and I'm probably missing all of my favorite shows to spend my time on the road with a couple of complete strangers."

"Then again," Tim said, "If this is real - Gemma, the case, and the agents - then you are part of one of the most important missions that the FBI didn't know it was running. The three of us are going to be responsible for making sure that this information isn't going to fall into the wrong hands."

"But whose are the wrong hands?"

Tim shook his head. "What are you talking about?"

"Who can we trust?" Dean said. "Who won't misuse this technology against this country? How do we know when it's safe?"

"I guess we'll just have to trust each other."

With a shake of his head, Dean stepped away and into the gas station. Tim followed behind.

Chapter 8

Tim stepped inside to the electric ding of the doorbell. Hiss eyes grazed over rows of metal shelves and racks stocked with snack foods, chewing gum and other consumables. He saw Gemma standing with a gun drawn and began to make his way to the bathroom. As he pushed the door open he stopped himself. In half a second he was running back to the lobby of the gas station. Stopping in the doorway of the hall leading back to the lobby, the sight met his eyes again. Gemma had her gun drawn and she was holding someone at gunpoint. Someone standing, unarmed, behind the counter.

"Do you always brush past people being held up at gunpoint?" Gemma's voice was strained.

"Well, when it's not me, I don't give much thought to it. At least I've never had to give thought to getting shot twice in one day." Tim looked at the unfortunate behind the counter. He was scrawny but tall for his size. Tim didn't doubt the young man could hold his own in a fight. He turned to Gemma.

"What did this guy do?"

"He was holding up the store."

"Oh. Is that all?"

She shrugged. "It's enough."

"So where's the clerk?"

"I told the clerk to phone the police."

With a glance to the shoplifter, Tim turned his back and stepped closer to Gemma.

"With all due respect ma'm, d'ya think it was a good idea to get the police involved?"

"What do you mean?"

"Well, when they see us, they're going to start asking questions. If they find the case in the back of the car, they'll be asking more questions - with us handcuffed to a desk."

"We were recovering the case."

"And why would they care to believe us if we told them that?"

The shoplifter's eyes darted back and forth as the two deliberated. He held his hands above his head. Once or twice, as he began to relax them a bit, but Gemma gave a shake of her pistol and his hands popped up again.

"We'll let the clerk take care of this." Gemma said. "We don't even have to be here when the police show up." Tim was about to retort when he head a door in the back click open. Turning, he saw Dean approach from the men's room.

"All right," he said to Dean, "tag me out." He passed by the man with a pat on his shoulder.

"Careful," Dean replied, "you may want to-" but Tim had already reached the restroom. Gemma looked at Dean and gestured to the men's room with her head.

"What was that about?" Dean only shook his head. He looked at the man behind the counter.

"Who's this guy?" he asked.

"I thought you knew."

"This lady's nuts." The man behind the counter said. "Look, buddy, you seem like a nice guy. I don't know what's going on."

"That makes three of us." replied Gemma.

"Look," he said, keeping his eyes on Dean, "I was minding my own business when this lady comes in here, points her gun at me and tells me to keep my mouth shut. Then she just stands there."

"What about the store owner?"

The man's lips pressed tightly together. His eyes darted between Gemma and Dean, but he said nothing. Dean gave a look to Gemma, then looked back to the man behind the counter.

"Phil is the owner's name, right?" The man nodded vaguely. "He runs this place? See I've known Phil for a while, and if I know anything about him, I'd tell you that you don't want to be messing around behind his counter. I tried pulling a prank on him once - and it was April Fool's day too - but he totally flipped out on me. Now I'm not one to make trouble, but I'm letting you know you don't want to get on Phil's bad side."

The doorbell rang. As one, the three of them turned to look at the newcomer. A silver-haired man stepped in, polo shirt and well-fitted jeans.

"Phil!" Dean cried, rushing over to the man. "Is that you?" he put an arm on the man's shoulder, slipping him a $20 with a wink. After an instant's hesitation, the man grinned, winked back and cried out "Of course it's me! Who else did you think it was?"

"Now I was just telling this young man here," Dean said, pulling him to the counter, "how you are about having anyone but staff behind the counter at your station here."

"Oh, we can't have that, can we?"

"No sir, we can't."

"And we'll have to come up with some kind of special punishment for this fella, won't we?"

"Yes sir, we will."

Dean glanced at Gemma to see her roll her eyes back into her head.

"All right," said the scrawny man behind the counter, "all right fine, do what you want with me? I'm telling you I didn't take anything. No, I don't work here, but I haven't stolen anything."

"No?" said Dean, looking at him. "Then you'll have nothing to worry about. We'll check things about and you'll be on your way."

The older gentleman looked to Gemma and gestured to the skinny man behind the counter.

"What did you find him doing?"

"I discovered him attempting to break into the cash register. I sent the clerk to go call the police, but I haven't seen anything of him. Hey Dean, check the back office, will you? See if he's got a hold of the police yet."

A bit of color drained out of Dean's face, but he nodded and swallowed.

"All right," he said, "let me go check on the clerk." He glanced around and, seeing the hall with multiple doors across from the restrooms, he made his way over to it.

"Dean." Gemma said, but the man kept walking. "Dean." He turned to look at her. She pointed at the near wall behind the counter. He nodded, turned around and stepped in that direction.

A door opened in the back hallway and Tim stepped out of the men's room.

"Dean, you could have warned me that you really let loose before letting me in there. I don't know how long it's going to take for them to clean that place out." Tim stepped into the lobby of the building as he said this. "I don't know how you managed it, but-" he stopped himself as he approached the counter. "Where's Dean?"

"He went to get the clerk."

"Got it. Who's this?" he said as he gestured at the man standing behind her.

"This- this is…" Gemma gave a sigh. "This is the manager of the building."

"Oh, why didn't you say so? Look, buddy," he said, turning to the silver-haired man, "you've got to do something about those toilets. They've got to be from, what, 1950?" He looked to Gemma and the shoplifter for support. She only met his gaze. The shoplifter shrugged. He turned back to 'Phil'. "I worked at a little office once that had the same problem – ancient plumbing work. It just couldn't handle-"

"Tim." He stopped and looked at Gemma. "He's not doing anything about the toilets."

"What are you talking about? He's the manager, isn't he? His job is to keep these things covered. Customer service, right?"

"We've got another problem on our hands." She nodded in the direction of the shoplifter.

"Who, this guy? He's not going to be any trouble. You won't be any trouble, will you?" The shoplifter shook his head 'no'. "What's your name, bud?"

"Angie." Tim stifled a laugh, but the sliver-haired man couldn't help himself. Angie got red in the face. "It's short for Angelo. I'd like to say 'Michelangelo', but my mom wasn't that clever. My buddies started calling me 'Angie', and I never said anything about it. That was as good as telling them to call me by that name."

"Where's Dean? I thought he went to look for the manager, not ask for a tour of the county."

"We need to get back on the road." Gemma said. "We're wasting time waiting here for something the staff can handle." But Tim knew she couldn't make good on that claim with a bystander like Phil, if that was his name, being another ordinary citizen. Then again, he was an ordinary citizen.

Tim stepped closer to her.

"So what's the game plan? We could leave Mr. Sunshine-"

"Angelo."

"Michelangelo, yeah, we could leave him here with our bystander and let the police take care of this when they get here. The sooner we get out the better." Gemma looked over the man and back to Tim.

"As soon as we leave this, we've abandoned a criminal to do as he pleases. I can't walk away."

"Why not? You've got this under control, it's clear that this guy isn't the bravest type. We need to get moving. The longer we stay in one spot, the easier it will be for them to find us."

"Who's gonna find you?" Tim waved Angelo off.

"Look," Gemma said, "I see what you're trying to do, but I'm going to make a different call. As long as I'm here, this is my responsibility. I don't know much about what responsibility entails wherever you work..." Tim didn't feel like volunteering that he designed packaging for blenders was his best card to play at the moment.

"And my point is that if we stick around here too long your first responsibility is going to go out the window." He didn't think it would be discerning of him to mention the case at this moment. He knew that he didn't know how the FBI handled sensitive information. Or how they handled sensitive information that they didn't know they needed.

Tim sighed and looked at the floor. If Dean didn't get back soon he considered leaving on his own and letting Gemma and Dean explain the situation to the police. He nodded his head to the side.

"Could I speak with you in private for a moment?" She looked to him, to 'Phil', to the shoplifter and back to Tim and nodded. She beckoned to the silver-haired man who stepped to them.

"What's your name?" she asked.

"My name is Leonard."

"It's a pleasure to meet you, Leonard." she said. "Could you keep an eye on this one for us?" she asked, indicated the man behind the counter. "We're waiting for a call to the police to come through so they can pick him up." The man smiled.

"You certainly know how to stay busy." he said. "I can keep an eye on him." She thanked Leonard and stepped aside with Tim, turning to face him.

"Look," Tim said, "we can stay or go, but if we stay, we can't let anyone find out about the case."

"I agree." Tim did a take.

"You do?"

"Yes. But we can't simply leave this situation as it is."

"Why not? The police are probably on their way, Phil-"

"Leonard."

"Right, Leonard has things in hand, and if 'Angie' tries anything he'll be outnumbered two-to-one until the police show up."

"But in any case we're caught. We've been seen by people, and if we run now, they'll think we have something to hide."

"We do." They stood and faced each other for a moment. Gemma sighed and shook her head.

"Let's see what Dean is up to."

Tim looked to the door that led to the back. It was painted a characteristic grey and was certainly uninteresting. Dean had been gone for several minutes. The hair on the back of Tim's neck stood on end. He stepped towards the front of the building.

A black SUV sat in the parking lot.

"Gemma." he said without looking at her. "Did you lock the car?"

"Of course I did." she said. "Why would you..." She stepped up beside him and stopped at the sight of the vehicle sitting in the front parking lot. She paused for a moment before speaking.

"But why would they park there?"

"What do you mean?"

"Why would they park in plain sight? Anyone in the front lobby could see them if they parked there."

"So you do think it's our friends from earlier?"

"That or someone else likes practicing their shooting on their own vehicle. But if they're parked out here..." She turned and moved toward the door leading to the office in back. Angelo spoke up.

"What are you..." Gemma held up a hand for silence. Tim and Leonard stepped closer, listening for whatever she heard. She turned and grasped the door handle with her left hand. She gestured for Angelo to join them. With a finger indicating himself, he stepped up to them with raised eyebrows. With a sweeping motion, she indicated they were to follow here. She counted silently to three and slammed the door open. No one was in sight. She moved quickly down the hall, keeping her gun in front of her. There was a small office on the right as she stepped into the hall.

Stepping into the office, she quickly found the video monitors.

"There." She said, pointing to one of the camera feeds. The television used to monitor the grounds was an old tube television set, with the different video feeds splitting the screen into four panels. Tim looked and saw a second SUV planted behind the gas station. It was backing up.

Tim turned and charged for the back door of the gas station.

Gemma turned in her seat and called after him.

"Tim!"

He didn't reply. His gut clenched as he charged down the hallway. As he went, he saw a body splayed on the floor – dead or unconscious, he didn't know. It was the clerk, he was sure. He was already too late, but if there was a chance he could do something, anything-

Tim burst through the back door to see the SUV accelerating as it pulled away. He began to move towards it, but saw a window rolling down as he did so. Knowing what would come next, Tim dove behind a dumpster as shots rang out behind the building. The tires squealed, resisting the car's forward motion, even as the car pulled away from the building. Tim looked out from behind the dumpster hoping to see something- anything- about the vehicle. The only sight he caught was of taillights.

Even if he could get to his vehicle in time he didn't have the key and the conversation that would have to take place for them to get moving would delay them further. The back door locked from the inside. Tim made his way around front. As he rounded the corner, his suspicion was confirmed. The SUV in front was gone. Tim stepped to the front door, his mind reeling. Less than forty-eight hours ago his life was perfect and perfectly mundane. He was designing packaging for blenders and appliances. Now he was considering life-and-death situations and whether or not to chase after deadly opponents holding his new friend captive as they worked to save civilization from collapse.

Life didn't prepare him for this kind of challenge. He had thought asking a girl to prom in high school was one of the most challenging things he'd have to face.

He stepped back inside the building. No one would guess what kind of events happened in ordinary places they took for granted. He stepped through the employee entrance again and into the control room. The group turned to face him.

"I have good news." Tim said. "The good news is that, as far as I know, we're all alive. The bad news," he paused for a moment. "the bad news is that these enemy agents have captured one of our own.

We still have no idea who they are or where they are from. And we don't know where we'll be able to find them.

> "The other bad news is that our car has been broken into. They have stolen the briefcase and are now in possession of a piece of technology which is capable of crippling civilization as we know it."

"So," he said, "if anyone has some kind of good news, we could desperately use some of that."

"Before you talk more," Angelo said, "could you guys tell me what's going on?"

"You heard him." Gemma said. "These men are chasing us because we have- because we had a piece of technology which could be used to cripple nations. It can be used to gather any kind of information from any computer which stores information. Passwords are nothing to this thing. Internet security will be a thing of the past."

"We need a place to crash and think things through." Tim said. He sat down on the edge of the desk and turned to Gemma when Angelo spoke up.

> "I might be able to help."

Chapter 9

"Are you sure about this?" Gemma said.

"Of course not. But what other choice do we have?" Tim glanced back at Angelo in the backseat. Phil had opted to stay behind and wait for the police. He was going to explain that the thief got away. But since Tim and Gemma were now employing the help of Angelo, it was clear that they couldn't be the ones to report a robbery. Especially when trying to keep some secret FBI tech from another unknown agency.

They had continued along the road they were traveling. A few miles down the way, Angelo directed them to turn off. They were following an old side road that looked like it led to the middle of nowhere.

Glancing to the back seat where Angelo sat, Gemma leaned over to Tim discreetly.

"I'm concerned about our choice of place to stay." Gemmas said.

"It should be all right." Tim replied.

"We have plenty of choices, and it doesn't have to involve going with a complete stranger to his house."

"You're right." Tim said. "We could have volunteered to jump in the back of that SUV with Dean to see where those agents would have taken us."

Gemma shivered and didn't reply.

They followed the old road down for half a mile before turning off again. Tim piloted the car along the way until Angelo indicated a house off the road. He pulled into the driveway, parking the car at the head and stepping out. Gemma stepped out of the passenger side and stretched. Angelo followed suit and walked to the front door, fumbling with a small ring of keys.

"How did you get to the station in the first place?"

"I had a friend drop me off. I'm sorry about what happened earlier." He rubbed the back of his neck. "This has been one of the weirdest days of my life so far."

"What made you think to go in and rob a gas station?"

Angelo shook his head as he flipped through his keys.

"I don't know. You get low sometimes, y'know? I guess I was looking for something to do. I didn't know what to do with myself." The door swung open. "Come on inside."

He gestured to the futon in the middle of the living room. "Make yourself at home. I think I've got some food in here. Leftover pizza. It's not fine dining, but-"

"It's fine, thank you." Gemma's response echoed what Tim was feeling already. Food was food. He turned in a little circle as he looked about the house. It was a single-story, with a main living area, an off-set kitchen and dining room, and two other rooms which Tim guessed were the bedroom and bathroom. From the abundance of Mountain Dew cans and Gatorade bottles on the floor, Tim guessed that the man was single, probably not dating at the time.

The house was clearly well-lived in. Tim wondered if Angelo was the first owner. From the estimated age of the carpet, he thought that was unlikely.

"So," the voice came from the kitchen. "You've got somebody after you. Well never fear, I've dealt with debt collectors before. They'll do all kinds of stuff to scare you."

"Like shooting at you?" Angelo looked at Gemma, shrugged and turned back to the refrigerator.

"I've had worse." he said as he dug around the inside of the fridge.

"Really?" Gemma stepped closer to him. "Because the last time I knew, the only thing worse than getting shot by whoever these people are would be to get caught by them. Like our friend."

Tim blinked. She had moved quickly from repulsion to acceptance. He heard that stressful situations could bring some people together. Like people stuck in a mining shaft - they bond through common experience.

"So what's going on?" Angelo asked, facing Gemma. "Tell me the whole story." Gemma sized him up before nodding.

"Tim and I are two of three surviving people who know about this case."

"Right. The tech that could bring nations down."

"Yes. We four are the only surviving people know about this. If these agents get their hands on the case- or on us- then the FBI will not know how this group managed to cripple the world, holding some information for ransom, threatening to release some information without payment - this is the information age, and whoever can manipulate that machine has stolen the whole deck of cards."

Tim stepped into the kitchen and grabbed a piece of the pizza that Angelo pulled out. He usually didn't care for olives, but he was too hungry to be picky at this point. The garbage can was half-filled with empty pasta and soup cans. Angelo was sticking some dishes in the dishwasher. From the look of it, Tim couldn't tell if the dishes in the washer were dirty or clean. He didn't think Angelo knew either, but it was only half full.

"We've got to get out of the state." Tim said, looking at Angelo. They were all gathered in the kitchen now. "The case has to be taken back to the FBI in Washington."

"They're not just going to let someone walk in and give them a suspicious briefcase." Angelo said.

"Unless you know an FBI agent, that's our only option at this moment. The only other people we know who are involved in this are the enemy agents, whoever they are."

"I was going to ask you about that. Do you know who they are?"

Tim shook his head.

"They killed an FBI agent. I managed to escape with the case before they caught me. Then Gemma found me."

"Well, you guys could try to catch a flight to Washington."

"That won't work." Gemma said. "We have to get through security. There's no way they'll let us board a plane with that thing. The security agents will just think it's a bomb or something." She sighed and looked between Tim and Angelo. "I think we're going to have to drive."

"Their vehicles." Angelo said. The other two looked at him. "Do you two know anything about their vehicles?" Angelo asked. "Those big SUVs?" They looked at each other and shook their head. "I know two things from seeing them at a glance. First, they're expensive. Second, those aren't easy vehicles to get. They're not on the open market."

Tim waved his hand a little.

"Meaning?"

"Meaning that whoever owns these vehicles is either part of a governmental organization, very wealthy, or part of a corporation."

"But these people were governmental agents, why would the government be killing its own agents in trying to get back it's tech?"

"Unless it's someone within the organization who has special interests." Angelo said.

"Could they have something to hide." Tim replied.

"Or something to gain." Gemma said.

"In any case it looks whoever is involved has money to spare."

Tim let out a heavy sigh.

"So the real question is, how are we going to face off against a very powerful entity as they have more weapons, manpower, and resources than we do."

They stood in silence for a few minutes, taking occasional bites of pizza. Tim took his food and sat on the futon. His mind raced to take in what was going on. His life had been turned upside down. A situation he had never imagined himself in was now his waking reality. He was waiting to wake up and find that he was just late to work.

"How did you know about the SUVs?" He asked Angelo.

"My brother was a mechanic. I learned all about different kinds of vehicles, makes and models."

"So what can you tell us about these vehicles?"

"Like I said, these are in a different class, used by those who can afford them, which is the very rich or those in government. Most vehicles are marketed to the general population base. A few are marketed to those who have more money to spend. You're not going to hear about these vehicles in your circles because they're made for those who can afford them."

Tim paused and Gemma jumped on the silence.

"So we're looking for someone who has the means and motivation to use this technology."

There was quiet again for a moment. Gemma settled in a chair by the futon. Angelo was on his second slice of pizza. Quiet settled on the room as each of them pondered their situation and considered their options.

"The way I see it," Tim said, "We're going to have to drive to Washington." Gemma nodded.

"Unless you want to walk, that seems like the most efficient way of getting there."

"Haha." Said Tim. Gemma turned to Angelo.

"What do you think?"

Angelo shrugged. "As far as I can see, this is your problem."

"What do you mean?"

"You guys got yourselves into this mess with these gunmen chasing after you-"

"Angelo-"

"If you guys want to run off with them chasing after you, that's your choice."

"Angelo, they've seen you with us. I don't know if you're going to be safe if you stay here."

"Well, it'll be safer than running off with you two."

"They'll find you wherever you are. It will be safer for you if you're on the move with us."

Angelo only shrugged and turned away.

"If they find you here," Gemma said, "You'll have nowhere to go and no one to turn to."

"I've managed on my own for a while. I think I'll be able to handle myself."

"Whoever these guys are, they are trained professionals."

Angelo didn't have anything to say to that. The three of them sat in silence for a while. Angelo turned the television on and watched some sports. Tim paced about behind the couch, thinking things over, a half-slice of pizza set on the counter where he left it. There really wasn't much left to discuss at this point. They were leaving in the morning and working to get to the FBI building to return this case. Tim imagined that this was going to be a long trip - several days long. He had nothing with him, except his phone, wallet, and the clothes on his back. His clothes served their purpose, but he knew that they would begin to smell. He would have to pick up some other clothing- and something to carry them in.

"So," Tim said, "there's no chance of getting back to my apartment?"

Gemma shook her head.

> "If they've figured out who you are, they may have already searched your home. They'll have people watching it to see if you do come home. If they catch you there, you're as good as dead."

Tim sighed and sat on a chair which was seated beside the futon at the moment. The more he thought about his situation the more his head spun. He had moved from having a nice job safe at a company designing packaging, and was now in a messy house built for two, currently with three people in it at the moment. He really had very little hope of getting the case back to its owners. But he knew that it was up to them. They were the three living people on the planet who knew of this technology that could cripple the world.

Chapter 10

Dean tried to raise his head, but shooting pain raced through it and he let it fall back and groaned.

"There he is." He heard a voice say. His seat had been reclined, and he felt it being brought up into an upright position. He opened his eyes again and looked around. He was sitting in a bucket-type seat in a moving vehicle. A man in a dark suit was in the seat next to him. Dean tried to shift his weight and realized that he was strapped to the seat. A canvas strap was buckled at his shoulders as well as his midsection. From the tension against his body he guessed it must have wrapped around him and the back of the seat. He realized that he had a splitting headache and that his mouth was dry.

"Where am I?" He asked, looking about him. At this point Dean noticed the others in the vehicle. The driver spoke quietly to a man in the front passenger seat. The man beside Dean grinned.

"America's great byways." The man said. "Don't worry. That headache shouldn't last too long, and the trip will be over before you know it." This wasn't reassuring to Dean.

"I suppose you guys list your employment status on tax forms as 'Alternative', huh?"

The man laughed.

"Hey fellas, we've got a comedian back here."

"Leave 'em alone." Said a voice from the front passenger seat. "We're a delivery service, not interrogators."

The man turned to look at Dean and grinned. "Our employer will take care of that."

"So they didn't tell you anything."

The man beside Dean looked at him. Dean shrugged. "Look," he said, "I don't know where you guys fall on the food chain at the organization you work with, but if you're in charge of pickup and delivery, but nothing else, I'm guessing there's not a lot they trust you guys to do."

"Will you guys shut him up?" The driver's tone had an edge to it.

The man beside Dean shook his head and turned back to him.

"He's a little on edge. He hasn't done this much before."

"So kidnapping is something that you guys do on a regular basis?"

"You mind your business and keep quiet." Said the driver.

Dean wondered whether they were paid to break people's knees. Whatever kind of work these men were paid in was certainly either under the table or labeled differently in their books, for whoever they worked for. Labels like "kidnapping and arson" hardly made a good impression on resumes.

Dean licked his lips again. His mouth was dry and he didn't know how long he had been in this vehicle. The sun was up, so it had been at least twelve hours since the attack at the gas station. He remembered being in the back with the clerk. He tried to remember what happened after that. Fire. No, it was an electric feeling. They must have tased him when his back was turned, and dragged him to their vehicle when he fell unconscious.

The guard must have seen him licking his lips again, because he brought out and opened a new water bottle. Dean's arms were bound at his sides, so he had to trust the man to direct water into his mouth.

The man was kind enough to allow him a drink. He followed this up with a dash of water of Dean's head. He chuckled a little.

"Never miss an opportunity." He said.

"For what?" The man wouldn't answer him.

"What happened to the others?"

"Your friends?" The guard beside him said.

"Shut up." The driver said. The guard beside him heeded his co-hort's advice and fell silent. Dean breathed a small sigh of relief. They weren't in his vehicle and if the guard beside him wasn't quick to brag about it, he guessed that Tim and Gemma were safe. Dean watched the cars flying by on his left side, each of them hurrying on to whatever track meet or conference they were obligated, not aware of the fellow human being in danger passing them less than a hundred feet away.

Dean's mind reeled as he tried to understand what was going on and why this was happening to him. He knew that it must be connected with the case that Tim found. Gemma said she was an FBI agent. Did she know what she was doing? Were his friends coming for him? If they hadn't caught this vehicle already, he wondered whether they could be close behind. But if the guards saw them, there was sure to be trouble.

He tried to remember anything he could about what to do in situations like this. Unfortunately all he could remember was stuff like advising joggers to carry mace with them. Or not to jog alone at night in the park. Or to jog in pairs. It was lots of stuff about jogging, and all stuff that helps before you're caught. It was nothing useful for his current situation.

Water was running down the back of his head and under his collar from where the guard beside him had doused him. If they had any towels or paper towels, Dean didn't think asking for any favors at this point would be a good idea. So he sat in silence. He looked around himself again. The straps around him held him tightly to the seat. He wondered if they were attached to the seat itself of simply held in place by friction. He attempted to learn forward slightly to feel the straps' strength. The straps held him tightly to the seat.

The two men in the front of the van were talking quietly between themselves. One of them laughed. Dean stole a glance at the guard beside him. The man seemed to be disengaged from his situation, looking out the front window. Dean wiggled his foot and discovered that this was chained to something underneath the seat, probably either a cross bar, or some part of the seat itself. He felt his breathing become shallow and swallowed as he tried to corral his racing thoughts.

He looked again to the guard beside him.

"I'm Dean, by the way." The guard looked at him, but didn't reply. He shrugged. "I didn't know if they told you my name or anything." The guard nodded at the driver's seat.

"That's Big." he said.

"I suppose he is." Dean said, with a glance at the man's bulging biceps.

"That's what we call him - 'Big'." Dean looked at the driver again and whispered.

"'Big', that's it? Not 'Big Boy' or 'Big Lump'?" The guard beside him grinned. "What about the other one?" The man in the passenger seat was not small, but he was well-proportioned - more lean muscle than bulk.

"He's the Grip." The guard said. "Retention is his thing."

"What about you?"

"Weapons specialty." He said. "I voted to be called 'Big Shot', but since he's 'Big', they just call me 'Casing'."

"Casing- like a bullet casing." The man nodded.

"So if you get any funny ideas..." The man swung his head towards the back of the vehicle. Dean craned his neck as far as he could, but only managed to glimpse just behind Casing's seat. Looking to the guard he shrugged as best he could. The man sighed and leaned in.

"In the back of this vehicle I've got weapons of several makes and models. This means that if I want to take a single shot at you over a long distance I could do it that way. Or I cold pull out a fully automatic weapon and let the spray of lead catch you as you try to get away. So don't get any funny ideas."

"I get funny ideas all the time." Dean said, his brain kicking into high gear. This only elicited a scowl from the man beside him.

Grip's look suggested he thought Dean admitted to stupidity. Dean shrugged. "I'm a comedian. My job is to come up with funny ideas."

"Will you two knock it off back there?" Casing's voice resounded from the front.

Casing fell silent and Dean went back to looking out his own window.

He must have dozed off, because the next time he woke up Grip and Casing were out of the car. Looking around, he saw that they were at a gas station, parked by the curb, out of the way of the fuel pumps. The sun was setting, casting a bright light across the earth. The sight comforted Dean. Whatever happened, there were some things that were constant in the world.

The two guards must have already been out for a little bit, for it was only a few minutes before they both returned. They switched seats, Casing taking the driver's seat and Grip settling in the seat beside Dean. The man was clearly careful about keeping in shape. Under the dressy-casual outfit, he could see the man's toned muscles pressing through the fabric. A glance in his direction and Dean knew what was going on. Try me, the man's glance said. He was sure that this apparently professional criminal wouldn't think twice about compressing his spinal column.

It quickly became clear that they were going to drive through the night. Dean spent his time trying to ignore the man beside him. He stared out the window at cars passing and saw the setting sun again.

God, if you're out there, I need help. I don't know what to do. I need hope. He felt the tension in his body begin to ease and he breathed a sigh. He wasn't sure what to think at this point. His family had been religious, but he didn't buy into it himself. Church was a place you went to see your grandmother at Easter and Christmas.

The sun began to dip below the horizon. In a few minutes the lights over the highway would begin to turn on, triggered by the setting sun's dying light. Dean kept his eyes on the sun as it dipped lower toward the horizon. The last red light of the day reached over the edge of the world.

Ninety-three million miles. The sun was ninety-three million miles away, and yet it's light reached the world, enough to heat it and allow life to flourish. And yet Dean never felt so alone in his life.

Chapter 11

Tim woke to the sound of birdcalls outside the house. He tried to remember the last time he awoke to the sounds of nature over car engines and sirens. The house was quiet. He stepped to the bathroom and washed his face, hoping that it would help him wake up more fully. He didn't know if Angelo had coffee, but he needed it. Tim had slept on the futon in the living room. At this point, since he guessed the others weren't up, he thought that the television might prove to be a nice distraction. Of course the noise could easily wake the others - whatever the architects had planned in building this house, it wasn't soundproofing.

He stepped to the front window and looked outside. The sun was just above the horizon. Turning from the window, Tim went to the kitchen to see about finding some coffee.

It was about half an hour later when Gemma emerged from her room. She looked subdued. All through the last day, she had always been at the head of the pack, calling shots. The most he could say now was that she was upright and appeared to be alive. She sighed.

"I thought that if I got up early I'd be the only one up. I guess I should have thought that I'd wake you up if I came out here." Tim waved the comment off.

"I was already awake." He said. She left it at that. Tim grabbed a few mugs from one of the cabinets and stepped to the coffee pot. "Trying to solve world hunger?" he asked. She looked at him and he sighed.

"I've been trying to wrap my mind around what's been going on. I'm still waiting to wake up and find that all this has been a dream." She nodded.

"I know what you mean."

His brow furrowed as he looked at her. "You?" he asked. "I thought you were a special agent. She shrugged and looked at her feet.

"It's just a title. Titles are empty." She said.

"But they're given to people who've earned them."

"Ah," she said, "and what does that entail? Some training regiment with weapons handling, gathering intelligence, mock trials. We go through the training, but does that somehow make us superhuman?"

"I see." He said. "I think I know what went wrong." She looked at him. "You got to the wrong training event. You were supposed to make it to the super-human training and only made it to the FBI training course." He shook his head with a sigh. "We'll just have to see if those skill will be of any more use."

She laughed. "Let's hope not."

They talked for a little while longer, about politics and religion and all the hot-button issues that society tells people to avoid. They disagreed strongly on some things but laughed about it as they did so. When Tim looked at the clock again it was 8:30 AM.

"I think we need to figure out what we're going to do next."

"What should we do next?"

Tim sighed and rubbed the back of his neck. "I would say we should go after Dean, but I wouldn't know where to start looking. And every day we spend with the briefcase is another day those agents - whoever they are - can track us down and take the case without a fight."

Gemma shook her head. "They've come after us twice now. They have us out-manned and outgunned. I don't look forward to running into them again." At this, she looked at Tim. Since he didn't know what else to do, he shrugged a little.

"What?"

"If we're going to keep doing this, with these armed people after us, it would be good to know that you can handle yourself."

"Driving's my thing, I much prefer sticking to that."

"You never know what kind of situation you'll find yourself in." she said. "You should be prepared for any kind of situation. You may have to fight." Tim swallowed and nodded.

After warning a half-conscious Angelo about what was going on, they stepped outside and around to the back of the house.

"All right." Gemma said. "What do you know about the use of firearms?" Tim shrugged.

"They kill a lot of people." Gemma laughed.

"First, let's be clear, people kill other people. And baseball bats are also responsible for a large number of fatalities as well. So, when you see another person intending to harm you, your goal is to keep him from harming anyone. You can do this in a few different ways. The first would be to get his weapon away from him. In our situation, he's not likely to be handing it over to you.

"The second method is some kind of body shot, harming him and keeping him from hurting anyone. The third would be a fatality.

"When handling a weapon, there a few things to keep in mind. Do not point the gun at anything or anyone until you intend to fire at something."

"What do I do with it?"

"Keep it trained on the ground at your side. Now," she said, pointing away from them, "let's say we have a shooter over there, maybe one hundred and fifty feet in that direction. If you plan to engage him, show me what you would do."

Tim took a moment to visualize the scene. Then he went for the quick draw, pulling and imaginary gun from his side holster he did not own.

"Pew-pew-pew." he said. "Did I hit anything?"

"Not yet. Let's talk about your form. When you fire the weapon, there's going to be a little kick, so you want to be ready for that. Plant your feet shoulder-width apart. That's right. Now, when you fire it, your hand may fly back, Remember, you've got something leaving the gun at 2,500 feet per second. To put that in perspective that's a little more than 1,700 miles per hour. If your hands fly back after the shot, let them do so over your shoulder. There's nothing like whacking yourself in the face with a blunt metal object propelled by controlled explosions."

Tim grimaced. "I can imagine a few things."

Gemma only shook her head. She continued to teach him, showing him the proper stance and grip when firing and talking about different situations when he might have to use a weapon.

"What about unusual uses?" He asked.

Her brow furrowed. "What do you mean?"

"Let's say they've got someone and I want to take them out, but I don't want to hit the person they're holding. They do that in films all the time. Is there any way it would be useful then?"

She shook her head. "Sorry bud. This thing is used to launch small pieces of metal at other things. Unless you're either a really good shot, or know something about advanced physics I don't know that it will do anything extraordinary."

Tim smiled and looked at the ground. "So how did you get into all of this?"

"All of what?"

"FBI, gathering intelligence, stopping terrorists and madmen - where do you begin if you're interested in something like that? how do you become interested in something like that?"

"It starts with people."

"People?"

"Yeah. I mean some guys come in looking for excitement, but they sober up pretty quickly. The point is, you have to know why you're doing something. Is it for the thrills and action? For the attention and glory?" She paused. "Or is it because you know that there are people out there who need you, who need help, and that your skills and knowledge can help change lives?"

"And now you're sounding like a College commercial."

She brushed a stand of hair behind her ear and remained silent. Tim quieted down too. He looked at her again. Her brow which was so often set in thought or concentration was soft. He stepped toward her and she looked up to his face. The air between them tingled.

"You know," he said, "if you're trying to save the world, you might need some help."

She shook her head. "I don't think you want to get involved in this. I shouldn't have pulled you into this."

He spread his hands. "I was already involved in all of this when you found me, there's nothing you can do about that."

Her head hung lower and she had no response to that. He looked at her eyes, but they were trained on the ground. He watched as thoughts flew through her mind, almost surfacing enough to be seen but then submerging themselves once again into her subconscious. One after another they flashed onto her face, a slide projection with her face as the screen. He waited, understanding that he could do nothing but wait.

After a moment she stepped away and walked back to the house.

"Gemma." he called. She stopped in her tracks and turned back to look at him. "You don't have to do this on your own."

She entered the house without another word.

Tim began walking, working through the situation in his mind. They would have to leave soon, since they didn't know who was after them, why, or when they would show up next. The trees behind the house vied for his attention. He began to wander, walking slowly away from the house itself and towards the wooded area away from the road. The grass was thick and trees were sparse at first, but he could see, ahead, that they grew thicker together. He let his feet lead, not caring where he went as long as he was moving. He found that whenever he was stressed that moving, walking helped him to process what he thought.

What did he think? He was on the run from all he knew with a complete stranger. The other stranger had been caught by an enemy of some kind whom he could not identify. He felt a breeze tickle his face and he smiled. He loved the outdoors. It was his haven. Whenever life became too much, getting out of the city was usually the cure for whatever thing was troubling him at the moment. He had spent enough time trudging down the sidewalk and longed for the feel of soft earth underneath his feet. Even the smell of the earth underneath him was a welcome difference from the scent of gasoline that seemed to permeate the city.

The boughs of the trees above him shaded him from the sun as he stepped down into a little gully and began strolling along it, keeping the direction of the house in mind. He knew he needed to get back to the house soon, as the group would have to leave. But he needed to sort out his thoughts. He took a deep breath and exhaled, imagining his neurons firing as he did so. Whatever part of his brain was responsible for understanding relationships was not the primary part he used in his life. Knowing that the first rule of any kind of social interaction is to "know thyself", Tim had made a habit of working to understand his own ideas, interactions and emotions.

He knew that men got a lot of flak in general for not being in touch with their emotions. They tended to be more practically minded. Of course this wasn't a rule, but if you asked a guy what he was thinking, most of the time it was about food, work, or something he wanted to do. To make generalizations of any kind was dangerous. So he got into the habit of trying to understand himself so that he could understand others.

All he had seen from Gemma had been business - getting the FBI case back to the FBI, escaping from the pursing agents, trying to find a safe place to stay, keeping a man from robbing a convenience mart - everything was about getting stuff done. From their conversation it was clear that he hadn't seen the whole story. Being in the dark was something that bothered Tim. He would rather know what was going on, even if it was a bad situation. Right now it didn't look good for them.

Chapter 12

Tim stepped into the house and found Angelo and Gemma talking at the table. He moved to the kitchen to get some coffee as they talked together. Angelo glanced at him, but didn't say anything. Tim poured himself some coffee and settled into a spot at the table. Gemma looked at him, but didn't say anything. Angelo had a slice of pizza in his hand. He gestured to the kitchen.

"There's more in the fridge if you want some."

Tim shook his head.

Gemma glanced out the window and stood, taking her mug to the kitchen and rinsing it out. Tim looked at Angelo and nodded towards Gemma. Angelo shrugged.

"Y'know," he said, "from all that I've learned in that last day, it sounds like you two could use some help."

Tim raised an eyebrow. "You hardly seem the type who's eager to volunteer."

"Do you think this is my eager face?" Angelo fidgeted. "Besides, I owe you one. After what happened yesterday, I started re-thinking things. If you guys hadn't come along, I would be just another petty thief, looking to rip off another convenience store. Now…" He looked between the two of them. "…I don't know if I'll be able to live with myself if I turned you guys down, or didn't help you. If this really is about keeping our country safe, then you guys are going to need all the help you can get."

"Thank you." Tim said.

"What's our plan of action?" Angelo asked.

Gemma cleared her throat. "As soon as we get the information to the FBI, we should be home-free. The key will be getting there safely. We don't know who's after us, what they know or where they are."

"Isn't there any way you can learn more about these guys?" Tim asked.

Gemma shook her head. "Until we meet them in person – which I hope we don't – but until we see them again, we have no way to know who they are."

"Or who sent them."

Tim spoke. "I have a question."

"Go ahead." Gemma said.

"Couldn't you just call it in?"

"I could." she said. "But there's no way to know if a phone we use is being traced. it's better if we get it there in person."

Gemma stood and the two men looked at her. "We'll need to get going," she said, "the morning is getting away from us."

In the next twenty minutes, Angelo went to his room to pack, and Tim went to the sink to wash his face. Gemma went to her own room. Tim had nothing to pack, so he spent his time in the living room, waiting for the others. The floor had a smaller number of old soda cans on it than when he first saw it. This meant that either Angelo decided to clean now that he had company or that Gemma got tired of them very quickly.

Angelo emerged from his room with a single duffel bag over his shoulder. He nodded to Tim and stepped out to the front of the house.

Tim followed him. They were broaching the subject of sports when Gemma emerged from the house. Seeing her emerge, Angelo made his way back into the house for a final check. After a minute or two, he stepped out again and locked the door behind him.

They climbed into the car, with Angelo in the back, and Gemma pulled the vehicle out of the driveway. The clock read 9:02 AM as they made their way down the road. They were quiet at first. Angelo started to make a conversation about sports. Gemma wasn't interested and Tim didn't track much with sports teams. It was about nine in the morning as they pulled away from Angelo's house.

"You know Angelo, this won't be an easy thing to do. It's not a quick fix that we're looking for."

He considered Tim's statement for a moment. "I knew coming into this that it wouldn't be easy." Tim nodded and they left it at that.

As they drove, he considered their options. He knew that they would certainly have to drive all the way to the FBI headquarters in Washington. No plane tickets, as even if they had the money for it, the case itself would raise too many questions. Gemma decided to keep to back-roads for the time being. Tim assumed that this would be to stay out of sight of whoever might be looking for them and the case. He found himself glancing over his shoulder out the back window. No one used the road they were on. Confident that Gemma knew what she was doing, Tim tried to get himself to relax. Thinking about how they were on the run only increased his tension.

Angelo was in the backseat, humming something to himself. Tim caught the tune, but didn't recognize it and didn't hear any words.

"What's that one you're humming back there?" He started the conversation to distract himself, as he had little interest in what song Angelo sang.

"You haven't heard The Cat Came Back?"

Tim shook his head. "No. Is that supposed to be representative of something?"

"No, man. It's about this cat that keeps coming around and bothering this guy. He keeps trying to find ways to knock off the cat, but the cat keeps surviving."

"That sounds like a sad song." Gemma commented.

Angelo shrugged, but Gemma couldn't see it. "It's supposed to be funny. Some people add verses to it. There's one about the apocalypse, where the nukes go off, humanity is wiped out, but the cat comes back."

Tim's brow furrowed. "That doesn't make sense."

"It's not supposed to make sense, it's supposed to be funny. The shock value of the cat making it through that is supposed to get a laugh."

"Yeah, but if I'm spending all my time thinking about how the cat would have-"

"If you say anything more about cat's dying, this trip is going to get unpleasant." The two men looked to the driver's seat.

"Our odds are already pretty bad." Angelo said. "I didn't think a little dark humor would be out of place in a situation like this."

"Humor about death," She said, "is always out of place."

They were quiet for a moment.

Angelo spoke. "Don't you find that you have to laugh at it sometimes, look at it from a different angle?" This prompted an irritated glance from Gemma. She turned back to driving without a word. "I think," Angelo continued, "that it's healthy to laugh at the things that we think so seriously about so often."

"So you think that I need to laugh about the death of people in my field. I'm too close to it all, is that right?"

He didn't reply. She turned to Tim. "Do you think this way?"

"That's not fair. You know that's not what he meant."

"For all we know, Dean is already dead."

"If they wanted him dead, they wouldn't have taken him. They need him for something."

"And when they don't?"

"We'll find him before then."

"What if that doesn't happen? Then I've pulled four people into this-"

"If you remember, I practically volunteered for this. Dean came of his own accord. He made that decision for himself."

"No one seems choked up about me risking my neck to help you guys." Angelo said from the back seat. Tim glanced back at him.

"Sorry bud. We do appreciate your help. The situation she found you in, though, wouldn't exactly endear you to anyone." Angelo's eyes dropped when Tim said this and he kicked himself for saying it. He turned back to the front of the vehicle and kept his eyes on the front glass.

They passed the next hour in relative quiet. Tim watched fields and trees fly by on both sides of the vehicle. Angelo kept humming to himself, switching from folk tunes to old tunes from the 60s and 70s. There didn't seem to be any rhyme or reason to his internal playlist, and Tim found it entertaining to attempt to guess what song Angelo would hum next based on his previous choices. His predictions were usually incorrect.

Gemma kept quiet as she drove. Tim soon began to wonder if her mood was normal or if there was something on her mind which quieted her. Whatever occupied her mind at the moment, she did not seem eager to discuss it with anyone.

Tim cleared his throat.

"It looks like it's going to be warm today."

Gemma kept silent.

"I heard the Bears are playing again this weekend."

This did not elicit a response.

"Have you heard of the new movie-"

"It's going to be a long drive." Gemma said.

He took that as a hint and quieted down.

A great spread of blue swept above their heads, a bright lining for the hills and fields to rest against. Bright green trees provided contrast to this. Some were flowering, and these flowers stood out like bright pinpoints against the green swaths.

The clock read 11:56 AM by the time they made their first stop. Gemma had already warned them several times to be cautious. The plan was to get gas, grab some food, and get back on the road. They had left Colorado behind them, and were making their way through Kansas. Aside from the occasional gas station or small town along the way, homesteads, fields and barns dotted the landscape. Some of the towns were probably officially villages for their size, and only took a minute or two to pass through, driving at a steady 25 mph. Once they were back onto the highways and county roads, Gemma increased the speed. Tim noticed that she didn't go over the speed limit, however their current errand pressed them. If they were caught by police who could investigate or confiscate their case, all could be lost.

As they stepped to the combination gas station and diner, Tim hoped that Gemma wouldn't take the law into her own hands again.

The old gas station confined itself to less than half a block. Tim wondered how many people had thought to abandon a place like this one. Or, worse, level it and build something new and exciting for the public which passed through once and then on to their destinations.

"Remember," he murmured to Gemma, "we want to get in and out, no trouble for anyone."

"Who said anything about trouble?" She said without a smile and stepped by the swinging doors. "In and out." she said.

Tim breathed a sigh. "In and out." He murmured to himself. "No trouble for anyone."

"You all right?" Angelo asked.

"Tim didn't reply. They stepped through the store's front door. Old swing music was playing over the speaker system. He couldn't imagine that there was much modern interest in the style of music. Whether the personal taste of the manager dictated it, or they decided based on having a diner attached to the gas station, swing was the music of choice for the establishment.

He grabbed a sweet tea and a boxed sandwich from the fridge on the wall and made his way to the front. As he passed the snack aisle, he grabbed some chips as well. Another man stood in line before him. The man must have had all the beef jerky from the display case. Tim wasn't sure how much that would cost a man. The customer in front of him finished up and stepped away and out of the building. Dean was still making his selection. Tim didn't know where Gemma was.

He stepped up to the counter and nodded to the cashier. The young man must have been sixteen, thin, angular jaw, blond hair. His hands seemed to move more quickly than the rest of his body.

"And how are we doing today sir?"

Tim had never liked that way of greeting people. The first way it might be used would be to address the royal "we", and Tim knew nobody the kid at a gas station saw would fit that profile. The second possibility was that the kid was referring to himself as well. But if the kid wasn't sure about how he was doing, why would he ask any customer about their current state of being?

"Fine, thanks."

"Did you find everything you needed?"

"If I hadn't I would still be looking."

"And is there anything I can help you with?"

Tim nodded at the products he had placed on the counter. The young man grabbed them and started to scan them. As he stood, his eye roamed the counter. Tim noticed some fidget toys in a display case. He looked away, but not quickly enough.

"Would you be interested in any Fidget Widgets today, sir?"

"No."

"As they say, the Fidget Widgets strengthen your digits."

"I'm not interested."

"We have a two for one sale today."

"If I don't want one of them, what would I do with two?" said Tim.

"I've heard it's great for stimulating the brain. These things help people focus if they've got trouble with biting on things, fidgeting with things, can't stop tapping pencils, can't stop-"

"I get the picture. How much for the fidgets?"

"Five dollars."

Tim waved him off. "Forget it."

"It's a two for one sale."

"Again," Tim said, "what would I do with two that I couldn't do with one?"

The clerk shrugged and looked at the counter. "You could give it to a friend."

Tim nodded. "That's not a bad suggestion."

"How many Fidget Widgets would you like to add to your order today, sir?"

Tim waved at the products on the counter. "Ring me up for this."

The clerk named the price for the food and Tim shelled out the cash. As he began to step away, the clerk began to speak again, quickly.

"If you're here for another second, maybe you'd like to try-"

"No, thank you."

Tim glanced around as he waited for Gemma and Angelo to finish getting their food. He scanned the room, trying to be aware of his surroundings. The man with the beef jerky had left already. Another man was at the back of the store, browsing the beverage section.

Tim stepped to one of the aisles near the front, working his way towards the man by the coolers. Tim saw Angelo already at the front, waiting to check out. He had three bottles of Mountain Dew along with some packages of chips and snacks with him. Tim glanced back at the man. He hadn't moved and looked nervous, glancing around him. Tim's gut tightened. He glanced around the store. Besides Angelo, himself, and the man, there was a woman near the self-care products, but she was much too old to be involved in anything like what they were doing.

His spine tingled. He turned where he stood so that he could get a better look at the parking lot. At first glance he didn't see any vehicles that he recognized from their first chase. He breathed a sigh. Maybe he was just being paranoid.

Tim stood at the end of the first aisle by the door and waited for the others to finish with their purchases. He took another look at the man by the coolers. The man was large, not a bodybuilder, but Tim guessed the man knew how to handle himself. Watching the man for a moment he could feel that something about the man threw him off, but he couldn't say what. After a moment, Tim took a breath, and walked towards the man.

He didn't know if Gemma or Angelo saw him, but assumed they hadn't since they didn't say anything. He stepped down the aisle to the coolers. The man was now about ten feet to ahead of him and had his eyes locked on the cooler in front of him. He was fidgeting with something in his pocket and didn't make eye contact, but kept his eyes on the cooler in front of him. Tim walked to the man, slipping around to his other side. As he did so, he took a glace at the man's face and head. The man wasn't wearing any discernable earpiece from what Tim could tell. The man was large, but he shifted where he stood, not budging from his spot in front of the coolers.

Tim nodded at the man.

"How's it going?"

The man shrugged and his eyes darted to Tim for just a moment before looking back at the cooler in front of him.

Tim cleared his throat. "I was going to say something that might be of interest to you, but you seem like a busy man, so I'll mind my own business. It was nice talking, though." Tim began to step down the aisle again.

"Wait." the man said.

Tim turned back.

"What do you have to say?"

Tim exhaled. "Well, I mean I was going to say I thought I recognized you. At least there was a buddy of mine who mentioned someone who could only be you, I'm sure. 'What's he look like, this buddy of yours?' 'Oh, he's about 6' 3", wears black a lot, has a penchant for funny kitten videos.'" The man stepped closer and Tim took a breath. They stood in silence for what felt to Tim like an eternity. Then the man began to laugh.

It was a breathy little thing at first, but as it picked up steam, the man's laugh began to resound throughout the building.

"Kitten videos." He mumbled.

"Say," said Tim, "I wonder if you've met a new friend of mine. He's a comedian. Dean is his name. He went missing just a day ago. We were minding our own business when these guys came out of nowhere, shot up the building where we were in, and dragged him out the back door."

The man's face dropped and turned white. A hardness come over his face. The man looked ready to reach for something in his pocket, when Tim heard a voice behind him.

"Hey Tim, how's it going over here?"

"Good." He said. "I was hoping I'd get to introduce you two. This is my new pal-"

The man's eyes darted between the two of them. Tim was ready to slug the guy if he tried anything.

"Mike." the man ventured.

"Mike." Tim said.

"It's nice to meet you, Mike." Gemma said, hand extended. The man took it warily. Her grip was firm, but no more than necessary. "Why don't we step over to the diner for a minute or two? You guys are old pals, right? You'd want to catch up." The man before them wilted. Tim looked over the man whose frame spoke clearly enough - this man would have no problem handling either of them. And Tim didn't doubt the man stood a chance against both of them. But whether "Mike" didn't want to make a scene in public or he doubted himself, he didn't seem eager to start a fight at the moment.

Gemma slipped around to the man's side and gently pulled, Mike resistant at first, giving in as she began to step away from the coolers. Tim caught sight of Angelo by the checkout counter. Angelo gave him a confused look. Tim nodded to the diner. Gemma led their unwilling volunteer to the diner and sat him down in a booth in a back corner. He sat against the wall, across from her.

"All right," she said, as Angelo joined them, keeping her voice down, "tell me what's going on here."

Tim nodded at Mike. "I believe this man knows something about where Dean is." They all looked to the man who swallowed, considering the choices before him.

"All right," he said, "I'll tell you what I know, just don't kill me. The guys who took your friend are part of a company called Singh

Industries. They're a technology firm named for the revolutionary Bhagat Singh.

Tim grunted. "Not exactly a typical role model."

"They invest in all kinds of technology." Mike said with a nod. "They're especially interested in new technologies. Singh Enterprises works with engineers and inventors to make prototypes and eventually marketable versions of these inventions."

"Who buys these things?" Gemma asked.

"It just depends." he said. "Sometimes it's stuff that companies use, computers, software, hardware, but the company's big enough to invest in all kinds of tech."

"Empty your pockets." Gemma said. The man cautiously emptied each pockets, putting the items on the table for them to inspect. A ring of keys, a cell phone, a wallet, some pocket change, two folded sheets of paper and a small device the size of a key FOB sat on the table. With a nod from Gemma, the man slid back into his seat. As Angelo began to go through the man's wallet, Tim took up the FOB device.

"I'm guessing that you weren't looking to unlock your car with this device." It was small, having two buttons on it, one on the top and a small one along the edge. There was also a small LED light. "What does this device do?"

"It's a-" the man cleared his throat. "that is a device which is used-"

"It's a tracker." Gemma said.

Angelo glanced around him. "Hey guys?"

Tim shook his head. "What would he be doing with a tracker?"

    "Guys?"

"The man is clearly involved in something tracking us, they're probably tracking him when he turns that on."

    "Guys?"

They both turned to Angelo.

"What?"

Silently, he held up a card for the two of them to look at. It was an identification card.

Gemma and Tim leaned in to look at the card.

"Michael Lefitt." Tim said. He shrugged. "What's interesting about the card?"

Angelo raised a finger and pointed it at the card. Tim leaned closer before Gemma grabbed the card from Angelo's hand. She was looking over it thoughtfully when Tim took it from her. Glancing up from the card to Mike, Tim smiled.

"Well," he said, "it looks like you might be able to help us with this. Technology and intelligence."

Mike glanced between the three of his captors but didn't reply. Beads of sweat glistened from his forehead, reflecting the harsh lights of the diner.

"Look," he said, "you seem like nice people, and what you're doing seems to be important, but we've got bigger things to worry about." He grabbed the FOB device before anyone could stop him. "You've discovered the tracking device. Any time I press that button it alerts working for Singh Industries that they need to intervene."

Looking at the device, Tim's gut clenched as he saw the LED on the device illuminated. He glanced around the restaurant. Mike set down the device and Gemma took it, asking "How long ago did you press that button?"

"Maybe ten minutes ago, when I first saw you."

Angelo looked to Tim. "What should we do with him? We've got him outnumbered three-to-one."

"I'm not a fighter." Mike said. "I just report what I see. If you guys are getting out of here you've got to move."

"What about the device?" asked Angelo. "What will they do with that?"

Mike shrugged. "They take it from me and deactivate it themselves."

"You said it's a GPS tracker, right?" said Tim.

"Yeah, it alerts them to my location when I activate it."

"Are you sure about that?" said Gemma. "Most GPS units are made so that they can send out a regular signal. You said that when you press the button it sends an alert to the corporation's agents. Do you know if that's the only time the GPS tracking is turned on?"

Mike's face wrinkled in thought and a look of worry came over his face. Gemma turned to Tim. "If that unit is letting off a steady signal, they'll know where this guy is at all times." She turned to Mike. "As long as he has it with him."

Tim stood and faced the table. "We had better get going. Now is not the time to find out if those agents have become better shots than the last time we encountered them." Gemma and Angelo stood as well. Mike looked at the three of them.

"What do we do with him?" asked Angelo.

Tim looked in Mike's face. There was fear in his eyes. He clearly didn't have the determination to try to do away with the three of them, if that's something he ever intended to do. Tim realized that this man worked as a kind of bounty hunter - if he saw the 'fugitives' wanted by the corporate agents, he signaled them, the three would be picked up, and Mike would get a hefty reward, if the corporation decided to pay him for his work.

Glancing around the restaurant, Tim only saw some casual diners, sipping coffee or dipping fries. Through the front window there was no sign of any suspicious vehicles- yet.

Tim lifted his hands in a little shrug. "I don't think Mike wants to hurt us. If you're looking for a safe way out of here you could come with us. It might not be an easy road, but we'll be looking out for each other.

If you come along with us we may be able to help you, or drop you off somewhere you want along the road we're taking."

"Are you sure about this?" Gemma murmured in his ear.

Tim turned to face her. "The man has made no attempt to either harm us himself. If we get rid of the tracker, that's his tie to the corporation that's after the case. He would be free like us."

"You don't know what you can promise him."

"We can promise him an opportunity."

Tim offered his hand to Mike. "Welcome to the team." he said. Mike stood and shook Tim's hand as he did so. They began to make their way out to the parking lot. Angelo sniffed. Gemma turned to him.

"What?" she asked.

"I didn't get a formal greeting."

"Sign up for the NRA if you want a formal greeting."

Chapter 13

Dean awoke to the smell of coffee. For half a moment he thought about a shower and getting breakfast ready. Then he remembered. He was strapped to a seat in the back of a moving vehicle with three formidable men who were delivering him to an unknown entity. He groaned in his seat. There was no reaction from the threesome. By this Dean guessed they were not in a good mood. He kept quiet for a little while, keeping his eyes shut as long as he could manage. He must have dozed because when he woke up again the sun was shining fiercely through the front window. East. They were heading east, into the rising sun.

"Here." He heard a voice beside him. Squinting against the sun's brightness, Dean looked to the passenger seat beside him. The one called Grip was beside him, holding some coffee. He offered the cup to Dean. He nodded at the offer, and the man directed the coffee into his mouth. Dean sighed to himself. However terrible his present situation, the taste of coffee in the morning eased some of his tension. At least something about this day could be normal.

"I suppose it couldn't hurt to ask where we're going." Dean said.

Grip shook his head. "You're right." he said, but was quiet after that. From this, Dean could tell that the man had a sense of humor. And that he shouldn't expect to get answers from any of the men in the vehicle. He decided on a different tack.

"So what's with the concierge? I didn't know the trip came with free beverages." The man beside him actually laughed and shook his head.

"What's got into your head?" he asked. "That you can joke at a time like this?"

Dean shook his own head. "I wish I knew."

About twenty minutes later they pulled to a stop.

"All right." said Grip. "We're giving you a few minutes to stretch. If you try anything stupid we shoot you. The boss doesn't need you that badly."

Dean wondered about that last statement. They had been driving all night to get him somewhere, and it was clear that they weren't stopping anywhere for long. Casing, in the front, opened the side door and kept a gun trained on Dean. Grip slipped to the back of the seat and undid the straps that held him firmly against it. His arms throbbed as blood began to rush back into the arteries in his arms and hands. Looking down at his hands, his fingertips were blue from a lack of circulation. He leaned forward with his elbows on his knees and let his body attempt to relax.

"Let's go." Grip said. "We don't have all day." Dean nodded and climbed out of the vehicle. He straightened himself up slowly and looked around. The day was beautiful even with the sun still rising. The wind carried a little chill from the night, but he knew that it would quickly warm up. Walking about, Dean raised his arms over his head and stretched his muscles.

The men kept a careful eye on him. He knew that any sudden movements would set them off, so he took it slow. He also knew that if he moved too fast he wouldn't be able to keep his feet. His legs felt almost like rubber. Ten thousand invisible needles seemed to prick his legs and he paced around the parking lot. It hurt to take a deep breath, but he did so anyways. The fresh air was wonderful, along with the sight of the rising sun. Using his feet again was also nice.

Able to see the men now, Dean could finally size them up. The one they called 'Big' was truly enormous. The man pushed the seven foot tall mark. He was muscular as well. Dean didn't doubt that the man would have no trouble, and take pleasure in keeping him in line.

"I know you guys aren't going to tell me about where we're going." he said. "But there's another problem you haven't thought about."

"And what's that?" Casing asked.

"What exactly is going to happen to me? I mean after you get what you want? I'm assuming you're looking for information. Otherwise, why go to all this trouble to get me halfway across the country in such a short period of time? If you wanted me dead, you've had plenty of opportunities do it that way."

Grip stepped up to him until they were nose to nose. The man grinned. "Who said we don't want you dead?"

Dean swallowed and kept eye contact with the man.

"Now look here." Grip said. "If you want to make your way through this with as little trouble as possible, you keep your mouth shut. We've been told to deliver you to our employer alive. That doesn't mean un-harmed." He saw the blood rush from Dean's face. "You understand." he said. "Our employer has heard nothing from us since we left to find you. Now if you were in tow and you had some broken bones, some bruises, the story would be that you fought back when we grabbed you instead of going down like a sack of lead." He looked into Dean's face, but Dean was looking at the ground. "Think carefully about your next move." he said.

Dean looked carefully around him. Casing and Big were standing off a hundred feet, talking. There was no one in sight, and Dean didn't think he could run fast enough to find help before the men caught him. He nodded quietly and looked at the man in front of him. Grip put on a small smile.

"All right." he said. He turned to the others, who caught his eye. With a gesture, they began to move back to the vehicle. Dean's legs felt bet-ter for standing on them for a few minutes. His back ached as did his ribs, from the constant pressure on them. He gave his arms another shake. Feeling had returned to them. His hands had that familiar feel-ing when blood rushes back into one's fingers. It felt like his hands were expanding and ready to burst if they kept it up. He shook them out again, stepping slowly to the vehicle. Grip smiled at the others. They ignored it.

Dean climbed into the back of the SUV and he sat once more in his seat, expecting them to strap him on, as they had done the last time.

"Put your seatbelt on." Grip said.

Brows furrowed, but not daring to disobey, Dean followed instructions. Grip climbed into the seat beside him. Casing kept a gun trained on him as Grip secured Dean's hands in front of him with zip ties.

"In case you get any funny ideas."

The other two climbed into the front of the vehicle. They pulled out of the back lot and onto the road again. The next hours passed in a long drone of sameness. Dean sat and watched the road go by. Beside him, Grip fell asleep in minutes. The two up front talked a little, but they kept their conversation quiet as they did so. Dean felt better for the stretch and walk around, but his situation was no better than it had been before. That wasn't entirely true. For whatever reason, they hadn't strapped him to the seat as they had done before. The zip ties pinched, but Dean was grateful that he could breathe more easily. With those straps holding him to the seat for hours, the man's ribs ached. Every breath in had been with tension, pressing against the restraints holding him to the seat.

He stared out the window, nothing different than he had been doing for the past day, wondering whether anyone would find him. From what little he could tell of the men in the vehicle with him, these weren't simply thugs off the street looking to earn a little pocket money. From the way they spoke it was clear that they worked for someone. That someone wanted Dean alive, but that wasn't much comfort. From what he could guess, Dean knew that they would want what little he knew so he could betray his friends, or he could face some kind of pain for not giving the information willingly. Grip's talk of broken bones didn't seem too far off the mark.

Dean tried to imagine whether there was anything he could do, but he couldn't think of anything. He was trapped in a moving vehicle with three guards who wouldn't think twice about injuring him. A doubt flashed in his mind and he looked at Grip. Another possibility was that Grip was bluffing to keep him in line.

Time had run together into one continuous stream, and Dean couldn't tell if it had been three hours or three days. He awoke to find the van stopped. The driver had stepped out of the car and was speaking with someone. Dean looked around. The vehicle was standing in front of a gate to what looked like an industrial area. He smelled something salty and realized it must have been a lake. Looking beyond the gate, he saw that they were in what looked like a shipping yard. Boats were moored about the harbor, some with great shipping containers stacked on them. Tall cranes dotted the area, set up to get the containers on and off ships as needed.

Why a shipping yard had been picked, he couldn't guess, but seeing that they were entering some kind of gated area, Dean guessed that they were about to exit the vehicle. He craned his neck and he heard and felt something pop. Stretching it back and forth he tried to work the kinks out from sitting in a car for so long. He glanced over at the seat beside him. Grip was there, and it looked like he has just woken up. He wondered how long they must have been driving.

The driver finished with the guard at the gate, who opened it up for them. Climbing back into the driver's seat, he pulled the car forward and into the expansive lot. They drove along the yard until they reached one of the warehouses. As they approached, the doors slid open and the driver pulled in directly. The door shut behind them, leaving them in thick darkness.

As he stepped out of the vehicle, Dean noticed some newcomers – he guessed they must have been guards, for they wore black and had weapons as well as utility belts. They had weapons trained on him as he stepped out of the vehicle. At first he didn't know why they bothered to do this. He wasn't skilled with any weapons or combat and didn't pose any threat to them. He had never visited a gun range, and didn't know the first thing about how to handle a gun.

After thinking about it, which he had plenty of time to do, he realized that they must not have known these things. The only thing that they could know about him was that he was traveling with a confirmed agent of the FBI who was in possession of a case with technology that could change the world. Playing through the story in his own mind,

Dean realized that there was no way for them to know that he was not an agent as well. Inwardly, he smiled to himself. He had always dreamed of being an agent.

The three men led him to a partition which was set up on one side of the warehouse. He heard no noise from it as he approached, but was prepared for anything. They stepped through a curtain set up as part of the partition and sat him down in a chair across from an oak writing desk, the kind with drawers on either side.

The chair on the other side of the desk was turned away from him. Dean almost felt like this was a confessional, a place to sit and talk to someone about his wrongdoing. Whether that was the intended psychological effect of the lighting and authoritative position of the person on the other side of the desk, he didn't know, but he squelched the feeling right away.

"So," said a voice from the chair, after a long moment. "I've heard you may be able to help us."

Dean was taken aback by the voice. His first thoughts were that whoever hired these thugs would be someone with experience, someone older. The person speaking sounded as though he was barely into his twenties. The second thing which caught him by surprise was that, for whatever reason, he had expected to hear a British accent. It may have been all the James Bond films he watched, or ideas of espionage, but the accent seemed to fit with his idea of secret agents, stealth, and big secrets kept from the government.

> "I apologize for the long ride. I admit that a flight would have been much quicker and more comfortable, but I've recently had a lot of trouble with keeping things quiet."

The chair turned around and Dean looked over the person in it. The man appeared to be in his mid-twenties. He was thin and from his size Dean guessed the man was very tall when he stood. He held a rubik's cube in one of his hands and was turning the pieces as he studied Dean. At Dean's expression the man smiled and stepped forward.

Chapter 14

"My name is Charles Destrier." The man said. "Yes, I don't exactly fit the grandiose stereotype of a thug you must have had in mind when you learned of my involvement in this case. Then again you hardly look like the type to be involved in espionage."

There was an awkward silence for a moment as the man studied Dean. Clearing his throat, Dean spoke.

"Y'know, I've heard conquering the world isn't all it's cracked up to be. I mean I heard of a few guys who tried it."

The man began laughing. "Oh, you're quick on your feet, aren't you? But not in the way of planning. World domination? What would I do with the pathetic thing once I knew I had conquered it? Do you know what work it takes just to maintain a country?

"No, I'm going to take the world economies and turn them against their own countries. Governments will try to keep their heads, but soon it will begin collapsing. Prices will fluctuate wildly and skyrocket. Vendors will realize that since their currency has no particular value they may as well charge as much as they can.

"This leaves those who don't have much money in a bind, and they'll begin bartering with others if they're civil. It won't take much before they resort to stealing. And, let's face it, if the next man is dead, who's going to defend his property?"

Dean's gut clenched and his brow furrowed as he looked the man in the eyes. "What do you want?" he asked the man again.

The man leaned in and smiled. "Anarchy." He whispered. "To see the world tear itself apart, and with only the slightest provocation. People say that people are good, but do you want to know the truth? There are no good people. A person will act good as long as others around him do the same. If others can't get away with wrongdoing, there's no way that he will either. But introduce a wild card and all those good people suddenly lose their smiles and concern with their homeowners associations.

"People will trample each other now in the streets for the most idiotic reasons – over tickets for their favorite concerts, Black Friday sales for things they wouldn't buy any other day of the year. Yet for some reason these items are suddenly worth more than the well-being of the other people around them."

"But you know," Dean said, "that those are hardly example of what normal people do at those sales. Those are only freak accidents not even once every year."

"Ah, so you rise to defend your people." He sighed. "True. If this were about a trampling every once in a while, this wouldn't be a reason for concern. But you don't think that I've spent my resources preparing something because a few people got knocked over in a checkout line at their favorite superstore, now do you?

"The world needs a reset button and I intend to push it. I have the means. Everything is in place. All I have to do is say the word I can have the world's economies beginning to collapse within twenty-four hours."

Destrier stood and walked around to the front of the desk, sitting on the front edge.

"I would like to think of myself as a man of patience." he said. "I've been planning this for a while now, but things aren't going to fix themselves. We have a problem. Of course you think that when I say 'We' that I really mean 'I' have a problem. But that's not true. Because as long as I have a problem, you, sir, are here to be witness to that problem." He nodded to the men behind Dean who pulled him up out of his seat. They stepped out of his makeshift office and out around to a side room. It's original intent was likely to be some kind of office for a manager at whatever facility this used to be.

As they walked, Dean felt dread rising in him. He tried to think back to what he knew about the case. He knew that he couldn't tell them anything. Innocent people would be harmed or killed if he let them know about the case.

They pulled him into the small room. It's layout was simple with a chair in one corner. There was a rope connected to a mount on the ceiling. What use they had for the rope he couldn't tell, but he supposed he was about to find out. They quickly led him to a spot underneath it. The ceiling was about ten or twelve feet high. Dean took a breath, but they were coming more quickly. He wondered if he was hyperventilating. Destrier took a seat in the corner.

Dean's hands were already tied with a zip tie in front of him. He saw one of the men reaching for his arms and realized what was about to happen. With a shout he gave a kick to the abdomen of the first guard, but was rewarded with a fist in his ribs from the second one. Dean sank to his knees, clutching his side. The first guard brought his knee up against Dean's head with a blow that made his ears ring.

The two men then pulled his arms upright and looped the rope between his hands, under and around the zip tie that held his hands together. The rope was then hauled up, pulling Dean upwards with it, until he stood, arms above his head, to face the man in the chair before him.

Destrier spread his hands. "So. Dean, is it? You've seen enough films and TV shows to know how this goes. You can give us the information we ask for and I can promise to let you go, or we can let the boys go a few rounds and see whether that will change your mind about how you want to get things done around here."

The second guard gave Dean a blow to the midsection that left him breathless. Destrier rose from his chair before standing in front of Dean, looking him in the face.

"Where is the case containing the technological hardware that I'm searching for?"

Dean shrugged. "Could be anywhere."

Destrier laughed and the guards followed suit. Dean wondered if that was in the job description - laugh along with the evil mastermind's diabolical laughter. Destrier shook his head.

"I want to help you." he said. "But more than that, I'm looking to accomplish my vision for humanity. Once in a while, mankind needs a reminder of the sorry state that it's in."

Dean looked up into the man's eyes. "Call me crazy," he said when he had caught his breath, "but I thought that destroying the world would put it in a sorrier state."

Destrier looked into his face and for a moment, Dean thought he saw what almost looked like a smile. Suddenly it was a gone, and he felt a series of jabs pelting his side again. Destrier stood, flexing his hand.

"It's your choice," he said, "you can cooperate or you can spend the rest of your miserable life as a human punching bag. The choice is yours." He stepped to the door, but not before nodding to the guards, who closed in around Dean. They asked him no questions and it wasn't long before he passed out with the dull thump of fists connecting with his body.

Chapter 15

They were on the road again. Gemma was quiet, but Tim could tell that she wasn't happy about his latest recruiting methods. Mike chatted with Angelo in the backseat. They had explained their predicament to him, part of which he guessed already. His vehicle was left back at the station, but he said something about a fine and left it, there, grabbing a few things out of it. From what Tim had seen, it looked like the man practically lived out of his car, or had been on a long trip recently. He wondered about the man's lifestyle, if he was just switching cars and company from what he had before, but keeping the same lifestyle that he had been staying with. Whatever was going on, he had not been hesitant to join them. Tim wondered why that was.

Mike seemed comfortable with them. Angelo and he were talking something about mythology in the backseat. From what little he knew about it all, Tim would have quickly been in over his head. He never would have guessed that Mike would be one to discuss mythology and folklore with anyone. He knew a little bit about common references, like Medusa and her gaze which turned people to stone, or the rid-dling Sphinx, but his knowledge was clearly dwarfed by these philoso-phers in the backseat.

"How did you learn about all this stuff?" He asked them.

Angelo turned to him. "What stuff?"

"All this stuff about mythology. Where did you guys learn about it? I never knew so many philosophers existed so close to each other under the sun."

Angelo laughed. "It's not about great thoughts or being a smart-aleck." he said. "It's about stories. I learned it from reading, mostly. The challenges the heroes face as they strive to find what they're looking for, as they strive against what stands in their way. I mean some of the stuff is interesting, but if it's a sight-seeing tour, why would we talk about it? We want to hear stuff about people who are in trouble, who have hard times."

Tim shrugged. "I guess that makes sense."

"Who wants to hear about the perfect date? All the stories we tell - the ones we love to tell - are the terrible ones, where something really bad has happened to us."

They drove in relative quiet for a while, the mile markers passing by. Gemma spoke up in the later afternoon.

"You know that we're going to have to find a place to sleep."

"You're right." Tim said. "We'll keep our eyes open for a place to stop. We've still got a few hours before we'll have to get off the road, though." he was quiet for a moment, before turning to Gemma. "What are we going to do about Dean?" He asked.

Gemma looked at him but didn't reply. Tim kept quiet, but his mind went around and around this question. He knew that he had a responsibility to look after these people. Dean had been captured on his watch.

Tim felt the responsibility of leading this group as his job now. While Gemma had the expertise and knowledge of working with the FBI, they were looking to him to make decisions about what they were going to do. He glanced in the mirror into the backseat at Angelo and Mike arguing. They had smiles on their faces, even though they knew that they were involved in a dangerous leg of a relay race. Without knowing who their enemy was or where he might come from, they would have to rely on Tim's leadership and their own wits escape this fiasco alive. As they pressed onward, they tried to learn about each other. At first Mike was quiet, but Angelo pulled him into the activities as they talked. Eventually they all wanted to learn about what Tim had done for a living before he got involved in this kind of espionage work.

Mike piped up from the backseat. "So what as your job?"

Tim shook his head. "Nothing important."

"C'mon." said Angelo.

Sighing, Tim replied. "I was – am – a package designer."

"I," he said, "am a package designer. I design packages and blurbs for packaging for household appliances."

Mike shook his head. "Appliances?"

"Blenders, coffee machines, toasters, microwave ovens- I oversee package design for this stuff. So when you walk into a store looking to furnish your kitchen with something new, the first thing you'll see is my world." There was quiet for a moment.

Angelo and Mike continued their discussion of philosophy, ranging from Plato and Aristotle to Benjamin Franklin and Russian philosophers that Timothy had never heard of. He was amazed again at the broad range of knowledge these men discussed. In their arguments they brought up books, of course, but they also quoted movies, musicals and theater.

From the corner of his eye, he saw that Gemma was watching him. He kept his eyes on the road at first, but eventually her gaze drew his in. A honk and the squeal of tires quickly drew his attention back to the road. Once he had complete control of the vehicle again, Tim relaxed enough to drop his hand off the wheel, leaving it by his side. Tim heard some noise from the backseat, but didn't pay much attention. He soon felt another hand clasped in his, warm, with slender fingers intertwining themselves between and around his own.

The moment warmed him more than her hand warmed his hand. He glanced at her once and again to see the same thing each time: she smiled at him. He shook his head a little as he turned his gaze back onto the road.

"What?" she asked.

"It's nothing."

He hardly noticed the next few hours pass. He spent the first part of the day driving and feeling like he was on top of the world. Whatever was going on would hardly have made a difference. The ground could be collapsing beneath him, and Tim didn't think that it would change how he felt in that moment. He felt warmth spreading from his hand up through his arm and through his body. As he drove, he felt Gemma's eyes on him. He suddenly felt self-conscious. Wondering what she saw, he thought about opening up the mirror on his visor to take a look. She must have noticed him stiffen, because she pulled her hand away and turned to look out her own window. Tim wished he had the courage to say something, but sat there in silence, staring at the road ahead of them.

If Angelo or Mike noticed anything they said nothing about it.

Miles passed and faded into more miles. They stopped at a restaurant for a break and for food. Tim didn't know if he would be hungry but as soon as he stepped inside the building, his stomach began to growl. The restaurant's mascot was a smiling cactus with a sombrero. Tim felt like he had seen it somewhere before, but couldn't put his finger on where it had been. The restaurant chain's lack of reasoning about their mascot was evident in the cactus, Tim thought. Why choose a type of plant which is associated with the desert rather than vacation spots? And on which is impossible to touch or embrace without injuring oneself on it? It was clear that Mexican food was served here, but why a cactus and not something pleasant? That was like a pet's grooming salon choosing a porcupine as their mascot. Or an aquarium with opportunities to cuddle jellyfish.

Though his hunger was now taking up a good bit of his attention, Tim kept his eyes open, scanning the restaurant as he stood in line at the front. A couple with their small child sat near the window, the father keeping the child entertained. A woman sat by herself in the far corner of the restaurant. She wore jeans and simple blouse, her hair neatly pulled back into a bun. He observed her as she sat, but she did nothing interesting, so he turned his attention back to the menu in front of him.

His spine tingled as he became aware that anyone watching them could be against them. Tim turned his head and glanced around the room again. He guessed that there were about ten other people in the room besides Gemma, Angelo, Mike and himself. Tim tried to convince himself that he was only spooked, that his group had made it safe so far, but he wasn't convinced. His cell phone rang.

Gemma glanced at him, then back to the menu. He pulled it out and looked at the number. He didn't recognize it. Swiping his finger across the screen, he accepted the call.

"This is Timothy Runn."

There was silence on the other end of the phone.

Tim cleared his throat. "Hello? Who is this?"

"Mr. Runn, who I am doesn't matter. What does matter is that I have your accomplice. If you comply with my request, you may have a chance to save his life. In twelve hours, two of my men will meet you at the park in Chicago at 10 AM tomorrow. Millenium Park, the northwest corner at the bike station."

"That gives us less than a day to get there."

"Then you'd better drive quickly."

"What about Dean? How do I know you'll return him to us?"

"My men will stand at the north side of the park with food in their hands. All of you will be watched. We will have guards posted around the park. You will not be able to identify them. If you try anything you are as good as dead."

"What makes you think I'm going to cooperate with this? Why should I trust you?"

"You don't have to trust me. But you have to save the life of this man whom you claim is your friend, then I suggest that you get moving. Or you can let him rot away, it is your choice. Turn around."

Tim, who was facing the front counter and the menu, turned to face the front of the store, the seating area.

"Do you see the woman in the corner? Wearing the white blouse and jeans?"

"Yes." Tim said.

"She might be a target of ours. At my word she could collapse. The autopsy would reveal nothing. Perhaps an allergic reaction to something."

"Ma'm!" Tim shouted at the woman, stepping in her direction. She sat up, worry evident on her face, her fight-or-flight response ready.

"Then again," the man on the other end of the line said, "she could be an agent of ours. I give her the word and she chooses the method she deems best to dispatch of you all."

The woman looked at Tim with a very worried expression on her face. He gave her a pained smile and turned away, walking back to the front of the building.

"You're insane." Tim growled as he stepped back towards the front of the restaurant. He kept his voice down, aware that he was now attracting stares from customers. Adrenaline coursed through his veins, amplifying everything. Closing his eyes, Tim tried to focus on the task at hand.

A cashier at the counter glanced over the register.

"Will you return our friend to us?" Tim muttered into the phone.

There was silence on the other end of the line for a moment. Tim was about to throw his phone against the wall when the voice spoke again.

"I make no promises. 10 AM, Millenium Park."

The line went dead.

Tim hung up and put the phone in his pocket, walking to Gemma and the rest of the crew. From her expression, he could tell that she had heard something already.

"What happened?"

He held up a hand as his mind reeled. Gemma gave him some space, but waited at his side as he began to process the information. He went to the front counter and ordered, feeling like he was listening in on a conversation.

Dean had been captured, they knew that already. What could this person want that they had? The only logical answer resided in the briefcase, which he didn't understand. 10 AM the next day. That didn't give them much time. They would have to keep moving and move quickly to be there in time for the meeting. But could they trust Destrier?

No, Tim was sure that they couldn't. But as the man said, they didn't have to trust him. But they didn't have to walk into a trap blindly either. He ordered his food and found the table where Angelo and Mike were sitting already. Tray in hand, he took a seat at the table. Gemma settled across from him. There was quiet as they listened to hear what Tim would say.

"Destrier, the man who sent those men after the case, called and said that we should meet in Chicago tomorrow at 10 AM in Millenium Park. He's telling us he'll release Dean to us then."

"He's going to meet us there tomorrow morning?" Mike asked.

Tim shook his head. "I don't think so. He seems like the kind of guy to let others do the dirty work. I don't trust him." Gemma was nodding. Tim took a breath and continued. "I don't think we have much choice about going after Dean. This may be the only chance we have to get him back. But I don't think we should walk into this blindly either. Walking in there unprepared is begging for trouble."

"What do we do?" Gemma asked. Tim noticed the deference, but said nothing about it. "I think," he said, "that we need to be prepared for whatever happens." He nodded to the woman in the corner table at the front of the building. "You see that woman over there?"

They nodded.

"Destrier has a sense of humor. He started by telling me that he could kill her with something untraceable, and that he could do it at any moment." The crew stole glances in the woman's direction but said nothing. "Then he flips it around and tells me that she could be one of his agents, ready to kill all of us when he gives the word."

Angelo shook his head. "Why are you telling us this?"

Tim was quiet for a moment before he spoke. "If we go further with this." he said, looking each of them in the eyes. "We need to trust each other. I'm sorry that you guys practically got dragged into this." Angelo and Mike shook their heads. "But if we're going up against this guy, we need to be clear about what we're facing. He has more men, more weapons and more resources on his side."

Gemma gave a low whistle. "You sure know how to bolster the troops."

"But with a group our size," Tim continued, "we may be able to catch him off guard."

Mike said "Even if we catch him off guard, how are we supposed to get your friend back? It's not like they're going to have him dangling on a string in front of us."

"There's a way." Tim said. "There's always a way."

Chapter 16

The food was delicious, but a little greasy for Tim's taste. He had ordered the chicken chalupa combo, one of his favorites. Having one of his favorite foods in hand brought back a semblance of normal life. After some discussion, they decided that it would be best to get back on the road as soon as they could. With the tight deadline, they would drive through the night, stopping for gas and to change drivers. Angelo volunteered to drive first, since Tim and Gemma had done all the driving so far.

The conversation on the phone kept bothering Tim, and his mind returned again and again to one point – would this egotist and villain actually kill someone as a demonstration, and could he? If he could it meant that one of his agents had to be in the room with them at the time, didn't it? If it was poison, something untraceable like this mastermind had suggested, then it would have been something that was put into the woman's food.

What if the second option was true? That the woman was one of his agents, ready to kill them? If she was, why hadn't she taken the opportunity to do so? The only thing that made sense to Tim was that the Destrier didn't want them dead.

Another thought occurred to Tim as well. If the woman was an agent who was in contact with her employer, he could give her orders at any time. Those orders could be to kill all of them - or to kill herself. People had died for causes in the past.

Would a person harm themselves to make their employer appear godlike in power? Tim shook his head. People had died for kings in the past. The Egyptians held that their Pharaoh was an intermediary between the people and their god. When a pharaoh died and was buried, they buried all of his possessions with him so that he could take them into the afterlife. Sometimes this included his servants, who were still alive.

Tim thought through what would have to happen next. Angelo was in the driver's seat, and Mike hopped up to the front seat with him. Gemma sat in back with Tim. For the most part she was quiet, looking at him once in a while to see what he was doing. He stared out his own window, his mind turning the problem over and around, examining it like an alien artifact. There was no way around it: they didn't know what they were getting themselves into. This was their one shot at freeing Dean from this mastermind's grasp, and they had to take it.

Gemma put a hand on his knee and he looked at it before meeting her gaze.

She said "I want you to know that I'm proud of you for stepping up today."

He laughed. "I just hope I know what I'm going."

She shook her head. "Nobody knows what they're doing. They just pretend like they do and hope that it works out in the end."

He said "In all the action shows you see, with people dealing with this crazy stuff – they're all over it, like they've seen this a thousand times."

"Those are actors, they don't do this job. I won't say they don't know what they're doing." He looked away, but he heard her speak again. "Don't worry about trying to figure the world out. People have been trying to figure that out for millennia. What you need to do is figure out what your part is and do it."

She made it sound so simple.

"I wish I could think like that." He said. "Just leave it to the big thinkers and work on our little part of the problem, is that it?"

"What more can we do?"

"I don't know. What we're doing just doesn't feel like enough."

"Well, just as soon as you find a sustainable source of food that doesn't cost anything that that everyone across the globe can have without having to buy it or fight over it, let me know. And if it doesn't start a war at its discovery that's a bonus. I'd like to end global hunger by this evening, if that's good with you."

He laughed at this point and she elbowed him.

It grew quiet between them before she spoke again. "I've learned on this job." She said. "You have to develop a sense of humor. You have to find a way to cope. If you don't, you'll have to let the pain build up inside you and gnaw its way from your inside out. People talk about soldiers with PTSD, but it's not limited to them. We face some situations as well. We're under a lot of stress. You have to find a way to deal with it, or it will deal with you."

"So that's what you do? Deal with it?"

"What else are we supposed to do?" she asked. "We can't ignore it."

He shook his head. "No. You can't do that, can you?"

Tim watched as rolling hills in the distance rose and fell gently with the forward rolling motion of the car. He thought of the hills as slow-moving waves, like flowing waves of the ocean which had been slowed to where each wave could be observed as it crested and surged forwards toward land. As they left the city, long grasses spurted up and almost brushed the side of the car. Tim felt like reaching out to touch them as they passed. Sitting on the passenger side of the car, he could peer out the window into the fields on the side of the road as the long grasses threatened to flatten because of the wind blowing over them. He sighed and wished that he was standing among them. He closed his eyes, seeing it in his mind's eye.

His feet pressed into the soft soil. The wind flew into his face and he stretched his arms and hands to the very fingertips to feel the grass blowing around him. A thousand individual strands of grass rustled about in the breeze, calling for his attention as he stood enjoying the wind in his face. The sun shone on him, caressing his face. His eyes were closed in simple enjoyment of the moment. He thought of being back home where he belonged. Society had called him, telling him that a desk job was a good and respectable thing. But his heart longed to be connected with the land around him.

The land provided a home for him. He had grown up with soil beneath his bare feet. Now he was walking through carpeted offices in his loafers. Something inside of him was longing for a chance to break free, to come awake and venture forth. He hadn't known what that was until the opportunity had presented itself.

It was terrible to think of all the people who didn't know what they wanted or needed until they had it. And once they had it, they regretted all the years of not having it. People striving after the latest HD flat-screen television or finishing their vintage collection of vinyl albums – whatever it was, it didn't fill them up because as soon as they had it, they wanted something else.

An understanding of this began to stir itself in Timothy's spirit. He didn't know what he was longing for, only that he was searching for something to satisfy him. He stood in the field, listening to the wind blow, feeling it on his face.

But no. No, he was in the car with his friends. Gemma was asking him something. How he was feeling.

"I'm fine." He said, but he didn't really know. She took this at face value and left him to his thoughts.

How was he feeling? He felt distinctly lost, suddenly realizing that he was longing for something. This was set against a sense of purpose, letting the longing drive him into something definite and new, something that would lead him onward with certainty.

Once again, Tim saw the field he was standing in, with the grasses swaying around him. He heard birds crying and looked up to see ravens flying around his head. I shall feed thee in the wilderness. Elijah had been fed by ravens in the wilderness. Tim remembered his grandmother talking to him about the Bible when he was a child. Elijah was a prophet of the LORD. When the LORD sent a great famine over the land, the LORD sent ravens to Elijah with bread and meat to feed him. I shall feed thee in the wilderness.

Tim exhaled and looked around. Nothing had changed, and yet he felt as if everything around him had changed. Sunlight streamed though the sky and clouds and into the vehicle. The sun was ninety-three million miles from the earth, and yet for all that distance, its rays managed to reach the earth to light and heat it.

He turned to look at Gemma, who smiled.

"What's going on?"

He shook his head and didn't reply. To tell her he would have to know what to say himself. Silence settled into the back seat and they sat and listened as Angelo and Mike continued to discuss the nature of man and his place in the world.

Chapter 17

Dean's eyelids fluttered and he tried to remember what was going on. He felt as though something important was escaping his grasp. A dream. He had a dream, one he had to remember.

His hands were numb. He looked up to see that he was still hanging from his wrists. Attempting to shift his weight brought shooting pain to his ribs and arms. Bent at the knees, he dangled with his arms above his head. His shoulders ached from bearing the weight of his body for however long he had been dangling.

He took a deep breath ad felt a stabbing pain in his ribs. The possibility of broken ribs occurred to him, but there was nothing he could do about that now. Using his raw wrists, he pulled his feet under himself. The effort took the wind out of him and he wobbled at the knees for a moment before he felt ready to try and support his weight on his own feet. Dean took slow breaths, hanging his head ad focusing on managing his pain. Any sharp or deep breath brought stabbing pain to his ribs. His head pounded as his heart pumped, sending blood through his body and up to his head, which throbbed. It would take someone sticking his head in a bass drum and pounding it for a few hours to produce a comparable result to this.

He stood for a moment and let the sensation dissipate. The room was the same as the last time he saw it. Despair crept over Dean as he stood in the corner of the warehouse. He was alone in some shipping yard in an unknown corner of the country. No one knew where he was, if they knew he was alive. If they did, they had no way of knowing where he was or who had him hostage. In any case, he didn't know how long he had to live.

The door opened and the three guards walked in. Dean looked up at them and groaned.

"More fun, eh?"

They were silent. Casing kept a hand by his hip. It was clear they didn't expect much resistance from him.

"So," Grip said, "the boss made a call." He stepped forward, brandishing a knife. Dean saw it and began to struggle. They laughed.

"Hey dummy," Big said "if you don't want yourself to get hurt, hold still."

Dean did as he was told – better to obey now and preserve himself than harm himself in useless defiance. Grip stepped forward and used the knife to cut through dean's bonds. The zip ties snapped as the knife cut through them like butter. Collapsing to his knees, he rubbed his wrists, glancing at his captors. They pulled him to his feet. He noticed that one of them held a stack of clothing. They handed this to him.

"Get dressed." Grip said. The trio showed no signs of removing themselves from the room. Dean said nothing but began disrobing. The new clothes were dressy-casual, on the higher end of expensive. What the purpose of the clothing was, Dean couldn't guess, but he pulled the clothing on without a word to the men in the room. The pants fit well. The men stood speaking quietly to each other. Dean pulled the shirt over his head and checked the fit. It was a little baggy, but that was better than being too tight.

Standing in his new duds, Dean glanced around the men standing around him. Grip gestured for him to follow and stepped out of the room. The other two waited as Dean stepped by them and out through the door. He heard their footsteps behind him, but didn't turn to look. It occurred to him that they might be leading him to be killed. But why would they put him in new clothes if they were just going to kill him? Something else was going on.

They led him around the side of the warehouse. As they walked, Dean saw that the place had been converted into a functional base of operations. There were offices and a cafeteria which looked ready to serve a hundred people. A counter in one area held a few sinks along with a coffee machine and cupboards, presumably for dishes. The threesome led him past all of these on to another part of the building. As they walked, he tried to imagine what his future held. From what pieces he could put together, he knew a few things. These people had grabbed him because he was involved with the case containing whatever technology this organization was after. And for them to hold onto him, they must have believed that he knew something about this technology or about the people who had it with them.

The other option was much less hopeful. This organization was after the case. But to catch the people with it, they would need something to lure Dean's friends close enough to catch them. Which meant that Dean was little more than bait for their capture. If that was true, then he figured that he would have to try something to save them. The only ways to do that would be either to warn them beforehand or prevent their capture. He could try to escape himself, but that didn't mean that the others wouldn't get nabbed by the organization.

"Why does the boss have us playing babysitter?" Big mumbled as they stepped across the converted warehouse.

"He's got a reason for it." Casing said. "You don't think that he'd leave his best lead in the hands of any goon standing around, do you?"

"Like one of those guys?" He nodded at one of the uniformed men standing beside a doorway.

Casing nodded. "Sure, one of those guys. I mean, they keep an eye on things but beyond that they're not useful for anything."

"Yeah," Big said, keeping his eyes on the guard beside the door, "except target practice." Dean glanced back to the where the men were standing, casting sidelong glances at the guard by the door. The guard kept a straight face, but Dean could tell the man was working to keep himself together. He wondered if this was a regular thing, whether this club of three agents, being a specialized team, were allowed on longer leashes, abusing other members of the organization. After another moment of leering at the guard, the men stepped onward. Dean watched the guard nearly collapse where he stood as he relaxed from the scrutiny. He wondered what the precedent for the abuse of employees was here.

Grip led them onward past the offices and to the side of the warehouse opposite the chamber where Dean had been kept before. Stepping to a doorway, he nodded to a guard and slid a keycard in a reader mounted on the wall. The light turned green and he pushed the door open. They stepped through and the door latched behind them. Dean was struck with how much quieter the area was than the modified office space. They were in a hallway with doors on either side, always opposite each other. The rooms were numbered like on a college campus, odd on one side, even on the other - 102, 104, 106, and so on.

Dean then realized that this was an entirely separate wing of the building. It must have been added on either after or during the conversion of the warehouse space. They led him to the middle of the hall. Grip stopped and gestured to a door on their right. 118. He opened the door, and waved Dean in.

"After you." he said.

Dean nodded and stepped into the room. It was simple, but clean and well-furnished. There was a bed with a proper mattress and clean linens with a pillow and comforter. A chair sat by a small table and there was a desk as well with a second table. A mini-fridge sat in one corner. Dean noticed that there was no sink. He also saw that, as he stepped into the room, there was no handle on the inside of the door. There was a small toilet in one corner of the room with a bit of tile around it. The rest of the floor was covered in short carpet that businesses use.

Grip spoke up. "If you have anything you'd like to tell us, let us know." he pointed to the upper corner of the room above the door. "We can always send someone down here to talk. If you remember something important, you can let us know. It might mean saving the lives of your friends."

The last line sounded scripted. Grip closed the door and Dean was left alone in his small, if relatively comfortable prison. He turned in place, making a sweep of the room to see what was what. But it was just as he saw it.

The door clicked shut and he was left alone in the room. He paced about at first, not speaking out loud, but inwardly cursing his fate that led him to this point. After a few minutes of that, however, he tired of it and decided to do something else. His grandmother had always warned him against that kind of fretting. But in this case, he didn't have anything else to do.

That wasn't true. Dean sat with a sigh on the side of the bed and tried to still his mind which whirled about his head at ninety miles an hour. At the moment it appeared that there was nothing that he could do, either for himself or to help his friends. As he thought through the problem, he came to some conclusions. The first was that, since the cell now confined him, worrying about trying to break out would be a waste of his time and energy. He would have to wait for a time when his enemy was more vulnerable - when they were going to move him somewhere.

Their choice to move him to a cell baffled him at first, as he assumed that they were simply going to dispose of him. But after their taking him to the cell, he now saw that they had some use for him. Which meant that, whatever went on, they were more likely than not going to try and preserve his life if they could. This presented advantages to him, not the least of which being that he keep living to plan for another day.

Curiosity eventually got the better of him, and Dean stepped towards the mini-fridge. He expected there to be rotten or moldy foods in there, either as an oversight, or as a cruelty. Each prisoner is provided with food - no provisions have been made that the food will be fresh. As he opened the door, he was surprised to find that it was full of fresh food. It consisted mostly of ready-to-eat meals and fruit as well as bottled water. Dean grabbed a banana and stepped back to the bed, peeling the fruit as he went. If he wasn't getting out of this cell soon, he figured it would be better to relax, save his strength for the moment when it counted.

When he sat, as the first time, his ribs ached. He wondered if the men had broken any bones. He had no way of knowing, but from the ex-posure his ribs had to the men's flying fists, he would not be surprised, later, at the doctor's report of cracked ribs. Arranging the pillows on the bed, he eased himself into a reclining position on the bed and took another bite of the fruit. His mind began to wander, not to events of the past week, but to other events of his life. Losing a baseball game for his little league team. The first time he put on a stand-up routine, and the audience's laughter at it. Memories began to wash over him and he submitted, letting himself be submerged in their flow.

Dean opened his eyes and looked around. Nothing had changed. He felt as though a few hours may have passed in his sleep. He glanced about the walls for a clock, but didn't see any. That was a tactic of some prisons - keep the prisoners off guard or off balance by depriving them of their accurate sense of time.

He had heard of studies of people who decided to abandon all conventional senses of time that society sticks to. What they called a 'sleep bunker' was made and they were provisioned with food, water, books and a place to sleep. Then they stayed in there for a while, maybe a month, and with a camera scientists recorded things like their sleep cycle, when and how long the subjects slept and when they ate. They found that most stuck to the circadian rhythm - a 24 or 25-hour cycle that the body has, telling the body to rise with the daylight, eat when hungry, and seek sleep in the evening.

Without a clock or change in sunlight, there wasn't any sure way to know what time it was. Dean checked his pockets. The agents had taken everything on him. The banana peel rested on the bed beside him. He sat up in bed, groaning as his ribs protested with the effort, and swung his legs to the side of the bed. Grabbing the peel, he stood and stepped to a garbage can where he disposed of the banana skin.

Chapter 18

"But we're not talking about the movement of matter through space, we're talking about sound traveling through space."

"Yes, sound travels just like matter and light do, doen't they?"

"It's not the same in outer space. Without an atmosphere to travel through, sound wouldn't be heard. Sound is the vibration of air around us. Without air, there's no sound."

"There's air in space. What do you call that vast opening above us?"

"There is a great opening in outer space, but that is not air - it is an absence of air. In fact, it's an absence of almost everything. There's nothing up there but bits of particulate matter from whatever meteor or asteroid last crashed around the vicinity of the earth."

"Which means there should be plenty of room for sound to travel around in. You'd be able to hear for miles."

"No, that's what I'm saying - it's not about space, it's about vibration. Think about a musical instrument. You can't have a violin sound without a string or a drum beat without a drum head."

"When did we get into music?"

Mike and Angelo's argument had been going on for a little while. Angelo was defending the idea that sound cannot travel through space due to a lack of air or, more specifically, any kind of atmosphere. Since the earth is surrounded by a cloud of gases like oxygen, carbon dioxide and bits of stuff like helium, sound has something to vibrate and, thus, travel through.

"It's like water," he said, "you can't make waves if there's no water in the pool."

Mike persisted in the idea that because of the open space up there, sound would have plenty of room to travel in. Tim was sure that Mike was just messing with Angelo. Whether Angelo was aware of it, or thinking that he was dealing with an especially thick student, he was determined to make his point known.

"We're not talking about music, this is all about vibration. Vibration comes from transferred energy, whether that's from a stick hitting a drum head, a bow running across a string-"

"Or someone shouting while in space?"

"Why would you be shouting? If you're up in space, wouldn't we assume that we have a communications array which is sufficient with communicating with our fellow explorers?"

"What if I don't have a radio? Or a suit?"

"First of all, that's hardly possible, as no one would send you into space without a suit. But secondly, even if you could be heard, you wouldn't survive more than a few minutes without it. Even if you didn't asphyxiate."

Tim's eyebrows went up and he ventured into the conversation. "What do you mean?"

"The temperature in space is below - 400 degrees farenheit. At that temperature, if there's any liquid on your body - around your eyes or mouth, any sweat on your body - that's going to start to boil."

"Can we please talk about something else?" Gemma put in. "I hate to interrupt your fascinating discussion, but I confess that, despite being a trained officer, there are certain things that I don't have the stomach for."

Tim said "What did they train you for?"

"Management of trauma, flesh wounds, CPR - stuff you'd run into at a gun or a knife fight." She leaned back in her seat with a groan. "I don't think I can handle this stuff."

"My point is," Angelo said, "that without the suit, your dead meat. Of course there's no way your body will properly decompose, since the extreme negative temperatures will freeze your body solid within an hour or two."

Tim nodded. "Good to know."

"That is after-"

"Angelo."

He glanced in his mirror to see Gemma staring daggers at the back of his head. "If I have to ask you to stop again, you're not going to remember me taking control of the vehicle. You'll have a much more secure ride in the trunk, however."

The two men in the front seat quickly changed their topic to customs of the ancient Egyptians.

"You handled that well." Tim said.

"What did you expect me to do?" Gemma asked. "I was gagging already and could hardly think. Who would want to know about all that kind of stuff?"

Tim shrugged. "Some people are interested in the macabre. Most people are interested in the bizarre."

"What about you?"

"Not particularly. I was never the one especially drawn to the dissections in biology class."

Gemma grimaced. "Oh, please, please let's not talk about that."

"OK, OK," Tim said with a laugh. "we can talk about something else. But what has you so put off about it anyways?"

She gave him a dark look.

"Right, sorry. Finding another topic."

"What about sports?" She asked.

He shook his head. "I don't follow sports."

Her mouth gaped. "Since when is there a man on earth who doesn't enjoy sports?"

"I didn't say I don't enjoy sports. I said I don't follow sports. Getting to a basketball court is fun once in a while."

She cocked her head and a grin spread to her face. "Oh, you play a little, huh? How good are you?"

He shook his head. "I don't think about that. You'd have to ask the other guys."

"C'mon you must have some idea."

He blew out a breath and thought for a moment. "Well, for each game we play i usually manage to make a few shots in, so I guess I'm not terrible."

"'Not terrible' - that's certainly a start."

They were quiet for a minute. Tim looked out the window and watched fields go by outside.

"Gemma." he said, as he turned to look at her.

She looked at him. "Yeah?"

"How do you think this is going to end?"

She shrugged. "What do you mean?"

"I'm just searching for what comes next. I'm trying to figure out what my life is supposed to be."

"Who said your life is supposed to be anything? Do you believe that life has some kind of hidden meaning we're supposed to search out? I can tell you it doesn't."

"And how would you know that?" he asked with a grin. "If you haven't seen something, that doesn't mean it doesn't exist. It just means you haven't seen it."

"I don't chase fantasies." she said, and turned away.

Tim watched as the sky outside his widow as the sun, glowing a bright orange, began to dip beneath the edge of the horizon and the sky began to fade to red, purple, and darker hues. The stars began to shine in the east. If stars were pinpricks in the sheet of the sky, Tim wanted to peek through one of those holes and see what lay on the other side of that sheet.

After a while, Tim looked over to see that Gemma had fallen asleep in the seat beside him. It was hardly nine-thirty, but with all of their running, he understood her urge to get to sleep as soon as possible. Mike succumbed to the same impulse for he soon began to snore.

Tim always thought of a snore as a loud, grating sound, but this wasn't the case. Mike's snore had a kind of whine to it. It didn't quite sound like a wheeze, but there was a whining quality which made Tim think of a rusting door hinge.

"Angelo."

"Yeah man?"

"Do you need me for anything? Co-pilot, cranking the tunes?"

Angelo let out as loud a laugh as he dared with the sleeping passengers in the vehicle.

"No thanks man, I'm all right. You should get some sleep. I'll be waking one of you guys to start driving. Besides that we've got a big day tomorrow. Don't want to approach that with only a nap to tide you over."

"Yeah, you're right." Tim thought for a moment. "So what kind of stuff do you read? You seem to know a lot about- a lot of stuff." he said.

"I used to read about all kinds of stuff. Especially in school. I had one teacher who got me onto reading. She started by talking about the stuff I was already interested in - like superman - and then tying that stuff to literature."

"Sounds like a good strategy." Tim said. "We do that all the time in marketing - use what the audience loves to help them love our product."

"Right. So she gets me from reading comic books to reading stuff like The Lion, The Witch and The Wardrobe, and The Hobbit and stuff like that."

"You liked fantasy stuff, huh?"

"Well, that's what she recommended. Since in the older literature there wasn't much on superheroes, she recommended fantasy, since that stuff was so different than the rest."

"I hear you." Tim said. "I think my family had a copy of those books lying around. I might have read them once or twice when I was in school too."

"What did you think of them?"

Tim paused, trying to recollect what he knew about the two volumes. What little he remembered wasn't coming easily. "I liked the Hobbit. I guess that was because all the girls around me in the school would be talking about romance and a that bunch of men-"

"Dwarves and a hobbit, but point taken."

"A bunch of men going on an adventure to kill a dragon and claim some gold sounded like a manly, exciting adventure that was different than what the girls were reading."

Angelo nodded. "What about the other?"

"The Wardrobe?" he asked, shaking his head. "When I first read that, I hardly knew what to think of it. I thought the girl was crazy, and that her brothers and sister were right. But then they went in the second time and all of them saw the magical snowy kingdom with the faun and other mythical creatures. At that point I didn't know what to believe." He paused for a moment. "It was then that I talked to the teacher."

Angelo grinned. "What did she say?"

"She said 'Don't be held back by what you think is possible. Let the story take you on a journey and see where you end up.'"

Angelo nodded. "Good advice."

Tim moved in his seat and tried to settle back in it. "All right." He said, "wake me up when you need to switch."

"All right. Get some sleep."

Chapter 19

As he slept, Tim had a dream. He was running down a street at night. It was dimly lit, with streetlamps shining down intermittently. A great shadow pursued him, a shadow that had mass.

A voice in his mind told Tim to stand and fight against the shadow. But he knew that the shadow was too great to fight against. He continued to run and it was gaining on him. There was no one on the street and no lights on in any of the buildings. No sign of human life appeared anywhere. As he ran, he looked for an opportunity to slip away and hide.

Spotting an alleyway, he darted down this and pressed himself against the building, hoping that the shadow hadn't seen him slip away. As he stood there, he felt it approach, a thick shadow, with a raucous cacophony of sound coming from it.

Tim pressed himself harder to the wall, wondering how long this would take to pass. Suddenly the feeling and noise passed. Just as soon as it was there it was over. He took a breath and looked out onto the street. The street was empty. But this unnerved him more than before. He took another step down the alley toward the street, head swinging, looking for anything out of place. As he did so, he felt a chill creep up his spine.

Behind you.

His head turned and his body followed, turning to see what was behind him. The shadow was there, massive, larger than before, drawing from the shadows that naturally occurred in the alleyway.

The quiet voice came again. *Stand and fight.*

Falling back a step or two, Tim turned and began to run out of the alleyway. But the shadow manifested before him. He was trapped. Looking back and forth, he saw the Shadow divided into two parts, cutting off both paths. For the third time, the unknown voice came to him again.

Stand and fight.

But he had nothing to fight with. As he watched, the darkness began to move in a way that made Tim think of water boiling. He turned to see that the bit of darkness cutting off his escapes to the street did the same thing. He was just about to turn when, suddenly, both parts leapt forward, knocking him to the ground. As he began to get his feet under him, another length of the darkness flashed out, like limbs without hands, striking him in the head. As he lay on the ground, he was vaguely aware of the sound of wings.

Chapter 20

Dean must have fallen asleep, because the next thing he knew, a knock at the door woke him up. He didn't know why they knocked, since he had no say about who entered or left his room at any time. The guards who entered this time were the kind he had seen stationed around the plant. The first two who stepped into the room did not acknowledge his presence, but stood on either side of the door. A third man stepped in, this one a head taller than the other two. His keen glance told Dean to stay on his toes. Accordingly, Dean sat up in bed and climbed out, standing beside the bed.

"Mr. Meare, is that right?"

Dean shuffled in place. "Yes sir, that is my name."

The man looked Dean over again. "You understand that while you are in my custody that you are in my command and will follow my orders or those of my men, is that understood?"

"Yes sir."

"Any attempt made to either disobey an order or to escape from our custody, forcibly or unbeknownst to us, will be considered directly disobeying an order. At that point, your life is forfeit. Is that understood?"

Dean nodded.

"For our purposes I will require a verbal acknowledgment from you."

Dean swallowed and spoke. "Yes sir."

He turned without another word and stepped out of the room. Dean's bewilderment must have been evident on his face, for one of the guards at the door gestured with his gun to the door. Dean stepped cautiously forward and out the door, following the scientist.

They walked down the hall and out through a corridor that Dean didn't recognize. As they walked, he wondered about where they were going and why. Why were they keeping him around, and where were they taking him now?

Dean told himself not to panic, that he didn't have any reason to panic. The change of guards meant something, he knew. Either the threesome who had escorted him unwillingly were called off for something else, or it was determined that they weren't needed anymore, and the job of watching Dean was left to these guards. Or it could be that the terrible threesome were somewhere else at the moment, to return to their stations later.

He wondered about the way this organization handled itself. Clearly its M.O. was modeled after a military unit. Was this whole operation in the giant warehouse something bigger than Dean knew?

Destrier had said that he wanted anarchy. What wonderful thing could come of riots in the streets? How could the government's overthrow help anything? What good could come of people starving in their own homes because a force decided that looking over the feeding of a nation was not its primary concern at the moment?

Dean stepped down the hall and jokes began to filter through his mind. He wondered if this was what would happen when he finally died - that his mind, rather than being filled with memories of his life, his family and the things he had done or wished he accomplished, his mind would be filled with jokes and corny one-liners. Was that the measure of a comedian? The number of jokes he remembered at his death?

Putting this out of his mind, he focused as they stepped into an office which must have been Destrier's. It was relatively small, but certainly not cramped, perhaps. Without a word he was made to sit in front of the desk that took up a good amount of the space in the room. Dean glanced around. It was sparsely furnished. There was one painting on one of the walls. It was an ugly thing, all painted in dark hues. Why, of all the paintings in the world, would Destrier pick that one to put in his makeshift office?

"You don't like it much, do you?"

The voice came from behind and caught Dean off guard while he was staring at the painting. He didn't reply to the question.

"I'll admit, it's certainly not one of the most beautiful works out there. However, if you take a close look at this one, it is full of meaning." He stepped up behind Dean's chair and pointed at the lower portion of the picture.

"Do you know what that bit is?" Destrier pointed at a lower portion of the canvas. He didn't reply. Destrier indicated a spot on the canvas again. Looking at it, Dean recognized what the abstraction represented.

"It's a book." he said.

> "That's right, Mr. Meare, it is a book. This is to represent the great works of western literature - Shakespeare, the Bible - whatever is well-respected in society despite the ignorance of the masses."

Dean looked again at the painting. While a few books sat intact, the rest had been spread across the ground in shreds, confetti. Destrier spoke again.

> "It is absolutely fascinating to see a people rebel against every-thing they love, which they've believed to be so good for them and for others. For the longest time that was what troubled me the most - people choosing their future for each other. Then I realized that wasn't really the problem - they had simply chosen the wrong future for each other. It was then that I realized all I had to do was figure out what was best for them. They don't

know what to choose for themselves. So I've made it simple and chosen for them."

"Yes, things will be thrown into chaos. But it is only in the fire that the true refining can take place. Then there will be time to introduce structure. But the lack of structure is a powerful tool, one which must be used carefully. It will only do good to introduce structure back into society when society itself is ready for such structure. So you see, of course, that I do have long-term plans and I do have a next step to my plan, unlike those bombers and protesters you see in the news.

Dean turned to his captor. "What do you want?

"What I want," the man said. "Is the power of a dream." he said. "The power to change the face of our world." he stepped around the chair and sat at his desk. "Do you know what it is that you are so stoically protecting? That you seem to be willing to sacrifice for?"

The man smiled at Dean's silence. "I thought not." He stood up from his seat. "Simply put, this case that your friends are so carefully guarding carries a piece of technology which would allow someone to freely access any kind of information stored online or on any kind of technology. Smart phone, computer, online, secure account, banking interface - all of it becomes an open book to read and write in."

"Now this is an incredibly useful tool for someone seeking to make any kind of social change in the world today. If you want to make change in society, you start in the part that will hit them the hardest the fastest – the economy. Specifically, the free market. If I can drive up the prices for consumers and the sellers at the same time, everybody loses. If I drive them up high enough quickly enough, and enough people get upset, people will get angry.

"Now if the thing they are angry about is the high price of the latest ipod people will complain, but they will do what they have always done – nothing. That's because it's all talk. People don't change over talk. But when the price of things they need start increasing – food especially – that's where things start to get hairy. Imagine a can of beans sitting at, what, eighty-eight cents or a dollar in some stores nowadays, right? Imagine that were eight times as high. Frozen food would skyrocket. And let's not even get into fresh meats, fruits and vegetables.

"Now what do people do when they can't afford something and can't get it?" The man grinned as he said this. "Supermarkets will have to start hiring security forces just to break even with all the looting going on. The markets in poorer towns will have to rely either on the mercy of the people or on the local police force. But once something as powerful as hunger begins to sweep the country – well, Black Friday rioting will pale in compare to what will take place.

"And that's just one step. There are many more pieces of this puzzle. I don't need to tell you that the price of gas has been high in recent history. People will talk and complain about it as they've always done. Until it becomes expensive enough that people will begin opting to walk everywhere, if not use bicycles. Or, in other cases, begin to steal or siphon the fuel.

"Above all else, however, if you want to the seeds of anarchy, you have to teach mankind one thing- that mankind itself cannot be trusted. That at its heart, mankind is deceitful and dishonest. If you tell people this, they may confirm their own suspicions of others, it never occurring to them that they themselves are part of the problem. With coalitions discouraged, it will be easier to speak to the people."

"For what purpose?"

"For the purpose of revolution. We will overthrow this old system of living and establish a new one."

Dean sat quietly as he thought about that. So the man wasn't a true anarchist after all, at least not for the sake of watching the world collapse around itself. So what did he truly want? Dean took a look at the man and was struck with an impression. Maybe he didn't know what he wanted.

Destrier spoke again.

> "I will explain the situation once. We will ask for your cooper-
> ation, but you are by no means required to give it. But if you'd
> like your friends to stand a chance at life you'll cooperate."

Dean was briefed on the situation and what was going on. He was
happy, first, that his friends were still alive and second that they had
stayed ahead of Destrier's forces.

He began to wonder about what was going on. If Destrier was telling him that his friends would need help, then he imagined that some
kind of trap was being laid. His mind returned to his earlier train of
thought. He had to find a way to help them, if he could. For the moment, he had to buy some time.

Chapter 21

Tim woke, his eyes darting about, looking around for an unseen ene-my. He sat up in his seat. The sky was dark. Mike was at the wheel now, Angelo was asleep in the front seat, snoring. Gemma slept in the seat beside him. He looked out the window again. Stars were in the sky, but they were beginning to fade with the approaching dawn.

His dream came back to him in fragments. Running from the shad-ow. Trying to escape from it. Being cut off by the shadow. There was a voice as well, telling him to stand and fight. But a chill ran down his spine. He told himself that fighting against this shadow would mean death.

He let his mind wander as listened to the car's engine. Mike was quiet at the wheel and didn't have the radio on. Tim guessed that the man used this time as space to think things through, whatever might be on his mind. Tim stretched his neck and heard it crack as he did so. Mike's large frame easily filled the seat in front of him. It was difficult to see around him, if Tim was inclined to try and get a view of what lay before the car.

Cars were scarce on the roads they took on their journey. Some of these back roads were completely deserted, leading through the mid-dle of nowhere. They had decided that some of these roads would serve them well over the highways, since the highways could often be crowded with traffic coming and going. Back roads served them well in that they were empty and, with little traffic and few dwellings in the area, they could pass unrestricted through the countryside. And they needed to get through quickly if they were going to get to the agreed-upon meeting place in time.

Glancing in the mirror, Tim saw there were bags under Mike's eyes.

"Not exactly what you signed up for is it?" he said, keeping his voice down for the others.

Mike gave a soft laugh. "That's for sure. Still, driving at night isn't bad."

"Are you doing all right? You should probably get some sleep while you can."

He considered this, then waved Tim off. "I'll be fine. I've pulled my fair share of late nights. Try to get another hour or two of sleep. I think we're getting close."

"Pull over."

In a minute, Tim had taken Mike's place and sat in the driver's seat. As he drove, his mind began to wander. He knew that their chances of getting Dean away from this group alive were slim, but what choice did they have? The man had involved himself with their cause - if they didn't look out for each other, who would?

Trying to get comfortable, Tim stretched his left leg a bit and sighed. So far it looked like things would be all right. As soon as they got to the meeting place, he knew that it could change on a dime. The captors could refuse to bring Dean with them, or not show up at all, or just catch Tim and his group without showing that they had Dean. There were any number of things that could go wrong.

At the same time, Tim trusted that there were ways that things could go right as well. He didn't have much hope for it, but realized that if there were chances for things to go wrong, maybe there was a chance for things to go right as well. If his group didn't have hope, what did they have?

After they got Dean, they would have to hightail it away and try to get off to the FBI headquarters as soon as they could. Tim hoped that the plan would go off without a hitch. He knew, though, that there was no way that Destrier would let them get away with Dean, especially if he didn't have the case in hand. His mind went around the problem circling like a bird of prey searching for any sign of life in the landscape below him.

He heard a screaming horn on his left and swerved to keep in his own lane. There were grunts and groans from the sleepy passengers.

"Sorry." Tim whispered, turning his attention back to the road.

"You all right?" Mike asked.

Tim nodded. "I'll be fine."

With a shrug, Mike sat himself back to try and sleep.

In his line of work, Tim found that observation played one of the most important roles. Whether it was surveying products in the marketplace for marketing strategies or observing a designer in their creative processes as they put together package designs, Tim was consistently using his powers of observation.

Tim turned again in his seat, trying to make himself comfortable enough to fall asleep. Instead, his mind wandered for another half hour and he decided that sleep was going to evade him. At this point he asked Mike to pull over and they switched places, Tim taking up the wheel, and Mike climbing in back to get another hour or two of sleep.

The stars on the western horizon continued to shine, even as the light began to grow in the east. He waited with baited breath for the coming moment. Little by little, light began to grow and spread from the eastern horizon ahead of them. Shadows were deep, and seemed to be impenetrable. They stood like solid objects, apparently immovable, like the great stones lying in some field. Though he knew that the sunrise was coming, there was a certain hesitation about the sun's rising that did not dissipate, but only grew as the light in the east grew stronger.

Then, in a glorious moment, the first great beam of light broke over the edge of the earth and into their visible spectrum. He took a breath. The sight radiated glory. Tim took another breath and gazed at the sight. Hues of red and gold mixed together as the sun continued to rise. The red began to brighten and give way to other hues, such as gold and yellow. Soon he would be basking in the light and warmth of the sun's light.

Slowing as he needed to, with the sun in his eyes, Tim looked out again at the beautiful range of colors scattering themselves along and above the horizon. At first there had been some dark purple hues that mixed with the darkness near the horizon. Deep red hues followed that, along with orange and yellow.

Tim took the sight in, letting his mind wander as he did so. He wondered about their chances of success at their intended mission. From his knowledge of marketing, he knew that nothing is simple. Anything that may appear to be straightforward may, in fact, have many factors underlying its structure underneath. While something as apparently simple as approaching whatever forces they were presented with and taking Dean and leaving seemed like a simple resolution to a simple problem, he knew that this would not be the case.

The first point was that Destrier would certainly be on the lookout for the briefcase that they had in their possession. If he didn't know where it was, he might be hesitant to step in and do anything to them. The second point is that whatever forces were deployed in the open air were certainly not going to be the only ones. Tim guessed that he might be able to spot a few plain-clothes agents but whether he would be able to do anything about them would be another question entirely.

Continuing on its ascending course, the sun rose further over the edge of the earth, it's light breaking along the earth's surface and into the atmosphere, illuminating the sky to a bright blue. The light permeated the atmosphere, illuminating it from behind, as the sun reached across the galaxy to shine its light onto the earth. The sun's rays blossomed, striking the earth's atmosphere and spreading throughout it, changing the sky's vibrant hues from red, purple and gold to magenta and blue. Tim gave the car a little more gas, aware that if they didn't make it to the meeting point in time, they would lose their only chance of getting away with Dean.

Chapter 22

"Hey guys, time to wake up." Tim said. Gemma groaned and turned over in her seat. She opened her eyes to see Mike in the seat next to her, snoring. Tim was in the front, at the wheel. She stretched and glanced around the cab of the vehicle.

"What time is it?" she asked, rubbing at her face. Tim glanced in his rearview mirror at her. Even with her slightly disheveled hair he found himself casting second glances her way.

"Time for some food." He said.

He was already in a line for McDonald's. They all narrated their orders, which Tim dictated to the cashier. Despite the early morning, the cashier tried to put on a happy face. Tim saw that she wasn't eager to be there. Her name tag said "Betty".

"Good morning Betty." He said, when they had pulled up to the window.

"That will be $27.98."

He offered his debit card. "I guess it gets pretty busy here, huh?" He could feel Gemma rolling her eyes in the seat behind him.

She shrugged. "Lunchtime is the worst. Everybody and their mom decides to eat here. We've got to take customers at the window and at the front counter. Then, if we get an order wrong, you can bet that some customer is going to come storming in here, screaming about or terrible service and asking to see a manager."

Tim shook his head. "It's that bad?"

Betty grinned. "No, not really. Once in a while we get a complaint, but we fix the order and they get on their way."

Tim thanked her, and she gave them their change before the cashier spoke again. "You guys are on a road trip, right?"

Tim asked her how she knew. She motioned to Gemma. "I know what it's like. You've been in the car all night, and can't get a chance to fix your hair."

Gemma touched her hair self-consciously but stayed quiet. Tim thanked Betty again, pulling forward to the second window to receive their food.

Tim passed the food to Angelo, who distributed it. Tim had ordered two breakfast sandwiches and a coffee. He didn't care for coffee much, especially stuff from a fast-food place, but after his restless night in the car and the day ahead of them, necessity overpowered personal preference. Angelo navigated as Tim drove and they made their way to Millennium Park. He pulled around the park once to see whether he couldn't spot anything out of the ordinary. As he discussed it with the others, they knew that the agents would be using some kind of ordinary looking vehicle for their own transportation, rather than something conspicuous.

At this point in the day, there weren't a lot of people in the park yet. The group sat in the car at the far curb of the street, waiting to see whether any sign of their adversary would appear. As they sat, some joggers made their way around the park, taking the sidewalks as their track. The park was in a residential district, with houses surrounding much of it. A few of the joggers had their dogs with them. Tim noticed one woman with an athletic stroller and wondered whether athleticism was genetic and if the child would end up athletic like his mother.

They all kept their eyes open for anything unusual, but for a little while they didn't see anything. Wondering whether they needed to tip the scale themselves and show their faces before their adversaries made the next move, Tim turned to Gemma.

"What do you think? Should we step out now and let them see us?"

Gemma glanced out the window. "Let's wait a few minutes."

Tim nodded and turned his attention back to the park. There weren't many other cars in the area. Save their own sedan, there were other vehicles parked in driveways around the neighborhood, clearly family cars. Nothing seemed out of the ordinary, which gave Tim a worse feeling than seeing his enemies face them head-on.

Suddenly Gemma pointed. "Look!" she said.

Tim craned his neck to see out the window.

"What?" Said Angelo. "I don't see anything."

"Over there." she said, indicating a place with her finger.

Looking closely, Tim saw a bench located near the center of the park. It was facing a monument in the center of the park. A man sat on the bench, facing away from their vehicle.

"I don't see it." Said Mike. "Are you sure you saw something?"

"No." said Tim, "I see it."

The man turned on the bench again, and Tim caught his breath. It was Dean.

Dean sat on the bench, hands folded, facing kiddy-corner away from their vehicle.

"He doesn't look hurt." Gemma said, withdrawing her hand. She turned to Tim. "What do you think?"

Tim paused for a moment, looking Dean over. He had hardly known the man before he was taken from them. Now that he could see Dean in the flesh again, it was like seeing a long-lost brother. Gemma saw Tim's hesitation but remained silent until he spoke.

"I think we need to be careful. Whoever brought Dean here is sure to be watching him. As soon as we approach him we're going to be targets." He paused, and the car's air conditioning sputtered before continuing on. "Our mission is to get Dean safely out of here without getting caught ourselves. If we can manage to do that, we'll be on our way to getting the case back to FBI headquarters. Above all else, we need to be sure that Destrier does not get ahold of the briefcase."

He turned a bit farther in his seat so that he could see them all more easily. "You all remember the plan, right?" They nodded. "All right." He said. Tim hesitated before he spoke again. "May God be with us."

It was a strange way to send them out, but it felt like the right thing to do. Gemma gave him a glance before stepping out of the car, waiting by her door. Mike and Angelo stepped out of the car as well. The twosome walked towards the bench. Gemma kept her eyes subtly on the men sent ahead.

"You do know that if they get caught we're in deeper trouble than we had before."

Tim didn't reply.

Dean sat still on the bench. It was clear that they would have to approach the bench to reach him. This made Tim nervous, and he said so.

"Well," Gemma said, "should we leave him?"

Tim realized she was being serious. Looking to her, she wasn't grinning or grimacing, but waiting for him to answer. He took a careful look around the park again.

"Let's go."

During their conversation the number of people in the park had increased. There were more joggers making their way around the park in their running shorts. Mothers came with their youngest children who ran eagerly to the play equipment, striving to be the first to the top, either to look out at the park in full or to get to the slides first.

With a glance around the park, Tim was about to say something to Gemma, when she spoke up first.

"We need to be sure about getting Dean out of here alive, and I'm not sure about our chances right now."

"When can we be sure about anything?"

"If you've got a plan B in mind, I wouldn't be disappointed to hear about it."

"I think you would. Let's keep our focus on the first plan for now."

They kept walking, keeping a not-too-straight course for the center of the park. Picking the center of the park had been a good move. Wherever they came from, it was sure that from the center of the park Tim and his friends would have the longest distance to run to their vehicle. Angelo and Mike looked like they were having a casual conversation ahead of them.

"I'd like to tell them to stay focused." Tim said.

"They're nervous too. Some people get chatty when they're nervous."

"You ever met any people like that?"

Gemma kept silent.

As they approached, there were trees dotting the landscape which made visibility a little tricky. Dean, however, had his eyes fixed ahead of him, on the fountain at the center of the park. As they came closer, Tim's gut clenched.

"Something's wrong." he said, and glanced around.

"You can't look suspicious or they'll know we're onto them."

"They already know that we don't trust them. They're letting us get too close. Why would they let us just waltz up and take Dean and run? Something's wrong with this picture."

Tim looked over his shoulder. He didn't see anyone following them or watching them. That only increased his anxiety.

"Hold up." Tim said. From her expression, Tim guessed, at first, that Gemma would snap at him. When she saw his expression, however, her gaze softened and she spoke.

"Do you think we need to pull back?"

Tim hesitated, but only for a second. "No," he said, "let's see how this plays out."

Angelo and Mike were talking and laughing as though oblivious to all around them. Tim knew they were nervous, and this lent energy to their conversation as they strolled through the park. If he didn't know what was going on, he would have guessed a couple of buddies were catching up on old times.

As they walked, they passed by others enjoying some time in the sun. The trees provided some shade, dappling the sunlight in places. Tim glanced behind them again, eliciting a growl from Gemma.

"You're making me nervous." Gemma said.

Mike approached the bench where Dean sat.

"Mr. Meare." He said. "You might want to come along with us if you want to get out of here alive."

Dean looked up. From where he stood, Tim saw the haggard look in the man's face. The man looked wilted, a plant left to languish in a dark cellar. Tim wanted to know what had happened, but there was not time for a discussion.

Tim and Gemma stood nearly a hundred feet behind the bench, eyes open for any sign of trouble.

Angelo beckoned to Dean. "Let's get out of here."

Dean nodded and stood. He followed Angelo around the bench and back toward the car. Tim dared to breathe a sigh of relief. Maybe they would make it away after all. All the worry almost seemed foolish at this point. Yet at the same time he knew something was wrong. The look in Dean's eyes spoke volumes. The five of them kept walking, but Dean was silent. The rest of them were quiet as well. They hurried, unsure of anything.

Gemma glanced over her shoulder and grunted, turning to face front.

"Don't look now, but we've got trouble at four o'clock."

"How many are there?" Tim asked.

"I saw two."

"Which means there will be more waiting for us somewhere. Did you lock the car?"

"Yes, I did."

They picked up their pace, moving quickly to the street where they were parked. Tim felt his pocket. The gun Gemma gave him was there. Tim took a slow breath.

Angelo began to sprint. Tim heard a shout behind him and reached for his weapon.

Mike shoved Dean behind a tree as Gemma and Tim sought shelter. Tim heard a shot ring out as screams began to echo through the park. Two more gunshots followed quickly after the first. Tim saw wood chips flying off the tree behind which he hid. He pulled out his gun, checked it, whipped around and fired off two rounds before getting back behind the tree.

He shouted to Mike and Dean. "Get to the car!"

He didn't look to see whether they had left or not, but turned his attention back to the fight at hand. Tim waited until after Gemma before attempting to fire another round, trying to keep the shooters busy while Mike and Dean got away. Another shot resounded and wood chips flew.

Tim glanced around his tree to see an agent creeping to his left, trying to flank them and cut them off from the vehicle. He raised his gun and fired another shot. The agent ducked behind a tree.

"Gemma." He said. "Get going." She hesitated for a moment, but nodded. Firing another shot, she slipped away. Tim fired on the agent learning out to take a shot at Gemma who ran. The man pulled back as Tim fired again. Tim glanced over his shoulder to see her running for the car.

Tim saw the man's attention drawn to her as Gemma sprinted away, but he fired off another shot. The man ducked behind the large tree hiding him again. Tim looked around for the other agent, but didn't see anything of him. Praying that this lapse would last, Tim sprinted toward their car and ducked behind a tree for cover. As he did so he heard another shot ring out. Keeping behind another tree he looked ahead of himself, in the direction of the car. The next part would be difficult. There was little cover, so he would have to keep behind trees when and where he could find them and keep moving so as not to be caught.

Keeping his eyes ahead, Tim gathered himself and began to sprint for the vehicle. As he did so, he heard another shot. He kept running and managed to get behind another tree where he looked at his arm. He felt a tightness in his left arm. Touching it, the arm felt wet. He blinked once, twice, inspecting it. There was no pain, but he saw that his jacket and shirt underneath were torn and it was red underneath. He had been shot. There was only shock as he stood there gazing at it.

His breaths were coming in shallow gasps. He looked up to the car, where the others were supposed to be gathering. Gemma was almost there, and he saw the others piling into the car. Looking around, he saw that there was another vehicle, a black SUV around the block. He knew that if they waited for him, there wouldn't be enough time to get away. Angelo was behind the wheel, saying something but Tim could only hear his own breath. In what felt like slow-motion, he waved for them to start driving. He was still a couple of hundred yards away with the two gunmen on his tail and at least one vehicle which could catch up with them in a minute or two.

He felt his mouth forming the words 'Go now.' but didn't hear anything. Angelo glanced around the cab, and Tim caught the man's mouth moving as he tipped his head around to speak with the people in the backseat. Gemma, who was in the front passenger seat, was about to step out of the car when a bullet ricocheted off a lamppost not six feet from the vehicle. She took that as a warning and stayed in the vehicle. Tim could see that she was shouting at the others.

Tim turned to face the gunmen, unsteady on his own feet. He now saw that he had been losing blood. As he turned the earth tipped and he vaguely wondered about whether the others would get away. He raised his gun on the first attacker, who was no more than a hundred feet from him now. He pulled the trigger only to hear it click.

The chamber was empty.

His head was spinning, but he was aware enough to hear tires screeching on pavement as the two attackers moved in. He raised his hands, aware that a fight at this point would only land him deeper in trouble. The two men stepped to him, stopping about ten feet away.

"Put the gun down and take three steps back. You try anything different and you're a dead man."

Tim did as he was told, taking his gun and setting on the grass in front of him, then taking three steps back, away from the gun. One of the attackers kept his gun trained on Tim while the other retrieved the weapon. Checking it, he turned to his comrade.

"It's empty."

With that confirmation, they moved in, one stepping to Tim's side, and the other keeping back.

"Let's move." the man said.

Chapter 23

They stepped forward, in the direction of the vehicles. Tim looked again to see that there were now two black SUV's pulled onto the street, and an empty sedan sitting where they had parked it. There were two more men standing out in the street. A few pedestrians were standing around, staring, but they clearly didn't know what to do about what was going on. Tim wondered whether the pedestrians thought these men were government agents. What would that make him?

He thought about yelling for help, but just as he was ready to open his mouth, he heard a voice behind him, from one of the men who had caught him.

"You try anything funny and I'll tell our men to kill all your friends on the spot. We can do this with one just as well as four."

The men moved him quickly across the park to the rear SUV and bound his hands, seating him near the back of the vehicle. There were three rows besides the driver's seat. The first man climbed into the vehicle with him while the other stepped around to the second car. Tim turned in his seat to see Angelo and Dean in the backseat. Angelo had a black eye and Dean didn't look well.

"Well," Angelo said, "I guess of all the things that could happen, this is as low as things can get, huh?"

Dean shook his head but didn't say anything.

Tim glanced about at their captors. There were four of them, three guards and a driver. Two of the guards sat in the front bench seat, while the third took the front passenger seat across from the driver. The vehicle was already moving, each SUV pulling down a different street, the neighborhood appearing already as though nothing had happened. The police would show up, find some marks on the trees from bullets, and claim that it was a drug deal gone bad, packing up before the investigation began.

Tim realized that if anyone was going to save them, it had to be themselves.

"Keep your heads up guys." he said. "We're going to have to find a way out of this."

"Hey you," said the guard in the front passenger seat. The man's voice was clear, his frame large, his hands scarred. "keep it quiet back there. We can quiet things down ourselves if we have to."

Tim looked again at Angelo and Dean. Besides Angelo's black eye he had a cut above his upper lip. Dean had a bruise on his temple, and he had already looked worse for wear when they had found him in the park. Tim wondered about their chances. From what he could tell just from Dean's appearance, he guessed that the stress of his situation had exacted a heavy toll on the man's well-being.

Angelo's eyes were aflame. In them Tim saw the drive to stand up and take action. But he shook his head barely. Not yet. They would have to wait for the opportune moment. The moment to take action against an enemy often came from an enemy's mistake. While their fate was uncertain, they would have to hope that a chance came for them to free themselves.

Tim's mind suddenly turned to the case. Had they found it? They had reached the car so it was possible. Why did Destrier have his men take them alive? Did he need information? Questions began a furious dance about Tim's head, one which he only managed to silence by distraction. It would do no good to waste his energy and thoughts on something he couldn't help. He would have to see what was going on and try to take action as best he could when the opportunity presented itself.

For now, the opportunity to take advantage of was to rest. Tim sat back in his seat and tried to relax. For all the uncertainty surrounding him and permeating his situation, he felt drowsy, as the adrenaline rush wore off and exhaustion overtook him.

Tim woke up once to find that they were still in the vehicle. He couldn't tell how long he had been asleep. From what he could tell of traffic around them, it looked as though they were headed away from the city. Traffic wasn't heavy and they got along at a decent speed as they rode along the highway. He didn't know how long they would be in the vehicle. He glanced back to his comrades in the back seat. Dean's appearance told that though his eyes were open he was not mentally present. Angelo appeared to be asleep as he rested his head against the window. Turning again to face the front of the vehicle, Tim sighed quietly and waited.

They approached a great warehouse sitting by the docks of a harbor. Gulls cried and water lapped against the pier. Waves crashing on the docks created a constant swishing noise as the water broke again and again on the dock's structure.

The area appeared to be completely deserted. They had probably come to the docks either to hide them for a few days or to kill them outright. Hiding their bodies wouldn't be difficult at the edge of the ocean. All of these thoughts ran through his head as they approached some outer gates which stood outside the warehouse the size of an aircraft hanger.

They approached the gate and a guard spoke with the driver of the vehicle. The discussion was short, but after the driver showed the guard his ID the guard waved them though. It occurred to Tim that the driver could park the vehicle inside the warehouse. He had seen that done in films and television shows. The bad guys pull into a warehouse with their car, open it up and there's the money or the hostage, or whatever the cops sought.

Pulling around to the side of the building, the driver stopped the car. The guards climbed out.

"All right," said the driver, "step out of the vehicle one at a time."

Tim climbed out slowly, his back aching from the running and pro-longed sitting. He stood quietly as they brought out Dean and then Angelo. The guards directed them to a side entrance of the hangar building. One guard led the way, the other two followed behind to keep them together.

Upon reaching the door, Tim saw that it was clearly reinforced. A keypad was mounted to the side of the door. The first guard entered in a long code and there was a tone followed by the sound of the door's lock clicking open. He stepped inside the building followed closely by the prisoners. They were in a roughly square room painted grey. There were no chairs, save the one that a guard sat on behind a console.

Seeing the structure of the room itself, Tim realized that the room would have been built after the warehouse was complete, as part of the conversion from a warehouse into whatever kind of base of operations the building was being used for at the time.

"So," Tim said to the guard behind the console, "I guess you don't see much action out here?" He was met with silence. The guards escorted them to separate cells.

As the door closed behind him, Tim took stock of the room. It was small, but certainly not cramped. He had seen smaller apartments. There was a proper bed and the linens were clean. There was a toilet in the corner. None of the amenities changed the fact that he was a prisoner.

He shook his head and sat on the edge of the bed. He couldn't imag-ine things getting any worse than this. The only people on the plan-et who knew about the technology to change the world were either locked away or had the technology and wanted to run the world with it. Tim had been entrusted with this case and had failed. He was the one who should have died in that alleyway, allowing the agent to live and complete his mission.

But he also knew that it was his duty to protect those who had come along on this journey. Their effort to rescue Dean had failed miserably and now they had all been captured by the forces they were hoping to outwit. It was over. The enemy had won. They now were in possession of the technology that would allow Destrier to throw the world into utter chaos, perhaps so that he could eventually take advantage of it, ruling the world himself.

Tim knew that he had failed. More than failing a simple mission, however, he had failed his new friends who were counting on him. Angelo, Dean and Mike were following after him. Gemma was following him too. What was her story? Tim suddenly realized that he knew very little about her. But he wanted to know more.

She kept her head in dangerous times. She trusted his judgment. By paying respect to him and trusting him, she had earned his respect as well. More than anything now, he wanted to apologize to her for getting her into this mess. He felt that if, somehow, he had done something differently that none of this misfortune would have come upon them. Dean's getting captured had happened so suddenly there had not been time to process what had happened. Now he felt guilty for not either sending someone else into the back of the gas station with Dean or making sure the enemy agents hadn't been in the back area where Dean had been grabbed.

He thought back to his life less than a week ago. He could hardly imagine his old life now, approving package designs, making sure that the package was something that enticed customers to buy their products. Now he was trying to make sure that his friends got out of this situation alive and unharmed, and unsure that he would be able to pull them through this experience.

For all his experience, being the leader of others who were relying on him for their lives had never occurred to Tim. He had been happy where he was, simply approving designs, living in his comfortable lifestyle. If he got out of this alive, he didn't know what he would do with himself.

These and other thoughts were running through his head when the door opened. A guard stepped in, making sure that the room was secure. Tim almost laughed at that, but kept quiet. A doctor stepped in, a young man wearing a white coat.

"Good afternoon." He said. "We're going to take a look at that arm for you."

Tim glanced at it before looking back to the man in front of him.

"You're a licensed doctor?"

"Yes."

"Of medicine?"

"Yes sir."

The man stood before Tim with hands folded, waiting for Tim's response. After a moment, Tim beckoned the man over. Why the organization would want to better him before they battered him was beyond Tim, but he didn't complain.

He had Tim remove his coat and shirt so that he could see the wound, which was on Tim's upper left arm, the outer part of the tricep. Except for the guard who stayed in the room, the doctor worked alone. He quickly cleaned the area, then anesthetized the area, stitching up the cut. The injury was not large, but the doctor was thorough. The bullet had only grazed the side of Tim's arm. He thanked the man.

"It means a lot to see that not everyone here means to harm me."

The doctor's face clouded for a moment with that statement. "I don't think you understand Destrier."

"Oh, is that right? And just what don't I understand about him kidnapping me and my friends?"

"I work for the healing and benefit of others."

"And is that how you justify your employment here?"

"Mr. Destrier has great plans for-"

"Mr. Destrier had his men kidnap my friend, use him for bait, shoot me, and catch me and the rest of my friends for whatever purpose he has in mind here."

"I know that beginnings can be rough, but with some time I think you may come to understand what is truly going on."

Tim spread his hands. "Enlighten me."

"Destrier is a man who understands many methods of accomplishing his tasks. You've experienced his use of force, of course, but there are many others; the manipulation of economics, the playing of governments against each other, the use of media to turn the people of entire nations against an idea. What Destrier is attempting to do is nothing short of revolutionary."

"It's interesting that you use that word like it's a good thing - 'Revolutionary.' Do you remember the French Revolution? I don't know how much you know about history, but almost everyone has heard of the French Revolution."

"Yes, the span of years which has produced some of our modern systems of government."

"And was responsible for the death of thousands. When the people stormed the Bastille and overthrew the government, they simply took the place of the rulers who were already over them."

The doctor gave a shake of his head. "But, like what Destrier has in mind, it was an entirely different system."

"There's no such thing as something entirely new." Tim said. "Old ideas are reborn and come back to different societies at different times and are given different names.

"This time it is different."

"Does 'different' mean better? And that notion is what led to the killing of thousands under the reign of terror."

"But we won't harm a single person." Said the doctor.

"Noble echoes of every revolution. But it never happens that way."

The doctor shook his head. "This is something where we give the people their own chance to behave as they choose, whether that's to help themselves and their neighbors, or to harm those around them for their own benefit. How many people would you get out of the way so that you would claim everything in reach?"

"So, in other words, you're going to start it, and let the people, and let the people start killing each other and roaming the streets in total chaos."

"If they roam the streets in chaos, that is their decision."

"But what if they didn't have a reason do it that in the first place?"

The doctor stopped talking after that bit.

After examining the arm, he bound it and left Tim on his own. The arm ached whenever he flexed it, so he left and tried not to use it for anything. He didn't know what would happen next. If his friends were all right, he had no way of knowing. Tim was isolated, and spent his time staring at the wall and talking to himself about his situation. He had no ideas about what would happen next. If the group already had the case, then they might just be waiting to kill Tim and his friends. So why bind his wound, then? Why not let him slowly bleed out? As he thought through it, Tim realized that the organization must have some reasons for keeping him around.

Tim paced his cell as his mind ran in circles. He currently had no way out of his cell, so he would have to wait until an opportunity presented itself. That might not be often. He didn't know how often guards came to these cells. The cell seemed clean enough.

His only guess about his friends was that they were in similar cells to his. He was sure that keeping everyone separated was intentional. If Destrier had allowed a few of them together, they would have the chance to talk and make a plan. Whatever Destrier was doing, he couldn't afford a wrench in his plan now.

Tim sat on the edge of the bed and tried to collect his thoughts. The group was now all being held captive by Destrier in the same building. They had no clear hope of escape. They had no clear idea of what Destrier wanted from them, except to get the case out of their hands. Now that he had it, what would he do with them? Releasing them was certainly something he wouldn't do. Either he would end up killing them or, perhaps, imprisoning them, locking them away so that they would not interfere with his intended plans.

Tim sat and thought then stood and paced and sat again as his mind ran in circles. The hours dragged on, and ideas were scarce to be found. He sat at the small table in the room and stared at the wall, willing himself to think of something which would save himself and his friends. But as much as he tried to think of something, nothing came to mind. Even if he could get out of the cell, the organization was already in possession of the case, meaning that they may have already begun to access the information that they needed.

One of the things he quickly found about his new habitation was that it was quiet. He didn't hear any noise from the hallway. When he had first approached the room, he noticed that other cells were adjacent to his. If anyone in the next room was making noise he couldn't hear it. He wondered about the rest of the rooms and the use of them, whether this organization kept them filled or if Tim's group was all they had seen in a long time. If they weren't the only ones, who else was being kept here, and for what reason? How long could the organization keep anyone here? People would come looking for them. But Tim realized that this organization, given the right resources, could wipe a person off the map. With the right tools a person could disappear from society without so much as a second glance.

He wondered about the people at the park. What had they thought when they saw a bunch of black vehicles come screaming up to the curb so that a bunch of men could jump out and drag some regular-looking people off to an unknown place and fate? Had they all thought that it was simply something that the government was doing? A test? Or did everyone assume the radical problem had been handled? In the end, no one did anything.

Chapter 24

It may have been a few hours or several, Tim was too disoriented to tell, when his cell door opened again. He sat at the small table at the back of the room. One guard stepped in and glanced around the room before looking at Tim.

"Mr. Runn." He said. "You are to follow me."

Tim caught the relatively formal address, but didn't say anything as he rose and stepped through the door. The guard was standing five feet before the door. Tim stopped before the guard and waited while the guard produced a pair of handcuffs. Bringing his hands before him, Tim watched blandly at the handcuffs were secured to his wrists. After checking over the prisoner, the guard stepped to and through the door while another guard took up the rear.

Tim's senses began to awaken as they walked down the hallway. He wondered if this could be his chance to do something. But a look around the hall told him otherwise. First there were a guard in front of and behind him. Even if he got past them the hallway appeared to be secure. The only doors in or out were either end of the hall. If he knew anything about security, the doors would be locked with controls for the bolts beyond the room itself.

The first guard stepped up to the door and Tim stopped as he stopped. After a moment there was a click as the door's deadbolt disengaged. The guard easily pushed the door open and stepped through. The guard behind Tim urged him onwards, and he stepped though the door as well. They stepped into a large open area which made up the main part of what used to be the warehouse before it was converted. It now functioned as one giant office space, divided by partitions and six- or seven-foot walls which had been put up to divide office spaces between workers.

Tim took a look around the giant room and observed its structure. The building was a warehouse which had been converted to a usable space, that much was plain. Looking at the walls of the original structure, he could see that there were doors of the warehouse itself which had been converted and which probably led to other types of rooms. Restrooms, storage rooms and rooms with other purposes surrounded him. As they stepped down the walkway which circled the building's edge, Tim saw a few people pass by. His first instinct told him to run, but he knew that he would likely be caught if he did that. His second idea was to employ the help of some other person working in the area. But he quickly realized that these other workers, though they did not work in the prison itself, were certainly aware of its existence, and not likely to help an escapee from such a prison.

Tim took a breath and tried to think of what he could do. He knew that it was not likely he would get help from anyone in the building. That meant he would have to rely on himself and whatever opportunity presented itself. Whatever happened, he determined that he would keep his eyes open for just such an opportunity. They passed several people, and Tim wondered how often these men led prisoners in handcuffs through the halls, because no one looked at him as they went by. Either they had seen many people in his position or there was some taboo about speaking with or interacting with prisoners. As they walked, Tim kept his eyes open for anything that would help him. The guards did not appear to be talkative, so he decided that any conversation or prying with them wouldn't be useful. They walked around the outer wall of the warehouse until they arrived at an enclosed office with walls and a locking door, as opposed to the superficial structures on the main floor of the building which provided the employees with a semblance of privacy.

The guard knocked before being prompted to enter. He cracked the door and hesitated for an instant before opening it fully and stepping through. The guard behind Tim moved and ushered Tim into the room ahead of him.

The room was small and well-furnished, with a desk and two chairs for guests. A painting hung on one wall, but Tim didn't give it any more attention than to notice its presence. The guards seated him in one of the chairs facing the desk. A man was sitting there. The man was young, maybe in his early thirties. Tim noticed at once that the man was keenly aware. His eyes darted everywhere, up and down Tim, around the guards, across the room – he was entirely observant. After a moment the man spoke.

"My name is Julian Destrier and though you don't know me you must at least recognize that name by now." He looked over his prisoner. The way he sized Tim up made him think that the man was hardly impressed by anything. "You must be Mr. Runn, the one who's been giving me all this trouble." The man stood and stepped over to where the painting hung on the wall. "Tell me, do you know much about art?"

Tim had been prepared to fight for himself, or to offer himself for his friends. The security of his nation was at stake, and the man had asked him if he knew anything about painting. Tim was silent.

"This one is by Camuccini. It's a print, of course. It's called the Death of Julius Caesar. It's the moment just when the conspirators come together to kill the tyrant in their hopes that doing so will restore their nation to the republic it once was."

The man turned from the painting and sat behind the desk again.

"Of course things almost never go the way we plan. After Caesar's death, those who hoped to gain from it had to give up or diminish what they gained from destroying Caesar's tyranny. What they believed would be a grand victory turned out to be a small affair, bartering for a few terms that they hoped to keep their nation as the Roman republic. Their victory was starved of all impressiveness they hoped for, the terms which they believed they fought for were sacrificed. Their victory was hollowed and it became only a semblance of what they envisioned.

"They saved their nation from a tyranny, only to trade the power of one man for the power of a council who decided that their terms were negotiable. Those who had saved their nation, who should have been regarded as heroes were now bartering for the vision of their nation."

The man studied Tim for a moment before he spoke again. "We have the chance to change not our nation but the world, and without compromise. We can set things as we please. The beauty of it is that the world begs us to do this already."

The man stood and stepped around the desk to stand before Tim. "The world will be in such chaos that they will beg for order. When we offer it to them, they will grab ahold of it greedily, eagerly. People naturally look for leadership. They talk about being free as if that is all they desire, but they don't know what they desire. People want to be ruled. Without being properly ruled, chaos ensues among the people. They don't know what to do with themselves. They need someone to oversee them."

"And I guess you're just the man for the job." Tim said. "There's nothing like a bit of tyranny to make people appreciate their status as slaves."

Destrier hesitated for a moment. Then a backhand flew and caught Tim across the face. He coughed and flexed his cheek a little. It stung and he felt a small trickle of blood. The man's ring on his finger had cut into his face, leaving a small gash across his cheek.

Destrier circled around his desk again, flexing his hand which he had used to strike Tim. He sank into his seat.

> "Your life is in my hands now. All I need from you, Mr. Runn, is information. If I don't get it from you, I may be able to persuade you. What do you know about the case which we found in your possession?"

Tim sat and considered his situation. He knew that he couldn't give the man the information that he was after. If he did so, his society as he knew it could come to an end. The other reason he couldn't help was that he simply didn't know much about the case. For all the trouble they had gone to, seeking to return the case to its proper owners, Tim and his crew had not had a real chance to sit down and examine the case. From what little chance they had to examine it when they first found the case, there was no discernible way to open it.

Tim guessed that Destrier had already taken a look at it and was having trouble. Otherwise he could have already found a way to dispose of him and his friends. But telling him the truth would do no harm at this point, would it? The truth was that they hadn't had any success with opening the case any more than Destrier had, or any of his people with their resources.

"I don't know much about it." Tim said. "We never managed to get the case open. I never saw any clear mechanism for opening the case. However it's put together, I never learned what it is."

"Who else knows about the case or what it contains?"

"Just my friends and I."

"Name them."

"Gemma is the one who I first met. Dean found us quickly after that. Then there's Angelo and Mike. They're the only ones who know about the case."

"And how am I supposed to believe you?"

Tim kept himself from grimacing. The psychopath was asking for something to verify that Tim was telling the truth? What about himself? On the other hand, with any person making themselves an enemy of others and lying on a regular basis, they become distrustful because of the nature of their business. Being engaged in untrustworthy activities, they began to look for verification that others are telling them the truth.

Tim shifted in his seat and considered the question.

"You can't." he said. "At least there's nothing I can do to make you trust me. Trust is a voluntary activity. If you're going to do it, you'll have to make the decision to do it yourself."

Destrier shook his head. "You're not used to arguing your own case, are you?"

Tim shook his head. "I hardly have experience being interrogated as a hostage so no, this is a new experience for me. That doesn't change my answer, though."

"Doesn't it?" Destrier appeared to be amused. "So you believe that trust is a voluntary activity, entirely on part of the individual to invest as they see fit, is that right?"

"That's right."

"What you forget is that entire societies shape the behavior of individuals. This goes so far to the point where their behavior isn't truly individual, but shaped by the society itself, by others around the individual. Trust is an empty word people use to say that we need to put up with each other's mistakes and not complain or retaliate when things go wrong."

"Trust is essential to any meaningful relationship." Tim said. "How can I say I care about someone if they have no way to trust what I say? My words to them become empty and meaningless. If that's the case, there is no way to build a foundation for a relationship because nothing has substance."

"But society doesn't need substance. The elements which drive societies - fear and force - are enough to push millions to take action. It is a society that determines the value of the individual and of the conglomerate. The individual has no place except among the masses of society at large.

"A society is the measuring rod by which the world can be valued. People are born and die every day, individuals pass away and yet the societies stand."

"Societies which are made up of millions of individuals."

Destrier sighed. "As interesting as this conversation is, there are other matters I'd like to discuss. Like the release of your friends."

Tim sat up and Destrier laughed. "That got your attention, didn't it?"

He remained silent.

"Here's what I'm going to suggest. I will provide you and your friends with the means necessary to get home to your families-" he waved his hand. "-whatever semblance of a family you have. You will have the means to get home and when you arrive there you shall be left in peace."

"You'll let us go home? Just like that?"

"Of course. Except for the woman, of course."

Gemma.

"What do you want with her?"

"Well I can't have her running around back to the FBI telling them everything about me and leading a team of armed men to come and kill me and shut down my operation, can I?"

Tim didn't know that the FBI would come in and kill the man outright. Destrier would have too much information that they needed about his project. There was no way to know for sure what the FBI might do if they knew about this building and the operations going on in it. Tim thought they would put a stop to it.

If they knew about it. The problem which had been confronting Tim within the last twenty-four hours was unavoidable. There was no way for anyone to know about their problem.

"Take me instead. Let the others go. Do what you want with me, but let her go."

"You know I can't do that." A grin came to Destrier's face. "You care about this woman don't you?"

Tim kept silent. The man laughed. "You thought you could love a woman involved in espionage and not pay the price for it?"

Tim had no response, which only prompted more laughter from his captor.

Eventually the man spoke again. "No. Whatever happens, she will not be leaving with you. One slip of the tongue could bring my entire operation down around me, and then where would I be? No, the only way out is forward. If you will not cooperate, then you may just have to grow used to my hospitality."

Destrier rose and the guards stepped up to flank Tim. He stepped around the desk to face Tim. "I am sorry about how this has gone, but you have left me with little choice. What else could I do after you managed to foul up my operation?"

"If it's any consolation, it didn't look like it was going well in the first place."

Destrier gave a sigh and looked at the ground for a moment, then nodded to one of the guards who slugged Tim in the side. Tim lost his breath and fell to his knees.

"Over the next few days I want you to seriously consider your situation. However desperate you believe your situation to be, you are only beginning to understand it. It's at this point that I'll entreat you to take advantage of my hospitality for a while."

Tim groaned and took a breath. "There's something to say about the hospitality here. Still, it's a roof over my head, and that's better than nothing. Not as nice as my own home, but that goes without saying."

The two guards pulled Tim to his feet and directed him to the door on his unsteady feet.

"And Mr. Runn." Rather than turning himself, Tim was turned by the guards. "I might remind you of the lives of your friends who are involved in this plight as well. Try to think of them before you make your next step, hm?"

The two guards escorted him back down the hallway and to the door of his cell.

There was a buzz, a click, and the door opened before the hand of the guard. They escorted Tim into the room and removed his restraints before leaving themselves. Tim slowly sank onto the bed and put his head into his hands.

Chapter 25

Tim, Gemma, Angelo, Dean and Mike were being held in separate cells in the same hall. Since they had entered the building they had not seen anything of one another.

Mike had been a watchdog for this organization. He was there to look out for them. Now he found himself in a cell. He wasn't employed directly by the company, but was a freelancer, taking jobs as he pleased. Or as he could get them. Less than a week ago, the organization had begun to offer a hefty reward for anyone who had seen something of a heavily reinforced case containing a breakthrough technological development by the organization. They were looking for the case itself along with two persons who had it at the time. Any information was to be reported, and they were to be detained.

That afternoon in the gas station he had seen them.

Imagining them to be desperate fugitives, he was ready to fight them. When they began to crowd him, suggesting they sit and talk, he was on his guard, but still uneasy about these newcomers. Now he was in their plight, risking his life with theirs.

———————————

Gemma sat brooding in her cell. She sat glaring at the wall, as though with concentration she would drill holes in the walls with her gaze. Then she would stand and begin to pace, silent, but her thoughts ringing loudly in her head. Across the room and back and across again and back, she began to wear on the old carpet of the cell. Fear began to get the better of her. She would push it back and her anger would double down at her situation and at her fear of the situation. Fear was the admission of weakness. Weakness wasn't going to help her out of this situation.

She was stuck. There was no way out of this prison. She would be staying there until either they didn't need her anymore, in which case they were sure to kill her, or until she wasted away. A small refrigerator hummed in the corner. As much as her stomach was growling, Gemma ignored it. She tried to focus on the problem at hand. There was nothing but the problem at hand. Each way she looked reminded her that she was imprisoned.

Angelo gazed around his prison cell from his seat at the little table. He had raided the refrigerator and found some pre-packaged food, digging in. As he sat and ate hid mind wandered over the last few days which had sent his life spinning in a wildly new direction.

Since he had been working at the gas station, Angelo had settled where he was. Any vision for his future was lost when he decided that his present situation was the one he would have to accept as it was. So he spent his days working a roadside convenience store. He had forgotten to wonder what else life held for him besides a small job and one long day following a series of other long days.

Dean lay in his bed staring at the ceiling. His body ached from the abuse heaped on him in the last week. He tried to think back to when his work was trying to make it in the world of comedy. He had been broadsided on that day when the shooting took place and he found himself mixed in with people who were looking to return a lost case to the FBI.

But he hadn't be mixed in, had he? Dean had volunteered. He had told them he wanted in. Shaking his head, Dean scoffed at himself for being so eager to get involved in something he didn't understand. He had gone from telling jokes and working nightclubs to running for his life on a desperate mission to return a missing case to the FBI.

Before they had headed to the park, Tim had suggested a plan to hide the case beforehand. In the very likely scenario that any of them were caught, they decided it was best if Destrier didn't get his hands on the case. Gemma argued against it, saying that if the case was left anywhere out of their sight that there would be no way to know if someone found the case and stole it before they could get it back. Tim had argued that it would be better to be caught without it and be unsure than to be caught with it and sure that it was in the enemy's hands. But Gemma persisted, telling them that there was no way she would allow them to leave the case anywhere out of her sight. So they had kept the case in the car, compromising as they all stepped in and worked to free Dean.

In the end it had worked against them. Since their car was spotted as soon as they approached the park, Destrier's men moved in as soon as Tim's team was out of sight of the vehicle. They then quickly and easily broke into it, finding the case in the trunk. Having been strictly warned to do nothing but deliver the case, they packed it in its own sedan and that vehicle drove off before Tim's team was grabbed.

So really, as soon as they stepped out of their vehicle, their plan had failed. Tim knew that moving in to save Dean would be a risk, but no one disagreed with his sentiment that it was their job to rescue him if they could do something about it. They all had some idea that if they didn't do anything about it, Dean would be lost.

———————————————

Now Destrier stood at a table looking down on the case he had worked so hard to bring into his possession. He allowed no one to touch it, having a guard deposit the case in his private office and exiting, leaving Destrier alone.

Destrier approached the case as one might approach a holy relic dug up by archeologists. This technology was the last piece of the puzzle and his plan was falling into place. He glanced over his shoulder once or twice before stepping up to the desk to examine the case. From all outward appearances it looked to be a normal briefcase.

He chuckled at the knowledge that there was nothing ordinary about this case.

It lay flat on the desk with the handle facing him. He stepped up to the desk and lifted the case so it sat upright, along its thin edge. Destrier ran his hand along the outer edge, where the seam of the case should be. Upon closer inspection, the seam was nearly invisible. He checked the topside and found that there was no apparent locking mechanism. Quickly scanning along the edge again, he found the hinges on the bottom of the case. These were inset. No screws appeared to be holding them in place.

He picked up the case, turning it over and over again in his hands, looking for some kind of clue about how it was to be opened. Seeing nothing he began to pry at the opening by the handle on the top of the case.

He might as well have been trying to peel apart welded steel plates with his bare hands. He kept at it for a solid twenty minutes but to no avail.

From every way he looked at it, there was no perceivable way to get the case open. Despite its ordinary structure the case's weight attested to being something more than ordinary. He hefted the case and jiggled it about. Nothing rattled, no sound issued forth from the case.

His already tried patience having reached its upper limits, he set the case down with a scoff and set himself down to consider the matter. It was clear that he did not have the expertise to handle an item like this. He opened his door and told the guard to call for an assistant. Within five minutes one showed up, an young woman who, though eager to please, knew how to hold herself.

"Mr. Destrier."

"I'd like a search made for locksmiths and safe crackers – experts."

"Yes Mr. Destrier."

"I want one standing here in my office within twenty-four hours."

She knew more than to ask any questions, but quickly left the room.

Julian had waited too long for this. He had been planning this for years and now the answer to his problem was within his grasp. But the obstacle lay directly before him, hindering him from continuing.

He sighed and sat back in his chair. The world was ready for a change and he was on the precipice of giving the world the change they needed. He was in a position to change the world and the world was completely unaware of it. Before the year was out the world would know his name and praise it. He would correct society as he saw it. The peoples of the world would give him free reign to do as he saw fit, once they saw that he had the knowledge to lead them forward into a glorious new order.

He sat and stared at the case, contesting it, engaging in a battle of wills. Anything that opposed him must, of course fail or fall. Having resources on his side, time was the only barrier to his goal of accessing the free world's resources. News organizations would run his stories and be the vehicle whereby he won over the people of the world. People blindly followed those who they believed to be in authority. So he would access that authority and use it to his purposes.

The only problem with asserting authority is that no one seeks out a leader if everything is going well. So the only option for him to assume power would be to create a need for him to step in and assert that power. Thus the case and the device inside would provide the means whereby he would win his position over the world.

He stood and paced before stepping back to the case. Hefting it up again, Julian examined it thoroughly. Besides a hairline seam running along the thin edge, there was no sign of any kind of opening or mechanism whereby the case might be opened. He set the case down again. Clearly, nothing would be gained by continuing to finger and fondle the object. He would have to wait until someone arrived who could take a look at the case.

Once he had the technology in his hands, the internet would become an open book for him to write in and edit as he pleased. Anything could be used for his own purposes. Social media and news sources would be especially helpful. Economic sites for currency exchange and relating to the valuation of currency would be useful as well in forwarding his plan. Once he had his grip on the foundations of society it would be a simple matter to tear the old down to establish the new.

Playing upon insecurities would lead to outrage and fear in the streets. People would begin to distrust each other and their government, moving on their own for their own behalf and calling for the collapse of the current government.

Once the kindling was in place, all that was left was to light the fire and watch it burn. Society would cleanse itself of the old which was no longer needed so that he could sweep away the old and build a new foundation with the people behind him. The people would rally behind him once they caught onto his vision. The fire would spread and the people would join with him in establishing his rule. Anarchy would be the tool with which he would establish his rule. Once established, it would have to be inarguable that he was in charge. He and the position of authority would have to be inseparable.

Destrier considered these and other issues as he sat waiting for a locksmith, hardly daring to leave his seat, not leaving his office for any purpose. For the next day he stayed put, having food sent to him, waiting for the news that someone had been sent to open the case.

Some hours after he gave the order for the search, the assistant returned to his office unbidden. Usually someone coming to his office unbidden would face consequences for their actions. In this case, however, he was so on edge that he welcomed the woman's presence, though he said nothing about it.

"Mr. Destrier, it has come to our attention that there is someone near who may be of some help to you."

"Good. And who might that be?"

"Dean Meare."

Destrier blinked stupidly. "The prisoner?"

"Yes sir."

"How did we not know about this?"

"He was caught for his involvement with the case, sir. No file was opened on him."

"But he is a locksmith?"

"He has experience in the field, sir."

Destrier considered the situation. Seeing that someone in the palm of his hand might have the knowledge base to help with the most vital part of his operation began to give him hope. It wasn't guaranteed that Mr. Meare knew much about locksmithry but the chance that he might have insight into the case sounded better than not.

Chapter 26

The room's constant light began to wear on Dean. The constant brightness kept him alert and as a result his body began to wear down before his mind did. Laying on the bed for hours without sleeping, staring at the ceiling, Dean bid his time.

His friends had come to rescue him and now they were imprisoned just as he was. There was no point in hoping now because there was no hope to be had. They were all imprisoned without a chance of getting back to the lives they knew. Dean almost laughed. He had been a comedian before all of this had happened. Now he had no reason to laugh.

But that was not true. A comedian doesn't just laugh because he feels like it. He finds ways to make others laugh. He looks for thinks that makes people laugh, searching through the world for things that he can elaborate on, invent or parody so that he can bring joy to others.

Dean hadn't had much reason to laugh.

He looked around his cell. The room was devoid of windows, forcing the occupant to rely entirely on the control of the guards and warden for his source of light and sense of day or night. The lights went down at the same time every night and turned on at the same time every morning. Dean guessed that they went down around 10 o'clock at night and up at 8 o'clock in the morning. This guess was arbitrary, but made sense to him, if they were going to try and keep the prisoners on a regular and reasonable sleep schedule.

When his door opened one morning, Dean was surprised. He did not move from his bed where he had been lying. The first guard stepped inside the door and stood aside while a higher-ranking officer stepped through and up to Dean.

"Mr. Meare." He said, looking the prisoner over. "I am to escort you."

The failure to mention where the guards were escorting him both scared Dean and piqued his curiosity. He sat up in the bed where he had been lying and stood. It had been about three days since his friends rescue attempt. He was still wearing the clothes that he had come to the prison in. They smelled at this point, as they had not allowed him to bathe, and no means of doing so existed in the cell.

If the guards smelled anything they had either grown accustomed to the smell or they were ignoring the stench. Neither of them reacted either to his appearance or to the smell. They cuffed his hands and ordered him to follow.

Dean stood and followed the guards out of his room and into the hallway. A thousand thoughts flooded his mind at this point. To run, attack the guards, make his escape. But these were quickly drowned out by the more reasonable way, to bide his time'. As he walked he glanced about his surroundings. The hall had doors without windows on either side standing like sentries. The guards moved quickly, Dean walking between them, one in front one behind.

After they passed through the prison section to the door and stepped through, Dean caught another sight of the office area. He saw again the open space which, he thought, was about the size of a football field filled with little cubicles. What the people did in these cubicles he didn't know. What does a hidden company do for a psychopath?

The guards quickly moved him to Destrier's office, entering with a knock and stepping in, one before Dean and one behind him. Bringing him into the office, they released him from the handcuffs and stepped aside.

"Mr. Meare." Said the man as the guards left the room. "I under-stand you may which may be of some help."

"That depends." Said Dean. "I'm not one for appraising art much, but I might be able to give you a

The man laughed, standing up from his desk. "So you do have a sense of humor. I wondered about whether we would get to see your talents in action. But I've called you here this morning about other talents." He stepped around the desk to stand in front of Dean, looking him over, sizing him up. "When we first got a hold of you, I thought of you as nothing more than bait. Now I realize that you may be more crucial to our predicament than anyone else."

Dean's eyes flitted about the room, then back to Destrier, but he said nothing. Destrier grinned.

"You're quiet. Some people say that quiet people are afraid. I disagree. I think they're smart. Careful."

He turned and put a hand on the briefcase. The briefcase which they had spent so much time looking to get to the FBI. Dean looked it over. It appeared to be normal. Destrier continued to speak.

"This case contains a breakthrough in the world of surveillance technology, a breakthrough that will change the lives of billions. With this technology in our hands we could affect change on a global scale, shape the world as we please."

"I've heard stuff like this before. It's usually called propaganda."

"We've got to start somewhere. I need what is in here but the designer of this case is one of the best in the business at designing secure locks and specialized safes like this. What I need is for you to open this." He gestured smoothly to the case and stepped back. Dean glanced at the man, who kept his eyes on him. Swallowing, Dean stood up and stepped to the desk, looking the case over.

"From all outward appearances it looks to be a normal briefcase." He turned it around to look at the sides and top. "There's no apparent mechanical lock on the outside. Whatever is keeping this shut is on the inside." Lifting the case, Dean examined the underside. As he expected, the hinges were not attached to the outside of the case. If they had been, anyone with a screwdriver would have been able to, potentially, unscrew the hinges and simply lift the lid off of the case.

Dean scratched his head and considered the object before him. Whoever designed this was not only good at their job, but clever – a puzzle-maker, one who could find a way to modify a simple briefcase into the conundrum before him. He picked the case up and looked it over. The immediate difference he felt was in the weight of the object. When he had first lifted it in the store when the first attack had come, he had hardly noticed the extra weight of the case with the rush of adrenaline coursing through his body.

Now that he had the time to consider it more carefully, he guessed that this was not the simple thing he imagined it was. He was now exploring the case driven by his own curiosity. His hands ran over the sides and edges of the case, trying to imagine how the case was put together. Who would build their own briefcase from scratch? Or modify a briefcase for this purpose? Looking over the case, he saw that there were no latches on the top of the case. Any kind of moving part, save the handle, had been removed from the outside and put on the inside.

"It looks here like you have a specially-made case. I don't know if this one can be opened by hand." Dean showed the top of the case to Destrier. "You can see here that there's no clear way to get the case open. No latches, no exposed hinges, no buttons, nothing on the outside."

Dean sat back in his chair and gestured to the case. "Whatever means there are of getting that case open, we don't have them here. The missing lock on the outside clearly indicates that someone has redesigned and repurposed this case for something."

"The technology."

Dean nodded. "Probably."

Destrier's eyebrow raised. "I don't like the sound of that 'probably'."

"In all likelihood this case has been specially made to contain this piece of technology that you're looking for."

"Yes."

"The other possibility…" Dean hesitated.

"Out with it."

"…is that this is all a prank on you." Dean watched the man carefully. Destrier smiled and began to laugh. But his complexion had paled, and Dean could see that the man was visibly shaken. For all of his dreams and visions of power it had not occurred to him that his plan might fail this way, that the case might not be what he claimed it was. Destrier laughed, but it was half-hearted.

"Do you think you can trick me with a ploy like that? You think I would believe your word about a case you've only seen for the first time just now?"

"This is the second time I've seen it. And you asked me to come in here because you wanted me to take a look at the case. So you expected to believe or consider something I said."

Destrier stayed silent and continued to observed Dean as he inspected the case. After a few more minutes of looking it over he set it down and spoke again.

"I don't see how there's anything more I can learn about this. It could be something really advanced with some kind of internal lock. That could be activated wirelessly by a computer, or by a magnet. Or this could all be a joke and the case could be filled with lead weights."

"You're lying to me. There's something you're hiding from me."

"There's nothing more to see. You've seen it yourself. It's just a briefcase that can't be opened."

Destrier's voice dropped to a hiss.

"Then find a way to get it open."

"Do you know what you get when you ask for the impossible?"

"Results."

"Disappointment." Said Dean.

Destrier glowered at Dean for a moment before his frown slowly turned into a smile. It felt like watching a snake.

"All right Mr. Meare. As you say it's impossible, I'll take that to mean you don't understand the case or how it works. How about this; I will give you the resources whereby you can either open the case or find a means of opening it. You'll have the time for that as your schedule seems to be clear. In return for this small favor I can offer something of value.

"Do this for me and I can offer you a painless experience here, perhaps one in which you won't have to die when I'm finished with you. In short, I'm offering you your life back if you do this favor for me."

Dean hardly thought this was comforting but said nothing in response. Destrier must have been satisfied, however, for he returned to his seat. As he considered this moment, something in Dean stirred. The case was going to be in his hands. Perhaps his moment of escape for the team was approaching. He knew that he would have to keep his eyes open. He realized that Destrier continued to watch him as he sat across from Dean at his desk. Dean nodded slowly. It wasn't much, but it was the beginning of a chance.

Satisfied with the man's response, Destrier called for guards. They came and Destrier gave them a series of short instructions. The guards escorted Dean out of the room and back into the main working area. Two guards escorted Dean, one on either side, and one took the case with him. They all stepped down the aisle-way to the cells which were becoming very familiar to Dean. He realized with surprise that the idea of going back to the cell didn't scare him. Having Destrier show up, no matter how simple his threat, with him not finishing the task at hand frightened him. He was going to find a way to get the case open,

They stepped through the first door to the prison block, and Dena anticipated approaching his cell door. When they reached it the guards kept moving. Dean didn't dare complain, but wondered about what was going on. They escorted him to a prison cell at the end of the cell block. Opening the door, the guards stepped through, bringing Dean with them. This room was different than the other he had occupied. It had a simple setup, with a set of shelves against the back wall and a single table in the center. Dean noted that the table was fixed to the floor. A single chair was set before the table as well.

The guard with the case set it on the table and stood by. Another guard released Dean from his restraints. He gestured to the table.

"Have a seat." he said.

Dean nodded and stepped to the chair, seating himself in it.

"This is where you will work." The man said. "You will have resources available to you. Simply ask and the tools will be delivered. You will work until the case is open."

The guard stood silently and observed Dean. Dean glanced about the room, from guard to guard. They stood watching him. He flapped his hands against his side.

"No 'Ready, set, go'? No other signal to start?"

The guards stood silently as they observed him. Dean knew to continue to delay working on getting the case open would only bring more trouble. He slid the case over to himself and began to look the case over again. Whether his examination would do any good he didn't know, but he could hope that he would find something that would get the case open.

Of course as long as he was working on getting the case open, they would need him alive, which meant he had time to think about what to do next. He had to make his next move before getting the case open. There was no way to know, however, when and how an opportunity might arise.

He looked the case over again and thought through how he would approach this project. He knew more about locks on doors than this kind of work. Apparently these people were going to take what they could get. Looking closely at the top of the case, near the handle where any kind of lock would be, he tried to see if there were any signs of any mechanism that was holding the case closed. There was hardly an opening between the two leaves of the briefcase and the seam was nearly nonexistent. But it did exist.

What did he know about the case? That it was shaped as a regular briefcase. The seam was small. It had a handle at the top. There was no clear mechanism which kept the case shut. Any case that locked had a lock on the outside. This case was also heavier than usual, whether due to the technology inside, the build of the case itself, or some kind of joke on part of the case's builder it could not be told, at least not until the case was opened.

Dean looked at the bottom of the case. He could see three thin hinges running along the bottom of the case, one on either end and one in the middle. From what he could see, the hinges themselves were attached within the case itself, whether on the inside of the case or between the case and the inner layers of the case's lining. However they were attached it would be relatively difficult to get it open.

He sat back in his chair and considered the task before him. To get the case open appeared nearly impossible and yet he was expected to get it done. As he looked it over he remembered what the guard had said.

"I'm going to need some more tools to work with. I'll need something to use that I can slip between the halves of this - locksmithing tools. Also, anything relating to metal work in a small shop, not blacksmithery, but things that could be used for punching or cutting."

The guard nodded and stepped to the door. There was a buzz and he pushed it open. The door swung shut behind him, leaving Dean with the two guards. Dean continued to work, though slowly. He didn't know how the case was put together. Because he didn't know how thin the walls of the case were, he didn't want to simply try to melt or cut through the case itself. If he did so and the walls of the case were thin enough, he could easily end up ruining whatever was inside of the case.

Chapter 27

Tim lay back on his bed, dozing. He didn't know what to think at this point. He knew that he had to hold onto hope. If he didn't find a way to see his friends through this trouble, no one would. But there was no way. Even if they let Tim and the others go, Destrier's promise to hold onto Gemma hung over his head.

He didn't know how late it was, but the guards had turned the lights off some time ago. There was a soft rap-rap-rap at his door and the door opened. Tim sat up, weary, not knowing what to expect. At this point he would not have been surprised to find that someone had been sent to kill him off. He was quiet as the door opened and a shadowed figure stepped into the room. The figured glanced around the room and strode before the bed, stopping before Tim.

A man in his late twenties stood at five and a half feet tall. He was dressed in a janitorial outfit with a cap and boots. His shadowed expression showed concern and some worry.

"Listen closely, I don't have much time." The man said.

Tim's ears perked up and his spine tingled at the sound of the man's voice. The man's tone and words suggested that he might be a man in enemy territory, surrounded by hostile forces, speaking with a lone friend he could trust. "You will have one chance. It will be unorthodox. Look for the signal. At the moment you will have to convince the others. We don't have time to approach each of you." He lifted his left sleeve to reveal a marking on his wrist. It was a tattoo, a small marking of a gryphon. "This is a sign of our brothers." He glanced around again. "Our time is up." He moved for the door.

"How do I know I can trust you?" Tim asked. "And who are you?"

"Call me Adam." The man looked like he was going to speak again, but grinned instead. "You could trust Destrier if you want, but I wouldn't recommend it." He pulled down the collar of his shirt to reveal scarring on his neck. It looked to be from burns or cuts, but in the dark the mass of tissue wasn't clear enough to see for him to judge what kind of wound had been inflicted. With the slightest wink he stepped through the door and let it close behind him.

Listening intently, Tim heard the man's footsteps recede down the hallway, and fade into nothingness, leading him to wonder whether the man had visited at all. But the memory burned vividly in his mind, especially the details; the Gryphon on his wrist and the burns on his neck. If nothing else, he knew this was nothing he had imagined, and had to be something tangible. Hope had come. Whatever form that took, he knew he would have to hold onto it. Now came the waiting where he would have to bide his time until this helper made his move.

Chapter 28

The door to Gemma's room had been shut for a while now. At first she wondered about it, but after a bit she knew it was pointless so she stopped. When she had set out to discover what had happened to the intelligence gathering program, she had been the sole agent on the case. Now she was no longer the sole agent, and apparently not in charge anymore. For whatever reason, these people who had her in captivity had not come to her to ask her about what was going on.

It was petty, she knew, but without something else tangible to focus on around her, her mind turned to the events outside her cell. What was going on with Tim and the others? Were they safe? Of course they weren't safe. They were all in the hands of a man who would do about anything to accomplish what he wanted with the technology he had stolen. She had spent several days tracking down Agent Williams who first possessed the briefcase. And when she arrived, the case was in the hands of a complete stranger.

With no outside stimulation and no one to talk to, her mind began to wander, looking for something to focus on. Things like the choices of colors for the room began to stand out. The walls were painted in mellow colors. The bare carpet was a dull grey and the ceiling painted white. An air vent was put in the middle of the room in the ceiling.

Sitting at the table, she considered the situation, but kept coming back to the same thing. They were stuck and unless either an opportunity presented itself or they took some kind of action, there was no way they were going to escape.

These and other thoughts were running through her mind when the door opened. Destrier walked in with two guards. He grabbed the second chair and settled himself across from her.

"I hope your stay has not been uncomfortable. We wouldn't want you to feel you were unwelcome here."

Gemma carefully looked the man over. He was well-groomed and wore expensive-looking clothes. The slacks and shirt were well-made. He had no coat or necktie. He sat upright in his chair, not slouching as she had expected. Silently, she sat and observed him as he kept his eyes on her. Neither of them spoke. He continued to study her as a sportsman studies his opponent.

"Have you been enjoying your stay?"

Gemma remained silent.

He laughed. "You have the right idea. It's a waste of time, really. People sitting and lying to each other, hoping that the others will think better of them. And if they did, then what? Now each believes lies about the other and thinks his friend is better than he, while harboring resentment and guilt about the very lies which provide the respect they seek." He slanted his eyes toward her. "Let's talk about truth."

"Truth." She said. "What do you know about truth? Working for yourself so that you can shape the world as you see fit? Anything that doesn't fit with your vision is thrown out. But what if you throw out truth with your list of unfit ideals?"

"Impossible."

"What if in rejecting the old you reject the truth?" she asked.

"As the great Pontius Pilate said, 'What is truth?'" He asked. "What is it, but excuses for people to keep from taking action and to lie to each other. They're not worth the time it would take to destroy them. That is why I will let them destroy themselves."

"You say that like it's their own idea."

"But it is their idea, isn't it? Mankind doesn't know what to do with itself so it engages in its own destruction. Take a look around you and what do you see? People harming themselves, people harming other people. They take from others for their own gain. They get low and they hurt themselves in a hundred ways. They invent new ways of escaping from their everyday problems. But a man helps himself to what is his neighbor's and the police get involved. Witnesses and alibis, evidence and court dates, the man's world becomes a long court session.

"Destroy something that's not your own and society steps in and tells you that what you've done is wrong. Why not let these people do this as they please? Society has been the master of the individual for too long. Now it's time for the individual to rise up and assert what is theirs by right."

Might makes right. The idea was hardly new. Gemma looked the man over as what started as a conversational piece became a sermon delivered with fiery passion. The man's advocation would have moved many if they didn't understand what he was talking about. Knowing his premise sent chills down her spine. She didn't speak for fear that her voice would betray her emotions and rile the man further.

Sitting in a kind of stupor for a moment, the man fell back into his chair, staring emptily before him.

"Then," he said softly, "then will the scales of society be properly balanced and set for a new age."

Chapter 29

A soft knock sounded at Tim's door. Half-dozing, his gaze roamed to the door. The knock sounded again. This time he heard murmuring voices. Rising from the bed, he stepped up to this cell's portal. The knock had been so foreign that it shook sleep from him. Whenever someone wanted to enter his cell nowadays they simply did so – no one knocked.

He pressed his ear to the door and listened for a moment. There was no sound. He was about to step away when he heard a human sound. It may have been a rustle or a cough, but it was a human sound outside his door. They hadn't opened the door which meant… what?

"Hello?"

There was movement outside his cell and a voice sounded again. Then, distinctly:

"Hello Mr. Runn. Are you alone?"

He looked around his empty cell and back to the door.

"Yes, I'm by myself." A joke about ghosts or silent, bodiless friends felt out of place at this point.

"…moment." He caught though the cell door. He waited for what felt like ten minutes before the door clicked and swung open. The janitor who presented himself a few nights ago to Tim stood before him now in the same outfit.

"Mr Runn." The man said. "Now is the moment." The janitor had a large laundry or garbage bin with him. He nodded to the next cell down the hallway. They began to move in that direction. Tim looked this way and that down the hall as they walked but saw no one.

"Isn't there supposed to be a guard?" he asked.

"No time to explain." The man said.

They now stood before the next cell. Adam spoke a soft verbal cue into an earpiece Tim hadn't noticed beforehand. About seven seconds later, Tim heard a click. At a nod from Adam, Tim pushed the door open.

Dean lay on the bed, exhausted. Tim couldn't tell the reason. The time from home under stress had worn on him. It had only been a few days since he had seen Dean last. Now that he looked at him with fresh eyes and the simple joy of finding him alive was gone, Tim observed the disheveled look, his slumped demeanor, the extra lines on his face.

Tim stepped up to the bed and laid a hand on the sleeping man's shoulder. With a shout the man was upright, squirming away from Tim's grasp.

"It's all right, it's all right." Tim said. "It's your buddy, Tim."

"Oh." Said Dean with a breath of relief and he sat up on the bed.

"Can you move?" Tim asked. "We've got to go."

"How did you get in?"

"A friend."

Dean looked unsure, but Tim quickly prodded him and helped the man to his feet. Once he was upright, strength seemed to flow back into him and his spine straightened. Dean held his head upright. They stepped out of the cell where Adam was waiting for them. He greeted Dean quickly and politely and then moved on, Dean casting occasional side glances at Adam. They opened the next door in like fashion to Dean's. Mike occupied the next cell. Of the three prisoners thus far, he seemed the least ill at ease. He was seated at the single table in the room a look of contemplation adorning his face. He looked up as Tim stepped in, gesturing over his shoulder.

"Time to go." He said.

Without a word, Mike stood and followed Tim out of the room. At this point Tim turned to Adam.

"So what's the plan for getting us out of here?"

He patted the bin which he pushed.

"You're looking at it."

The threesome started at it for a long moment.

"No." Dean finally said. "I'm not riding out in that thing."

Tim looked to Mike, who shrugged.

"This is your ball game, just tell me what you want me to do."

He looked between the men then down the hall. "Let's get the rest of the crew out first." They approached the next door and waited a full minute for the lock to disengage.

"How did you find us?" Dean asked the man. "Who are you? Why are you helping us?"

"Dean," Tim said. "now's not the time."

"Now's not the time? Just when is the time?" The expression of anger stopped Tim, who shrugged.

"I'll tell you if I know when it comes."

Dean was quiet as they continued.

Angelo's door opened and Tim stepped through, leaving the others in the hallway. Angelo sat on the bed, looking forlorn. Glancing up, he did a take. In that brief moment, Tim saw the expression of a relatively innocent gas station attendant minding his own business as he kept shop. Relief swept over the young man's face as he stepped out of his cell.

In that moment, with his friends looking at him, Tim came to a full realization that they were now looking to him for direction and answers. He took a breath to steady his nerves and spoke.

"All right, one more."

They moved on to the last door and waited as Adam spoke into his radio once again. After a moment there was a click and the door opened as Tim gave a tug. He stepped quietly into the room, glancing about as he did so. Gemma sat at the table. She looked up. No response registered on her face as he stepped further into the room.

"Gemma." Tim said. "Time to go."

She looked at him ashen for a moment. "I thought you would never come."

Tim spread his hands. "What can I say? Good work takes time. Come on, we can talk later." She stood, but hesitated.

"This isn't a trick, is it?"

"No." Tim said. But his hesitation was enough to set off her internal alarms.

"How much did they pay you? What do they want? Why did they send you? You of all people, I should have known…"

Tim stepped up to her and gently laid his hand on her shoulder.

"Gemma." He said. "this is not a great time or place for panic." He pointed to the door. "Out." He said. She gathered her nerve and followed his prompt out of the room.

"What now?" said Angelo as Gemma and Tim stepped out from the room into the hall.

Gemma looked to Tim for an answer. He gestured to his new acquaintance.

"Everyone, this is Adam. He is the one who has initiated this escape." He nodded to the man who acknowledged Tim back.

"We have little time, so this will be to the point" Adam said. "Two or three of you will hop in here if you want to escape unseen." The others looked amongst each other. "We don't exactly have time for a conference. There is one hitch." He said. "If there's any point in helping you all escape we need the briefcase." The group was silent for a moment.

"All right." Tim said.

"Gemma, Angelo, you get into the bin. Mike, you're with me."

Gemma spoke. "You're not ditching me."

"No, but I need someone outside this compound with a cool head who can lead." Gemma caught the sarcasm in his comment and remained silent. Adam spoke again.

"Your other friend is being held with the case itself. Apparently it was discovered that he is a locksmith."

They looked at him for a moment in silence. "So," Adam continued, "we can get your friend and the case at the same time."

Tim spoke. "Where is he being held?"

"There is another set of rooms on the west side of the building. The group running this operation has converted much of this building from its original structure for their own purposes."

"All right, so how do we find him?"

"He'd be surrounded by guards. Look for the most heavily-secured area. Other than that, you'll just have to keep your eyes open. The security should tip you off."

"Right. Destrier won't trust anyone – they're all supposed to keep an eye on each other I guess."

"Unless you're either more heavily armed than I knew or you're superman there's no way you'll get past those guards on your own." The man's tone made Tim guess that the man wasn't despairing.

"You've got some ideas?"

Adam smiled. "I've got a few."

Chapter 30

"I don't like it."

"You don't have to like it, you just have to follow it."

"I still don't like it."

"Unless you've got any other bright ideas you saved for this moment you're gonna have to stick with the plan. If you wanted to do something different you should have said something earlier. Now's not the time to improvise."

Timothy and Michael were making their way through the complex, trying to appear as at-ease as anyone else in the building. Tim, however, was having some second thoughts and voicing these to Mike.

"It's a terrible plan." Tim said.

"It's not great." conceded Mike. "But unless you come up with something better in the next ninety seconds it won't make a difference."

"I'm thinking, I'm thinking."

"That was not a challenge to come up with an alternate plan, just because the plan is terrible."

"I don't care whose plan it is, I don't like it."

"Too bad, we're here."

Tim groaned inwardly; if he hadn't decided to be a Good Samaritan for the day when he saw the agent running, he could have gone home with a heavy conscience but an easy step. Mike reached forward and knocked on the cell door. Footsteps sounded from inside the room and a gruff voice called out.

"Who's there?"

"Security, open up." Mike said.

The voice on the other side of the door mumbled something, then replied.

"We are the security here. Who are you?"

At that point, Tim would have changed his story, or perhaps run in panic, but Mike calmly reiterated what he had said the first time.

"We are Plant Security. Destrier has requested an immediate transfer for the prisoner."

There was silence for a moment and Tim felt sweat beading on his neck and forehead.

"Why's that?" Asked the inner guard, his voice on edge. Tim nudged Mike and gestured that they should get away while they could. Instead to his horror, he heard Mike laugh.

"Are you kidding?" he said. "Who can tell why the man does anything?"

It was quiet for a moment and they waited with bated breath. Then from the other side of the door Tim caught the mumbled words "guess so" from the guard. Soon he heard the interface of the inner lock and the door opened.

Tim stood in front of Mike, so he was first in line to see what the room held. He and Mike were ill-armed, but the small number of guards caused Tim to wonder about their chances of pulling this off. At first they thought that if things went smoothly they might be able to talk their way through this, taking Dean and the case with them without violence. It might be more convincing if they had uniforms, but no opportunity had presented itself for them to disguise themselves. So they decided that they had take full hold of the one advantage they had over their adversaries – surprise.

The door opened and Tim leapt in with Mike right behind him. It was crucial that they give the guards no time to think. Wild jabs from a guard were much better than hearing an officer direct the guards to deliver them back to their waiting cells.

Tim went in hard and slugged the first guard that come into his sight. The man caught the blow across his jaw and staggered back half a step before finding his feet again. The second guard, seeing Tim's charge, was not caught unaware when Mike came hurtling in, but the Mike's magnificent size dissuaded him. Knowing his duty, however, he put up his dukes, ready to fight.

Glancing around, Mike caught sight of the guard and laid him out in a swift moment. Falling onto his back, the man didn't stop struggling as Mike let loose with a few more blows before the man fell unconscious to the ground. Mike had scarcely looked up when he saw two more guards approaching. He pulled out the small club clipped to his left side. Standing quickly, he moved for the guard on the right. A glance to Tim assured him that the marketing designer was all right.

Mike moved in, relying not on agility but on his own size and weight to carry the battle. The other man certainly was not small, but would not have the chance to meaningfully throw his weight around much if Mike got his hands on him. So he kept the guard on his toes with swings which nearly connected and kept the guard moving back. The guard slunk this way and that as Mike took a few swings at the man's head.

Meanwhile Tim looked up from the unconscious guard before him to see Mike locked in combat with another guard and a third on the ground. The fourth guard was caught between Mike and Tim. He had his eyes on Mike and was reaching for his belt. Tim saw that the man had a club clipped to the back of his belt. Getting to his feet, Tim launched himself at the man before he could swing at Mike.

He caught the man upside the head with his fist and made a grab for the man's baton. But the guard saw him coming and swung low, catching him across the left knee. Tim grimaced, but tried to catch hold of the baton before the man could swing again. The man was too quick and swung again, hitting Tim in the side before he got his hands before he got his hands on the baton. Then it was a matter of wrestling it from the guard's grip as they each took swings at each other' sides and heads. Tim caught a blow across his jaw. The guard received a gash across his eye. Tim, after a moment, wrestled the baton from the guard's grip and quickly dispatched him. Mike was standing over the body of the guard he had wrestled with.

Looking to Mike, Tim confirmed that the man was all right. At the back of the room was a long workbench covered with circuitry and electronics equipment. A few laptops were there as well. The briefcase Tim had spent so much time thinking about lay on the bench off-center to the left. Dean sat behind the bench on a tall stool staring at them. The expression on his face suggested that he was observing some aliens invading his own home. Tim gave a little wave as he approached. Dean waved back.

"Hey Dean," Tim said, stepping towards the bench. He saw that the man was chained to the desk and moved to the guard to get a key. "Are they treating you well here?" Dean shrugged and turned his attention back to the desk and the tools in front of him.

Drills and bits of various sizes were laid out on the table as well as simpler tools such as screwdrivers, hammers and chisels. Tim imagined, however, that Destrier would want the case opened without the technology inside being damaged.

The room was quiet, save the steady hum of the laptop on the workbench in front of them. Tim walked up to Dean with a key in hand, which he nabbed from a guard, to unlock Dean's chain. Dean looked between the two of them and cracked a smile.

"Aren't you going to introduce me to your new friend?"

Tim shook his head. "Dean, this is Mike. Mike, Dean."

Mike nodded. "Pleasure to meet you."

Dean leaned in. "Where did you find the big guy?"

"We picked him up along the way." Tim said as he worked at the chains. Seeing the chains fall off, Dean flexed his wrists around and sighed.

"It feels good to be free of those things."

"We're not quite out of here yet. We have a ride, but we need to meet up with them."

"If we want to get out of here, now's the time." Agreed Mike.

Dean nodded and glanced around the room as though the light had just come on. He saw the room for what it held and not its capacity or purpose. Spotting a laptop on a table, he closed it and grabbed it as well as the unopened, mystical case as well.

Seeing their opportunity, Tim and Mike quickly crossed to the unconscious guards to check their sizes. There was one, fortunately, whose sizes looked as though they might just fit Mike, the big man. Tim was easier, having no extraordinary features and he quickly found an outfit to match. They pulled these on over their own clothes. This was relatively difficult, as the outfits were not made to be pulled over, but to fit against the skin. Nevertheless the two managed to wriggled into the uniforms in record time.

Tim turned and examined the table again, noting all the different hardware.

"What's the laptop for?" he asked Dean.

"If we get the case open, and it contains hardware we may want to interact with it. Besides, having a laptop could come in handy."

Tim breathed a sigh. "All right." He took the laptop, handing it to Mike and grabbed the case itself. Tim then crossed to Dean.

"Clasp your hands behind your back." Tim said.

"What are you doing?"

"I'm getting you out of here."

"You don't think people are going to fall for this, do you?"

"I expect that people will not ask to many questions and we'll be out of here before they get a few words in."

Dean took the hint. So, with Mike holding the case, Tim the laptop, Dean between them holding his unbound wrists together, they left the room and make their way across the complex.

When no one instantly accosted them, Tim decided that either the organization was very large, where not everyone knew each other or that the uniforms were enough to command respect from the other employees. Either way, they met no obvious resistance, and no one seemed to notice them.

Tim and Mike kept close, nearly side by side behind Dean to hide the fact that their prisoner lacked proper restraints. Tim kept his eyes and ears open for stray glances in their direction or questions. But no one challenged them.

He had to remind himself that they were, in fact, undercover. He felt as if the walls around them were pressing in around them; walls covered with eyes demanding to know the reason for his presence. He took a breath and kept walking with Mike's pace. The man was quiet enough, but when he decided to move he trucked along. It was a wonder he didn't plow over Dean as he rolled along.

"I need a breath." Dean said.

"You can get a breath in a minute." Tim replied, pushing him along. "We're almost there."

Dean didn't reply. The door stood within sight. Tim heard a commotion behind them. Dean began to turn but Tim restrained the man and whispered to him.

"Keep walking. No one knows anything yet."

As they moved farther forward, Tim was instantly aware of voices behind them. This was not the general murmuring of hushed conversation but that of a hushed dialogue of importance of those in no mood to stop. They had been discovered. Their only chance would be to slip into a quiet spot quickly and hope the pursuers followed them. He wished at this point that they had radio contact with the others, so they could warn their comrades of impending danger.

They stepped to the door and waited for a moment, hoping that their own saboteur hadn't been caught and was still behind the controls at the guards' room.

Fear began to build in Tim's consciousness as he stood there. Slowly overwhelming his mind, it began as a seedling of doubt, growing into observations around him and accusations about his situation. He fully expected strangers, enemies to come barreling down on him at any moment. He was nearly ready to bolt when the lock of the door released.

Mike pulled the door opened and they swept though. Tim shut the door behind them. Feeling the security of the door behind them, Tim turned his mind to the next stop and their reunion with Gemma and the others. They stepped down the hall, looking for anything conspicuous. The hall was straight, so if there had been anything, they would have seen it the moment they walked into the hall.

"Start checking the rooms." Tim said softly. He began looking into the window ports of the doors on his right side. The first cell was empty the second cell had a lone occupant. Whether Destrier simply didn't have an abundance of prisoners or he simply had an abundance of space they didn't know about, one prisoner to a cell seemed to be the norm in the facility.

Tim observed the prisoner carefully. He wanted to be sure of the what he was dealing with before taking action. It was a man who appeared to be between the ages of fifty and sixty. He was emaciated , but if he had been well-fed, Tim would have imagined the man to be lean in any case. His hair was grey and though his face was lined. The man sat at the table his brow slightly furrowed. His thumb and forefinger were pinched together and he wiggled them about on the table. Nothing was in the man's hand and nothing was on the table. Tim watched for a moment, trying to understand before he realized what the man was doing. The prisoner moved the phantom pen as though writing with ink and paper. His movements were definite, conscious, not heavy-handed but with purpose.

Tim hesitated before he moved on to the other cells in the hall. Each was empty and he was almost ready to call off when he heard Mike call him.

"Over here."

Tim came jogging in their direction. Mike slipped into a cell which Tim could see was just held open a crack – as he walked the walls pressed in oppressively in around him. Stepping to the door he pulled it open and, with a glance over his shoulder, slipped inside the cell.

Though spacious enough, with group of six the room had become much smaller in the last few minutes. There was certainly standing room, but now a good amount of that was taken up by the laundry hamper.

"I hope nobody notices this thing is missing." Tim said, indicating the bin.

"We brought it in for this." Adam said. "It makes things easier, in some ways."

"All right. Who's going first?"

"Whoever goes first need to take the case with them." said Gemma. "We can't afford to leave it here any longer than we need to."

"Now here's another question I have." said Tim. "Once the first group gets out of the building, what do they do?"

"We'll have a vehicle waiting for you in the back. Hopefully our plan has few enough moving parts to keep it form failing."

Mike spoke. "How about we talk about something other than the plan failing."

There was a lull in the conversation.

"All right." Adam said after a moment. "Dean, Gemma and Angelo, you're up first. Tim and Mike keep quiet and wait for me to return. I can't promise I'll be back quickly, but I will be back here to pick up you two when I can. Any questions?"

The collective group glanced around the room for another questioning eye, but no one either had a question or was bold enough to speak again.

The next order of business consisted of getting the escapees into the bin. This was not an easy task, because of the different masses and configurations of their body types. For instance, Angelo's slim figure might easily be fitted in a tight space around others. If there was some kind of awkward setting he might be able to flex his body a bit more then the others and save them a bit of trouble.

Gemma's trouble was not so much in physical positioning as in the managing of the situation. Hearing someone say that they will use a laundry bin to smuggle you out of a hostile environment is one thing. Climbing into an old piece of canvas which has been strung up on a metal frame on wheels is something else entirely. Tim wondered at this, but didn't say anything.

Dean, for this part, was compliant with Adam and the others. His question was about the order of entry and positioning of everyone in the car and how they would fit. Would they all be able to fit if they sat around the sides? The problem with it was that the cart was essentially a sack so anytime anyone shifted their weight the whole thing moved thus, as he began to step into the cart it upset the others who complained though minimally.

Once they were in, Adam pushed them down, gently, to make more room. He then put large laundry bags in on top of the three escapees. These bags stank. The weight made Angelo squirm, which prompted complaints from the others. Tim wondered how they managed to find such filthy clothing. The passengers grumbled at first, but quickly took the hint from Adam and quieted down.

With a last spoken word to Tim and Mike to stay low, Adam gave a command into his earpiece. In a few seconds, the lock to the door, which had been closed, clicked opened and he wheeled the cart out of the room and down the hall.

Tim watched the proceedings with a kind of distant hope that it would work out in the end. Mike looked at Tim.

"Now what?"

Tim shrugged. "Now we wait."

"At least we're safe."

"Safe in whose hands?"

Chapter 31

Adam pushed the cart casually down the corridor. The laundry bags in the cart reeked to high heaven. He wrinkled his nose a little but paid no other heed to it. One of the cart's wheels squeaked in protest as he pushed it down the hallway. As long as nobody looked too closely he would be fine. But one nosy no-good could cause more trouble than any bureaucrat in office.

If, for instance, one especially cocky patrol officer decided that he didn't like Adam's look, he could stop him for any reason. No one did it much, simply because it was inefficient and wasted time. Yet, somehow, Rudolf Graham decided that he wasn't seeing enough appreciation on Adam's face as he walked by. So he called the laundry boy to a halt. He asked him to identify himself.

"Adam."

'Adam' is not identifying oneself. Adam who?

"Adam Meyer."

And what was Adam Meyer doing today wandering this part of the complex?

"Taking out the laundry to the delivered."

But didn't he know that the laundry was to be removed in properly-sized canvas bags?

"Yes, and those bags have to be moved in this." He patted the cart. "Unless you'd like to accompany me to hand-deliver these and account for my tardiness?"

Mr. Rudolf Graham became much less interested in laundry at that point and let Adam pass on unhindered to the rear, where the loading dock sat. Adam had passed through the most thickly inhabited space in the building. This part made him the most nervous because of the open floor plan of the back part of the building. If anything went wrong there was nowhere to go and nowhere to hide.

He pressed onward, deliberately slowing his pace, keeping a cool head and not allowing his nervousness to show. In the end, he slipped across the room, pushing the cart through huge back storage rooms. They offered little excuse or place to hide except behind another shelf. But if they got caught in the back, the security force was very thin and unlikely to present much trouble. Adam would tell whoever asked that he was delivering laundry and wouldn't they like to smell it? The smell had been a clever idea in the planning process as they hoped to deter the less stout-hearted of the guards and employees working at the plant.

As he walked, he murmured to the cart, being sure no one was around.

"We're halfway there. Keep your chins up, heads low."

He heard a muffled rustling but nothing more. Adam kept up his pace, keeping an eye out for employees and guards. The back of the building was only lightly patrolled. From his time spent working at the facility he knew that there would only be one or two guards in the back area of the building. The trick here would be to get out without having too many questions asked. Hopefully he would be able to slip out without being seen at all, but he didn't like the idea of being unprepared so he kept his eyes peeled for any sign of life.

And so he continued, walking and hoping against hope not to run into something perfectly reasonable in any large establishment: a security patrol. The back of the building was laid out with tall shelving set up all throughout the storage area, sans the last fifty yards, which was simply a large open space, allowing for people and goods to move about freely. Despite the size, the place was quiet. Adam's footsteps resounded through the room like the slapping of a soft book against a hard table. He glanced around himself to see whether the sound of his slapping feet or the noise of the wheels' soft rattle had been heard. But nothing sounded: no creature stirred. Adam almost dared to breathe. But he did not stop moving. He neared the end of one stack of shelves and passed an aisle which crossed the warehouse before the next set of shelves began their run of the room.

As he approached the cross-aisle, what he feared revealed itself in all its terror. Emphasis on 'guards' is important as well as an understanding of the expectation one usually has – men well over six feet tall, 300 lbs., unusually muscular, although if one guard has a bit of body fat on them that is acceptable as well. These men who are thoroughly trained will have either no idea what to do with anyone who is the focus of a tale, or will be otherwise incompetent in some capacity.

This particular guard at this particular facility was of an average build, on the leaner side of 200 lbs., well-built but certainly not specimen of the WWF. In short, a well-built man who was able to pass a simple physical examination and fitness test during the hiring process.

Adam tried to think quickly about what to do. The guard walking around the corner was alone. He certainly appeared able to handle himself. Adam's best bet would be to stay relaxed and feel the situation out.

"How's it going?" the guard said, spotting Adam.

Adam shrugged. "Can't complain."

"You can't, huh?" said the guard, falling into step beside Adam as he made his way down the aisle. "I'll be you could, though. What keeps you going? Hold on." He stopped and Adam stopped with him. The guard was studying him intently. "Nah." He said after a moment. "You don't seem like the type to live for a paycheck. So what motivates your laundryman here?"

"Sundays." said Adam.

The guard laughed and shook his head.

"Sounds good. I'm Neil."

"Nice to meet you." Said Adam as he continued to make his way down the aisle.

"How's the work here?" Neil asked.

Adam shrugged. "It's work, what can I say?"

"I know how it is. You get the job with high expectations, but it's just to pay the heating bills really."

They approached the end of the aisles and Adam's mind scrambled desperately for any kind of distraction for this tagalong. If they were caught and outnumbered their chances of getting out alive were next to none. He doubted that the guard would simply let him walk away without a word of explanation. He glanced at the guard. He didn't appear to be suspicious of anything, which was all the better. Adam felt the weight of the cart in his hands as he pressed forward with each step.

The cart's weight was enough that when he pushed it took nearly his whole body weight to get started or stop. This meant that as he went, every once in a while, he put his weight behind a great push to keep the cart rolling. Whatever happened, then, he would not be able to get as quickly as he would like, unless he found a way to turn the situation around. As they made their way down the aisle, Adam tried to gauge the man beside him. This guy seemed relaxed, which was better than dealing with a high-strung guard. There didn't appear to be anything extraordinary about the guard. He wasn't clearly left-handed or a trained martial artist.

Adam took a breath as they walked. If there was one rule in society it was that the more people became involved in something, the more complicated it became. More people involved simply meant more irritation and complications along the way. And in Adam's case, it meant winding up either dead or imprisoned.

They stepped out of the aisles and into a large, open area in the back. The ceilings were tall. People were scarce to be found, which meant Adam had something to be thankful for. He and the guard strode side-by-side to the garage doors which lined the back of the warehouse. Some of these were open, giving them a clear sight of the back parking lot. Here Adam caught sight of the utility van, parked before one of the garage doors, waiting to serve their purposes. It wasn't the latest model, but it was certainly functional. As they approached the vehicle, Adam nodded to the utility van.

"You want to give me a hand with this?"

"Are you serious?" The guard's head bobbed back a little as he said this.

"I'm afraid not. We're a little short-staffed right now."

"Short-staffed? How short-staffed can you get? It only takes two to do a job like this, getting the bins into the van's back. Tell me your van's got a lift."

"Sorry."

The guard sighed and took a long look around the empty hall which served as the back room of the facility. To say the room was spacious was to say the moon was a far walk from your house. The vaulted ceilings made quite an impression. The spaciousness of this back area resulted in the room feeling more like a dockyard than the inside of a building.

Adam wheeled the bin to the back of the utility van. His counterpart stood back a few feet, watching as he wheeled the cart up to the back of the vehicle.

"Well," said Adam as he gave the bags a slap. "I'm gonna need some help here. Any volunteers?" He gave a pointed look to the guard.

Half-mumbling to himself, the guard stepped the rest of the way up to the rolling cart as Adam opened up the back doors of the vehicle. Taking a whiff of the bags, the man gagged and bent halfway over, supporting himself with his hands on his knees.

"You go digging in dumpsters much?"

"This is what we're hired for. Laundry cleaning services. They've got to be loaded up, unless you think we should take 'em back and tell them they're too dirty."

The guard groaned and stood upright, approaching the cart more slowly than he did the first time.

"What is that funky smell?"

Adam shook his head. "I almost wish I could tell you. It could be any number of things. We pick these uniforms and clothing items from all over the facility." He righted one of the bags, giving him a view of one of its passengers. Angelo gave him a dubious look from the bottom of the bin. Adam gave an indicating nod to the guard, whom Angelo could not see from his vantage point. 'Be ready.' He mouthed as he took up the first bag and tossed it into the back of the van.

The guard stepped around to the other side of the cart and grabbed at another bag of laundry. He didn't gag or double over this time, but shook his head.

"I can't imagine what this stuff has been through to make it smell this bad. It almost smells like rotting food."

He hefted up a second bag and was turning to put it into the van when the first blow fell, striking him in the ribs. He turned to find Angelo struggling out of the laundry bin not four feet from where he stood. The guard dropped the bag, and as he turned, Angelo struck again, catching the guard in his stomach. Adam saw that the guard reach for his belt. Moving the bag of laundry from his shoulder, Adam quickly got the bag into a better grip and swung it in the guard's direction. He was already trying to strike Angelo when the laundry bag made contact, knocking the man on the head and off his feet.

The man collapsed to the ground and he struggled to rise, but another blow laid him out. Gemma rose up from the belly of the cart gagging at the smell of the bags. She quickly ascertained what was going on, hopped out of the cart and pulled more bags out, pulling Dean up so he could get his bearings and get out of the cart.

"Where are we?" she asked as Dean climbed out beside her.

"We're at the back of the building." Adam said. "This is where I'll have to leave you for a bit. I'm going to have to go back to get Timothy and Mike and come to meet you here. You have the case, right?"

Gemma reached down into the cart, pushed aside a few laundry bags, and pulled up the enigmatic briefcase. Adam nodded.

"Good. I'll get the others and be back here as quickly as I can without drawing a crowd."

"And if you can do this without getting noticed that would be good." Adam looked at Dean.

"Right, that's what I'm saying."

"Right."

They worked to put the laundry bags back in the bin. Gemma looked it over.

"You all set?"

He nodded. "I think so."

"What do you want us to do here?" asked Dean.

"Just sit tight." Adam said. "Hardly anyone comes back here. If you hear anyone, get in the car and keep quiet. Whatever you do, don't fight. We don't want escalation. We got lucky this time. This guy-" he indicated the guard on the ground "- was alone and didn't call for help. He could have brought every guard in the building down on our heads. The chances of being that lucky twice in a row aren't great."

"We'll keep our eyes open." Gemma said.

With a last check of the bags, being sure they were arranged in a satisfactory manner, Adam turned his cart around and made his way again into the labyrinth of the facility.

Chapter 32

"How soon do you think he'll be back?" Timothy asked.

"I don't know."

"There's got to be something we can do."

"Yeah, we wait here until he gets here."

"No I think we're going to get caught if we wait too long here."

"Tim, we're in a cell, why would they come and look in a prison cell? They know that this place is secure. Besides that, he's got his friend in the control booth who's looking out for us there. We need to wait. Even if we wanted to get out of here now…"

Mike went to the door, grabbed the handle and gave the door a rattle. "The door's locked. We're not going anywhere. We're going to have to wait here until he gets back. Why are you suddenly so nervous?"

"I'm not nervous, just- expectant. Why are you so talkative all of a sudden?"

Mike spread his hands. "Do you see anything else to do?"

"Look, just because you can talk doesn't mean you should-" Tim waved it off and stepped back to the table, turning away from the doorway. Shaking his head, Mike looked back to the door.

The two waited in silence to be released from their cell. Tim tried not to imagine what might go wrong or how Adam may already have been caught by the guards. The last thing they needed was to be caught again by the guards running the facility. Tim tried to think about their next steps. Immediately before them, they had to get out of the building. Beyond that, they would have to find a way to get to the FBI headquarters and return the case to them. If Adam was telling the truth, they already had a car to ride in. They would have to get out quietly if at all possible.

Breaking out of the facility was one thing, but it would be best to do it without guards on their heels. If they ran to the FBI with guards following, they would have to find some way of ditching the guards. Getting out of a prison was not as simple as breaking out of a cell and walking away. Tim tried to think through other details of their plan. He assumed that Adam had some other ideas, but at this point, having his own ideas wouldn't hurt anything.

Once they got clear of the building in their vehicle, he wondered whether switching their license plate would be worthwhile. If it was something which threw off the company's search for them and their vehicle it would certainly be a help to them. Tim couldn't imagine what kind of resources Destrier would or could send after them if they ran away, but he was sure that the man would certainly send some force after them if they managed to escape from his clutches.

Mike spent his time standing, walking a little bit, but mostly standing in the room and examining things about the room. He did not seem anxious in the way that Timothy felt. Timothy felt as though he was going to burst if he didn't get out and do something. Mike, on the other hand, puttered about the room, looking at this, then wandering to that. It drove Timothy crazy. He couldn't stand to sit still at this time, especially when the others had left and were risking their lives. Now here he was waiting in a prison cell. It hardly occurred to him that this was an unusual situation. Less than a week ago he was at his desk looking at blenders and making sure that the designs for the package were all right. The room's single bed and small table with a chair made him think of an espionage agent at work.

Either being caught and put in a small cell like this or working at an office with a place to sleep and eat did not seem out of line. The two men waited for a half hour before they heard anything. There was a soft rapping noise at the door and a spoken word. Considering their situation, Timothy figured that a guard would not be the one to knock.

"What do you think?" he asked Mike. Mike shrugged.

Tim moved to the door and listened. "I don't hear anything."

"What are you going to do?"

"I'm going to let them know we're in here."

"What if it's a guard?"

"What are they going to do? We're already in a cell. If it was a guard, they wouldn't be messing around with our cell door in the first place."

After a moment's consideration Mike agreed.

Stepping up to the door, Timothy spoke.

"Adam, it's Timothy. Mike and I are the only ones in here."

Timothy listened for a reply, but heard nothing from the other side of the door. After a moment he shrugged.

"I don't know. We'll have to wait and see I guess."

"Well what are we supposed to do? What if it's a guard? Shouldn't we be prepared?"

"That wouldn't be a bad idea but like I said before, we're not going anywhere. At least not in their heads. Why would they come charging in inspecting us if we're clearly stationary?"

"But are we? What if they've found out about the others?"

A scowl crossed Timothy's face.

"Then I guess we'll just have to hope they put one of them in here so we know they've been caught. Otherwise we'll sit here for a couple of weeks thinking that Adam's running around trying to find us. 'Now where did I put that cell? I suppose it must be around here somewhere. It's sure to turn up sometime or another. Well if I can't find it, maybe I should sit here and wait for the cell to show up. Ah, no wait, there it is! Right where I left it. I sure hope my friends are still inside. I'll hope, too, that they're still alive.'"

Timothy turned and threw himself down into a chair. The room was quiet for a moment. Mike stepped up and looked down at Tim. Tim looked at him, but didn't say anything.

Mike shrugged. "Now what?"

"Now we wait."

The men sat and talked for a few minutes, stealing glances at the door, wondering if it would fly open to reveal Adam standing there commanding them onwards at any moment. Timothy found it important to keep listening and he found himself replying less and less to the stimulus of Mike's attempted conversation. Timothy heard a clicking sound near the door. There was a moment's pause and he held his breath. Then the door opened.

Adam peeked through.

"Well guys here we go. Don't come too quickly."

Timothy gave Mike a look before walking to the door and stepping through, quickly and quietly. Mike grabbed the laptop from the table and followed suit. They were in the hall now and Adam stood there with his cart and laundry bags which still smelled to high heaven. Mike and Tim were looking up and down the hall, but Adam didn't pay any attention to it.

"Relax." He said. "I have an operative who's taking care of security risks. Help me with these."

They quickly removed several bags from the laundry cart to make space in the bottom of it. Tim's eyes scanned over the cart, judging the size of it. His eyes went over to Mike and his large frame. The man was well-built, certainly a powerhouse. Not necessarily a body-builder, but not overweight. Mike caught the glance from Tim.

"What?"

"Nothing."

Mike looked over his own frame, then looked back at Tim.

"You don't think I'll fit?"

Adam spoke. "Ladies, please, you're both beautiful, but we've got to keep moving or we'll get caught, I'll have to answer some awkward questions, and either join you in your cells or leave you all to figure out a second chance out of this place. You'll both fit."

They quickly got the rest of the bags out of the cart and onto the floor.

"All right, in you go." Said Adam.

After some back and forth discussion Mike slipped in first followed by Tim. Tim was met with the feeling of the canvas underneath him stretching as he shifted his weight.

"Now look." Adam said. "I know you guys are buddies and love to chat, but this part is serious. You have to keep silent when we get moving. These walls you're in are canvas- not sound-proof. Got it?"

Adam began to arrange the bags on top of the two men in the bottom of the cart. They tried to adjust the positioning of some of the bags but that proved difficult in their positions. Mike was in a semi-fetal position on the floor of the cart. Tim laid on his back with his head resting on Mike's feet. He attempted to turn sideways once or twice, but the cart's size wouldn't allow for both of them to lie fetal-position in the bottom of the cart. Tim imagined them showing up as shapes on an ultrasound and the announcement from the ultrasound technician. 'Ma'm you've got a six footer and a near seven-footer.' Tim tried to un-imagine their shapes as an ultrasound.

Chapter 33

With a thump, Adam settled the last stinking laundry bag on top of their already cramped bodies. Bending down he brought his mouth close to the canvas.

"Remember – not a peep."

He heard two taps on the canvas from the inside. Nodding to himself, he started down the hallway out of the cell block. With a tapping on the door, he let his friend know that he was ready to be let out of the cell block and onto the main floor.

"OK Lorenzo." he said into his earpiece. This was their last stage of the operation. If this went smoothly, all that was left was to get out of the building, which should be easy enough.

There was a wait. Adam was anxious. He knew that his counterparts in the basket would be even more anxious than he was, so he kept his head and waited quietly. The last thing he needed was to draw attention to them. He waited for another minute or two before going to his radio.

"Lorenzo, what's the situation?"

"Sorry, but we've got a lot of activity on the other side of your door."

"Do they suspect anything?"

"No, they're just passing through. I figured it's best to wait until you've got a fairly clear path to get to the van."

"All right, but let's not wait much longer."

The wait lasted another minute and a half before he got another signal.

"OK, it looks like we're good to go. I'm opening the door now. Remember, head out right, then down the hall. The door you want will be on your right."

"Got it."

He heard a tone as the doors' locks were released. The pneumatic locks were more than enough to keep prisoners in. Seeing the size of the place, Adam wondered about the material and locks, if they were designed for large groups, assuming a chance that a group of prisoners managed to get out of their individual cells and get past the guards. In any case it wouldn't have been possible to slip out of the cell block without someone planted in the guard room. He also thought about the legality of privately detaining people against their will.

Adam waited for the door to slip fully open and stepped through and into the hall. Then he turned and made his way in the direction of the back hallway which would take him to the waiting van. He could only hope no one would find the piles of dirty laundry in the hampers throughout the building. He began his hike down the open hall, keeping close to the wall so as to keep away from prying eyes. He came to the hallway where the back storage was and glanced about. There was no guard standing around. With a glance behind him, Adam made his way forward with the rancid laundry. The shelves were lined up on both sides of him, passing him in unison. As he went he heard a quiet shuffling from the inside of the cart.

"We're almost there guys." He said, keeping his voice low. "Just keep it down for another minute or two." Adam pushed ahead and was about to tell the men they could relax as they were approaching the vehicle, when he heard footsteps behind him.

"Halt." Said someone behind him.

Adam slowed the cart and came to a stop about a hundred feet away from the open garage door and the parked van with the rest of his new friends in it.

"What is this?" The person behind him asked.

"Laundry." He said. Adam's voice echoed through the room.

"And what are you doing with this laundry at this time?"

The voice moved as the guard stepped around Adam. the guard was a thin man with neatly-combed hair and a small mustache. "Do you have a permit to transport it off the premises?"

"I don't need a permit, it's my job. I'm a laundryman. Still, if you want to talk to my boss you can. I can tell you he'll be really mad, though. We were supposed to be out of here fifteen minutes ago and we just found out that you guys had a second load-"

"All right, I see."

"-of laundry to pick up. So I had to go back and get it-"

"Yes, that's enough."

"-and load up the entire basket-"

"Quiet."

"-and bring it all back here."

"Be quiet!"

Adam quieted, hoping his companions had caught wind of something going on outside of the vehicle. If they were laying low, the best thing they could do now would be to lend themselves as a distraction. That did not seem likely right now.

"Can you please show me some form of identification, sir?"

"All right, that's no problem sir." Adam said, reaching for his wallet. "To tell you the truth," he said, hesitating, "you did make me nervous there, for a moment. We've heard all kinds of crazy things around here lately, like there are some officers who aren't really officers here who work at this plant."

"Sir, we aren't really officers."

"Do you mean to tell me that you are impersonating an officer of the law?"

"No, we're not police officers, you should know this. We're security guards. We take some courses in handling weapons and how to deal with security breaches and things like that, but we're not full-blown police officers."

"Oh." Adam said, dropping his hands. "Then what am I doing here, waving my hands like I just don't care?"

"You've got your hands up because I asked you to stop. I was going to ask you a few more questions, but you began rambling on about police officers-"

"You're the one who said you weren't a police officer."

"I am a security officer here to be sure that this area is secure."

Adam looked around the room. "Well, I mean it looks like it's pretty well-enforced. You've got brick walls and those will be hard to get through. Those garage doors will be trouble if you leave them open long enough."

"All right wise guy." The guard said. He had already drawn his gun and was holding it, albeit with the barrel pointed at the ground. "What's in the laundry bin?"

Adam shrugged. "Laundry, for the most part. Sorry about the smell, but most of the inmates don't have access to clean clothes or a washing machine. I don't know the last time was when these were washed."

"What else is in the bin?"

"There's nothing else."

"No goods, substances or people?"

Adam shook his head.

"Step away from the laundry bin."

"All right." He said. "Don't say I didn't warn you."

Adam stepped back from the laundry cart and the guard stepped nearer. He winced at the smell, but had no other discernable reaction. After looking the cart over, the guard spoke again, raising his voice and speaking with immaculate diction.

"This is security for Destrier Industries. We know that you have commandeered the laundry cart. Come out slowly with your hands raised. Your counterpart has been caught as well."

No response came from the cart. The guard glanced at Adam, then spoke again.

"I will give you ten seconds to comply."

A rustling came from the bottom of the cart. When he made the announcement, the guard made the mistake of standing directly next to the laundry cart. Mike reared up from the cart. At the same moment, they heard a door slamming open. Gemma crouched in the back door of the utility van, gun drawn, surveying the situation. As he reared up, Mike managed to snake his arm around the guard's neck and another around his gun hand. Mike's arm tightened like an anaconda. Unfortunately for the guard, he didn't think to fire before asking questions.

"Now," said Mike with a grunt as they struggled, "we can do this one of two ways. You can drop the gun and they can find you later and send you off to your quarters to pack your things and find a new job for getting caught off guard. Or we can take a chance and have them find you and send you either to the hospital or to the morgue, whichever way it ends up. With you waving that gun around, I'm probably going to do this quickly." Mike had one arm completely wrapped around the man's neck and the other wrapped the other way, countering it.

The man wriggled in his grasp, but said nothing.

"Drop that gun."

The gun fell to the floor. At this point Timothy had climbed out of the cart and stood to the side watching the exchange between the two.

"Tim." Mike said. "Get the man's radio, please."

Tim nodded and moved to the guard, unclipping the guard's radio from his belt. They proceeded to relieve the man of any potentially dangerous materials in their situation – pepper spray, his cell phone, his baton, and his knife. Checking his boots as well, they found a second knife there.

Tim said "Do we have anything to tie him with?" Gemma made a search of the van and found some tape. Mike kept his grip on the man while Angelo bound the man's wrists in front of him. At this point Mike deemed it safe to release the man. Seating him on the ground before them. Congregating around the guard, they took a look at their captive.

"Do you think he'll cause any trouble?" asked Gemma.

"I don't know." Said Tim. "He doesn't seem like the feisty type."

"We can't let him loose." Mike said. "We'll have to leave him here to be found. I'm sure someone will be around to find him or relieve whoever's supposed to be on duty."

After a short conversation, however, they decided that if he was left in the middle of the floor their getaway might be discovered too quickly. They pulled him over to the side of the room and bound his legs as well. Adam made sure the man's bonds were secure and they high-tailed it to the van. As they prepared another man showed up, Adam's assistant in the guardroom. He was a small man who did not introduce himself at once. With all that was going on at the moment it was fine by Tim, who made it his duty to be sure that everyone was in the vehicle. He also made sure that they had both the case and the laptop with which they hoped to interface with the technology in the case, somehow.

With that, they were off. The garage door was already open, the van parked in the stall. Adam pulled out, his companion in the front passenger seat keeping an eye out, both through the front windshield and through the passenger side. So far there was no sign that they had been spotted. Adam eased through the back lot and out the driveway. There were some guards posted around the building, but they hardly paid any attention to the vehicle as it made its way out of the lot. Tim kept glancing back over his shoulder expecting guards to come running or to hear the sound of guns firing at them from behind. But he heard nothing except the quiet idling of the vehicle's engine as they rolled forward on the asphalt.

Chapter 34

"Keep your eyes open." Adam said as he pulled the car around the building and out into the front lot. "The last thing we want to happen is to be caught off guard." He kept the van crawling along at an appropriate speed with the foot traffic outside the complex. With their first entrance into the area, Timothy had hardly noticed that there were other buildings in the area which might be purposed by Destrier and his company. From the outside it was impossible to tell what was being used. If building was being used, it was also impossible to tell what the building was being used for. Each of the passengers kept quiet in their seats, keeping their eyes open for trouble. But so far none had come. Timothy had nearly expected guards to come out running with guns blazing as soon as they left the building. Of course the guards would have to know they had escaped to do anything about it.

Timothy turned back to Gemma.

"Do we know that the one guard we left is the only one who knows we left?"

Gemma hesitated. "Say that again?"

"Is the guard we left behind the only one who knows we left?"

She thought for a moment then said "Yeah, he would have to be. No one saw anyone leave the cells, and the only place anybody was revealed was right by the trucks. The only person by the trucks was the one guard we took care of."

"I guess that makes sense." Tim said, nodding.

They spent the next few minutes in furtive quietness, wondering and keeping their eyes open for any signs of telling activity outside their vehicle. As they approached the gate, they discussed what they were going to do.

"We can't let them see us." Gemma said.

"What should we do?" asked Mike.

"I think," said Angelo, "that if we just stay hidden and Adam doesn't draw too much attention to himself we could slip out of here without much trouble." Tim saw him look about the cab of the utility van they occupied to see the others' reactions.

"I agree." Tim said. "If we keep quiet and unseen they won't have any reason to ask questions. If they see a bunch of people they don't recognize coming through the gate who they don't know they'll be sure to turn us around."

"And if they find that we've just come out from Destrier's place," Mike added, "I'll bet there'll be more waiting for us there than solitary confinement."

In a matter of seconds, they got the fugitives moved to the back of the van. Timothy thanked God that the vehicle wasn't a passenger van with glass on both sides. To see into the back, the guards would have to come to the back of the vehicle and actually open up the back doors. Otherwise they would be blind to everything in the vehicle except Adam and his companion in the passenger seat. As they sat in the back, Tim watched as the two men spoke quietly before pulling up to the stop at the front gate. As they sat, Timothy's mind began to wander and focus on the idea that the back of the van acted as an audio amplifier- being made of large plates of sheet metal, sound would simply reflect off the surfaces and bounce around the back of the car.

Adam pulled up to the front gate. The guard at the front greeted him.

"You look like you've had a rough night."

"I can't say it's been an easy one."

"Yeah, we all have one of those, right?"

Inwardly, Tim breathed a sigh of relief. It sounded like everything was going fine. He heard a slight sniff beside him. They would get through this all right. The sniff became a heaving breath of a kind. Tim glanced over from his reverie. Angelo was in the middle of a mouth-open approach and it was too late to stop. Tim looked to Gemma and Mike, across from him, only to see their desperate stares, but it was too late. Angelo's explosive sneeze resounded through the back of the van. It might as well have been a gunshot. Tim thought to look for a gun himself, but didn't have the capacity in the moment to follow through. Everyone in the back of the vehicle was frozen

Tim just caught the conversation from the back of the van.

"What was that?"

"What was what?"

"That noise from the back of your vehicle. I thought you told me you had no cargo or people in the back of your vehicle."

"I… don't."

"Well what was that noise?"

"That was… that was my…. Grandmother."

"Your grandmother?"

"Yes, my grandmother. I promised to take her to the doctor, only she lives two hours away. The only arrangement that made sense was for her to come to work with me."

"You do realize that with your twelve hour shifts you would have to have your elderly grandmother in the plant by herself for twelve hours."

"Is that all? Oh, she manages longer than that at home."

"At home?"

Another explosive sneeze sounded from the back of the vehicle. From his vantage point, Tim could just see the guard lean to look towards the back door of the vehicle.

"Oh, no, you don't want to go back there. You see I took my grandmother to work with me because today I have to drop her off at the doctor's office. She's really sick, you see. I'm not really sure yet, but it could be tuberculosis."

Tim heard a third voice entering the scene.

"What's going on here?"

"This man is telling me that he has his grandmother in the back of the vehicle."

"Yes sir," Adam said, "I took my grandmother to work with me because she lives two hours away from here and the nearest medical center is an hour away from here in the opposite direction of her house."

"So," the second guard said, "your grandmother needs medical attention?"

"Yes." Adam replied.

The second guard turned to the first one. "The why don't you let the man through? He's clearly on important business."

"Because something doesn't line up here. It was only after I heard a noise from the back that he began telling me this story about the grandmother."

"You didn't ask." Adam said.

"The man's mother could be dying-"

"*Grand*mother," Adam said. "and she's not dying, just sick. But I need to get her to the hospital for proper treatment. If you don't mind wrapping up the conversation so we can get on our way, I can get out of your hair."

"What about the sneezing?" said the first guard.

"I told you, she is sick." Tim could hear Adam's patience wearing thin. "That's why I'm taking her to see a doctor."

Tim didn't catch the next part of the conversation, but the vehicle was soon moving forward and through the gate. He glanced over his shoulder, hardly believing that they had made their way through that last obstacle. Turning to Gemma, Tim spoke.

"Did that just happen?"

She nodded. "I think so."

He turned to Angelo. "Do you have allergies?"

The man shrugged. "I might."

Tim kept his eye on Angelo.

Angelo shrugged again. "I might not."

"Ladies and gentlemen, Harborside theater presents for you tonight - The Enigma. Does he have allergies? Will he find the girl of his dreams? Does he not have allergies? Did his dead uncle really leave him a million dollars or is it all a huge joke by his uncle who's still alive?"

"Dean, you have the strangest sense of humor."

"Next up, please stay tuned for a special presentation of Mr. Baxter's who is the world's greatest llama impersonator."

Gemma spoke. "As long as he doesn't spit."

Tim crawled to the front of the vehicle. Seeing him, Adam gave a little wave. Tim nodded and spoke. "How are things going up here?"

Adam blew a sigh. "Not too badly. We don't seem to have anybody on our tail, so that's good news. However terrible the grandmother story was, it was either brilliant enough to work or stupid enough that they took it as a joke and dismissed it. In short, it looks like we're doing pretty well."

Tim nodded and thought for a moment. Then turning, he remembered the man in the seat beside him, Adam's companion. He offered his hand.

"I'm Tim. Timothy Runn."

The man smiled and took his offered hand, but didn't speak. He was small in build, quiet in his movements and conduct. Tim glanced to Adam for an introduction, but didn't receive one. Tim tried to satisfy himself remembering that this man had risked his life for him and his friends. Having an unnamed person in the vehicle who would remain unnamed was such an unnatural thing that it lingered on his mind. Tim crawled back the back of the van and made for a spot next to Gemma. Seeing him coming, Mike gave up his spot and shifted, moving around the laundry bin so that Tim could settle in next to Gemma. She turned to Tim.

"How's our driver doing?"

"He's all right. No one's on our tail, which is the best news I've heard all day."

"That's good." She said.

"We're going to have to get to the FBI headquarters as soon as we can. The question is, how are we going to get the case to them?"

"Simple." Mike said. "We take it inside and tell them what it is."

"No, it's not that simple." Said Gemma. "Do you know how many times a week the FBI gets tips that a briefcase someone has contains secret information that must get to the head of the department, or to the President, or contains a bomb? If we came to their doors with an unidentified briefcase, they'd go nuts. There would be a complete lockdown. They would start asking who we're working for, who we know, what tactics we use, with what purpose we entered the building – anything and everything would be on the table."

"And if Destrier gets wind of it," Tim said, "he could get away and we might never find him again."

"Wait," said Dean, "find him *again*? You mean you would deliberately come back here and try to come after him?"

"Who else is going to do it?" said Gemma.

"The FBI." Said Adam from the front seat. "That's their job to gather evidence and stop criminals, not ours."

"We're witnesses." said Tim. "We've seen and heard firsthand what he plans to do, what resources he has in hand."

Gemma spoke. "Then we get to the FBI and go from there. They'll be able to help us. I know some people there, they'll be able to do something about this."

The group was quiet after that, each keeping to their own thoughts. Tim turned the question over in his mind again and again; how would they approach the FBI with a case which they would not accept? He turned his mind to more familiar things and realized that he missed his home. It had been such a string of events that had kept him occupied that his desire to be home once more had intensified.

He never imagined that he would have been caught up in an adventure like this one. To be on the run from an organization like the one Destrier ran and doing it for the FBI, even though the FBI had no knowledge Tim and his friends were doing so boggled his mind. But he found himself already caught up in the middle of the journey and so settled himself further back on the floor of the moving utility van and tried to imagine what he would tell his neighbors had happened.

What, I was gone for two weeks? No, it wasn't for family. Nothing's wrong, I just got caught up in things. What kind of things? Developing things…

He realized that anything he would try to tell them would sound stupid, whether he told them outright or tried to hide the fact that it was for the FBI. If he told people he knew that he was involved in a case for the FBI he would be labeled as the local nut or as a comedian. He didn't want the first label, and the second wouldn't be good because he knew some friends who would continue to goad him into learning jokes and gags to appease their sense of comedy, their especially bad sense of comedy so that they could say that he was, indeed a comedian they said he was. With that kind of friend anything they said in that way was a kind of self-fulfilling prophecy if they pushed hard enough.

"So," Adam said "what's the plan?"

Tim turn around to look at the rest of his crew. He smiled a little bit. "How about lunch?"

Chapter 35

It was late in the morning, but since they were all exhausted and agreed that they could use some food, they sought out a place where they could find a bite to eat. The consensus came in that they needed to keep moving, so drive-through was best. With that in mind, they decided on a burger place. Some disagreement broke out about favorite places for burgers, but having an odd number of people settled any ties in the voting process.

So, at about 11:30 AM, they pulled up outside a Burger King, Adam with a story ready, the crew in the back ready to stay quiet and to stifle Angelo should he have another sudden allergy attack. After a moment of static, a young woman's voice came in over the intercom.

"Welcome to Burger King, order whenever you're ready."

Adam proceeded to read off an extensive list for the seven members of the crew in the vehicle. After he did so, silence emanated from the intercom for a moment. Then the voice proceeded to read the list back to him, in order, just what he had ordered. He then confirmed that they had the order correctly entered. After being told their total, Adam pulled around to the payment window.

As they approached the first window, Adam glanced back to be sure that his passengers were behaving themselves. It was quiet enough. It didn't matter much at this point. But having some report of a utility van with seven people in the back without seats or seat belts wouldn't be any help, even if such a report might not lead Destrier to them. He pulled up and nodded to the cashier. She had to be in her early twenties, he'd guess. At first glance, she appeared to be entirely bored with her job. He rolled down the window and her mouth inched up into a smile. She brushed her ponytail behind her shoulder as she did so.

"That will be $45.98."

"All right." He pulled out the cash and passed it along.

The young woman grinned as she took it. "I've heard some men eat big, but you must be a boy with a big appetite."

Adam tried to turn his grimace into a smile. "Just picking up some food for my buddies at work."

"Mm." She said. "And we want to be sure you've got enough to feed those great big muscles of yours." The young woman behind the counter glanced towards Adam's biceps and a small flash of disappointment showed that he wasn't a professional bodybuilder. Why she didn't notice this before she thought to mention his 'great big muscles' was beyond Adam, but he shifted in his seat.

"Can I get my change please?"

She gave a little gasp and he hoped that this had upset her enough to move on.

"So well mannered!" she said. "I'm sure you're parents brought you up right." She handed him the change with one hand, which he accepted, and offered him the other one, palm down, batting her eyelashes. A flirtatious smile adorned her mouth. He hesitated for half a second, unsure of how to proceed, before taking her hand in a firm handshake. The corners of her mouth dropped and she turned briskly back to her work. Adam smiled to himself and pulled forward to the next window.

After picking up their food, which consisted of three large bags, several cups of coffee and a few other beverages, they pulled away and got back to the road. As they drove, discussions arose about what to do next and their approach to the FBI. Again they didn't know how they would leave the case for the agency.

Then talk fell to other things. Casual conversation went to sports and movies. They hadn't had a chance to sit down over a meal. There is something humanizing about gathering around a meal, even if it is in the back of a moving vehicle. No matter where you come from or what your belief system is, everyone has to eat. So they ate and talked about where they came from and what they thought about the world. There were some stark differences and some close agreements. Some close alliances were formed, through the love of sports teams, love of books and films, actors and actresses.

As Adam drove, he found himself glancing back, every once in a while, at this ragtag team that had been spliced together by chance and misfortune. It seemed that Misfortune had come along and decided to play a trick, taking these five individuals and putting them together in each others' lives, making them dependent on each other, giving them chances to trust each other. As they did so, the bonds of friendship would go, strengthening each of them in turn.

He knew it would be more than difficult to explain to his superiors how he ended up in this position. Adam tried to image what would be going on if he hadn't stepped in at this point. Right now he would probably still be a maintenance man at the docking area-turned-base of operations. People would walk the halls, politely greeting him. He would nod or murmur a word in reply.

As he expected, the conversation eventually turned to him and how he found them, and what he was doing at the plant in the first place.

"How did you find me? And what were you doing at the plant in the first place?" said Tim.

"I am a private investigator. I hire myself out to individuals who have suspicions either about other individuals or about a company. I got myself hired as a maintenance worker at the plant, so I have keys to practically every room in the building except the head manager's office. While I'm on the job I try to keep my ears open about what's going on. Sometimes I chat with some of the guards and officers and find ways to get news of what's going on in the building.

"As I'm working one day, I get word that they have two vehicles coming in with five prisoners. Now you don't hear the word 'prisoners' everyday, and my thought process is that to have prisoners you need some kind of jurisdiction for that, but I keep quiet about that. So I listen in on them as they talk and they go back and forth for a bit, and talk about picking you up in the park and who did the work and how it was simple enough to surround you all and get you out of there. Nobody asked any questions, and they just stuffed you away, took the other vehicles and left."

Gemma spoke. "Was this the first time you heard of something like this from them?"

"I've only been collecting intel from this company for some three or four months." Adam said. "But no, I'd heard nothing about stuff like this before."

Tim said "Do you think they might have done this in the past?"

"It's possible," Adam said "but there's no way to know right now. They would need some strong reason to do so. That briefcase is one of the strongest reasons I've seen so far."

"Which brings us around to the issue we haven't addressed yet," Gemma said, "we need to decide what to do with the briefcase."

"Let's get to the FBI building," Tim said, "and decide when we get there."

Gemma shrugged and muttered to herself. "Or we could just waltz right up to the building and take it inside."

They settled into another time of quiet conversation, some duets and trios talking about film, others talking about their home life. No one wanted to talk about what had happened. Not many of the people in the van were eager to discuss what they were to do with the case, besides taking it to the front desk. No one else could think of what else to do with it. Their unsolved problem of restoration without arrest would remain until they tried it out. They burned away the time with food and conversation.

It was another few hours before they heard any word about being close to the J Edgar Hoover building. It was decided by the rest of the group that Timothy would be going in to deliver the case. Since the case had been given to him, it only seemed right that he deliver the case to the proper authorities. If a long passage of time went by without him emerging then someone would be sent in to inquire after him. Tim didn't know how this would help, since he might be in some back office or, worse, in some dark questioning room answering some agent's string of questions to which he might or might not know the answers.

Tim felt like the sacrificial lamb being led to the slaughter. The problem with the metaphor, Tim thought, is that most of the time the lamb has no idea anything is wrong. In this case he knew well what was going on but could do little about it. He thought through the problem, wondering whether there wasn't another way to return the case. But the same problem faced him no matter which way he looked at it – there had to be a human agent delivering the case to the agency. And that human agent would be suspected of theft, if not worse. He had no guarantee that he would walk away from the building without some kind of prison sentence.

But the security of his country was on the line. He knew that this was something into which he had been placed. Tim turned and looked at the people around him. Gemma noticed him.

"What?" she said.

"I can't imagine doing this without you all." Tim said.

"Aw, thanks." Said Dean.

"No, really." Said Tim. "If it wasn't for you guys I could opt out of this."

"I thought you were the one who said that we should go to the FBI headquarters to get the case back to the authorities."

"I did say that. I just think that we should go and give the case back to them. To have one man walk in by himself unidentified with a single briefcase – does that make anyone think of suspicious behavior?"

The vehicle was silent. Tim groaned.

"Look," he said, "if I go in by myself I will have no one to vouch for me."

"But you'll have us to vouch for you." Angelo said.

"And how will you do that from the car?"

"If there's any trouble we'll come and vouch for you."

"So after the fact?"

The van was quiet again. Apparently they hadn't thought it through much.

"Gemma, what about you? Aren't you an agent?" Tim said.

"Yes," she said slowly," but if you recall, no one knew about Agent William's work. Williams was the agent who did all of the research and created the technology in this case we're carrying. So my claims about it will be scolded for not doing the work I have been assigned."

"You're assignment?"

"Yes," she said again, "I was working on another assignment which I put aside when I caught wind of Agent William's work."

"I see." Tim said. "And what would we have heard about this mission? Anything in the news?"

Gemma shook her head. "Nothing much."

It was clear that she wasn't going to say anything else, and no one else in the vehicle felt like they had the privilege to pry any more, so they spoke of other matters.

Chapter 36

The J Edgar Hoover building imposed to say the least. A mass of concrete sitting on its own city block, a massive monolith, it was a monument unto itself and to the work that went on inside it day in and day out. The square windows peered out like dark eyes searching the streets below for the lost. Two visible pillars held up part of a lofty structure which rose above the rest of the building as a series of upper floors rose into the sky.

Tim stood for a moment, alone, gazing up at the building. He tried to imagine the work that went into building such a monument. Shaking his head a little he stepped forward and into the front doors of the FBI building. As he came inside, he met his first obstacle. Security stood ready to search each person as they passed by a metal detector. Tim took a breath and approached the metal detectors.

The worker at the near metal detector nodded as he approached. Tim nodded back.

The worker spoke. "Please step through the gate."

Tim hesitated, but complied, knowing that disobeying orders at this point would only cause more trouble than was necessary. As he stepped through the alarm went off.

"Step over here, please." The worker said.

Tim followed quietly as the worker led him over to a table at the side. The worker indicated him to set the case down on the table, demonstrated that he was to spread his arms and began a pat-down, having him remove his cell phone, some pocket change and some other paraphernalia.

"May I ask what's in the case?" the worker said as he stepped around and began to examine the strange briefcase.

"Yes, it's the reason I'm here." There was only the slightest hint, but Tim could see the worker bristle. "I'm returning this case. It was three days ago when one of your agents, Williams I think his name was, lost this case and I told him I would return it for him."

The agent held up his hand. "Please wait here for a moment." He stepped over to a pair of well-equipped security guards standing in the corner making a hurried and, if Tim would be so bold, erroneous explanation to them.

The male security guard was the first one to get to the scene.

"Sir, I appreciate your patience with us. Can you explain your story to us again, and how you came upon this case?"

"Yes, sir, thank you. I was minding my own business, walking down the sidewalk, when I saw a man running-"

"Which way was he running?" the female guard said.

"Down the sidewalk toward me. There were two men chasing after him-"

"How large were these men?" asked the male guard.

"About six feet each, I don't remember. I didn't take out a tape measure and offer to measure them. They were following after the man who appeared to be wounded, so I followed him into the alley where he had ducked to lie low-"

"Don't you think this job is overrated?" The female guard had turned to the male guard.

"I had been told there would be lots of action." He said. "Instead I get paid to say 'How do you do Mr. Hawthorne.' 'Very nice to see you Ms. Macy.' 'Looks like it's going to cloud over again Mr. Norris.'"

"Oh, I know. And the mundane conversations you have to carry on as you go through the morning rituals drive me crazy. I can't tell you how many times I've said 'Yes Mr. Smith.' 'True, Mr. Gruver.' 'I'm sure they are Mr. Dartmoore.'"

The chatter continued for a solid two minutes as the twosome voiced their gripes about the staff. The first security worker listened and Tim waited for them to continue their process with him. But they didn't. Seeing his opportunity, he waited for a moment when the security officer was distracted and grabbed the case, quietly heading further into the building.

As he moved forward, Timothy tried to be fully aware of anything that could stop him from returning the briefcase. So far no one seemed to be paying any particular amount of attention to him. As he walked in, he saw that the main floor of the building bustled with activity. People came in and out of the building, come to the front desk, left it, headed to their offices or out of them, reported to their senior officers or went to file reports about whatever work they were doing at the moment or had been assigned to look into. Seeing the front desk, Tim headed for a receptionist who didn't appear to be particularly busy at the moment.

Tim stepped up to the receptionist who smiled and spoke. The man's nametag said Joseph.

"Hello, how can I help you today?"

"Hi," said Tim, "I came here today about an important matter, both as an informant- well not really an informant- I mean- what I really mean-" Tim trailed off and tried again. "I came here to return something." Tim explained himself and showed the receptionist the case. "It is critical that this is returned to the proper people." He said. "I've heard that this thing has the potential to infiltrate any database, any website, anything which can connect to a wireless router. This is a matter of national security."

Joseph looked Tim in the eye. "Well," he said. "I'd better get someone right on it."

"Really?" asked Tim.

"Of course." Said Joseph. "This is a matter of utmost importance." He said as he lifted his phone receiver. He looked into Tim's eyes for just a moment and Tim felt his as though his own soul was touching this man's soul. Then the man was laughing. Tim blinked. Joseph was laughing hard. A few people glanced in his direction but didn't pay any more attention than that.

"What's going on?" asked Tim.

"Are you kiddin'?" Joseph said. "Do you know how many tips we get a day about national security, not to mention people walking in here with all sorts of crazy things telling us that aliens and men in black gave them to us and that the world is going to end if we don't take action now? I've had three people tell me in the last two days that either Mahatma Ghandi is coming back, that crop circles are the universal roadmap and that we must start the worldwide initiative to take to the stars and abandon the earth entirely within the century, and a third tip that children's television contains the keywords which may be the secret to unlocking unlimited sustainable energy. So I get my fair share of strange tips."

"Then take this one that's not so strange. Agent Williams gave me this case to return to you. Its research he was doing on internet security." Tim said.

"Why didn't we know anything about it?" asked Joseph.

"I don't know." Tim said. "But he told me that no one knew about his research. And that a man by the name of Destrier was after it because he's looking to create havoc with our society. I need to speak with someone who will listen to my story and take me seriously, not someone who deals with a tip line about aliens and the return of Mahatma Ghandi."

As he spoke, Tim heard a shout from across the room. The two guards from the entryway of the building were coming after him. Tim raised his hands to show his intention to go nowhere.

"Well," said Joseph, "I think that's settled."

Chapter 37

The guards grabbed the case and took it away to another part of the building. They put Tim into a holding room which was not inhospitable. There was some coffee. The chair's back dug into his spine a little so he found himself shifting in his seat often. The room's interior was cold, but the coffee helped. It served as a warm handshake, though shaky and unsure at this point.

There was a large picture window which was dark and slightly reflective. He sat at a table with a chair on the other side. A door was behind him, solid walls around him. If he had been claustrophobic, he would not have liked to spend a lot of time in this room. Still, here he was, waiting for the next step. He couldn't imagine that the next step would be good if they had him in a waiting room like this.

Within ten or fifteen minutes the door opened, and a man walked in. He was lean and fairly young, not much older than thirty. Timothy smiled and nodded. The man smiled as he entered the room and walked around the table to sit across from Tim.

"Well, let me see here Mr…" he picked up the file folder and opened it to read what was written inside. Tim knew that the man knew his name, and that this was for theatricality. He didn't know why the man decided that he had to be a showoff, but the man waited a full ten seconds before he spoke again. "Mr. Runn." He looked up to Timothy. If the effect was to scare Tim into thinking the man didn't know or had forgotten his name it hadn't worked.

"My name is Agent Manning. I know that all of this is a bit confusing-"

There was nothing confusing about it, they were threatened because they didn't understand what was going on.

"-but I'm sure we'll soon get all of this cleared up and you'll be on your way." The man smiled. Timothy tried not to shudder as his first thought was of a hyena.

"So Mr. Runn you say that you are returning this case which one of our agents gave to you?"

"Yes," Timothy said, making eye contact with the agent, "a man who only identified himself as agent Williams passed this case onto me and said that he was doing research and that this case contained technology which had to be passed on to the FBI as soon as possible."

"And you questioned nothing about this?" the agent asked.

"I questioned a lot of it. But what could I do? If I was to believe that this case contained something which could be dangerous, I had a responsibility to return it as quickly as I could." Tim said.

Agent Manning nodded. "What is it that you do for a living, Mr. Runn?"

"I am a marketing director." Tim said.

"A marketing director?"

"Yes, I oversee package design as well as some commercial design for a company which produces small household appliances. Toasters, blenders, things like that."

Agent Manning nodded with his mouth pulled into a firm line. "I see." He said. And how did you get involved in this... escapade?"

Tim took a breath. "A mistake. I was shopping when I heard a commotion on the sidewalk. I saw a man who looked like he was in trouble. Two other men were chasing after him and he appeared to be injured. He ducked into an alley, so I followed him. He said his name was agent

Williams and that he was on the run with some important research. The men after him had already wounded him. He passed the case onto me and asked me to pass it on to the FBI."

"Well, if your story wasn't so wild, much of it might be true, except for one point, your agent Williams."

"What do you mean?" Tim said.

"He's dead."

Tim shrugged. "Well, we knew that."

Agent Manning smiled. "What you didn't know is that he's been dead for nearly seven years. If you ran into an Agent Williams, it's not him. Or it's not the same Agent Williams."

"It had to be someone. I don't know what else to tell you. He gave his name as Williams, and had no reason to lie as he was dying. I had to stand and watch from the end of the alley as they approached and were about to kill this agent. If he wasn't Williams, then I don't know what to tell you." Tim said.

Agent Manning pressed onwards.

"What about these friends of yours, where did they come from?"

Tim shrugged. "Where don't they come from? Dean is the comedian we picked up at a coffee shop. Angelo is a gas station attendant working at one of the places where we were attacked. Mike was a hired gun to keep a lookout for us."

"You mean you hired him to keep a lookout?"

"No, he was supposed to be looking for us. We caught sight of him at another rest stop, acting funny, Gemma starts talking to him, easing him down a couple of notches, and he decides that rather than reporting us to a questionable organization he's going to help us do a good deed." Tim said. The expression on his face showed that he had forgotten his own situation and had caught himself in remembering past events.

Agent Manning pressed onwards. His questions were repetitive and circular, leading Tim to repeat what he had already told the agent. This frustrated Tim, as he felt that he was being held in a room while answering a tape recorder which had three or four variations of the same message being played on it all at the same time. Tim told him all he knew, all he had heard from Gemma about the case, what she had told him about it's potential use. When he spoke Agent Manning sat silently, taking notes on a legal pad. He sat and endured the line of questioning from the Agent, wondering when it would be over, focusing his attention on each question as it came up.

He had not seen a case like this before.

He had not met Gemma before their first encounter in the alley.

He did not know what else Destrier was involved in.

He did not know the names of Destrier's accomplices.

Though the Agent asked a question or two about Destrier, he never said any more. Tim would supply fodder with his answer to a question, then Agent Manning would ask more questions based on the answer to the question Tim had just answered. What was apparently a string of nearly unending questions had suddenly ended. Agent Manning had stood and was headed for the door.

"Mr. Manning."

The man turned to look back at Tim.

"Thank you."

Agent Manning nodded and exited the room.

Chapter 38

Agent Tonya Nimmons sat and watched the interrogation from the control room and thought through the questions. Most of it was standard. Go over the events leading up to the event, go over the relationships of the suspect. But there was something else Manning hadn't touched on and with which she was not satisfied.

This mention of Destrier bothered her, and how quickly Manning moved on from it. In all their speaking, Tim had nearly spoken for half an hour about the man, and Manning had dropped the subject. She turned to one of the younger men in the room. He sat at one of the computers.

"Hey Mickey." She said.

"Yeah?"

"What do we know about this character Destrier?"

"Nothing, really. Could be a fantasy. Half of this stuff could be drug-induced. Forensics is working on the briefcase." He said.

"Do you mean that they are working on it now, or they'll be working on it sometime?"

Mickey shrugged and went back to his work.

She looked back at the room. The man tapping his fingers on the table didn't strike her as the type to be caught for substance abuse.

"Mickey." She said.

"Yeah." He replied.

"Could you do a little digging for me? See if you find anything about this character Destrier?"

"I'm on it." He said.

"Thanks." She said.

Tim was introduced to a cell where he sat brooding about his situation. Now he truly felt alone. No one was coming to rescue him, the only people in power to do anything about the case were either accusing him or laughing at him, and he was halfway across the country from home. He sighed and lay back on the thin mattress that he had been provided with. No one else occupied the cell.

He was about to doze off for lack of anything else to do when a knock came at his door. He didn't know why the person bothered to knock, since he couldn't open the door. But the door opened the door a moment later. A woman strode into the cell and took a look at Timothy, who sat up.

"Timothy Runn." She said.

"Yes." He said.

"My name is Agent Nimmons."

"I heard you've had quite a rough day."

"You could say that."

"I understand that some of our agents have already questioned you."

"Yes they have."

"And they've asked you several questions concerning this brief-case you've brought in."

"That is accurate, yes." He said.

"In your time here you haven't talked much about the events which led up to your bringing the case in to the FBI building here. But you did mention the name of one man – Destrier, correct?"

Tim became quiet.

"Mr. Runn, is that the man's name?" she said.

"Yes, it is." He replied.

"And what is his involvement in this- escapade?"

"When I found the case, I took it from Agent Williams who was dying. When Destrier heard about it, he took one of my friends and held him for ransom so we would return the case to him." Tim said.

"Did you ever find Destrier?" Nimmons asked.

"He led us to him. We came to pick up our friend and he collected my friends and me. It's only by a miraculous chance that we found a means of escape." He said.

Her brow furrowed. "What do you mean?"

"Someone was already there – a private investigator. He saw what happened and offered a chance for my friends and I to escape. We slipped out pretty quietly."

"Do you know anything about this man who helped you to escape?"

Tim shook his head. "Not much. He went by the name 'Adam' and had a partner he worked with. Medium height. I didn't notice any accent."

"And his methods of working?"

"Pardon me?"

"Some people might choose to use explosives and run for the nearest exit. Others might try for stealth. Some might rely on technology or blackouts. Every person running some kind of operation like this has their particular method or methods that they may fall back onto."

"Adam slipped us into a laundry cart, covered us with stinking laundry bags and rolled us out to the back where a van was waiting already. Why does this matter? Do you know something about this guy?" Tim said.

"Can you tell me anything else?" Nimmons asked.

"He had someone who was working with him. Another man. He was pretty small, didn't speak much. Adam had him in the control room while we were on the floor. Even when we were in the van, however, he hardly spoke. I wondered whether he even spoke English."

"You have no idea who this second man is?" She asked.

"No, I don't. Adam didn't tell us who the man was, so I figured it wouldn't be appropriate to ask." Tim said.

The woman nodded. Tim watched as she stood by the door.

"I'll ask again about Destrier, only because I think it may be important. Is there anything else you can tell me about him?"

"Not off the top of my head." Tim said but hesitated. "I think he's an anarchist. He wants to collapse the worlds' economies."

"Collapse them?"

"Yes." He said. "He was talking to me and said something about causing the economies to collapse."

She studied him for a moment. "Mr. Runn, how have you managed it?"

"Hm?"

"How have you managed getting through all of this?"

He shrugged. "Faith, I suppose. My parents raised me in the faith, and I've always held on."

"God stands with those who seem to be alone." She said.

Tim looked up to the woman who was now smiling down at him. Now he saw a friend looking down at him. He smiled as well. She turned to leave the room. As he sat, Tim tried to think through all that had happened to him in the past few days. He put his head in his hands and began to pray.

Chapter 39

"What were we thinking?" Dean asked the air as they sat in the van. It had been three hours since Tim had entered the building and he had not emerged. After the first half-hour Gemma had insisted that she go in but they all said no, wait it out. Now it had been three hours and they were still waiting it out.

"I'm going in." Gemma said. "That's it. I'm going in, no questions about it and no one's going to stop me." No one stopped her, but she didn't go in either.

"Didn't you say you work here?" Angelo said.

"Yeah, that's what she said." Mike said.

"So, why isn't she going in to vouch for Tim?" Angelo said.

"Because if I go in there now, they'll be sure that I'm involved with the death of Agent Williams." She said.

"In any case," Adam said, speaking up for the first time in nearly an hour, "we can't stay in this spot much longer." They had been moving their van about the city, trying to stay near the building, but attempting to remain inconspicuous, which was difficult to do for a van with a driver who didn't come out from his vehicle.

"If we want to keep from getting caught we're going to have to move again." He said, shifting the van into gear.

He pulled away from their spot which was parallel to the street on the far side from the FBI building at one of the back parts of the building. They hoped that Tim would be clever enough to, if he got out, walk around the back of the building. Pulling away, Adam drove out and around the block and out past another block or two.

"I hate to say it, kids, but if we're going to come back, it will have to be in a different mode and in a less conspicuous manner." Adam said. "Our big, white van doesn't exactly whisper anything. Every minute we spend here is advertising ourselves for them to check us out and ask why someone is spending three hours staking out the FBI headquarters."

"Where do you suggest we spend our time, then?" asked Gemma.

"Somewhere," said Angelo, "where we can regroup."

Adam pointed at the gas station attendant. "I like the sound of that. This van is getting too small. Let's find a place to stretch out and talk."

It occurred to them that a restaurant might serve as a place where they could talk. There they could also get some food, as was pointed out by Dean and Angelo, and was not argued by any of the others. Throughout the entire conversation, Lorenzo stayed quiet. Though they had decided on the type of place they wanted to stop at, they could agree on little else. They all could not agree on what kind of food to stop for. Eventually, Adam said that he had to stop for gas, so he did so and the others climbed out of the vehicle.

"Don't wander too far," Adam said, turning in his seat. "This escapade isn't over yet." Nods and shrugs were the only response he received.

Adam hopped out and shut his door with a surprising amount of energy. Dean shook his head.

"I don't know how he does it. How does he get through a day like this with so much energy?"

"He doesn't talk so much." Angelo said. "That's got to be the equivalent of a 40 MPG vehicle while we're chattering away at 28 MPG."

Gemma turned to him. "Angelo that has to be one of the strangest human-to-vehicle metaphors I've ever heard."

Dean was distracted with his own thoughts. They could hear Adam just outside their van as he pumped the gas into the vehicle. The afternoon was relatively quiet, the sound of car sirens was quiet at the moment and traffic was slow for the time being. The crisscrossing byways bustled with traffic as cars worked their way up and down the highways of Washington D.C.

Dean spoke up first about the topic which was on all their minds. "What are we going to do about Tim?"

"That is the question, isn't it?" said Gemma.

"Isn't there a way to get him out?" said Angelo. "Aren't you an agent?" he said to Gemma.

"Yes." She said hesitantly.

"Well can't you just go and get him out?" Angelo said.

"It's not that simple. There are agents who rank higher than I do. And he's now in the custody of the federal government. If they're going to release him they've got to decide either that they're done with him, or that he's been pardoned, if they think he's guilty." Gemma said.

Dean said "And if they do think he's guilty, how long do you think he'll be in there?"

"The real question is how are we going to get him out of there?" said Gemma.

Mike spoke up. "It's going to take getting inside the building."

"And once we're inside the building we're going to have to find out where in the building he is." Angelo said. He turned to Gemma. "Do you have any idea where that will be?"

"Of course I do. But I can't just waltz in there and ask for someone being detained to be released. There's a process for everything."

"We'll have to find some kind of cover." Mike said. "If someone other than Gemma is going in we can't just waltz in there without some kind of cover. I don't think I should be going in there, since I was a hired gun, they'll pick up my face and have me on the floor before I make it to the lobby."

"That leaves Dean, Angelo, Adam, and his friend." Gemma said.

"Lorenzo." The man said.

"I'll go." Said Dean. "And let's take Adam with us. I feel like we could use his smarts in the building."

"Thank you sir." Said Adam, who had long since got back into the car and pulled away from the gas station.

Dean spoke again. "That leaves Angelo, Mike and your friend to be ready for us when we come out."

"All right." Said Angelo.

The van remained relatively quiet for about ten minutes until Adam spoke up as he piloted the vehicle.

"It looks like we might have trouble."

"How so?" said Dean.

"We've got someone tailing us. I don't know why. It might be your friends from the bay area, but I've got no idea how they found us so quickly." Adam said.

"Just when you think you're having a good day." Mike said.

"If we don't lose them," Angelo said, "I'm going to guess they'll end up shooting at us."

Adam nodded. "It's likely enough."

"So," said Dean, "what are we going to do about it?"

278

Horns blared as Adam jerked the wheel to the left and darted into the next lane. He slowed the van right in front another car, leaving no room for the tailing vehicle, forcing it to come up alongside them on their right side. As it did so, Adam and Lorenzo saw the driver and passenger of the next vehicle clearly – men in suits, crew cuts, sunglasses on a day which was not excessively bright.

As he looked, Lorenzo saw the passenger bring his arm down over the driver of the next vehicle.

"Get down!" He shouted.

Adam hit the gas and bent over as all the passengers in the back of the van bent over as a gunshot pierced the afternoon. The van roared forwards, pushing the car ahead of them forward and out of the way as a bullet thudded into their vehicle's side. Mike turned to Gemma.

"Don't you have your gun with you?"

"They took it, remember?" She said.

"That's right, they did."

The van swerved around another car and sped forward as the pursuing vehicle tailed just behind them. It was a mad race simply to get out of the way, or to get caught up with the other vehicle. Tim tried not to imagine what would happen if they got caught. The newly-named Lorenzo leaned out through his window and, seeing the pursing car ducked back in again.

"It might be helpful," he said, "if we had something to fend them off with."

A collective 'Oh!' sounded through the room.

"What about a positive attitude?" said Angelo.

Those in the back of the van looked at him with blank stares and grimaces. Angelo shrugged. "It never hurts."

"He's right though." Gemma said. The rest of the group stared at her.

"It is the end times." Dean muttered.

"We've got to find something with which we can fend them off." A nervous chuckle ran through the vehicle. "Check the van. See if you've got anything you can use to target them. Remember, we don't want to cause a pile-up, we just want to slow them down enough for us to get away."

Keeping down, the crew began searching around the back of the van for anything that might be useful. The one obvious thing that came to mind was the bin and the laundry bags within.

"But let's leave that." Gemma said. "If we use it right, we might not have to use it more than once."

The van was built with a sliding side door and two doors on the back which swung open opposing each other. As they scrounged around the van, they discovered that there wasn't much to be done except to hang on for the ride.

Adam, in the meantime, was spending his time weaving in and out of traffic. He had a delicate balancing act to engage in – keeping their own vehicle from colliding with any other vehicles and keeping it far enough away from the pursuing vehicle that they wouldn't get shot or rammed into.

At the moment, he was on the second end of the spectrum, with the pursuing vehicle right on their tail.

"Hey Gemma," he said, "if you guys have any crazy, fun ideas for getting this guy off of my tail, it would be much appreciated."

Gemma got to the front of the car and looked out of the front of the windshield. She grinned. "I've got an idea." She turned to Adam. "Get over into the left lane."

"The left lane? Why would I need to-"

"Just do it. And try to keep them on your right flank or behind you if you can."

Adam pulled the van around another vehicle and looked up to Gemma for just a moment. "Would you like sunny weather with that, or does it matter?"

"On your right flank." She said. Gemma worked her way to the back with the others and looked at them. "All right," she said. "here's the plan."

She explained it to them in a fifty-words-or-less manner. "Does that make sense?" A glance around the group showed that there were no lingering doubts or nagging questions. "Then let's get going." Gemma and Angelo began to empty the cart of its bags of laundry, piling them by the door. Every once in a while, a gunshot would echo through the city. The group would keep low and keep working.

"All right," Dean told her after moving the cart, "we're ready."

"All right Adam," Gemma said, "we're all set."

"That's great that you've got your little party set up back there. It's not like I've been skirting death or anything. But y'know, you live some, you lose some."

"Are you done talking or are we going to do this?" she said.

"Whenever you're ready." He replied.

Adam looked out his window. "They're behind us now. Would you like fries with that?"

Gemma moved to the back of the vehicle, and waited.

"Here he comes... there he is." Adam said.

Gemma and Angelo pulled the side door open and found a black car running alongside them. One by one, Gemma and Angelo began to throw the full, old laundry bags onto the car. As the first one landed, the occupants of the other vehicle shouted. Keeping an eye on the driver, Gemma saw him gesturing to the man in the passenger seat. The driver backed off on the gas a bit. Angelo took advantage of this moment to throw one of the bags onto the front windshield. The driver, who wasn't looking at the windshield at that moment, swerved and nearly rammed into a car in the lane to his right.

"Get ready," Gemma called to Dean, "I think this one will do it."

The driver was already slowing his pace. Having the laundry bag slide off onto the road at his right side, the driver pulled up alongside the van again. Angelo hefted up a third bag to throw it and was met with the sound of a gunshot. Gemma dropped to the floor of the van, as did Angelo. As the van swerved around a corner, he felt himself sliding and would have nearly slid out the door if he hadn't caught ahold of the passenger seat. As he came to a stop within the vehicle, he looked down, through the door's opening, to the rolling pavement beneath them. He pulled himself into the protection of the van and waited through the barrage of bullets.

It did not last long. Either the gunman had to reload or the driver had to get back to driving and insisted that he couldn't do that with the gunman's arm across his own arms. At the moment when he felt it was safe, Angelo, in one smooth movement, hefted up the bag and slung it out and against the pursuing vehicle. The laundry bag slammed against the driver's door and the car went careening into the next lane on the right before the driver hit the brakes.

"All right, here he comes." Gemma said.

Mike and Dean were watching from the open back doors of the van as the pursing car careened around them and into the lane behind them. At the moment it settled into the lane, they gave the laundry cart a push and it went rolling out towards the door. That stage hardly lasted, however, for it quickly hit the bumpers then tumbled out of the car.

One side of the cart fell down against the ground. The car's nose quickly ran into the bin of the cart, driving the bars of the cart into the road and throwing sparks everywhere.

The material on the car, though industry-standard, was not made to withstand being exposed to constant sparks. After a few moments, the pursuers had regular flames going under their vehicle.

"Adam, we'd better get going." Mike said.

"You've got it."

Adam hit the gas and their vehicle flew forward on the highway. The men in the car behind them were jumping out of their stopped vehicle. The man in the driver's seat was running across lanes of traffic away from the flaming vehicle. The second man leapt out from the vehicle and was nearly hit by an oncoming car. He ran past two lanes of traffic to get to the side of the road.

"Who was that, then?" Asked Dean.

"Those were more of Destrier's men trying to get us back and get the case or to get more information about the case and where it is." Said Gemma.

Mike said "If they're smart they'll think twice before coming at us again." A few people laughed and applauded his comment.

"No," Adam said, "if they're smart they'll come at us right away."

The group became quiet. "If they're smart they'll try to catch us while we're on the run, away from home, with no weapons, no friends, no resources, and while we have no better means of keeping them off than some old laundry bags. When we're in this position they have almost every advantage."

"So," said Dean, "what are we going to do about that situation?"

Gemma turned and looked at the others in the vehicle, realizing that they were waiting for an answer from her. Without Tim there, they were waiting for someone to step up and take the lead. She sighed.

"Let's get to a place where we can stop and think for a little while before we move on."

Chapter 40

It was hardly two o'clock when they all sat down at another fast-food restaurant for a break. Some of them were already getting hungry again and ordering more food. The place was hardly crowded except for a few mothers who decided to meet there with their young children in the play area. This was built off at one side in a glassed-off room holding a few small tables. The room itself, save the play equipment, was claustrophobic, however, and the mothers preferred to stay out-side of it. Every once in a while a small child or two would come out to voice a complaint or ask about when they would leave. The child would be reassured in some cases, chastised in others, by the mother before being sent back into the play area.

Gemma was sipping on coffee while Mike worked on a burger. Angelo had a small fry. Lorenzo abstained, Adam took a small fry, and Dean didn't order anything. They sat quietly for a little while as each of them ate, thinking about the mission, if it was a mission. They sat and talked for a while about nothing important, and they talked about more important things. The subjects ranged from politics to media and television to favorite books and movies.

They sat and talked they got no closer to solving their problem. What would they do to help Tim in his plight? He was trapped in the FBI headquarters and they were the only ones who could help him. Willing as they were, they were unsure about what to do next.

"The only way this is going to work." Adam said. "Is if someone goes into the building."

"Right." Said Mike. "We need an inside man." He glanced at Gemma. "Or woman."

Gemma sighed. "All right." She said. "Supposing I do go in there, exactly how would we pull this off?"

Adam cocked his head a little. "What do you know about the organization, about the building that we don't?"

She shrugged. "I could tell you where things are and I could guide you around inside, once we're in. But getting into the detention center is going to be tricky. There'll be guards."

"Aren't there always guards?" said Adam.

"Well-trained guards." She said. "These guys don't just fall over when you jumpscare them. They practically expect something to go wrong on a regular basis."

Dean's eyebrows went up. "Do things go wrong on a regular basis?"

"No, but they have to be that ready."

"All right," Mike said, "tough guards. What else will we have to deal with?"

"Security. Getting in and out of the building. If I come into the building with someone other than myself I'll have to have a good explanation to them for what you're doing there. And you'll have to have identification." She said.

They considered this and continued to discuss their various options. Many ideas were slapped down, despite rebuff. During the course of their conversation, Adam kept an eye on the television sitting in the room. As they spoke at one point, Dean and Mike were heartily into one debate when he stopped them.

"I think it would be a good time for us to get moving."

"Why is that?" Said Angelo.

All of the group looked to Adam for an explanation. He glanced to the television as an explanation.

A report of a federal investigation underway was being played as a special report. Apparently there was 'no cause for alarm' but the federal government was searching for a group of people responsible for aiding one Timothy Runn who was in custody of the federal government. What he was responsible for was not yet known, but it was vital that people let the federal government know if they had seen anyone from this group of renegades.

A picture of each of them came up on the screen, likely pulled from employee records. The only one for Mike was a surveillance footage from one of the gas stations they had been at during the past week. The group sat and stared for a moment before quickly rising and clearing their table of all their trash and food they had purchased.

"Don't leave any receipts behind." Adam said.

After making sure that each one had their own food and no one had left anything behind, they quickly left the building and pulled away, hoping that the staff hadn't noticed a group which matched the call on national television for six fugitives sitting in their restaurant.

———————————

"We should ditch this vehicle." Gemma said.

"Why is that?" said Mike.

"Destrier's men could be looking for it." Adam replied.

"And the federal government," said Gemma, "could know about it after we split from any location with access to cameras."

Dean spoke. "So we'll have to dump this car and move around by public transportation, unless anyone else knows of a car lot where we can get another car for a steal, and get it quickly."

Angelo turned to Dean. "Sprechenze English?"

Dean looked at him. "Huh?"

"What did you say?"

"I said we've got to get a new car."

Mike laughed. "For all the words that came out of your mouth, you could have fooled me."

Dean lifted his hands. "What? Haven't you guys learned anything about our language as well?"

"Yeah," Angelo said, "and I could have said the same thing in half the time."

"Everybody has a gripe." Dean groaned. "By the way," he said to Angelo, "how long did it take you to learn?"

Angelo's brow furrowed. "How long did it take me to learn what?"

Dean gestured. "Y'know. How long did it take to learn…" Everyone in the van was looking at them, so there was no way of escaping the conversation now. He sighed and committed to the conversation. "… to learn English."

"English?" Angelo laughed. Everyone else in the car laughed as well. Dean stood and chuckled a little.

"I thought- y'know, with the foreign name, you might be from another country or something."

"I see, I see." Said Angelo. "So." He said, and he suddenly had a thick, put-on accent. "You thought that you come to me and tell me that you knew who I was. You were sure of yourself, that I came from the homeland, and not from this America. In fact, you were so sure that you were ready to risk embarrassment in front of all your friends here. Well, Signor, I am here to tell you that you are gravely mistaken. I am, in fact, am American.

"So, Signora, Signors, what is to be the form of his punishment? For there should be some kind of punishment, for this disgrace no?"

The others were in hysterics at this point, and Dean himself was laughing.

"Dean. Do you want to know why you do not have friendship? Why you don't have more money? Why you don't have more fans? It is because you don't ask with respect." Angelo's impression was not a good one in particular, but the rest were willing to forgive him on that point.

After the laughter had settled down, quiet descended over the group as they began to think through what would come next for them. Now they were on the run with no one to turn to.

"We are going to have to get this started without them knowing we're in the building." Dean said. "If they catch us, I don't think they're going to give us 5-10 years."

"Who knows what they're likely to do?" said Mike.

"They'll lock you away in a little cell somewhere until they decide what to do with you." Said Gemma. "That's until the hearing. The hearing itself could take weeks. Once they sentence you it could be years. If they suspect that you've been preparing for an act of terrorism, the maximum penalty you can receive is a life sentence."

"But this isn't anything like terrorism." Mike said. "That was us trying to return a briefcase with unknown contents to FBI headquarters."

Gemma looked at Mike who hesitated with words on his lips.

"And they have no way to be assured that whatever is in the case is not a bomb or weapon of some kind." She said.

"Point taken."

They drove for another half-hour or so, talking about what must have happened to Tim inside the FBI building. Through all that had happened so far, they hadn't actually discussed what they thought might have happened to Tim to keep him from coming out to them again.

"It's clear that the FBI must have thought that the case was his." Gemma said. "Or they kept him for questioning."

"The question is," said Lorenzo from the front, "what will they do if they get all of us?"

"Sentence us all to prison." Said Adam.

"Let's try to focus on the positives." Said Dean. "Like I'm positive we've been driving around in circles for the last fifteen minutes."

"I've been trying to find it…Aha! Here we are."

Adam pulled into a small lot with some worn-out looking vehicles, most of them dating within the last forty years. As they pulled in, they saw the cars lined up along the lot, some of which Dean swore were older than the building.

The place was put together poorly. A flimsy chain link fence ran around the place, as if anyone would want to come and steal these cars. The lot, save the cars was empty, except for a single trailer sitting by itself in the back corner, like a rat in a cage. The crew piled out of the car. Gemma sidled up to Adam.

"Are you sure you can afford this stuff? It looks pretty suave to me."

Adam ignored her comment.

The group began to meander about the lot, looking at the different cars, seeing what was available. For the most part, if it was a mid-range car manufactured before 1990, there was a fair chance of seeing it on this small lot. Adam kept an eye on a good, tall van with passenger seats all the way back.

At that moment the door to the trailer in the back opened, which did not disturb them, but the voice from the back of the lot did.

"Well, well, well good afternoon ladies and gentlemen, or should I say Gentlemen and Lady?"

The man was short, not much above five feet tall, had medium length blond hair which he used an excessive amount of styling products on to pull it back. His taste in fashion was nothing to mention. The man's stride was quick and everything about the man was definite. This man did not hesitate in much of anything.

"My name is Barnes, Reginald Barnes, but you can call me Reg. Are you all just visiting our wonderful state of Washington?"

"Yes we are." Adam said, taking the man's fast talk in stride.

"And are you all looking to visit any historic sites during your stay? There are quite a few."

"Not today, we're just looking at the different cars you have here, if that's all right."

Reginald gestured to the vehicles. "By all means, take your time. Let me know if you have any questions."

"I do have one before you leave." He said. "How much does this van run for?"

"This one is a 1975 Chevrolet G20 Beauville Extended van. May I?" He said.

Adam indicated for the salesman to proceed. The man circled around the vehicle and opened up the driver's door. As he began to explain the features, the others gathered around and looked over the vehicle as well. He showed Adam everything the van had to offer, and must have been hoping hard to make a sale, for it seemed as though he ran out of subject matter and he was back at the front of the vehicle.

Still, Adam hardly said a word about it. He had been shown the back swinging doors, as if those were a new feature, the side doors which opened opposite to each other. Adam stepped around the vehicle and looked at it for himself.

"I don't know what you think of it." Said Reginald, drops of sweat coming off his forehead. "But I'm sure you'd love it if you wanted to take it for a test run. 'Only the best at Barnes', that's what they say."

"Is it?" said Adam.

"Yes sir." Said Reginald.

"And you clean the inside of the vehicles, you said?"

"That's right, we clean them up when we get them."

Dean nudged Gemma and shook his head. "Adam's got this guy eating out of the palm of his hand. I've hardly seen anything like it."

Gemma shook her head. "Being loud doesn't usually mean much. It's that old saying 'His bark is worse than his bite.' This guy must have had a hard time getting heard. He grows up and finds that it helps to be louder than everyone else around him. So instead of developing strong character, he gets louder. It's like a light show, it gets people's attention"

The others looked at her. She shrugged. "I'm not saying he's not a good guy. I'm saying there might not be substance under all that chattter."

"All right," said Adam, "I think this one will do nicely. How much will this one run for?"

"Well," Said Barnes, "why don't we step back into my office and talk it through?"

Adam stepped away with the salesman and they headed back to the small trailer. Dean was sure the man's bed was in that trailer as well. Adam stepped to the trailer, keeping up a conversation with the salesman.

Mike had wandered over to a few old sporty-looking cars and was gazing lovingly at them.

"He'll have to use a different name." Gemma said.

"And he can't use a credit card." Said Angelo, who had remained quiet until this point. He stepped closer to the group and looked around at them as they spoke. "He picked the van?"

"Yeah." Said Gemma indicating the '75 Beauville on the lot. "Unless he pulls something tricky in negotiations and is looking at a vehicle that we haven't noticed or considered yet."

This comment pulled a few glances around the lot, searching for a vehicle which might be the one that Adam may be secretly gunning for rather than the Beauville. But whether they could decide on what it was or agree, there was simply no way to know. They would have to wait until he showed up with the license in hand, having made the purchase - or walked out of the deal with the Beauville or without a car.

They spent some time exploring the lot and trying to look inconspicuous. There were a few families in the lot looking at vehicles as well. One of them was a couple with a few small children. The mother and father in getting on in years, the father's hair starting to show a few wisps of grey. The mother appeared anxious, but after watching them for a little while, Dean concluded that this was were normal mode of operation. The children were young, one was about eight, the other around five years old, both girls.

The other family consisted of a father and son duo, and it was apparently the big day for the son. Dean guessed he was, probably seventeen. The kid was looking at hot rods, and the dad was trying to point his attention to station wagons and mini-vans. As he walked, the dad kept wiping his hands on his pants, as if he had handled a dead fish and wanted to get fish guts off of his hands to dry them. The young man would stand over a mustang, gazing at the interior, and the dad would come up, motioning at another vehicle. The kid would vaguely shake his head. The father would insist, and the kid would sigh and roll his eyes before tramping after his father to look at a more moderate vehicle.

Dean looked out to the road at the cars passing and saw the flow of traffic passing by small car lot they were now inhabiting and thought of the FBI investigators who were now chasing after them.

Chapter 41

Inside Barnes' trailer, he and Adam were talking through the paperwork about the two vehicles.

"Now Stephen," Barnes was saying, "with the trade-in, you will save a bit on the price of your vehicle, but…"

"Come on now Mr. Barnes, we both know that your van's price has been bumped up, and mine is more than enough to cover the worth of that van twice." Adam said.

"That's not quite true." said Barnes. "We stick with the industry standard for the prices of all-"

"Oh don't give me that nonsense about the industry standard, we both know that you'll jack up the prices." Said Adam.

"-all of our vehicles on the lot at all of their different price points." Finished Barnes.

Adam sighed. "Well how much will I get for turning in the first vehicle?"

Barnes dug through some papers, looked at some, took a bit of time, scribbled on a notepad, and passed a note to Adam, who raised his eyebrows.

"Good news Orville," he muttered to himself, "looks like we won't have to sell the farm after all."

After some more discussion, and some thought of bartering on Adam's part, and some haggling, they finally settled on a price which was more to Adam's liking. It was certainly less to Barnes' liking, but he ended up settling, whether in respect to Adam's persistence, or for the trade-in, it couldn't be said.

Adam, however, was getting anxious to move, and he was sure that the others would be feeling the same way when he finally showed his face. When he finally emerged from the dealer's office, he found his friends waiting anxiously.

"What have you been doing?" asked Gemma when he was close enough to speak quietly. "I thought you said you were going to buy a car, not tell him your life story."

"I did buy us a car." Adam said. "But I had to get him to come down on the price. That takes time."

"Time which we don't have." She said.

"We all have time." He said. "We just have to decide how we're going to use it."

'No," she said. "we have an insane anarchist and the federal government after us. We're a small desperate band of renegades trying to break into one of the most secure buildings in the world."

"Well, I'm only using my life savings to rescue this friend of yours from the federal government after having already rescued him from this radical anarchist. At least we're on the same page." Adam said.

Barnes' walked to the '75 Beauville to get it ready for them.

"Come on guys," Adam said, "let's get our stuff out of the old van."

It took them a good ten minutes to be sure that they had everything out of the old vehicle to get everything that they had left. They wanted to leave the vehicle clean for the next owners.

Once they had everything out, it was a matter of a handshake, thanking Mr. Barnes, who gave them the key to the new vehicle. Their new vehicle was older than their first vehicle, but no one complained in the parking lot. They piled into the van and got settled in their seats.

"Now Mr. Reginald Barnes has assured me that this machine will work." said Adam. "And that if there is any trouble we are to bring to him and he will fix it himself."

"That's generous." Said Mike.

"I don't care either way, as long as this car runs. Let's get out of here and back on the road." Said Gemma.

Adam put the key into the ignition and turned it. The engine turned over and started beautifully. The crew breathed a collective sigh. It occurred to Adam that test-driving the van before buying it would have been a good idea.

Pulling out of the parking lot, he glanced both ways and across the road for anything out of the ordinary. Seeing nothing, he pulled out and onto the road.

"Gemma, could you keep an eye out the back, just in case someone tries to tail us? I wonder whether anyone found us while we were waiting at the car park there."

She shook her head. "It's possible. I don't know though. With Destrier tailing us, and the first car after us, I can't imagine that a second car is far behind. And with the federal government after us, I imagine that they have people everywhere."

Gemma looked out her window at the cross streets as they passed. She felt on edge, but there was little way to prepare except to keep watch. The suede interior of the vehicle annoyed her, but she could do nothing about that, especially since she hadn't purchased the car, it belonged to Adam. If she was going to be sure about what was happening and her 'gut feeling', an uneasiness that she couldn't explain, only made her unsure about her sense which she could be sure of, then it would be best to leave the feelings out of the picture entirely.

What does your gut tell you?

Chapter 42

The memory sprang from the past. The man's voice echoed through the hall where the trainees stood at the teachers insistence. He said that you can't teach a self-awareness class for agents if they're not on their feet.

"What does your gut tell you?" He said

Several students shrugged. It was safe, they said. Nothing was in the room, no sound came from the halls.

"Good," he said. "Now-"

He pulled out his gun and leveled it at one of the students.

Two of the students jumped in front of her, one dropped to the ground, and many shouted, in nearly perfect unison

"Put the gun down."

"Aha, so your guts are working just fine." He said, turning the gun about the room so it pointed at various people.

"Well that's all right then. It will serve you well."

With that. He flipped the gun in the air and caught it again, then knocked it against the table.

"It's a prop," he said, "borrowed from the local college's theater department. I wanted to make a point, but no matter how much I scared you, there's no sense in putting anyone in harm's way. Now," he said, "what is this?" he asked, waving the gun around his head.

"A gun."

"A weapon."

"Evil."

"The enemy."

He shook his head. "You all are trained agents. Think objectively."

There was silence for a full minute where no one spoke up. Then a voice from the back spoke.

"An...idea?"

The teacher gestured in the direction of the voice. "Who said that?" The people split like the red sea to reveal a young woman, well built, in her late twenties. "Why do you say that?" he asked.

"It can't do anything on its own. Not unless someone is behind it."

He pointed his finger at her. "Bingo." He said. "Inanimate objects will remain inanimate unless set into motion by an outside force."

The class laughed, but he looked at them seriously and they quieted. "People will apply attributes to objects all day long to control them, to get them banned, to promote their own ideas. But a person's character will be a consistent signifier of their actions."

"How did we get on gun control?"

"We began with talk about trusting your gut and that's what we'll end with today. Good work today people." The teacher watched as the students filed out, all but one, the young woman who had answered his question.

"So you run your class by having us all jump on each other?"

"No, I do it by having you follow orders. Go ahead to your next assignment."

Gemma was seated in the Beauville '75 as her mind wandered back to the present. To initiate the new vehicle, the men were trying their best impressions of 70s impressions and songs. Ain't No Mountain High Enough assaulted her ears at the moment. She stayed quiet as they found a way to induct the vehicle into their crew.

Of course to her ears some of the noise was terrible, and some of the others said so, especially when the high notes were too high. But they kept singing and enjoying themselves.

Gemma considered what they would have to do next. The attack worried her. Switching cars didn't mean that they wouldn't be found even though it did lessen their chances of being spotted by an enemy. Considering their desperate situation they weren't doing too badly – most of them were together, no one was injured, all of them were alive and they had a general idea of what they had to get done.

"So," she said when their next terrible rendition was over, "where will we be crashing for the night?"

"I thought we could crash at a hotel." Adam said.

Gemma glanced around the car to see what the others were thinking. They were quiet, but didn't offer any protest to the idea. She shook her head.

"No, that's not a good idea."

"Well, unless you can pull a safe house of your back pocket we don't have a lot of options." Said Adam.

"But if we check into a hotel, we've just set up a beacon for anyone to track us down." Said Gemma.

"It's not nearly that obvious." Said Adam.

"Really?"

"Really. I've been on several cases where I've checked into a hotel with no trouble of being tracked or spotted."

"And on how many of those visits were you being hunted by the FBI?"

Adam sighed and shook his head. "Again, unless you have any other ideas we're going to have to settle somewhere."

Dean spoke up at this point. "I do have a cousin who has a place where we might be able to crash."

Everyone turned to look at him.

"Why didn't you say something before?" asked Mike. "Do they have enough space for all of us?"

"Oh yeah." Said Dean. "Plenty of room."

Everyone looked at Adam who shrugged. "Sounds good to me. What's the catch?"

"Catch, what catch? She's got plenty of room and would be happy to have company." Dean said.

"Where is it?" Adam asked.

"California."

Mike laughed, Lorenzo just shook his head, others laughed and groaned or rolled their eyes at the joke.

Chapter 43

It was getting late in the afternoon when they pulled up to a hotel. They all piled out.

"All right." Said Adam. "Stretch your legs, but keep it quiet and stay outside. I'm going to check things out and check us in. We'll use three rooms. Mike, do you want to tag along?"

The large man made no sign other than to raise his hands, as if in protest, before following Adam into the hotel.

It was a good mid-level work, keeping families and business travelers comfortable, while those who were used to extravagance would be left wanting. A glassed-off room near the front of the lobby allowed the guests to view the pool. This wasn't a good idea in design, Adam thought. As soon as you step into a hotel, you should think about relaxing. When you step into this hotel, you see folk wearing swimsuits that are either too old or too new and are ill-fitting.

The lobby was decorated well, though. The management had clearly decided to stay away from using live plants to decorate, so the few plants in the building were clearly fake. The wooden front to the desk at the front nicely blended with the dark stone top to it. There were pamphlets in a transparent rack at the near corner, resting near the door for visitors to discover and peruse. Unfortunately, whoever picked up these brochures found them in the wrong places. They were all for thrift stores and second-rate diners, nothing to suggest that the hotel was something worthy of recognition. The cheap brochures drew attention to other flaws in the building.

The carpet by the front door lay waiting to get replaced. Scuffs and marks around the lower edges of the walls from shoes, luggage carts and perhaps from heavy luggage showed that management spent no time taking care of cleaning up after the mess. The pens on the counter were chewed on the ends. Marks on the counter from pen scrawls gone astray crossed in miniature trails on the countertop. These and other small signs were like a slow-creeping vine, something beneath the surface of the water, suggesting that the hotel was not what it appeared to be.

Yet the hotel stood as a refuge off of the street for the crew. So Adam stepped to the desk to seek accommodations. A clerk greeted him with a dispassionate smile.

"Hello, and welcome to Turner's Towers, where we'll make up for your stay…" The clerk trailed off at this point and mumbled something else that they couldn't hear and stood there in silence. Taking that as their cue, Adam spoke.

"Yes, we're looking for three rooms."

The man nodded and entered some information into his computer. "For how long?"

"Just overnight."

Adam provided the rest of his information and it came time to pay. He pulled out some cash. At this point he saw Gemma standing casually by the glass doors. She was subtly beckoning him with both of her hands over her head.

"Sir?"

Adam looked at the clerk. "Yeah, all right." He went back to counting the cash. Gemma's beckoning from the front door continued. He groaned and handed the cash to Dean.

"Can you finish this up?"

Dean looked to the clerk, down to the cash, then back up to Adam's face.

"What was the question?"

"Just finish paying."

"Oh, right, I can do that."

Adam nodded and turned for the door. Stepped outside he found Gemma waiting for him, standing near the entrance of the building. As he stepped out of the building, she silently strode toward the van. He dubiously followed behind her.

"What's going on?" he asked her. She wouldn't respond. He shook his head and followed her to the van.

When he arrived, he found the other three men sitting in their seats and avoiding eye contact with her. Standing at the door of the van, she gestured at them as he stood.

"Talk to them." She said.

"What am I supposed to talk about, the weather?"

Gemma turned to them. "Is no one going to say it?"

"This is your fight." Angelo said. "If you want to get riled up about it, you can but I think you're fighting an uphill battle."

"Anyone else?" she said.

The others were quiet. Gemma turned to Adam

"We need to take the next step." She said.

"We are taking the next step, we've found shelter-"

"You know what I'm talking about; we've got to get Tim out of FBI custody."

"We'll work on that. But we can't work on that if we're on the streets." He said.

"So that's it? We sit around and wait?"

"No," said Adam, "we wait and figure out what the next step is."

Gemma opened her mouth and closed it before opening and closing it once more and striding away to the hotel. Adam shrugged and looked back to the others in the van. Lorenzo spoke up.

"Dean is checking us in. We'll have three rooms; Gemma in one, Lorenzo and I in another, Dean, Mike and Angelo in the third."

They nodded and began to climb out of the vehicle. Its age meant there was no key FOB, so he had to manually lock the doors with the key, or lock them before he closed them, as he did with the passenger doors. Since they had no personal belongings there was nothing else to do but follow the others into the hotel. He followed them and stepped into the hotel.

Dean had finished with paying for the rooms. He handed out keys which appeared to be at least thirty years old.

"We're in the same hall." He said. "I don't know how you want to split us all up." He said.

"We've been given room assignments." Gemma said. She took one of the key cards. The clerk had written the room numbers on the envelopes which the key cards came in. Adam took another key card.

"You'll be with your buddies." He said and passed by on the way to the elevator.

Mike, Lorenzo and Angelo passed him on the way to the elevator and Dean trailed after them. Filing in, they took this to the fourth floor. During the ride, Adam observed the elevator. The mirrored surfaces were smudged in places that weren't easy to clean. The carpet was wearing down. The buttons were also grimy. All of these pointed to a lack of initiative and a bad cleaning staff.

They stepped off of the elevator and out into the hall, looking to locate their rooms. He had given them three rooms, two of them side-by-side, the third across the hall. They called a conference in the third room and talked about what had happened and tried to think about what they would do next. But try as they might, they could think of nothing to do to get Timothy of out the custody of the FBI.

"I don't know." Seemed to be the common response.

"We could try to get in." Angelo said.

"How are we going to do that?" Dean asked.

"I don't know." Angelo repllied. "But they've got a front door. It can't be that hard. You figure something out."

And so the conversation would fall to arguing about getting in, disguises, means of breaking Tim out, and they would talk in circles, but what it all came down to was that they just didn't have the means to get the man out of custody.

After some more talk, they decided that all they could do for the time being was to get some food and spend the night in their current position quietly, trying to keep from attracting attention to themselves. The fight with Destrier's forces had rattled them.

Since Adam and Lorenzo were the only ones left with their smartphones, they did the research for food in the area.

"Now there's no way we should be all be seen outside, especially together." Said Gemma. "So if we go to pick something up, just one or two of us should go."

"What about pizza?" said Angelo.

"That's fine by me." Said Mike.

"No." said Gemma. "It's all carbs and grease, there's nothing else to the meal. Let's find something different."

"You could get a salad with it." Angelo suggested.

"But that's the cover-all for any food sin." Said Gemma. "I don't want a salad. I don't want the pizza, so I'm expected to eat the salad."

Dean rotated his head to look at her from where he was lying on the bed. "What's wrong with salads?"

"Nothing except everything right now." Said Angelo.

Dean nodded at the man's clarifying statement. "Got it."

"I mean, what is it with society, skinny women and salads? Why can't they leave women alone, let us eat what we want, and we'll see that we'll stay away from carbs on our own because news flash we can think for ourselves, we don't need to be indoctrinated. Why is it that every time I turn around, there's some stick figure of a woman pushing salads at me, on the TV, at the store – even at some restaurants!"

Gemma continued talking in this way about the price of gas, about pushy salespeople, and about the price of a new mattress as well. She continued for a solid three minutes before finishing and dropping down into a chair in the corner. There was silence for a moment.

Then Dean began the slow applaud.

"That's right." He said. "You tell 'em. Say what needs to be said. No holds barred."

"Thank you Dean." She said. "But I'm not sure about applauding now. Nothing has been done. We haven't even decided what we're going to eat."

Nate spoke "Deciding what we'll do next about the plan is very different than deciding where we're going to get our food from."

There was quiet for a minute before Dean spoke up again. "What about Chinese?"

Chapter 44

The group ordered from a Chinese restaurant and had it all delivered to Adam's room so that everything would be consolidated. When the waiter-turned-delivery boy arrived from the restaurant there had been a knock at the door.

"Order for Adam."

Adam opened the door and paid the young man.

"You're not having a party in your room are you?"

Adam's eyebrows went up, and he hesitated before he spoke..

"No." he said. "I just have some friends that ordered with me."

"The last time this manager had to clean up after a big party like this there was trouble the next day."

Adam's brow furrowed. "How do you know all this?"

The young man grinned. "I've been delivering food here for several months now. You can usually tell when you've got a single man on a business trip and when he's got some of his friends hiding in the room with him." He held up the two bags of food. "The amount of food here is enough for at least four men, probably more if they eat regular portions of food and don't stuff themselves."

Adam took the food, thanked the young man for his service, and closed the door behind himself. As they ate conversations came up about the food, about next steps, and about what they had been through so far. Some people asked questions about those who had been working with the case from the beginning. They heard of Tim's involvement, as thoroughly as they could for not having been there themselves.

Adam whistled when he heard about Tim's first encounter with the briefcase.

"It takes guts to duck into an alley with a total stranger on the run. But that's hard. That man could have been lying to Tim."

Little boxes sat on the floor beside a few of them, like Angelo who sat by the window, finishing off the last of his fried rice. Now the group sat with bags and boxes scattered across the room. Silence filled the space, creeping in from every corner. They sat and considered their situation, most of them thinking it hopeless, six of them hoping to infiltrate one of the most secure buildings in the country. They knew that somehow they had to find a way inside and get their friend out. All sorts of plans were suggested and strategies put forward.

"What about the classic Trojan horse?" Dean said. "A few of us will bring in a gift or something with someone hiding inside. Then, when everyone has gone home for the evening, the person inside will spring out, rescue Tim and get out of the building."

"Supposing we did this," Gemma said, "what kind of object would they hide in? And how would we get it inside?"

Angelo spoke. "And how would they convince security to let them through with it? The security force at the FBI building would be checking an odd-looking briefcase, how in the world would they not check out a coffin-sized object?"

This and more or less ridiculous plans were put forth by various parties to no avail. Either the plans were no good, or the team couldn't agree, or they simply didn't have the resources available to them. The one thing they could agree on was this: that if they did go in, it would be blind and they would have to make up their plan as they went along.

Gemma knew the building best, so she would be going in. Other than that, there was no definite plan. Eventually the talk died down as each person turned to their own thoughts. After their prolonged discussion, the sun's rays cut a nearly horizontal track across the sky. They shot ninety-three million miles through space, bending through the atmosphere of the earth, where the angle of the surface of the earth at this moment caused the usually white light of this giant gaseous flaming ball to turn red.

Mike, Dean, and Angelo went back to their room as did Gemma. The hall became noisy as people passed by, and quiet again as they settled into their rooms. The sun set and the people grew relatively quiet in their own rooms. As it grew darker outside, all the crew could do was wait until morning. So they began to settle for the night.

Dean and Angelo flipped through the channels arguing about which ones to watch. Mike, however, was restless.

"I'm going to go outside."

Angelo looked over at him. "What?"

"I'm going outside." He said again, gesturing at the door.

"Don't you know how many people are after us?" Said Dean.

"I know and I don't care to hear it right now. I need to get out and stretch my legs."

Angelo looked at Dean.

"It's not a good idea." Said Angelo. "You know how many people are after us, and that they have got more weapons than we do. If you go out there alone there's no way you'll be able to take care of yourself if more than one person comes after you."

"I beg to differ." Mike said. "I'm the only person of this group with any kind of training."

"Except Adam." Said Dean. "He's the private investigator."

"I remember. You do remember that when you found me I was hired as a bounty hunter, right? I track down people on a regular basis, some of them being criminals who may resist with deadly force?"

They shook their heads.

"But," said Dean, "you're not working for a police department, you're working for an individual and whatever company he has set up. That means you aren't under the jurisdiction of the local government. Which means that saying that you're a bounty hunter is a misnomer."

Mike hesitated before he spoke.

"What does it make me, then?"

Angelo looked to Dean and spoke. "Dean, you don't have to do this."

"He's talking about being a bounty hunter. That's at the time when he found us, and not under the government. We knew something was going on."

Mike shrugged. "You want me to tell you again what I told you before – that I worked for Destrier to track you guys down so that I could bring you back to him? It's not the latest news update. News flash – he just imprisoned me along with the rest of you; if I'm not one of you now, I don't know what I am."

The two of them looked at him blankly. He spread his hands. "So that's it? The jury's out?" He waved it off. "Never mind. I'm going to get some fresh air. It's starting to reek in here."

Mike stepped out of the hotel room and strode down the hall at a brisk pace. He flew down the steps. His gait through the lobby had heads turning. His breathing was shallow and quick as he stepped out of the building.

Mike stood on the pavement before the hotel. He tried to slow his thoughts down and catch his breath. Though Dean's accusation came off as harsh it was true – they all knew that when they found him, he was a bounty hunter searching for them so that he could sell them off into Destrier's hands. Harsh. However he looked at it, he was not in a good situation. Going on meant either getting arrested or killed. Going back meant going to a criminal life. He needed a third option.

Mike looked out along the street as he stepped down the pavement. The sun was nearly set and the streetlights were on now. The shadows deepened as the sun's light continued to diminish. Shadows now melded into one with the darkness surrounding them. People passing on the sidewalk dipped in and out of shadows, their hues varying by the degree to which the darkness overshadowed them.

The shadows around the buildings glowered in the dark. A dim light caught Mike's eye. He stopped where he was and looked about before looking again. A car was parked along the sidewalk. Whoever had parked the car had stayed out of the streetlight. This wasn't surprising – no one could plan ahead for everything. But their headlights were off. He wondered what had caught his attention. He checked up and down the street, but no other cars had their headlights on.

Looking again, he saw that this vehicle was a black sedan. He began to walk towards it. As he did so he saw what must have grabbed his attention the first time – someone inside the cab of the car was using a flashlight. That told him a few things. The first was that they were looking to lay low. The second was that this was a professional – not a junkie or renegade prankster. He wished he had a weapon on him. He steadied his breathing and stepped across the street four cars behind where they were placed.

He glanced behind himself to see whether anyone was tailing him. No one was there. Even as he approached he knew it to be a bad idea. He stepped up to the window of the vehicle in question. Knocking on it, he waited for a reply. A raised voice from inside was a reply. The man in the passenger seat held conference with the driver. The passenger rolled the window down. Mike took a breath.

"Luis." He said when he saw the man's face, "and Benny, it's good to see you both. I couldn't help but notice someone was on duty out here, so while I was stretching my legs I thought I should check it out."

The driver, Benny, spoke softly into his radio while the passenger maintained eye contact. Mike drummed his fingers on the hood of the car. "Look, there's no easy way to do this." He said. "My position is difficult to say the least, right? You'd give me that much, wouldn't you?"

There was no response from either of them.

"The point is, I've dug myself in rather deep and I think I need to take a step back from things."

"Take a step back from things?" Benny said. "Take a step back? Where do you think you are that you think you can take a step back from? Do you think that you've had one slip-up with the boss and you can straighten it up if you work real hard? Get in a few hours overtime and you'll solve the problem?

"You've made yourself an enemy of the state."

Mike glanced around. "With the U.S.?"

"No you idiot! With Destrier."

At that moment Mike felt a hand on his shoulder. He tried to whip around, but it was too late. Benny was talking again, but he didn't hear. Cars were pulling up by the door of the hotel. FBI vehicles had arrived. They had come for Mike and his friends. Something struck the back of his head and he didn't remember any more.

Chapter 45

Adam lay on one of the beds, exhausted. He had trained for long days but this was one of his greater challenges. To run around with a bunch of people who were civilians or half-trained agents was beyond his experience, especially as his expertise was in working alone and reporting in once he was finished with his work.

Nate sat on one of the chairs nearby watching television. An episode of the old show "I Love Lucy" was playing. At the moment, Lucy and Ethel were desperately trying to keep up with a conveyer line of chocolates as they came out one end and approached the other. The twosome were supposed to wrap the chocolates as they came along before the got to the other end, but the sweets came too quickly, so the girls began taking the chocolates and stuffing them in their mouths and hats, knowing that if even one stay piece was found they would be ousted.

"What do you think of this bunch?"

Nate turned to Adam, surprise evident on his face. Adam lay on the bed still, but turned himself a little so he could see Lorenzo, who shrugged.

"I don't know. They seem like a pretty nice bunch."

Adam *humphed*. "Nice doesn't get you through a life-or-death situation in one piece. What do you think about their capabilities?"

Nate shrugged. "The lady seems like she has her act together pretty well. The big guy-"

"Mike."

"Yeah, Mike is well-trained. The skinny one and the comic..." said Lorenzo.

"Angelo and Dean."

"They have no idea what they're doing, do they?"

"Well, I've seen worse instincts before." Said Adam. "I'm not saying they're A-quality material, but they haven't gotten themselves killed yet."

"What are we going to tell our customer?"

"The truth."

"And how are they supposed to believe the truth?"

"It's not our job to convince them of the truth. It's our job to tell them what happened." Adam said.

"Or we could drop off the face of the earth," Lorenzo said. "and go in to hiding. See if we can't escape."

"No, we're not running." Said Adam, ignoring Lorenzo's attempt at humor. "The thing is we're stuck in this to see it through."

"No." said Lorenzo." "You can pull out at any time. It might not be easy, but you could do it."

"I don't think so. There's no way I could walk away from this situation and not blame myself afterwards. I know there are other cases for which I blame myself. The Willie Martin case was skewed from the beginning. There's no way we would be walking away from this one without some trouble."

"Shh." Lorenzo said, his face suddenly wrinkled with concern. But the vocalism had little effect on the quickened pace of the private investigator's train of thought.

"Every case we run into there's some kind of trouble that comes out of left field."

"Be quiet."

"Why is it that every time go to follow a lead, there's some thug waiting around the corner, or some hired hand waiting to give me a broken wrist?"

"Maybe it's because they can hear your brain rattling around in your head." That last comment caught Adam off guard. He stared at Lorenzo who looked him in the eyes. Lorenzo held a finger to his lips and mouthed someone outside. Adam glanced to the door and listened. At first it was quiet. If he wasn't determined he would have stopped there but he kept listening. As he did so he heard quiet hurried footsteps in the hall. Looking to Lorenzo, Adam shut the lamp off and rolled out of bed. Lorenzo left the TV on and grabbed his wallet off of the bedside table.

A knock at the door sounded.

"FBI. Open up."

Adam and Lorenzo looked at each other. Was it a ruse? It couldn't be Destrier's men, could it?

A moment later a thud sounded and the door shuddered. Another thud, another shudder. Adam and Lorenzo stood in place, waiting for the arrival of the agents. A third thud and the door flew off its hinges. Agents in black gear flooded into the room like locusts. They were shouting orders. Adam had his hands over his head. He turned and saw Lorenzo was saying something to him through the chaos. Adam saw tactical gear and weapons pointed at him. Not anarchists' gear – they had hand-cuffed him and had him kneeling in place on the floor.

Gemma, Dean, Angelo. The others had to escape if they were going to have a chance of getting Tim out.

As Adam and Lorenzo talked, Gemma sat in her room thinking through all that had happened. She had been trusted with a single task of keeping this case safe. If it hadn't been for this stranger and his friend, there was no way she would have been able to keep it safe or get it back. But now that it was back and her mission was complete it felt as though her soul had been wrenched from within her.

She took a breath and stifled her tears. She climbed off her bed and stepped to the door of her room. Footsteps resounded down the hall. Trained footsteps in boots. They weren't Desterir's men. Grabbing her shoes, she ran to the window and looked out. There was no sign of a fire escape or any other means of descent.

The window itself would have to be pushed out of the frame. She quickly undid the latches and opened the window. Knowing she was on the third floor of the building, a straight jump to the street below would not be feasible. Turning Gemma stripped the bed of its sheets and began to tie them together. She heard a thud from down the hall. Adam and Lorenzo's room. She closed the shutter and locked the door behind her.

Gemma stepped onto the balcony outsider her room overlooking the parking lot. Having tied the sheets together, she quickly improvised a rope and tied it to the balcony railing outside. Throwing the sheet over she took a look down and took a breath. A breeze ruffled her loose hair. She hoisted herself up onto the railing with the tied sheet in one hand. Keeping a firm grip on the rail. Keeping a steady grip on the rail, she clambered over the rail until she stood on the floor with her feet on the wrong side of the guard rail.

"FBI. Open up." When they received no response the door shuddered.

Gemma took another breath and let her weight down. If nothing else, the sheets would allow her to slow her descent. Looking below her, there appeared to be another balcony directly below her own. Having nothing else to aim for, she let herself down with the intention of heading for that balcony.

The thudding continued for a slow moment, prolonged by not knowing what was going on. The thudding stopped. Gemma let herself down, remembering that when she landed she would have to bend her legs as she did so, to flex her body which would help absorb the impact of the fall. As she guided herself down her makeshift ropes, she saw that she would miss the balcony. With a bout of strength, she pulled her legs up and caught the rail of the second story balcony. With a fierce grip on the sheets, she flexed her legs to pull her body up and into the embrace of the balcony.

Landing safely on the second story balcony, Gemma managed a sigh and waited for a moment, listening for the agents on the story above and for anyone occupying the room of the balcony for which she stood on. All was quiet on her own level. She heard the heavy tramp of feet and knew that the agents were in the room upstairs. Pressing herself against the archway, she tried to imagine herself as small as possible. The sheets would be a giveaway, but no one would follow after her, so she might have a minute or two.

On cue, she heard the sliding door open above her. She pressed herself further into the corner and prayed, wishing that she was invisible.

"Sir. You need to see this." A voice, a young man, perhaps in his late twenties, called from the balcony above.

A moment later she heard another voice, a man in late thirties, joined the first one.

"What do we have?"

"Whoever we had seems to have escaped this way." The young voice reported.

"Bed sheets. They may have made it out this way."

Gemma noted that the second voice was more cautious in coming to conclusions. A tied sheet to the rail did not mean that someone had escaped.

"Get someone on the ground." The second voice said. "Tell them the suspect may have tried to get out by means of the window." There was a slight pause. "A drop of that height is likely enough to break your leg."

After that the door closed again and she was left alone in silence.

Craning her neck, she looked up to see that no one was standing on the balcony above her. Looking at the glass door beside her, she saw that the lights were off. Whoever rented the room last, or currently, had left the curtains open. Either the no one rented the room or no one was home at the moment. She stood up and stretched her muscles. Halfway through the agents' conversation her back had begun to cramp from her doubled position in the corner.

Moving quickly to the edge of the balcony, she looked down. The street was still two stories below her. She had to move quickly, though, as anyone could come back at any time, and the agent's order would have someone on the ground level looking for her soon.

She straddled the rail and looked for something to break her fall, such as a tree or an awning. Nothing like that appeared, however. Dropping off the balcony might be an option, providing she hung close enough to the ground. It would have to do. Gemma swung her other leg over the rail and was about to make a move when she heard a noise. For an instant she froze, which was the one thing she knew not to do. Either get out or hide. She decided to get out. If someone saw her, she could say that she was practicing extreme parkour – in the middle of the night. On someone else's hotel balcony.

She worked her way down to the lower part of the balcony and had her legs dangling above the ground. Gemma supported her weight entirely with her arms at this point and was working at getting herself lower without a sudden drop and a twisted or broken ankle.

The door opened fully and a woman stepped into the room, dressed in business casual. She reached for the light switch. The lights came on and the woman stepped slowly in the direction of the window.

Little by little Gemma lowered herself until she gripped the balcony by her fingertips. The woman was at the window now, getting ready to open it. Gemma let go and felt the rush as her body accelerated toward the ground. She landed on her feet and flexed her hands as she began walking. She knew it that to keep moving at this point would be best. The last thing she needed was a crowd of people standing around, asking if she was all right, drawing attention to her.

She considered her options. She thought about going to pick up their new vehicle. If she did that, however, it wouldn't be long before the agency would be onto her and tracking her wherever she went. They could track both the license plate and the vehicle model itself. It would be best to find another vehicle that she could commandeer for the time being.

Walking toward the back of the building, she spotted no sign yet of any FBI agents. A glance over her shoulder told her the same. Pulling a tie out of her pocket, she put her hair into a ponytail and she pulled her sleeves up, despite the cooling weather, making herself look as different as possible from when she was last seen on the streets.

Keeping her eyes open, she looked for a car that she might be able to use. There was a Mustang, which would be nice, but too difficult to hotwire. A few other sedans and vans lined the street, but they were relatively new, and she didn't want to risk setting off a car alarm. She was keeping her eye open for something special.

Body language is important. She kept her head down, hands in her pockets and kept her pace up. No one wants to bother someone in a hurry. Some people passed her on the sidewalk, a few of them bothered to nod or say 'Hello'. Gemma would nod and keep moving.

Eventually she found an adequate car. Looking up and down the sidewalk, she had to wait until the sidewalk was clear of people before she got to work.

Slipping around to the passenger side door, it wasn't long until she got that side open. She always kept a set of tools on her for picking locks in case of emergencies. This car didn't have a particularly good lock and she picked it for that along with other reasons. Slipping into the driver's seat, she bent over and said a double prayer, both hoping that she could remember how to do this and that she wouldn't be spotted and caught before she got away.

After a moment of digging around she found the tools she needed and got to work. It was in under two minutes that she had the engine running and she was shifting into gear. Glancing over her shoulder into oncoming traffic, she pulled onto the road. With a deep sigh, she flexed her fingers and glanced about the interior of the car. Now it was just about getting to where she needed to go.

As she pulled down the block she saw the first thing she should have expected to see – a blockade. Cars and barriers were set up in the middle of the intersection. Men and women walked about, some giving orders, others directing people. Several worked as crowd control. Anytime there was some case where people needed to stay back, people naturally tended to move towards it. As Gemma began to pull down the street – she wouldn't turn around now – she noticed one agent in particular.

A woman stood by, speaking into a radio. Her hairstyle made Gemma think of the eighties, with her hair pulled back into a simple ponytail. A business suit among the police told Gemma that this woman was likely a federal agent.

Cars were lined up in front of Gemma so she had nowhere to go, but plenty of time to think. The vehicles were civilian cars and Gemma guessed many of the drivers were getting home from work. As the cars crawled forward, she wished that they would move at the speed limit. That way, the FBI agents ahead wouldn't pay so much attention to each car. But because they were paying attention to each car, the line was moving slowly and holding things up.

She let the vehicle crawl forward and looked around the open area of pavement where the FBI had set up their Base of Operations outdoors. Several trucks obscured the road. Gemma glanced out her window at the people walking on the sidewalk. It would be faster to walk through at this point, until one got to the mess of negotiating one's way through the FBI's setup.

When the next car had made its way forward, Gemma dutifully pulled forward, and up to the inspection line.

"Good evening Ma'm." said the agent. "We're just running a check, that's all." The man continued to talk about their procedure and how this wouldn't hold her up much if she would help them for just a moment. "Can I have your name please?"

At this point, the agent Gemma had noticed stepped up. she recognized the woman as Agent Tonya Nimmons.

"All right, now who do we have here?"

She looked into the driver's window, then drew her gun.

"Gemma Erskine step out of the vehicle with your hands in the air."

Gemma considered her options. She could gun the engine, but she didn't know how far she could get, or if Nimmons would fire if Gemma didn't listen to her prompt.

She raised her hand, opened her door and stepped out or the car, hands high in the air.

"You have the right to remain silent. Anything you say can and will be used against you in the court of law. You have the right to an attorney…"

As she felt her hands being cuffed behind her, Gemma wondered about how the situation had turned around, from working to carry out the last work of Agent Williams, not only to honor his death, but to save the lives of countless people. And that last task had still not been accomplished.

Chapter 46

Dean and Angleo sat back after Mike stormed out of the room. Angelo turned to Dean.

"That was a bit hard, wasn't it?" he asked, looking at Dean sidelong.

"I had been wondering for a while." Dean said with a shrug. "I thought it was important that we know."

"He doesn't have to tell us." Said Angelo.

"You're right." Dean said. "And he didn't." Angelo groaned, but Dean continued in his discourse. "When I asked him directly about whether he was working with a police department or whether he was a bounty hunter he didn't respond."

"He had told us already that he worked for Destrier and that he was hired to track us down. We knew that when we met him the first time." Said Angelo.

"I'm just saying we could do with a little more transparency." Dean said.

"Transparency? What are you on? We've all been honest with each other. Tim is a marketing director. Gemma is part of the FBI. I know you're supposed to be a comedian. I used to work a gas station. That feels like ten years ago. Adam's a private investigator, Nathan helps him, and Mike used to work for Destrier. That pretty much sums up the group."

"And there's another thing; just how is this group supposed to pull off this mission? I mean usually you have a trained team go in and rescue fugitives. Not that I know anything about professional operations of government agencies." Said Dean.

"What is your problem?" asked Angelo. "I thought that three hours ago we were all on the same page; that all of us knew what we have to do. We're not sure how to do it, but we agreed on what we have to do."

"Excuse me for expressing some doubts." Said Dean. "I just think that I'd like a chance of getting home again instead of being locked away for a crime I didn't commit, or for trying to rescue someone and save our nation before that nut job runs rampant with the untested technology that the FBI can't keep track of."

"Tomorrow we get to FBI headquarters, find a way in, and get Tim out. Then we find a way out of there. Afterwards we can worry about stopping Destrier." Said Angelo.

"You're still thinking about Destrier?"

"Yes." Said Angelo.

"Why?" Asked Dean.

"How can you not be thinking about it? This guy is determined to cause chaos throughout the country, if not throughout the world. And we're some of the few people who know about his plan."

"So what?"

"Have you ever heard that old saying that 'knowledge is power'?"

"I've seen it on some school posters, yeah." Said Dean.

"Since we're some of the few people who know about what's going to happen, we're those who have power over what's going to happen

326

next. That means we should be doing something about it." Angelo said.

They were quiet for a moment. Dean and Angelo sat, each engaged in their own thoughts.

"I don't know about responsibility," said Dean, "but…" he trailed off, seeing the look on Angelo's face. "What is it?" Angelo held up his hand and stepped toward the door. As he moved to the door he was vaguely aware that something had changed. He looked around the room.

"What?" Dean said.

Angelo peered around the room before he realized what distracted him. A few minutes ago he heard noise outside their room, noise of people passing and talking in the hallway. Now it was dead silent.

Suddenly a voice called out from the other side of the door.

"FBI. Open up."

Dean looked at Angelo, who shook his head. "What are we supposed to do?"

"Open the door. It's the FBI. They're going to open the door if we don't."

Angelo looked around the room. "We could go out the window."

"What?" Dean's brow furrowed as he spoke.

"We need to find a way to get out of here." Angelo said.

A heavy thud sounded and the door shuddered.

"Are you crazy?" Dean said. "The FBI is at the door, they are looking for reasons to arrest us, and you seem to agree with them. Am I the only person on the premises who is not looking for us to get arrested?"

Angelo swung around to look Dean full in the face. "If we get caught by the FBI there is no way that we can help Tim or get him out of FBI custody. For all they know he stole that case. Destrier is a figment of his imagination to them, so until we can release him we have no evidence and no way of proving to them that Destrier does, in fact have a plan. If we can't get them on our side then we have no resources at our disposal. We may have to work without those."

Another thud sounded at the door and it shuddered once again.

"Unless we can release Tim and get back to that lair of Destrier's and find a way to stop him in his self-appointed quest, then I don't see what our future holds." Angelo rubbed at his forehead in irritation. Dean shrugged.

"Why didn't you just say that ten minutes ago?"

The door crashed open.

"Get on your knees! Get on your knees! Hands behind you head. No sudden moves."

Dean and Angelo dropped to their knees in the middle of the hotel floor as a troop of FBI agents in full gear stormed into their hotel suite in tandem with two other groups entering the others' hotel rooms. They would find one occupant missing, the next would find two men, as expected, and the third would find the room empty, but would begin a search of the streets for the woman they expected to find in the room they swept.

"Things could be worse." Adam said.

"That's the understatement of the year." Dean replied.

"I mean really. We've made it into the building."

"In custody of the FBI." Dean said. "That's a vital part of the picture, we're in the custody of the- why don't you tell him, Angelo, maybe he'll listen to you."

Angelo didn't reply.

"Oh now you're quiet. You had a rousing speech prepared when we had to face a slew of agents storming in on us but now you're quiet."

The dim cell was clean but bare, serving only as a functional holding space. The light above held steady but didn't reach quite to the corners of the room. Adam imagined the darkness as a physical object looming there, a living growth on the walls, reluctant to leave. A faint buzz emanated from the light above, serving as a constant irritation for his already uneasy state.

Despite what he had said, Adam had lost hope. He had stepped in to help this band of misfits in their self-assigned quest. He had seen that they were the only people who might accomplish this task before them. Now because of it he sat locked away with them in a government cell, the government who would assign someone to question him about what had happened. Then after evidence had been collected, a jury would be called, a lawyer might be assigned and his case tried and the court might hear his pleas, but they would mostly hear of his involvement in some scheme to take a piece of government property to misuse or resell it to an anarchist, someone would say. If it wasn't said in the courtroom it would be said on the streets.

There was a sound from the door. Adam looked to see it open and an agent walk in. A guard joined him as well.

"Adam Hayner."

Adam nodded at the use of his name. The guard stepped forward and put handcuffs on him. Submitting to the proceedings, Adam did not resist as they led him out of the room. He was taken on a short route to a small room with a large mirrored window on one side. A table stood in the middle of the room, along with a chair on either side of it. They seated him in one of the chairs and left him. Having more time to himself, he continued to reflect on his situation and was just getting back to bouts of self-pity when the door opened again.

"I'm glad to see that they left you in one piece." A woman's voice said. "I will say that your work had me worried."

Stepping around his chair, Tonya Nimmons smiled at the man as she took a seat in the opposite chair.

When he managed to shut his mouth again, he took a breath and tried to form a sentence.

"This is… It's a uh- you really caught me off guard I didn't know that you- how long have you… I didn't know that you were a… uh- an FBI agent." He rubbed his brow with his right hand, forcing him to bring his left up with it. She laughed a little.

"I can't say that's the reaction I usually get."

"Why, what's the usual reaction?"

She ignored the question and opened a filing folder she carried with her.

"Now Mr. Adam Hayner, you are a private investigator for hire. Your last, current case is much more involved than the usual P.I. You infiltrated a guarded base of operations of a suspected terrorist? Despite what this may appear to be, we believe that this may be a front for an extremist agenda.

"When I last spoke with you I gave you the means to be employed by this company and left to you get in and discover what you could. What have you found so far?"

Adam shifted in his seat.

"It appears to be as you've said. Destrier is certainly an extremist in the category of anarchist. He is setting up plans to collapse world economies and governments."

He paused here.

"His plans seem to revolve around a piece of technology that we've had our hands on and only returned recently to the FBI."

For an instant he thought he saw a flicker of recognition in her eyes, but no other facial expression.

"Tell me more about it."

"Gemma, one of our companions, was apparently supposed to hold a rendezvous with the agent who had this piece of technology. But Destrier's men nearly got there in time."

"Wait," she said, "if agent Erskine didn't get there and the enemy agents didn't get the case, then who did?"

"A bystander."

She nodded. "All right."

"Timothy Runn."

"What do you know about him?"

Adam shrugged. "Not much. I think he works a desk job."

"Does he have any family that you know of?"

"He hasn't talked about it, so I don't know."

"What kind of training does he have?"

"Training?" he asked.

"Is he a veteran? Did he serve in our military or overseas or at least attend training camp somewhere?"

"No." Adam said. "He hadn't said anything so suggest that he has done any of these things."

"Then what would take a marketing director out of his home and on the road against armed gunmen to return a missing case like this?" she asked.

"I can't tell you." Said Adam.

After some more questions concerning their adventures, she turned the topic. "After what you've said, it appears to me that you all may be released. But we still have your friends to deal with."

"We know about Tim, but who else are you talking about?"

"We did not find Gemma or your other friend – the large one – at the scene. Michael is his name, I believe."

"Mike." Adam said under his breath.

"When we went to the rooms we only found four of you – we were expecting six. Taking to the streets we found agent Gemma Erskine. But we still have found no sign of your other friend."

"Before we picked him up he was working with Destrier's team." Adam said. "I wonder if they found him."

"That would put them right outside the hotel if he went on foot. There's no way he could have got far by himself."

Chapter 47

Tim sat and thought through what had happened. He told himself it had been a mistake. But he couldn't find a spot along the way where he could tell himself there was a blatant mistake he had made along the way.

But now he was in custody of the FBI. Now his friends were probably on the run from the government. And now an anarchist would be one step closer to setting fire to the economies and governments of the world. With a few keystrokes he could access the inner workings of any government on the planet and decide to collapse their economy. Within hours prices would soar. Within days their currency would become meaningless and people would resort to bartering, stealing and looting.

The implications of using such a piece of technology were beyond reckoning. Tim tried to grasp the different possibilities in which the technology might be used, for good or evil, but kept coming back to the same idea – that the same amount of power in the hands of one man was simply too much. For one person to make the decisions for an entire nation or multiple nations was absurd. But Destrier wanted to go beyond that. He had said so himself. He wanted to collapse economies. He wanted to see the world fall, simply for the sight of it falling, not to raise it up again.

Timothy was thinking of all this to himself when a noise came to his door. It opened and a guard stepped through, followed by a young agent. The agent was well-dressed enough, though he had shed his coat.

"Mr. Runn." He said. "If you will step this way."

The guard produced a pair of handcuffs. Tim sighed but complied. As they stepped down the hallway, Tim glanced at different doors and guessed what the rooms behind them might hold.

They stepped into the room and he was seated at the first chair. The guard and agent left him alone. The table and two chairs alone furnished the room.

The door opened and Agent Tonya Nimmons stepped in.

"Mr. Runn." She said. "A pleasure. I hope they are treating you well."

Tim shrugged and looked at the ceiling. "Well enough, I suppose."

"I apologize that it has been such a wait for you, but you understand that once we had detained you we had to do some investigating ourselves."

"It makes sense. Someone walks into your building and says that they've got something of yours, except you don't know that it exists."

"Exactly. Well, you'll be happy to hear that the first part of your story checks out. Our agent Williams went out on a mission which was not reported to the agency through the normal channels. He did not report in. It was only after you came in with the case that we began to suspect something more serious than a delay in research."

Tim didn't speak at once. "So you've heard nothing about what I said when I first came to you. That Destrier intends to use the technology to collapse governments – societies. This isn't about national security it's about international security. As soon as he gets his hands on that thing he can blow us all out of the water."

"Mr. Runn what exactly is in this case that he so desperately desires?"

334

Tim looked up at her. "Excuse me?'"

"What is in the case?"

"You don't know?'"

She shook her head.

"You have an international security threat on your hands-"

"Which is why, Mr. Runn, you would do better if you would move to the part where you tell me what this is."

"It's a device which allows a person to access any other computer connected to the internet. Any amount of security becomes absolutely useless. It's the greatest brain put inside of a digital hacker. Hook it up to your computer and start surfing, you've got access to files, computers, software, databanks – anything on an electronic device that could be accessed through a connection to the internet."

The woman sitting across from Timothy flipped through the files again, remaining quiet as she did so. She kept her eyes down for a moment, examining the papers in front of her.

"Ma'm."

She looked up.

"If there's any chance of doing something about this, it has to be done soon."

A wry smile came over her face. "I'm quite aware of the idea, Mr. Runn. You can be sure that the agency is capable of deciding about when to move forward with its decided course of action, however it has been advised."

Tonya looked over the papers again. "From earlier talks, it was noted that you were in captivity in Destrier's facility, correct?"

"Yes, that is correct."

She set down the papers and looked at him.

"We need to get to that facility and put and end to his plans. But we need a guide in. Ms. Erskine is a trained agent, but you've also had an encounter with Destrier, and I wonder whether you may also be of some help on this mission."

Tim looked over his shoulder, half-expecting to find that the woman was speaking to someone else in the room whom he hadn't seen until now. But there was no one else.

"How would I be involved?"

"As a guide. We would keep you off the field, but we would use video monitoring, if possible, to guide the team in. With their visuals you could then direct them from a safe distance away, with the help of a technician."

"Adam would be of more help than me. He was there before we were, working as a janitor."

"But from what you told us, Destrier also showed you into his own office. He hasn't been in there and you have."

"I don't think that the fact I've been in there makes this a good idea." Said Timothy.

"Whether it is or not you've been elected as a guide for a squad of FBI agents who will be taken in to pick up the case, disable the systems that Destrier has in place and pick up the man himself."

Timothy nodded. It sounded like a straight-forward deal. But a knot was growing in his gut. There was no way to know how this would turn out.

Chapter 48

Destrier stood over a technician who had the case open and a computer connected with the nearly-mystical device. The technician was attempting to get the computer and device to cooperate which was proving to be difficult.

"Well? What can you tell me?"

The technician held up his hands in a state of befuddlement.

"It's difficult to say. Whoever put this together built it from the ground up."

"So?"

"So that means that trying to get this device to interface with the computer in the way we want can be very…tricky."

"An English paper is tricky."

"Yes sir. What I'm trying to say is that whoever designed this has both a facility for electrical engineering beyond mine and a greater understanding of programming."

The man sat back in his chair. "Without understanding the designer I don't know if I'll be able to understand how this machine works."

"You had better find out how it works." said Destrier, turning away. "Or you're fired."

"Was that a threat?"

Destrier stopped in his tracks. "What?"

"Was that a threat disguised as an offhand comment, like 'I hope you don't have a bad day tomorrow'?"

"No. Why do you say that?"

"Because everyone's using that one now. Especially since dead people can't work."

Destrier waved the man off, and the young technician turned back to troubleshooting the hardware and software which was vital to his own plan. Once it was functional there would be no barriers left between himself and his goal of destruction.

He had received a call with a tip – someone had caught an old turn-coat. Destrier made his way down the hall to the prison. The guard searched him, as was his policy. He has established and enforced this, that all personnel be searched when entering or leaving the prison ward, including himself. If he wasn't going to be searched there was no point in establishing the rule, since everyone else would resent it or refuse to follow it.

Stepping through security, he made his way to the last cell on the left. This cell was built to be larger than the others, so that they could either hold more people in it or for other official purposes. As he made his way into the room, Destrier saw that two guards were already busy with the deserter. He waited a moment until they threw Mike down to the ground, before holding up a hand.

Immediately the guards stopped and came to attention. Destrier stepped around the man now lying on his side on the floor.

"So," he said as he looked over the man's massive frame, "my stray employee returns to me again. Should I reward him for his independence?"

The two guards didn't laugh or respond at this, but their grips tightened on their clubs where they stood. One club whipped out though the air and caught him on the back. He groaned where he was, but hardly moved.

"I could employ him again and give him the chance to prove his loyalty to me. But that would only be a chance for him to disappoint me again."

Destrier nodded to the guards who whaled on Mike once again. He cried out and struggled but made no attempt to fight back. Waving the guards off again, Destrier spoke once more.

"So for now you're just a bonus. I'll have to find something appropriate for you when I'm finished with more pressing business. Once I have my plate clear I'll come up with something appropriate for you."

He turned and left the room.

Chapter 49

At headquarters, an agent stepped into the holding cell with Dean, Adam and Angelo.

"Well, there's good news. It looks like you all have been cleared. I can't imagine how it happened with the ruckus you caused yesterday, but it's official. You are all to be released and allowed to go home or wherever you please. Transportation is provided since you don't have any."

Angelo looked at the man.

"Something seems too easy about this." He said. "Is there something more to this? Are all of us to be released?"

The agent blew out a breath.

"Well, not exactly. The agency has requested the help of Timothy and Gemma to stop this anarchist from destroying this nation and other nations as we know them."

"Then we'll be here to help." Said Adam. "There's no way we'll back out now."

"Unfortunately that's not your call."

As they spoke a guard who had entered with the agent unlocked their chains and allowed them to stand and move.

"If you all will follow me." Said the agent.

Since there was nothing else clear to do, they followed after him. The agent, who soon introduced himself as Mr. Caleb Newman led them down a hall or two and into what appeared to be a lounge. There Lorenzo and Gemma were already waiting for them. The lounge had chairs and couches as well as a table. There were bunks all around the room, stacked one above another on either side of the room. The room was certainly functional rather than designed to imitate the home. It could be imagined as an apartment or a dormitory and appeared to be comfortable.

Gemma spoke first as the threesome stepped into the room.

"Well, it looks like most of us are together again."

"For the moment." Said Adam. "I hear they're taking you out on an assignment."

"They asked nicely."

"And what are we going to do in the meantime?" Angelo said. "I thought we were in this together. We can't let you go in alone."

"Relax, we're professionals. You do remember that I'm an agent too?"

Angelo nodded, but didn't say anything in reply.

"What's the latest on Destrier? And where's Mike?" said Dean. The expression on the faces around him echoed this statement.

Agent Newman spoke at this point. "At the time of your apprehension we did not find your friend Michael. There were no traces of him and your vehicle remained where it was. If he left the area on his own it was on foot."

"He had just stepped outside." Said Angelo.

"We checked the tapes inside the hotel and found footage of him approaching a vehicle on the street opposite the hotel. In short, he stands and speaks with someone for a few minutes, then two figures – large men, even compared to his stature – come up behind him and incapacitate him with a blow to the head. Then he is put into their car and it drives away."

"That's a riddle." Said Lorenzo. "Why did he stand and talk to these people if they were hostile? Why did they attack him? It doesn't make sense that he would hold a conversation with them if he recognized guards if they were from Destrier's troop."

"Again, begging the question, why did he talk to them?" said Adam.

"I'm not sure that is the right question." Said Gemma.

The others, who had been caught up in the questions, turned to look at her. She shrugged a little. "We don't need to know what they were talking about or why Mike spoke with them. We just need to know where they went." She paused for a moment. "If I know Destrier well enough, his ego was wounded when we escaped. His ego was greatly wounded when we escaped. So any chance of getting back at us would be something of a reprieve for him, even while he works at trying to collapse nations."

"Wouldn't the collapsing nations come first?" asked Dean. "If I was planning something big like that, I think that I would put that first on my calendar."

"But you're not an egotist." Said Gemma. "An egotist puts himself first. He always seeks a way to mend his wounded pride. He has found a way to harm someone who has embarrassed him. Someone he had securely locked away, and yet who escaped. Someone who had been an allegiant of his, and yet gave up that allegiance in favor of fighting against his former employer."

At that moment the door swung open again. The room grew quiet as Timothy stepped into the room, looking back at the stares with which the rest of the people greeted him. He shrugged a little as he stepped into the room.

"What? Was I supposed to bring a dish to pass?"

It was late at night and the group was in the lounge talking about all that had happened in the time that they had been separated. They recounted back their own adventures to Tim and he sat, taking it in.

"So what about this mission we've heard so much about?" Angelo asked Tim. Gemma had retire to her own room at this point. "In all the talk going around maybe you've heard something about it. They're going to go and try to get the case back and-"

He hesitated with a glance to the others. Tim looked up at this point, catching the cue in his voice.

"What else is going on? No one has said anything about Mike yet."

They told Tim what had happened to Mike, both what they knew themselves and what they had been told by Agent Newman.

After all of this, they asked him what else he knew. He sighed and spoke up.

"They want me to go on the mission. They think what I know will be of use to them."

The talk died down for a moment as they thought through this. "In the morning," he said, "I'll be heading out with the team. I won't be on the ground with them, they'll have me off-site with a feed from their cameras so I can see the site and advise them about special locations on-site."

"Are you sure about this?" said Lorenzo.

"They're trained professionals." Tim said without conviction. "They know what they're doing."

"But do you know what you're doing?" said Lorenzo.

"Give the man a break." Said Adam. "The FBI is requesting his help. Does he have much of a choice?"

"Yes I do." said Tim. "But I know I shouldn't say no."

"What are your chances of walking away from this?" asked Angelo.

"I'd say they're pretty high." Said Dean. "He said himself that he's going to be away from the fighting."

The conversation then wandered away into tactics of the FBI and into the plans for the next day. Tim hadn't heard any specifics. All he could guess was that their plan was to get the case back and to try to find Mike and bring him back with them, arresting Destrier and shutting down his operation if possible.

Since they had told him nothing, Tim could only guess about what their plans were and make assumptions. The other men soon turned in, save Angelo who was used to a different sleep schedule. He stayed up longer than the others. He and Tim sat for a while in relative quiet. Eventually, he turned to Tim with an earnest expression on his face.

"Hey Tim, have you every thought about…"

Then he censored himself and stopped.

"What is it?" said Tim.

"No, you wouldn't want to hear."

"Go ahead."

Angelo bit his lip before continuing. "Have you ever thought about an afterlife? Like what happens when we die?"

Tim laughed a little and Angelo turned away, his face flushed. Tim quieted, realizing how serious this was to the man beside him.

"I've thought about it a little bit here and there. I know my grandmother had a strong faith. She was a Christian. She used to quote from the Psalms all the time. 'Yea, though I walk through the valley of the shadow of death I will fear no evil, for thy rod and they staff, they comfort me.'"

Angelo's eyebrow's came together. "What in the world is he talking about there?"

"He's talking about a shepherd. King David of Israel, the author of many of the Psalms, relates God to being a great shepherd over us, his sheep who he guides and cares for. When he talks about the rod and staff, those were used to guide and protect the sheep. It was used to keep the wolf and other beasts away. If the sheep got stuck, the shepherd would use the staff's crook to pull the sheep out."

"So this- big shepherd is watching over this King of Israel."

"Right. And He is the same God who watches over us now. There is an afterlife. We have a choice between life and death. Jesus, God's only son, was sent and took on our wrongdoing for us. After that he was crucified – execution chosen by his own people – and he died and was buried."

"Then he's just another man, right? One who came and died."

Tim looked up and smiled. "But he's not. On the third day, after he was buried, two women came to prepare his body properly but they found the tomb wide open. Their Lord had risen. He later appeared to his disciples, telling them to spread this Gospel, this Good News, that salvation had come by his sacrifice and that all who believed on his name would be saved."

Angelo's eyes were down on his hands as he sat bent.

"It can't be that easy." He said. "There's something I'm missing. Maybe if I-"

"Angelo. Many people have tried to live their lives earning God's love and their own salvation. There's no way to do it. The only way is to accept it, believing that Jesus gave himself to pay the price for your sin. Do you believe?"

Angelo sat in silence and Tim waited. Finally Angelo spoke.

"I do. I want to believe."

Tim smiled. "All right." He said. "Then let's pray."

Chapter 50

Tim sat in the back of a large vehicle with a dozen or more agents in full tactical gear. They had given him protective gear as well, but no weapons. At the front of the vehicle was a set of screens which showed a relay of what was being fed through the small cameras the agents had mounted to their helmets.

It was every boy's dream to be involved in stuff like this. To be a secret agent or to be a soldier. To run out onto the battlefield and fight bad guys. Running into a great big fortress to find and shoot bad guys so you could shut off to super-weapon before it was too late; this was the stuff that kids dreamed about. Now that he was on the edge of it all, it held a vague terror for Tim.

There were several vehicles, including the command vehicle from which Tim would watch the day play out. As they rode down the last few miles to the facility, Tim began to pray quietly to himself. This elicited a few glances from the agents, but no comments. He could imagine that some of the agents themselves prayed before and engagement like this.

Riding up to the lot, there was a call to stop and pull off to the side. Two agents stepped out of the vehicle, one of them carrying a case with him. The air stilled after they closed the door behind them. When they left the vehicle, the whole team sat and waited for about five or ten minutes. As he sat, Timothy heard a sound similar to a gunshot, but very soft.

In a few moments, the two men re-entered the vehicle and it continued forward. They trundled forward and Tim's mind wandered over the task they had before them, whether they succeeded or failed, their responsibility to attempt it was clear.

As the vehicle kept moving the men were quiet where they sat. Tim wondered whether this was normal, but these were trained agents. He looked to the agent across from him. The man's eyes were locked on a point on the floor in front of him.

Timothy heard his voice called from the front of the vehicle. Standing, he made his way up to where a technician sat at a bank of screens.

"This is our monitoring system." The man said. "We should have a live feed of every agent on the field through this set of monitors in front of us."

Looking over the different monitors, Timothy could see different shots of the interiors of vehicles. From one or two he could discern what his own figured looked like from behind. He wanted to look over his shoulder, but he refrained from submitting to the impulse.

"Now we'll have you with us in this vehicle," the technician said, "keeping an eye on things. If you see something that looks important or that you think we need to know tell me and I can pass it on to the team."

"All right." Said Tim.

The technician held his hand up and gestured to a man standing beside him. The man was well-built, in his mid- forties, probably.

"This is Agent Downing. He is our team lead. You'll hear his voice over the radio as he takes the team out."

Downing reached out and clasped hands with Tim. The man's grip was firm, but Downing had an awareness not to use his strength to crush the civilian's hand in this iron grip.

After showing him a few more details, and small talk the technician sent Tim back to his seat and Downing went to prepare for the raid.

A seat stood open next to Tim's, but they would wait until the agents entered the area for Tim to sit there.

The vehicles stopped. The doors opened and the men filed out. The doors closed and the vehicle was occupied by Tim, the driver and a few technicians.

"All right," said the first technician, "now this is your live feed. You can see the feed from each of the agent's cameras here."

The men filed out of the vehicles and onto the pavement, moving towards the building. Having studied plans for the building as well as images, they had a good understanding of the layout and where things were. The team leads used specialized equipment to take the doors down and the rest followed in quickly behind them. As they stepped inside, they swept across the visible space.

A crude office space was set up in the front part of the building. There were some people moving about this space, dressed as anyone else would for any office job. Seeing these people, the agents moved in.

"FBI! Get on the ground!"

Most of them complied. One of them tried to run for an exit and was shot. He fell to the floor and cried out as he grasped his arm where the bullet had hit his tricep.

Two were sent to sweep through the labyrinth of cubicles which were set up in the center of the room. Continuing to sweep the area, the rest worked their way down and through a series of rooms along the outer wall, most of them unoccupied.

A shot echoed through the building. The agents turned about, looking for the source of the sound.

"Status report." Downing said. "I need your status report."

Another shot rang out. The building's cavernous interior only served as an echoing chamber in which the sound resonated. One of the agents named Kendrick darted toward the cubicles.

"What's going on out there?" said Tim.

"I don't know." The technician said. He pressed an intercom switch. "Can we get an update? What's going on out there?"

There was a third shot. This time a scream followed, but from one of the illicit employees who was lying facedown, hands bound by the agents on the floor.

"Tell me what's going on!" Downing said.

"We have someone unseen at play." Said one of the other agents. "A wild card. He's firing on the employees, I repeat, the shooter is firing on the employees."

"Well where is he?" said the team leader. "And where is Kendrick?"

No sound came from the cubicles. The team leader spoke into his headset.

"Kendrick, report. Kendrick, where are you?"

The team leader received no reply.

Tim pointed at one of the live feeds. "What is this one supposed to be? And why is it blank now? Is t used for aerial views?"

"No," said the technician, "that's Kendrick's feed. It's gone dead." The technician was then back to his headset, talking to the team. A second tech handed Tim a pair of headphones. Nodding his thanks, Tim put the headset on and was bombarded with voices.

He stood and listened to the voices in the headset as they attempted to gain control of the situation.

Downing spoke into his headset. "Tell me what's going on out there." His gun was leveled.

In his earpiece he heard the voice of the first technician respond. "We've lost the feed for all three of the agents who entered the cubicle area. Be advised there may still be hostiles in the area. I repeat there may still be hostiles in the area."

"Thank you for that, I am advised. Hostiles still in play."

Downing spoke again. "I am moving in toward the cubicles. I need two backup." Two men quickly stepped in behind him.

The agents moved to the set of cubicles and began their search, sweeping each cubicle as they came to it. The cubicles acted as a screen, standing at nearly six feet. The agents kept low, moving quickly. Reaching one of the cubicles they stopped.

"Mission control, this is team lead. We have three bodies, all allies, one of the Kendick."

One of the agents moved closer to the bodies and examined them. It was clear, from a distance, that their injuries had not been sustained from a gun. The agent who examined them looked up.

"All three are dead. Their throats have been slit." The agent said.

"Keep moving." Downing said. They moved through the rest of the cubicles, finding nothing. A shot rang out, this one from a door opposite the entrance. Then a second shot rang out rang out from the same doorway in quick succession. The agents dove for cover, finding it behind filing cabinets and columns.

"Command, this is Team Lead. We may have a wild card on our hands. We have three agents down. Their throats have been slit. There are no signs of gunshot wounds. Kendrick is one of them."

Agent Downing looked back and found that the full group, less three was now in the vicinity. Looking ahead, he trained his weapon on the door in front of them. The shots had stopped firing. He waved the group ahead. Two agents moved to the door. He stayed just behind them, keeping his weapon trained on the door.

They kicked the portal open. Shots were fired as the agents moved into the hallway. It was three-on-one as the FBI agents stepped down the hallway and a single renegade stood at the end of the hall.

"Drop your weapon! Lay your weapon on the ground! Hands behind your head!"

Seeing the FBI agents storming in was clearly different than whatever he must have imagined, for the man quickly lay his weapon down.

"Get on the ground! Get on the ground!" The agents shouted. The man stepped out from the doorway where he was hiding and got down onto his face on the ground. The agents moved quickly to where the man was. As one of the agents searched the man. Another agent covered the detainee while a third agent covered the guard. The agents swept the room as they moved into it. It was a long hallway with doors on either side. They began to move down the hallway, checking the rooms on either side as they did so. Looking into one of the rooms on the left, Downing looked and saw furnished cells. He grasped the handle and gave a tug. The door held firmly. Muttering to himself he began to move down the hall.

"Check each room as you go." He said. "I don't want to come back and find that there's someone we didn't know about in a room we've already checked."

The team began their trek down the hall.

"What in the world would anyone need with a private prison?" a young agent asked.

"Well, when you want to control people, and asking nicely hasn't worked, some people find other ways to manage." Downing said.

He moved forward with the team, examining each room as he came to it. Each room was empty, save the furnishings. He wondered at this, since it was clearly not necessary. Were these rooms designed to be used as simple prison cells? In most prisons they gave the prisoners a cot and a toilet. If this wasn't designed as a prison, why did the rooms have locks?

He kept the group moving to the end of the hall, but discovered nothing more. They moved down the hall to the last door on the left. Looking in, Downing saw a body.

"I've got something." He said to the others. "There appears to be a male, on the ground. He appears to be unconscious."

He backed up and one of the other officers stepped forward. "This is the FBI. Can you hear me?"

The man didn't move from his spot. He lay on the ground, on his side.

Downing turned to a few of the others in the group.

> "Why don't a few of you see if you can find a control room for this place? Keep low and keep quiet. We need to find a way to get these cells open without blowing every door off its hinges."

The agents confirmed this and Agent Downing confirmed with them that they would stay in radio contact. With this done they turned, moving back down the hallway they had just entered. Downing watched as they exited the hallway on their search for the control room.

Downing pounded on the door again.

"Sir, this is the FBI, can you hear me? We are working on getting you out of there." The man in the room did not stir from his place on the ground.

Downing posted two agents at the door and kept moving through the door at the end of the hall. This led to an outer hall which ran around the premises. They took the hall, checking each room as they went, trying each room along the way. The building wasn't heavily manned.

As they worked their way around, they found no sign of any illegal paraphernalia. As they went, Agent Downing told the teams to keep their eyes open.

"How's my team working to find the control room?"

"It looks like we may have found something promising. We will investigate and report when we have something. Over."

"Good. Control, do we have any update or new information on the hostiles?"

"Negative. Anything we've run only lines up with the old information we've already established. We will keep looking to see if we can't find something. Over."

"Thank you control. We are now sweeping the outer hall which runs about the premises. We will report if we find anything suspicious. Out."

"FBI, we have a warrant. Open the door."

No one responded. Moving to the door, a young agent by the name of Wilkins moved up to the door. At Downing's signal he kicked the door down. Wilkins and Emery, moved into the room one at a time, setting themselves up at a split team angle with each of them in an opposite corner on either side of the door.

Downing strode in, followed by two more agents. They swept over the room, their lights illuminating the whole of the room and what occupied it. This room was filled with weapons. Guns of all sorts were on racks throughout the room. Cases were stacked throughout the room, filled with clips of ammunition.

"Clear." Wilkins said.

"Control, it looks like we've found something." Said Agent Downing.

"Agent One, this is Control, go ahead."

"We have a storeroom full of weapons, I repeat, a storeroom full of weapons."

Emery stepped down the aisles, his weapon down at his side for the moment.

"There are AK-47s here, some automatic rifles. These are cases, I don't doubt that they hold pistols of some kind."

"What was the man going to do?" said Wilkins, "Start his own war?"

"Or supply it." Said Agent Downing. "Let's move."

He and the other two agents were already near the door. Wilkens and Emery had their weapons up. Using the Buttonhook method, one of them swung out of the door and around the wall to the hall. Another agent followed, coming out of the room and keeping an eye out on the other end of the hallway. The rest of the agents filed out of the room. Moving down the hall, the agents continued their search of the building, keeping their eyes up and their minds open.

Chapter 51

"Boss." One of the thugs that Destrier found necessary to employ came charging into the room. However counterintuitive, the room from which he intended to work his scheme was not, in fact, very large as only two, now three with the guard, occupied it.

"What is it?"

"We've got a raid happening."

Destrier turned to look at the man.

"I've only just heard." The man said. "SWAT teams are moving through the lower floors."

Destrier's face deepened to a darker shade of red. "What?

"They're sweeping through the different rooms, and they'll be up here soon. You've got to get out of here."

The technician at the computer looked up at Destrier, who gave a nod. Folding up his laptop, the technician, whose name was Archie began packing up his necessities.

"Also, sir…" the guard started, but trailed off.

"What is it?"

The man stood there for a moment, but said nothing.

Destier rolled his eyes. "Did you go to another Redskins game?"

"Yes they did, and in the last quarter-"

"Let me explain something to you. You don't need to explain how much you enjoy going to see your team play. They are this state's team, so if you go and speak to ten people, eight people will say the same thing. If the Redskins had an unfortunate meeting with a truck-full of redskin potatoes on the road that would be something to comment about.

"Get everyone together, keep out of their way, get out of here, and do not get caught."

The guard nodded and hurried out of the door. The SWAT team was already making their way through the lower rooms, but there would still be time to watch if he moved quickly enough. Destrier looked about the room. The technician was packing up the device, the nearly-mystical device which endowed Destrier with the power he sought to release the world from the straight-jacket it had put itself into.

He grabbed a few necessities and, seeing that the technician was finished, folded up the case itself. Now that they knew how the case worked he could open it wherever he pleased.

Passing out of the room, he stepped away from the stairs and, instead, moved towards a small laboratory down the hall. Once inside, he began to peruse the different items on the counters. His bearings held as though he were visiting a store or a shopping mall. Eventually the technician cleared his throat.

"Sir?

"Hm?"

Destrier turned from looking at the glasses and objects on the counter. "Oh, yes, just a moment."

The man then moved to a corner and grabbed a broom as through he would begin to sweep up. Suddenly, with a scream, he whipped the broom handle through the glass equipment, sending it flying across the room.

"What are you doing?" cried the technician, but the animal rage continued as the man leapt onto the counter, letting the broom handle fly again.

The technician stood in terrified fascination as the man leapt around the room, smashing everything that was not tied down. Liquids were hissing and fizzing on the countertop and floor. Light twinkled everywhere as glass shards had scattered all across the room. Small fires burned here and there.

Destrier stood, as though in a daze, staring at the far wall. The man's hands quivered at his side, his long fingers jumping in coordination with each hand. He stood there in silence as voices echoed from the floor below. The technician stood in silence for a moment, watching his leader as his leader's mental capacities began to break down. After a moment of quiet standing, Destrier walked to the door with a flip of his hand. The technician followed behind. There were evacuation protocols but those called for the staff to go to the roof. Somehow he doubted that would happen now.

Chapter 52

"Here it is, here it is." Angelo said.

"It told you I know the way." Said Dean.

"Well if you two could keep quiet this would go more easily." Replied Gemma.

"Hey Gemma," said Dean, "thanks for getting us out of there."

She shrugged. "Well, you guys had already been released. I figured it was time for you to get out of there. I just passed on a few words to a friend or two."

They pulled up to the old docking yard.

"Now remember" she said, "we're here to help Mike if we can. If there's anything concerning the case we can do, we step in. Got it?"

The others nodded. "And don't get in the way of the SWAT team, they know what they're doing. All right, let's do this."

The group occupied their retro van at this point and were approaching the dockside warehouse which served as a base of operations for Destrier and his host. The trio continued down the dilapidated road which led them between other warehouses. Dean looked about as they went, scanning the different buildings they passed by.

"Are we sure they haven't used these other buildings for anything?"

"If they have we're not finding out today." Gemma said.

Dean nodded. "Got it."

They kept on until they reached the front gates. She slowed and was about to speak when Angelo pointed.

"Look there."

She leaned forward in her seat. "There's no guard."

Dean leaned between the front two seats to get a look but didn't say anything.

Angelo pointed to something else in the open yard before the warehouse. Gemma nodded. Dean looked between them. "What?"

"One of the SWAT vehicles has posted itself in front, outside of the building. We don't know where the others are, or if they're here yet."

Gemma stepped out of the vehicle and towards the building. With a glance at Dean, Angelo shrugged and opened his door. Dean sighed and followed the other two towards the building.

"I don't know what this is, but it feels like a mistake."

Chapter 53

The guard jogged his way down the corridor, hearing voices echo up from the floor below him. He only had to keep just ahead of the SWAT team and they could make it out of the building without being caught. What Destrier was planning he didn't venture to guess. Destrier didn't let anyone into his planning sessions.

With a quick pounding, the guard pushed through the door into the control room.

"There's a SWAT team downstairs and they're about to take the building."

The man at the board, Jennings, turned from his seat. "What?"

"Destrier has ordered an evacuation."

Jennings nodded "We'll see to it." His oversized, outdated glasses slipped as he said this. This could have been due to his greasy nose which shone, even in the dim lighting. The guard knew better than to question Jennings, despite his appearance. The guard turned and ran on. Jennings turned back to the people in the room and began calling out orders.

"Wipe the memory of the databanks we can't take with us. If we can't pack it up in five minutes burn it. Everyone is taking something. Let's move."

The room sprang to life as fifteen people began to work at consolidating an incredible amount of work. Typing at computers, printing out papers, and calling out orders were only part of the work that went on in this room. There was a business that came after the announcement which did not result in panic, but in a concentrated energy. All of the workers coming together to accomplish a single task of getting the information in a state where it would be ready to be taken out of the building, hidden, or destroyed so that it would not be found.

"How many copies of this building's floor plan do we have?" Jennings called out. One of the workers, a small woman who asserted herself around the office with her dominant personality and intelligence, passed Jennings a copy of the floor plan.

"Here," Jennings said, "here is where they will enter. Which means that, in all likelihood, they haven't thought about..." he became quiet, inviting a guess.

The other staff members became quiet as Jennings stood there, waiting for a response. He looked around the room but, seeing no one who either had an idea or who was willing to speak up, he spoke for them himself.

"They have not thought of us exiting through the windows."

There was quiet as the people who worked in the department looked at one another, trying to tell whether the man was joking or not. Did he mean simply leaping out the windows and landing on the pavement below? Was a required leadership trait here being insane or unreasonable?

"Perhaps, sir," said one of the young technicians who cared nothing for social class, "you're referring to the fire escapes."

Jennings hesitated. "Yes, that's right the fires escapes, we'll use the fire escapes."

There was a common murmuring throughout the room. 'Why didn't he just say that?', 'Don't the fire escapes lead to the roof?', and other similar comments.

The group was packed up in about seven minutes.

"No one has anything left?" asked Jennings as they stood outside the doorway. There was no affirmative reply, so he proceeded to the next phase. Taking a bundle of C4, he peeled off the adhesive strips attached and stuck it to the underside of a desk. Wiring it up, he set the timer for enough time to clear the building. Having started the timer, he stood and moved to the door. With one last look around the room he nodded and closed the door behind himself.

Chapter 54

Tim sat in the van observing the different screens, trying to track what was going on. He watched as they stormed the building and took down the employees, and the fiasco with the unknown assailant in the cubicles. Then they moved on to the cells and he saw Mike lying on the ground, unresponsive. In that moment his understanding of the situation went from seeing a cartoonish villain on television looking to cause trouble to seeing brutality caused by another human being determined to harm another.

He knew at that point he had to do something. Sitting in the vehicle simply to be an advisor wasn't enough when any of the SWAT team members had a question or him wasn't enough for this event. He knew that he had to go and do the one thing they hadn't asked of him, which was to go out into the field and help them. The way the SWAT team approached the situation, they would take things room by room, and Destrier would simply escape while they were clearing the rooms below. If Tim didn't move now, Destrier would move now and all of his friends would escape with him.

There was no way, however, that these agents were going to let him out of their sight. He needed either a diversion or an excuse to get out of their sight, and he needed it soon.

Tim stood and stretched. "So, how long do these stints go for?"

The technician turned to him. "It really depends. If the building is small, say a drug raid on a house, the could be in and out within a few minutes."

"And larger buildings?"

"It really just depends on the size. How many rooms are there? Are they running into any hostiles? Any obstructions? There are a lot of factors that can change the time frame."

"Thank you."

He moved away from the technician and toward the door of the trailer, but stood, looking towards the back, not ready to spring out. If he moved now they would be sure to chase him. He began to fiddle with something in his pocket and glanced over his shoulder. The technician was busy at the board, keeping his eyes on the screen. Tim hoped that the technician wouldn't be interested enough in him to notice what he was doing. He edged himself closer to the door while keeping an eye on the technician. There was no response from the technician. He was reaching for the door handle when he heard the voice of the technician.

"What are you doing?"

"I was just stepping out for a minute."

"I have strict orders that you are to stay in here until the operation is complete."

Tim glanced at the door, then back at the technician and nodded. "All right, that sounds good." He kept himself from goose-stepping to the chair set up for him behind the screen. Sitting down, he took another look at the display and tried to think through the situation. The only thing that came to mind was that he had to get out of the truck.

He took a breath to say something, but the something never came. Instead he heard a vehicle pulling up outside the vehicle he was in. He glanced toward the front of his vehicle. The driver didn't hear it and the technician kept his eyes glued to the screen, calling out a few words to the agents on the field every once in a while.

Sitting in his seat, Tim almost thought of risking another chance at the door and was just about to stand, when there was a knock at the door. He had nearly been ready to push onwards with or without help from the FBI. Of course help from the FBI would have been much more preferable, but he strongly felt that if he did not go now, Destrier would get away by himself. The knock startled Tim, but didn't seem to phase the others much.

"Get that, would you?" said that tech.

Tim nodded and moved to the door. Opening it, he found that he was face-to-face with-

"Tim." Angelo said. "Hey buddy, could you come outside for a minute or two? We've got a few things we want to talk about."

Tim glanced over his shoulder again No one was paying him any attention. Tim glanced abut one more time as he moved towards the door. Angelo stepped away from the door and down to reveal that he had not come alone. Tim took several steps away from the FBI van. Seeing the threesome standing before him, he laughed a little.

"What's all this?"

Angelo spread his hands. "You needed some backup."

Tim pointed to them. "And this is it? You're backing me up here? I have to stop Destrier because by the time the SWAT team gets to finding him he's going to escape."

Gemma looked to the building and back to Tim. "What do you need from us?"

"I just need people who are willing. That's all I can ask."

Gemma sighed and shook her head a little. "Yes, but what do you need?"

Tim paused for a moment. "I'm going after Destrier. I'm going to need eyes in the building to see whether he tries to escape via a different route than I take. I want to keep an eye out for Mike, though I think that the SWAT team will be going to try and find him anyways."

The group nodded.

"Well," said Dean, who had remained quiet up until this point, "I think we should try to find some weapons of some kind. I don't want to go in there and find out, too late, that I'm unarmed and I should have been armed."

"Or," said Angelo, "you go in there and find out that they had ninja warrior guards who make quick work, with a katana, of taking your arms off so you really will be disarmed."

Despite the humor, Tim gave Angelo a hard look. "You're not helping."

Angelo shrugged. "I'm just saying we should be prepared."

Gemma moved towards one of the other FBI vehicles which was parked on the premises. Getting inside, they discovered that weapons were stored in the back. Showing her clearance badge to the agent in the vehicle, she procured three weapons and clips for her companions. With these in place, they quickly moved onwards to the building.

As they stepped inside, Tim noted that it was not as dark as he anticipated. He also noted that there were bodies scattered all over the floor. At first he thought that these were dead bodies.

Then, as he walked along, he nearly screamed when he saw one reach up. They – he turned his attention to one of them lying on the ground. They appeared to be fine. He kept moving, keeping his eyes open for Mike, for Destrier, and for any more bodies lying around the atrium.

The group quickly moved through the atrium, staying close together.

"Any ideas?" Tim said to Gemma as they moved.

"Two." she said. "It's no good trying to hole himself in, since the FBI has all the resources at their disposal. That means that he'll be trying to get out. Either he'll be running for the roof or he'll find some other way out of the building. But he won't come out on this floor."

"Sounds like she has lots of ideas." Said Dean.

Tim glanced in his direction. "She usually has some ideas."

They kept moving forward. There were noises coming from the back of the building, but these didn't appear to be anything happening in the main atrium.

"What's the plan?"

Tim glanced at Gemma, surprised since the question had come from her. "We've got to find Destrier, and I doubt that he's hanging out down here to get caught by a SWAT team. What we probably want to do is check out that office of his, and then head upstairs, where he's likely to go in case of an emergency like this one."

Gemma nodded. "Sounds good. You take Angelo and head upstairs. Dean and I will check out his office down here. You have your phone on you, right?"

Tim felt in his pockets. "No, I don't."

"Then we'll meet back here in fifteen minutes if we can, assuming that we're not caught, either by the SWAT team or by Destrier."

Tim looked around the group. The others nodded, as did he. "Sounds good."

As they stepped away from the others, Tim noticed that Angelo held his arm out straight and stiff from his body. He laughed a little.

"In all your time working a gas station, Angelo, haven't you had to use a gun?"

"Not really. I mean not like this. I've had one guy show up with a knife on him, telling me to give him all the money. I pull out the gun and he doesn't give any more trouble. There was another case or two when some guys came in with guns but once they saw that I had a gun as well, they usually started running.

"These guys who come into the gas stations to rob it don't expect there to be a fight, they just want to grab the money and leave. That's why one of these is such a great deterrent. I show it and they run. Or else they drop the gun and put their hands in the air, waiting for the cops to show up."

Tim and Angelo moved through the building to the nearest stairwell, working to get to the upper floor as quickly as possible. They moved along the outer wall, realizing that any staircase would be there. Quickly finding this, they made their way up the staircase.

Keeping his back pressed to the wall, Angelo nearly stumbled over his own legs once or twice. Tim looked back to make sure he was all right.

"You sure you don't need any help back there?"

"I'm fine, keep moving. We need to keep out of the line of fire if anyone comes along."

They came up to the top of the stairs and Tim held up a hand. Angelo stopped behind him. Tim leaned out around the corner to see what was happening. A gunshot went off and he drew his head back behind the wall.

"Apparently they are armed."

Angelo rolled his eyes. "No kidding."

Tim got down on one knee and peeked around the corner again. There was no shot this time. He looked back to Angelo.

"I guess they've moved on."

Angelo shook his head. "Don't be too sure. I wouldn't count on these guys being dumb, typical criminals to keep running with no rear guard."

Tim looked again. "On my count – here we go." He got up and began to move down the hallway with Angelo behind him.

The hallway was dimly lit by lengthy lamps suspended from the ceiling. The grid-like cage around the bulbs was uninviting. Paint was flaking from many surfaces on the walls. There seemed to be a disheveled nature to the building's age.

They looked into the first room they came to. Angelo shook his head. "Nothing. That figures." It was an empty room, set up like a college laboratory, with counters running around the outer wall and a counter in the center. There were cabinets that ran around the upper wall at opposing walls and in the lower portions of the cabinets. Nothing sat on top of the exposed counters.

Tim shrugged and looked at Angelo. "Makes you wonder what they were doing in here."

They moved down the hall and approached the next room.

"What can you see?" said Angelo.

"It looks like a bunch of computers." Tim replied. "Desktops. Whoever worked in here spent some serious money on whatever they were doing. They weren't going halfway."

"What do you mean?" Angelo had his gun out, looking down the hall in the direction they had been heading.

"There are cables everywhere, but half of the computers are missing."

Tim stood up and stepped around the corner. Angelo glanced back and forth before following Tim's lead into the room.

The place looked like a disaster area. Cables were left everywhere unplugged, running to nothing, monitors blinking, and computer mice dangled by their cables. If the room had been ransacked the place could hardly have looked worse.

Angelo stepped past him and walked up to one of the computers which still appeared to be functioning. Quickly typing something in, he began to fiddle with something on the screen.

"What are you doing?"

"I'm trying to see what they were last doing here." Angelo said. "We might find some clue about their next step."

"Next step? Destrier's a nutcase – how do we know he's got a next step?"

"We don't, but we might find out…"

Angelo continued to type at the computer and click though the computers menus and icons. "Aha!" he said.

"Did you find something?"

"No, they use Windows XP. Who still uses that operating system?"

"We're kind of on a time crunch here." Tim said.

"Right sorry."

"And since when do you know much about computers?"

"Call it a hobby of mine." Said Angelo.

A minute later he had pulled up three image files. "They're blueprints."

"Blueprints?" said Tim, stepping closer to Angelo, who stood bent over the screen. "What would he need blueprints for?"

"Well I thought-"

Angelo dropped silent. Tim was ready to speak, but Angelo held his hand up to keep him quiet. Keeping his eyes open, he quickly scanned the room. There was no sign of anyone there. Glancing to Angelo, the man indicated, with a nod of his head, the hallway. Nodding back, Tim turned his attention to the computers again. Leaving the one that they had accessed, they moved back to the entrance of the room. With one last glance across the room, Tim was sure that no one else would surprise them from inside once they left the room.

Stepping to the door, Tim listened intently. As he stood he could hear what he intended to catch – the faint sounds of a person in the hall. The twosome stood and listened for a moment before looking at one another.

"What should we do? We can't be found out now." Said Angelo.

"We've got to catch them off guard." Said Tim.

"I don't like it."

"You don't have to like it."

"You're liking it doesn't make it any better."

Tim listened again. "He's getting closer."

Tim swung out of the doorway and fired on the person who was approaching down the hallway. The sound of a returning gunshot resonated through the hall. Tim stumbled back into the room.

"Remind me never to do that again." Said Tim.

"Never do that again." Said Angelo.

Angelo peeked around the corner and fired off a shot toward their intruder.

"I thought you might be back."

The voice resounded through the hallway. "I'm glad you showed up. It will give us a chance to finish things. Resolution is so much better than leaving things hanging like they did."

Tim tired to look around the corner, but Destrier fired off another shot in their direction.

"It's no good." Tim said. "There's no way to see out there. He's got the shot from where he's standing."

"There's really nothing left to do." Destrier said. "Everyone else has moved on, so I just have to deal with you cretins. I never believed that a few people meddling could do so much to interfere."

Tim turned and looked around the room. "isn't there any other way out of here? A window? A duct?"

Angelo glanced around and shook his head before turning back to the door.

"There is only one way this ends, Mr. Runn. This is about you and me. I've put aside the rest of the urchins who would be here. They would only have stood in the way."

Tim stood at the doorway. "This is over Destrier. The SWAT teams are here and will be upstairs at any minute. You can surrender yourself now or risk the consequence or fighting further."

The man laughed. "You think you can scare me with consequences? You've already lost this battle, when you decided to fight against me. You can stay in there as long as you like, but every moment will bring you closer to death. Come out now and I won't kill your friend. He may have a chance to live."

Tim looked at Angelo beside him, realizing that he didn't have any other way to respond. He stepped to the doorway.

"Tim, what are you doing?"

"Stay here."

He stepped out of the room and into the hallway. Destrier stood several paces down the hallway. The man's stature lent to his egotism. He held his head high, even in a situation when most men would have long given themselves up.

"Drop your gun." He said, indicating Tim with his own weapon. "And no tricks."

Tim nodded and slowly bent over, dropping the weapon on the ground.

"Kick it over here."

Tim sent the weapon sliding to Destrier's feet.

"Now this is how it should have been: with you standing at my mercy. But fate has ever come to try and set straight the inadequacies of human development, societies in general, and yours in particular."

The man held up a gun, directing it at Tim.

"I am Fate, and today this inadequacy will be set straight." He said.

Angelo leapt from the doorway, firing as he did so. Tim lunged for his own weapon on the ground, even as Destrier turned to face Angelo.

A series of shots fired. Destrier collapsed where he was. Tim turned to see Angelo, who lay in the fetal position on the ground facing away from Tim. Tim checked Destrier to see his condition and found that he was, in fact, dead where he lay. But there was no time to breath a sigh. Tim ran to Angelo's side.

"Angelo. Angelo buddy, tell me what's going on."

Angelo looked up at Tim, but said nothing. He was still breathing. Tim examined the man and found that he had bullet wounds on his torso.

Tim, supporting Angelo's head, spoke again. "Do you want to tell me a terrible joke?"

The man looked up at Tim. "What's black and white and red all over?"

Tim laughed. "I don't know, I newspaper?"

"No, man, a blushing penguin!"

They laughed together before Angelo became quiet.

"Is it true?"

Tim looked at him, but didn't say anything.

"What you told me before we came here? That I'm forgiven?"

Tim nodded. "God has redeemed and forgiven you. And if-" Tim caught his breath. "If this is it, then you'll see our Savior face-to-face."

Angelo nodded, drawing breath as his physical body responded to the trauma of the event, his mind grew easy at rest. And as he lay his breathing quickly grew shallow and he breathed his last.

Chapter 55

"Dean, come on."

"Right, right, I'm coming."

Gemma was leading the way down the side of the atrium, where the doors to various rooms stood. Dean glanced over his shoulder again. No guards followed them, and there had been no sign of hostilities, but he felt nervous.

"Do we know what it's supposed to look like?" asked the comedian.

"No." Gemma replied. "But the man up top has made it his own domain and he's an egotist, so it can't be too hard to spot."

They quickly found the office and mad their way inside. Making a quick search of the room, didn't bring up anything interesting at first. Gemma said they should search again, being careful to look for cubbyholes or clues to secret places to stow treasures or oddities.

After a second search, Gemma spoke.

"Got something." She held up some financial documents. "These look important."

"Look at this." Dean said, setting an odd-looking book on the desk. From it he withdrew a trinket.

"What is it?" Gemma asked, stepping toward him. He held up a small broach of a fox with diamonds for eyes.

"Come on," Gemma said. "We can talk about this later. We still have to find Mike."

After poking around, Gemma and Dean discovered a back room whose door was shut. Gun drawn, Gemma flew into the room to find Mike tied to a post in the middle of the room. He had a black eye among other injuries.

"What did they do to you?" Dean asked.

"Get me out of here." Mike replied.

They loosed him from the post ad helped him out of the room.

Finding nothing else of value, they left the room in search of their friends. Coming around a corner, they found Destrier collapsed, and Tim on the ground supporting Angelo's body.

Chapter 56

Seeing what had happened, Gemma spoke up.

"What's happened with the case? Has anyone dealt with it yet?"

Tim looked up at her and shook his head and stood.

Gemma spoke. "I don't know how quickly the SWAT team is getting on. We may have to take care of that before they do if they don't get to it first."

She started walking. "Where in this building would Destrier keep a piece of technology as vital as that?"

Tim shrugged. "I don't know, there are a lot of spaces that could serve that purpose."

As he got up from his spot on the floor, an explosion rocked the building. The ground under their feet vibrated.

"It looks like somebody's up to some mischief." Said Dean.

"Let's keep moving." Said Gemma. "If this place comes down I don't want to get stuck here because we spent too much time chatting."

After checking several rooms, they came upon the deserted room which held the case, which was now open. On the inside, the case contained a series of circuit boards and wires. It was hooked up to a computer

"Here it is." Said Tim. "Let's take it and go."

They turned to find a man wielding a knife standing between them and the door. There was blood on the knife as well as on his hands.

"And who are you?" asked Gemma

The man waved the knife at Dean. "This little fella knows who I am."

Dean looked attentively at the man's features, the large frame.

"Oh yeah," said Dean, "this is one of those big thugs that grabbed me when we were at the gas station. The one where you met Angelo."

Grip grinned. "The gas station, that's right."

Dean pulled out his gun and grinned. "Do you have any second thoughts?"

Grip's grin disappeared. "That's just not fair."

Tim laughed. "What they didn't give you one? If they're going to have you doing dirty work, don't they trust you with something more than a pocket knife?"

The knife shook in the man's hand.

"Put it down." Gemma said. "All of us are armed, you're just asking to get shot."

Desperation read in the man's eyes, enough that Tim was ready to fire on the man. But after a moment he wilted and held out his hand, dropping the knife.

In a split second he has snatched the knife from the air and was lunging forward towards Dean. The report of two weapons went off. Grip clutched at his midsection and collapsed to his knees.

At that moment, SWAT personnel came racing up the stairs, shouting at the people to drop their weapons and get on their knees with their hands on their head.

Tim paced the pavement outside the building. Seeing who he was, and that he had already been excused by the FBI, they let him roam, for the moment on a short tether within sight of the trailers and other vehicles.

He felt and hand on his shoulder, and turned to find Gemma behind him.

"I just wanted to say thank you for all you've done for us." She looked down at her feet. "For me."

He nodded. "You're welcome." They began to walk together. "So, where are you headed after this?"

"Oh, they've got me on assignment. I can't say where though." She looked at him. "Not too far."

"I see."

"What about Dean? Do you think he's caught the spirit of adventuring?"

Tim laughed and shook his head. "I don't think so. He's talking about getting home and getting back to doing comedy."

He glanced back and smiled. "Gemma. Through all of this, I never got to ask you something."

She looked at him as the wind rushed past, blowing hair all over her face. "Yes?"

He brushed the hair from her face. "Does the FBI have an academy?"